CW01507993

Middlebrow Literary Cultures

Also by Mary Grover

THE ORDEAL OF WARWICK DEEPING: Middlebrow Authorship and Cultural Embarrassment

Middlebrow Literary Cultures

The Battle of the Brows, 1920–1960

Edited by

Erica Brown and Mary Grover

First published 2012 by
PALGRAVE MACMILLAN

Palgrave Macmillan in the UK is an imprint of Macmillan Publishers Limited,
registered in England, company number 785998, of Houndmills, Basingstoke,
Hampshire RG21 6XS.

Palgrave Macmillan in the US is a division of St Martin's Press LLC,
175 Fifth Avenue, New York, NY 10010.

Palgrave Macmillan is the global academic imprint of the above companies
and has companies and representatives throughout the world.

Palgrave® and Macmillan® are registered trademarks in the United States,
the United Kingdom, Europe and other countries.

ISBN 978–0–230–29836–1

This book is printed on paper suitable for recycling and made from fully
managed and sustained forest sources. Logging, pulping and manufacturing
processes are expected to conform to the environmental regulations of the
country of origin.

A catalogue record for this book is available from the British Library.

A catalog record for this book is available from the Library of Congress.

10   9   8   7   6   5   4   3   2   1
21 20 19 18 17 16 15 14 13 12

Printed and bound in Great Britain by
CPI Antony Rowe, Chippenham and Eastbourne

Contents

II: US

Part III Categorization and Valuation

List of Figures

Acknowledgements

This collection draws on current debates about how tastes of 'the middling sorts' have been shaped in anglophone cultures. That a wide range of scholars has been able to participate in these debates owes much to the success of Faye Hammill at Strathclyde University in securing funding from the Arts and Humanities Research Council in the UK to establish the Middlebrow Network, a transatlantic, interdisciplinary grouping of researchers. We are grateful to Strathclyde and Sheffield Hallam Universities which have hosted both the network website and two of our conferences and also to Adrian Bingham and Sheffield University for hosting the 2008 conference 'Historicizing the Middlebrow'. We have also appreciated productive interactions with members of the Space Between Society and participants at the 'Masculine Middlebrow' conference, organized by Kate Macdonald and Mary Grover in 2009.

An earlier version of the essay by Joan Shelley Rubin appeared as 'Reprocessing the Cozzens-Macdonald Imbroglio: Middlebrow Authorship, Critical Authority, and Autonomous Readers in Postwar America' in *Modern Intellectual History*, 7, pp. 553–579 (2010), © Cambridge University Press and Nicola Humble's essay appeared in *Working Papers on the Web*, 11 (2008), Sheffield Hallam University; we are grateful to the editors of both journals for permission to reproduce these works. Rubin acknowledges the permission of the President and Fellows of Harvard College and the Princeton University Library to quote from the James Gould Cozzens Papers, Manuscripts Division, Department of Rare Books and Special Collections, Princeton University Library. Sharon Hamilton acknowledges the permission of the Enoch Pratt Free Library, Baltimore, to use quotations from the writings of H. L. Mencken, in accordance with the terms of Mr Mencken's bequest. She also acknowledges permission to reproduce the following artworks: Figures 8.1 and 8.2, front covers of H. L. Mencken and George Jean Nathan's *The Smart Set* magazine, March 1922 and October 1914, provided by the George H. Thompson Collection of H. L. Mencken, the Sheridan Libraries, Johns Hopkins University; and Figure 8.3, homepage of www.thesmartset.com, 22 November 2010, courtesy of *The Smart Set* from Drexel University.

We are particularly grateful to Jayne Waterman, who had the original idea for the collection, and to John Baxendale, Faye Hammill, Chris

Hopkins, Derek Grover and Jonathan Wild for their comments on the project. We would like to thank all participants in the network for their generosity to each other, which ensured an open and exploratory exchange of material and ideas. The contributors to this volume have not only shared their work with us but also have helped us think through the sources of the violence underlying the rhetorics of distaste.

We would also like to thank Derek Grover and Maurice McCabe for their patience and encouragement, without which this project would not have been embarked upon or completed.

Notes on Contributors

John Baxendale is Visiting Fellow in the Humanities at Sheffield Hallam University. He is the author of *Narrating the Thirties: A Decade in the Making* (with Chris Pawling) (1996) and *Priestley's England: J B Priestley and English Culture* (2007).

Adrian Bingham is Senior Lecturer in Modern History at the University of Sheffield. He is the author of *Gender, Modernity, and the Popular Press in Inter-War Britain* (2004) and *Family Newspapers? Sex, Private Life, and the British Popular Press 1918–78* (2009).

Kristin Bluemel is Professor of English at Monmouth University. She is the author of *George Orwell and the Radical Eccentrics: Intermodernism in Literary London* (2004) and the editor of the collection *Intermodernism: Literary Culture in Mid-Twentieth-Century Britain* (2009) and the interdisciplinary journal, *The Space Between: Literature and Culture, 1914–1945*.

Erica Brown is Associate Lecturer at Sheffield Hallam University and Administrator of the Middlebrow Network (www.middlebrow-network. com), funded by the Arts and Humanities Research Council. She is the editor of 'Investigating the Middlebrow' (2008) *Working Papers on the Web*, vol. 11, and recently completed her PhD 'Comedy and the Middlebrow Novel: Elizabeth Taylor and Elizabeth von Arnim'.

Janet Galligani Casey is Professor of English at Skidmore College in Saratoga Springs, New York. She is the author of *Dos Passos and the Ideology of the Feminine* (1998), for which she won the Modern Language Association Prize for Independent Scholars, and, most recently, *A New Heartland: Women, Modernity, and the Agrarian Ideal in America* (2009). She is also the editor of *The Novel and the American Left: Critical Essays on Depression-Era Fiction* (2004).

Mary Grover is Senior Lecturer at Sheffield Hallam University, where she promotes research into the special collection of popular fiction: Readerships and Literary Cultures, 1900–1950. She is the author of *The Ordeal of Warwick Deeping: Cultural Embarrassment and Middlebrow*

Authorship (2009) and 'The View from the Middle: Godden and Her Literary Landscape', in *Rumer Godden: International and Intermodern Storyteller* (2010). She is currently working on establishing an oral history project on popular reading in Sheffield 1945–1965.

Sharon Hamilton is Academic Dean at The International University, Vienna. Her chapter on 'American Manners: *The Smart Set* (1900–29); *American Parade* (1926)' will appear in the forthcoming second volume of Andrew Thacker and Peter Brooker's (eds) *The Oxford Critical and Cultural History of Modernist Magazines*.

Nick Hubble is Senior Lecturer in English at Brunel University. His publications include the monograph *Mass-Observation and Everyday Life: Culture, History, Theory* (2006, second edition, 2010) and two guest-edited special issues of the online academic journal *Literary London*: 'Intermodern London' (March 2009) and 'Middlebrow London' (March 2011).

Nicola Humble is Professor of English at Roehampton University. Her publications include *Mrs Beeton's Book of Household Management*, edited (2000), *The Feminine Middlebrow Novel 1920s to 1950s: Class, Domesticity and Bohemianism* (2001) and *Culinary Pleasures: Cookbooks and the Transformation of British Food* (2005).

Victoria Kingham's PhD, entitled 'Little Magazines, Commerce, and the Avant-garde: New York 1914–1922', was awarded by De Montfort University in 2010. Recent publications include a chapter in the forthcoming second volume of Thacker and Brooker's *Critical and Cultural History of Modernist Magazines*, an article on *The Pagan* (1916) in *The Journal of Modern Periodical Studies*, and diverse reviews.

Caroline Pollentier is a doctoral student at Paris Diderot University and will shortly submit her thesis, which focuses on the aesthetics and politics of the ordinary in Virginia Woolf's essays. She has published a chapter on middlebrow essayists in *The Masculine Middlebrow, 1880–1950: What Mr Miniver Read*, edited by Kate Macdonald (2011).

Candida Rifkind is Assistant Professor at the University of Winnipeg (Canada), where she specializes in modernism and anti modernism in Canadian literature and culture, popular and political writing, and graphic narratives. In addition to numerous articles on Canadian literature and women writers, her book, *Comrades and Critics: Women, Literature, and the Left in 1930s Canada*, was recently published.

John Shapcott is Honorary Research Fellow at the Research Institute for Humanities, Keele University. He has edited a series of new editions of Arnold Bennett's works, most recently a volume of 41 previously uncollected short stories from 1892 to 1932. Currently he is editing a centenary edition of *The Card* and working on a book-length study of Melvyn Bragg's fiction. Previous publications include articles on Jack Kerouac and spontaneous improvization, Indian Ocean politics and the book for the stage musical *Heaven Sent*.

Joan Shelley Rubin is Professor of History at the University of Rochester. Her publications include: *Songs of Ourselves: The Uses of Poetry in America* (2007); *The Making of Middlebrow Culture* (1992); and *Constance Rourke and American Culture* (1980). Co-editor, *A History of the Book in America*, vol. V (2009); Associate editor, *The Oxford Companion to the Book* (2010).

Jonathan Wild is Lecturer in English Literature at the University of Edinburgh and the Deputy Director of Edinburgh's Centre for the History of the Book. His publications include *The Rise of the Office Clerk in Literary Culture, 1880–1939* (2006) and a variety of articles covering the literary history of this period.

Introduction: Middlebrow Matters

Erica Brown and Mary Grover

The aim of this collection is to demonstrate that the middlebrow *matters*. The term 'middlebrow' itself, first used in the 1920s, is the product of powerful anxieties about cultural authority and processes of cultural transmission. It is a nexus for prejudice towards the lower middle classes, the feminine and domestic, and towards narrative modes regarded as outdated. Unless the rhetorical uses of this term are understood, the material culture from which any text in the twentieth century has been generated, the way that most American and British readers come to those texts and the way we teach canonical literature from the period will not be fully informed. The essays in this collection address the period 1920–1960, when the 'battle of the brows' was at its height. However, the cultural anxieties of this time continue to inform our attitudes to literary culture today.

> But what, you may ask, is a middlebrow? And that, to tell the truth, is no easy question to answer.[1]

As Virginia Woolf suggests, it is very difficult to say exactly what 'the middlebrow' *is*. It has been defined through its consumers, argued to be members of the anathematized lower middle classes. This is the view that Graham Greene took, associating the middlebrow with 'straphanging' typists commuting to and from the new suburban wastelands of interwar Britain.[2] Others have defined it as a conservative realist form, aiming for moral complexity and artistic merit but really just easy, middle-of-the-road stuff: what Q. D. Leavis called 'the *faux-bon*'.[3] Virginia Woolf herself, struggling to pin down the middlebrow, defined it by what it is not – not the emerging avant-garde of the 1920s, nor the honest lowbrow; instead characterizing it as something caught uneasily 'betwixt and between'.[4] For the American Dwight Macdonald,

1

writing 20 years later than Greene, Leavis and Woolf, it was associated with a dull and mindless 'matron' greedy for indifferent literature.[5] From whatever source, whatever the prejudices evidenced, one element remained constant: this was a pejorative label, its dismissive effect designed to credit its users with superior powers of discrimination which would place them safely beyond identification with the 'calves-foot jelly' (Woolf) or the 'tepid, flaccid' spread (Macdonald) of the dreaded middlebrow.[6]

The urge to define has had a recent resurgence, especially in America. For example, a recent column in *The Atlantic* notes that 'it takes time and millions of dollars, and possibly risible branding campaigns, to turn quintessentially middlebrow secondary reads into upper-middlebrow must-reads'.[7] This tone of spurious definitiveness ('quintessentially'), and the absurd exactness of the sub-divisions work to obscure the fact that, as Joan Rubin notes in this collection, 'cultural authority, while it may appear entrenched, is often precarious and always open to renegotiation on the basis of the anxieties in play at a given historical moment'. The middlebrow is difficult to define, therefore, because as a product of contested and precarious assertions of cultural authority, it is itself unstable. This instability and historical contingency is our focus in this collection. These essays do not attempt to find a fixed, essential meaning for the middlebrow. Instead they address questions of temporal, geographical and formal specificity, and identify how the term was understood in particular contexts.

The collection begins with two ground-breaking essays: the first argues for the central role of 'the middle' in teaching students about vital issues of cultural hierarchy; the second brings a fresh perspective to the influential work of Pierre Bourdieu by demonstrating the cultural specificity of his theories of 'la culture moyenne'. The second section of the collection offers detailed analyses of influential periodicals and individual 'taste-makers', which together productively compare the differing US and UK contexts. The essays in the third section of the collection develop thinking on middlebrow literary form beyond a simple realist/modernist dichotomy. They demonstrate how other aspects of form, such as illustrated texts and serial publication, are similarly devalued and complicate the notion of the middlebrow as straightforwardly realist.

Contexts

Janet Casey opens our debate by arguing that the middlebrow is central to the entire enterprise of literary studies. A literary pedagogy that confines itself to canonical texts 'robs students of the opportunity to encounter cultural jockeying in action, to make applicable connections to their own cultural moment, and to understand literary value as relative and situational rather than timeless and absolute'. Investigating the middlebrow leads students to consider the politics of literary evaluation and to reflect on their own reading and evaluative judgements. The texts that many students choose to read for pleasure may be considered middlebrow, and by teaching this literature we invite them to question what we read and why. Teaching the middlebrow often highlights the ambivalent relationship that most academics have with 'reading for pleasure'.[8]

Many of the readers of this essay collection will, in probability, have made the exercise of literary tastes one of the foundations of their sense of professional and personal selves. The resurgence of the word 'middlebrow' as a dismissive term may owe something to our sense that in a digital age, those with a passion for reading can feel, as Virginia Woolf and the Leavises did, that we are now part of a beleaguered minority culture who need to distance ourselves from a dominant majority who threaten the value we set on our tastes. We are likely to be professional teachers and researchers, and as Pierre Bourdieu rather sternly puts it, those whose chief source of capital is cultural tend to 'elevate its particular interests to a superior degree of universalization and invent a version of the ideology of public service.'[9]

It is therefore as tempting for us as it was for the early scholars of modernism to act as guardians of the arcane and difficult. Douglas Hewitt argues that the natural tendency of academic critics is to 'concentrate attention upon what they themselves can do and what the general reader cannot' – theorize 'difficult' works – having 'the effect of making the tradition of modernism seem not merely one tendency among a number but the only one'.[10] Geoffrey Crossick, Arno J. Mayer and Rita Felski link academic reluctance to explore this under-researched area of culture associated with the lower middle classes with the question of class origins.[11] Felski points out that many of the traditional values of the lower middle classes 'are closely linked to educational aspirations' so, unsurprisingly, many academics emerge from such backgrounds. She asks, provocatively, 'What happens then, when individuals from such a background find themselves in an academic milieu that disdains lower-middle-class cultural values?'[12] A reluctance to acknowledge the ways in which we have acquired our own cultural competencies is a persistent feature of bids to all sorts of sophistication, as Faye Hammill demonstrates in her recent study.[13]

It is always tempting to represent our gifts of discernment as just that: gifts, rather than painfully or, even more suspect, pleasurably acquired competencies.

The author of the satirical column entitled 'Charivaria' in *Punch*, 23 December 1925, defines the genesis of the term thus: 'The B.B.C. claim to have discovered a new type, the "middlebrow". It consists of people who are hoping that some day they will get used to the stuff they ought to like.'[14] In this early usage the middlebrow is regarded as a hapless aspirant, lacking in cultural confidence and reliant on the authority of his or her betters. Immediately we encounter one of the key anxieties which lurk behind identifications of this 'new type': fear of cultural change and hostility to vaguely illegitimate processes of cultural transmission. That the term appeared in *Punch* is significant: the magazine was a key component of what Françoise Baillet terms 'le paradigme bourgeois'.[15] Traditionally it satirized both the pretentious (the aesthete in the late nineteenth century, the highbrow in the 1920s) and the less educated; this it continued to do until its circulation started to diminish in the 1940s.[16] However, in the early part of the twentieth century *Punch* was performing a cultural confidence which implied that its readers had no need of a centralized arbiter of taste as the BBC was widely represented to be. This apparently casual definition of 'the middlebrow' conceals anxieties about a democratization of access to high culture by attempting to fix the identity of this group of newly aspirant individuals and by homogenizing their supposed tastes. The reader of *Punch*, an individual with innate abilities to make cultural distinctions independent of guidance, is constructed in opposition to a reader from a notional lower middle class allegedly without this independence and individuality.

However, British readers were also addressed by 'taste-makers' more sympathetic to those who, precisely because of their initiative and independence, were seeking to explore cultural worlds unfamiliar to them. Adrian Bingham's essay is the first examination of the construction of cultural hierarchy in the daily newspapers of interwar Britain. The attractiveness of small magazines as a site of cultural debate is obvious: they represent a discrete and hitherto hidden pocket of culturally significant data. However, as Bingham points out, the newspaper was a key signifier of its reader's cultural status during this period and the 'relentless' expansion of the daily press was a source of deep anxiety to both leftist and Leavisite cultural commentators. Bingham's work, here and elsewhere, has done much to break down assumptions about the monolithic identity of papers with mass circulations.[17]

Similarly the essays by Jonathan Wild, John Shapcott and John Baxendale show that the cultural aspirations of British readers were taken seriously by key 'taste-makers' who addressed an imagined community of readers whose tastes were far from monolithic. Wilfred Whitten is not a name as well-known as Arnold Bennett or J. B. Priestley, but the 'unassuming' editor of two inexpensive literary papers, *T. P.'s Weekly* (1902–1911) and *John O'London's Weekly* (1919–1936), enabled lower middle class readers, most excluded from higher education, to access literary pleasures otherwise out of reach. Jonathan Wild describes how Whitten seeks to banish what he characterized as 'the bogeys of correctness and completeness [that] are responsible for a great deal of shivering on the brink of literature'. With a weekly circulation of 80,000 at its peak, 'John O'London' helped aspirant readers throughout Britain and its Empire take the plunge into Conrad's *Nostromo* or the works of the French critic and historian Hippolyte Taine but declined to condemn readers' enthusiasm for the novels of Charles Garvice, for example. As Wild demonstrates, Whitten did not ignore his readers' cultural anxieties but negotiated them with a quiet confidence and generosity of spirit rare in any kind of literary endeavour and certainly absent in the rhetoric of middlebrow's detractors.

One of the new writers championed by Whitten was Arnold Bennett. Hugely popular as novelist and critic on both sides of the Atlantic, Bennett was said by Virginia Woolf to be a 'materialist' whose fiction was shallow, unadventurous and aesthetically outmoded.[18] John Shapcott investigates Bennett's contribution to the Book Review columns of the *Evening Standard*, 1926–1931. Rather than taint Bennett by association with the Beaverbrook press, Shapcott examines the terms that Bennett set himself. Like Whitten, Bennett worked to bridge cultural divides, aiming, as Shapcott puts it, to make 'it possible for the clerk and his wife to read both *The Yellow Book* and Mrs Henry Wood without fear of embarrassment'.

Bennett's successor at the *Evening Standard* was J. B. Priestley. John Baxendale, whose 2007 study demonstrates the generous but contradictory nature of Priestley's vision of an inclusive culture, here focuses on Priestley's explicit defence of what he perceived to be an increasingly democratized and thereby enriched culture.[19] Baxendale traces the public skirmishes between self-styled highbrows such as Leonard Woolf and curmudgeonly middlebrows such as Gilbert Frankau and links them with *fin de siècle* hostility to aestheticism. He makes the important point that hostility to the highbrow preceded and was more generally pervasive than hostility to the middlebrow.

Outside the pages of the democratizing columnists and editors, the pejorative connotations of the term 'middlebrow' rapidly intensified in ways often connected with the professionalization of literary criticism. Those such as F. R. and Q. D. Leavis, founders of the influential literary magazine *Scrutiny* (1932–1953), sought to build a canon of 'English literature' suitable for analysis by the new, academically disciplined literary critic. The Leavises deplored contemporary journalism yet they, like the writers and cartoonists of *Punch* who were likely to be eking out a precarious living in Grub Street, were not culturally secure and in the interwar period were not fully accepted by the academic community. Both the Leavises and these journalists sought to bolster their authority by adopting a language of pseudo-science in constructing their taxonomies and by mocking or lambasting aspirants to high culture. And again, as with the journalists of *Punch*, it is not simply the nature of the supposedly middlebrow culture that the Leavises found risible or lacking, but the vaguely illegitimate way in which those tastes were acquired: Q. D. Leavis's polemical *Fiction and the Reading Public* (1932) castigates the middlebrow as 'touching grossly on fine issues'.[20] The implication is that those whose sensibilities are 'gross' should limit their aspirations, whether as writers or as readers. Ironically, for one who, with her husband, was to be responsible for the pioneering ethos of generations of English teachers both in Britain and the country's former colonies, it is the middlebrow writer's attempt to exceed his or her grasp that appals her, unless, of course, that attempt is guided by a professionalized literary elite uncompromised by links with journalism or commerce.

Commercial projects offering guidance to the earnest self-improver were a matter of grave concern to Q. D. Leavis. She noted that the Book Society (established in 1927) chooses:

> novels of such competent journalists as G. B. Stern, A. P. Herbert, Rebecca West, Denis Mackail…, sapless 'literary' novels, or the smartly fashionable (Hemingway, Osbert Sitwell). By December 1929 the society had nearly seven thousand members, and it is still growing, from which the unbiased observer might fairly deduce two important cultural changes: first, that by conferring authority on a taste for the second-rate […] a middlebrow standard of taste has been set up; second that middlebrow taste has thus been organised.[21]

Her attack reveals the way in which those setting up the middlebrow as antipathetic to their own cultural identity erase the particularity and diversity of such tastes. Writers such as Hemingway, West and Herbert may seem diverse to us but Leavis found this selection typical of the 'second-rate' quality of the Society's book choices. Like the Book Society, the BBC was regarded as a middlebrow institution, yet Jane Dowson's analysis of the poetry published in the *Listener* (the BBC's weekly magazine 1929–1991) demonstrates that the BBC, instead of imposing highbrow tastes on a dim and pathetically aspirant reader as the *Punch* definition suggests, in fact broadcast a wide range of types of poetry.[22] This contradiction was not lost on contemporary commentators. In the 1920s, J. B. Priestley argued against the homogenizing term 'middlebrow', advocating the use of the more expansive and heterogeneous 'broadbrow'.[23] However, this term never gained currency. It is the term 'middlebrow' that peppers the reviews, letters and novels of a vast range of writers of the period.

Of the three chief scourges of the middlebrow in Britain (Virginia Woolf, Q. D. and F. R. Leavis), Woolf retains most authority. Her disgust at the 'betwixt and between' is as violent as anything written by the Leavises but was usually expressed in private; the infamous letter to the *New Statesman* in which this phrase appears was never sent so cannot have contributed to public debate at the time.[24] Woolf privately acknowledged that her distaste for fiction designated as middlebrow was so violent that it could not be contained, as Q. D. Leavis tried to contain hers, within an apparatus of rational argument. In a letter to Hugh Walpole (himself a prolific middlebrow novelist), she acknowledged the disproportionate nature of her response: 'I explode so easily against fiction that I have hardly any trust in my own vehemence.'[25]

It is tempting to regard Woolf as confident of her own cultural worth. Daughter of the eminent scholar Leslie Stephen (compiler of the *Dictionary of National Biography*) she was a close friend of writers associated with the development of modernism. Yet recent research by Christine Kenyon Jones and Anna Snaith has revealed that despite the assertion of Virginia Woolf and her biographers that she was largely self-educated, in the years 1897–1901 she attended numerous classes at the Ladies' Department of King's College London, taking examinations at degree level.[26] The first draft of her essay 'How Should One Read a Book?' begins with a disarming admission to the schoolgirls in front of her: 'In the first place I am going to confess a crime – not my own doing however – I have never been to school.'[27] Though strictly true, the reader is led to infer that her education was entirely informal and independent. No doubt her reluctance, and perhaps that of her biographers, to accept the educational debt she owed to public channels of education rather than to privileged and private access to her father's study, had much to do with Woolf's own distaste for the educator as a trader dealing in cultural goods. Woolf argues in *Three Guineas* (1938) that examinations in English literature should be resisted 'to keep one art at least out of the hands of middlemen and free, as long as may be, from all association with competition and money making'.[28]

Though the Leavises and Virginia Woolf were suspicious of access to cultural goods organized by commerce or the state, both set up 'organized' ways of asserting such control themselves: Leonard and Virginia Woolf with the Hogarth Press and the Leavises with the journal, *Scrutiny*. However, Woolf's hostility to the middlebrow is linked, in a way that the Leavises's wasn't, to an antipathy towards representations of the world that could be described as 'realist'. In her critical essays 'Mr. Bennett and Mrs. Brown' and 'Modern Fiction' she famously took issue with the Edwardian writers she terms the 'materialists': H. G. Wells, John Galsworthy and Arnold Bennett.[29] Human nature has changed, she asserts, and their nineteenth-century realist mode, building books packed with material detail, can no longer convey life. The time has come, she argues, for the young writers who attempt to come 'closer to life [...] even if' to do so they must discard most of the conventions which are commonly observed by the novelist.[30] The emerging modernist aesthetic is thus constructed in opposition to realism, and during the 1920s this realism became persistently identified as middlebrow. It can therefore be argued that 'the middlebrow' is in fact not a new part of the cultural landscape; as Nicola Humble observes in her influential book *The Feminine Middlebrow Novel, 1920s to 1950s: Class, Domesticity and Bohemianism* (2001), 'the stylistic and thematic blue-prints of the sort of literature that came to be seen as middlebrow [...] are little different from the conventions that dominated the mainstream novel throughout the nineteenth century'.[31] The 'middlebrow novel', therefore, is not a newly emerging literary form in the 1920s, but a critical term emerging as a consequence of contemporary literary developments.

As such there are certain narrative forms which from the outset of the term's use were associated with it. Candida Rifkind's essay, focusing on the Jalna series by the Canadian Mazo de la Roche, details the disdain for the serial shared by high modernists and Marxists alike over much of the century: repeated and repeatable pleasures are suspect, and the serial is seen as repetition motivated by profit. The repeated pleasures offered by the serial were bound to diminish the cultural capital that adheres to the unique and unrepeatable. It is thus, Rifkind argues, not only the form of the individual novel that can render a text middlebrow, but also the publishing format. Kristin Bluemel's essay on P. L. Travers's *Mary Poppins* (1934) uses theories of visual–verbal relations to understand why and how illustrated texts are consistently devalued by literary elites. The status of the text as both children's novel and illustrated text may lead us to consign it to the bland and reassuring middlebrow, but closer attention to the materiality of this chilling book and to its narrative strategies reveals a disconcerting and almost modernist identity. Both Bluemel and Humble's studies in this collection show how once a narrative form is devalued, texts defined as outmoded or unsophisticated invite misreading.

In her essay Humble challenges the notion of the middlebrow author as clumsy and unknowing. In the work of a number of popular authors (E. F. Benson, Mary Renault and Nancy Mitford) Humble teases out the characteristics of a camp sensibility: 'it is a mode of aestheticism; it emphasizes style over content; it converts the serious into the frivolous'. Crucially, Humble suggests that the 'double lens of camp' is 'entirely within the control of its author'. It is not unconscious, as Susan Sontag contends, but is a sophisticated stylistic choice by the author that allows the middlebrow to 'negotiate the prickly terrain between high and low culture'. As Faye Hammill observes, 'much middlebrow writing has been ignored by the academy because of a misconception that it is so straightforward as to require no analysis, while in fact, its witty, polished surfaces frequently conceal unexpected depths and subtleties'.[32]

Though Woolf drew a strict line between the middlebrow and new modes of representation, Nick Hubble finds complex interactions between middlebrow culture and avant-garde aesthetics through his analysis of the Mass-Observation project, begun in 1937. The Cambridge-educated founders of the project were profoundly concerned by the gap that had opened up in the 1930s between the masses and the intellectual and cultural elite, and therefore set up Mass-Observation to be an inclusive mass movement. In an early statement they asserted that 'it does not set out in quest of truth or facts for their own sake, or for the sake of an intellectual minority, but aims at exposing them in simple terms to all observers'.[33] However, these 'simple terms' did not preclude using modernist techniques. Unlike those intellectuals who sought to defend the avant-garde from the encroachment of the masses, the founders of Mass-Observation actively promoted the use of these techniques to their (predominantly lower middle class) observers.

The middlebrow has not only been persistently identified with devalued forms but also with female consumers: George Orwell considers that 'what one might call the average novel – the ordinary, good-bad, Galsworthy-and-water stuff which is the norm of the English novel – seems to exist only for women'.[34] Similarly, Q. D. Leavis, in identifying reasons for the decline in the 'critical intelligence' of readers, notes darkly that 'women rather than men change the books (that is determine the family reading)'.[35] The middlebrow is not simply tainted by a female readership, however; despite Woolf's focus on male writers in the essay 'Modern Fiction', some feminist scholars have argued that the middlebrow is a feminine form, written predominantly by women, and having a 'particular concentration on feminine aspects of life'.[36] In the last two decades feminist critics have led the way in examinations of 'middlebrow', finding, as nineteenth-century scholars have with 'sentimental' and 'sensational' fiction, links between gender and cultural devaluation. Alison Light, for example, has suggested that constructions of modernism are gendered, associating literary value with masculinity and exile, and thus implicitly associating the feminine and domestic with the devalued middlebrow.[37]

The compulsions in Britain to anathematize a formal, class or gendered 'other' as middlebrow are not neatly paralleled in interwar America. Indeed, the American culture industry was regarded by Q. D. Leavis as partially responsible for the acceleration of the commodification of culture and dissemination of the *faux-bon*.[38] Unsurprisingly, the relationship between the two cultures is by no means straightforward: John Baxendale has shown how Priestley, while mourning the lost vitality of Britain's indigenous popular culture, to some extent celebrated American mass culture as a revitalizing and democratizing force in contemporary Britain, and one which established higher production standards than what he regarded as the rather amateurish BBC.[39] However, Lawrence Napper, in *British Cinema and the Middlebrow in the Interwar Years* (2009), argues that much of British interwar literary and cinematic culture dismissed as middlebrow reflects an indigenous and democratizing resistance to US consumerism and a championing of broad cultural tastes.[40]

One of the first commentators to compare texts on both sides of the Atlantic that were soon to be described as 'middlebrow' is the American Montgomery Belgion. Writing in a journal for American teachers of English in 1928, Belgion does not use the term itself but makes a distinction between the omnivorous appetite of the American reader for all sorts of fiction, constantly moving from one author and one type of novel to another, with the British reader who attaches himself loyally to a particular author. Belgion associates the greater catholicity of the American reader with a stronger expectation of social mobility and of the power of new cultural goods to further economic advancement. The British reading public, by contrast, is more fixed in its preferences and hence more stratified.[41] As Joan Rubin has demonstrated, American promotion of 'high' culture was not, in the 1920s, constructed on a ground of hostility to the 'low'.[42] To a greater extent than in Britain, the guardians of the 'genial middle ground' (as Van Wyck Brooks termed it) were drawn from universities.[43] The relationship of the universities to commercial culture in the two countries is a key factor differentiating American and British discourses about the middlebrow. From the outset of the formal study of 'English' in Britain the boundaries between the academic and the non-academic were fiercely contested. In the 1920s, the authority of the English Literature degree at Cambridge University was predicated on its links to the established authority of the Greek and Latin classics, and the new criticism of I. A. Richards insisted on its kinship to the intellectually respectable field of scientific enquiry. In America the role of public educator of the middling sorts was taken on, in a way it never was in Britain, by the universities, in partnership with commercial organizations such as The Book of the Month Club, subject of Janice Radway's study of middlebrow culture *A Feeling for Books: The Book of the Month Club, Literary Taste, and Middle-Class Desire* (1997). The American Book of the Month Club drew its selectors from both academia and journalism, and the readers reliant on their choices were not as openly derided for their incapacity for independent discrimination as were those caricatured in *Punch*. The language of democracy, cultural aspiration and social change was readier to hand than it was in Britain, and downright hostility to supposedly 'middlebrow' consumers surfaced later in America, after the Second World War.

The reasons for this lack of synchronicity are complex. Cultural aspiration was viewed very differently in the two countries during the interwar period, as the juxtaposition of studies of American and British magazines in this collection shows. Though American literary culture was derided by Gertrude Atherton at the turn of the century for being 'the most timid, the most anaemic, the most lacking individualities, the most bourgeois, that any country has ever known'[44] (terms that anticipate Q. D. Leavis's), 20 years later the wit, cultural plurality and ease performed in magazines such as the *Smart Set, Vanity Fair, The American Mercury* and *Esquire* show how publications aimed at a wide, if not a mass readership, can, as Seldes puts it, be 'intellectual in its looser sense'.[45] The first two of our essays on the American middlebrow deal with American magazines in the first quarter of the twentieth century.

Victoria Kingham roots her discussion of the range of different types of American magazine in an examination of the terms used by two key American commentators on the state of American literary taste: Van Wyck Brooks in his essay '"Highbrow" and "Lowbrow"' (1915) and Gilbert Seldes in his essay collection, *The Seven Lively Arts* (1924). Brooks is contemptuous of the philistinism and associated materialism of the American middle classes, but sees the possibility of weaning them away from the lowbrow by fostering a respectable middling sort of culture. Seldes, however, deplores the existing cultural tastes of contemporary middling sorts, supposedly in thrall to the deadening 'genteel' American tradition. In contrast to Brooks, Seldes advocates a 'lively' eclecticism of taste in which high and low are combined to create a sophisticated and knowing readership. Kingham shows how the ease and confidence of highbrow commentators in magazines which set themselves apart from middle-of-the road culture is linked partly to the all-pervasive and widely shared referents of cinema and popular music, the vitality of which is held to express the youth of America as a nation and therefore to be celebrated rather than deplored. Yet this celebration had limits and Kingham shows how racial prejudices checked Seldes's proclaimed emancipation from Middle America. She argues that despite the egalitarian rhetoric, both magazines with highbrow aspirations and those which were more overtly commercial (the *Smart Set* and *Vanity Fair*, e.g.) 'painstakingly maintained control over their position in an intellectual aristocracy of refined taste'.

Published between 1900 and 1923, before the term 'middlebrow' was used, H. L. Mencken's magazine, *The Smart Set*, made intellectualism attractive to a diverse readership. Mencken managed to introduce his readers to icons of modernism such as Ezra Pound and James Joyce alongside frolicsome short stories such as 'Lady Marjory's Undies'.[46] Sharon Hamilton here analyses a number of comparable magazines and various facets of their production: advertisements, illustrations and juxtaposition of material. Though the frequent playfulness of Mencken's tone might seem to suggest that American readers were more at ease than their British counterparts with cultural plurality and divergent status, Hamilton demonstrates how both the advertisements and articles engage with deep-seated cultural insecurities among the magazine's readership. It is a mark of how differently notions of the middle were constructed in the States that the *Smart Set* itself became a marker of cultural distinction, a phenomenon enjoyed by no comparable British publication that attempted to mediate high culture for a wide readership.

Dwight Macdonald's writing is energized by a vitriol that fully matches that of Woolf and Leavis 30 or so years earlier. Joan Rubin's essay in this collection argues that the famous 'Masscult and Midcult' essay of 1960 should be read in the context of Macdonald's extensive engagement with popular fiction in the 1950s. Rubin shows how the mutual antipathy of Macdonald and his *bête noir*, the best-selling novelist James Cozzens Gould, was animated by their own cultural, political and racial insecurities. By detailed examination of the reception of Gould's best-selling *By Love Possessed* (1957), Rubin demonstrates how mistaken Macdonald was in attributing the novel's success to a conspiracy of reviewers hostile to modernism. This essay's method of analysis exemplifies one of the ways in which study of middlebrow matters. Literary critics, from Matthew Arnold onwards, have been tempted to place the role of the critic in a far more central place in relation to cultural change than is warranted by historical evidence. It is an awareness of this actual marginality that contributed to the intellectual paranoia experienced by Macdonald and the Leavises, who demonized those who resisted or ignored attempts to guide their tastes.

Two key critical texts on the relation between the brows in the United States, Peter Swirski's *From Lowbrow to Nobrow* (2005) and Lawrence Levine's *Highbrow/Lowbrow* (1988), omit the middlebrow from their titles, perhaps, like Seldes, attempting to wish it out of existence.[47] Levine mourns the loss of cultural fluidity in twentieth-century America, arguing that the discourse of the brows led to a decline in the cultural eclecticism and openness that characterized popular culture in the nineteenth century. Swirski argues, rather differently, that twentieth-century American fiction tends to a hip synthesis of high and low, thus shimmying past the 'flaccid' middlebrow; and indeed it would be difficult to imagine a British equivalent of the kind of modal conjuring trick pulled off by Cole Porter in his 1934 celebration of high and low 'You're the Top', in which he lovingly conjoins the 'feet of Fred Astaire', 'an O'Neill drama', 'Whistler's mama' and camembert.[48]

Despite their unabashed appeal to readerships that were stigmatized as 'middlebrow', it is arguable that the greater earnestness of the British taste-makers in popular periodicals reflects a project less intimidating to the aspirant middle class than do Mencken, Nathan or Seldes's bravura performances. Certainly, the British taste-makers discussed in this collection – Bennett and Priestley in their weekly columns in the popular daily the *Evening Standard*, and Whitten in his editorial guidance of *John O' London's Weekly* – reached a wider readership than any of the so-called 'smart' magazines. Whereas the cool of the *Smart Set* and *Vanity*

Fair may be more beguiling to a modern scholar aiming to redefine the middlebrow as a source of hitherto unsuspected sophistication, Bennett, Priestley and Whitten treat the cultural aspirations of their readerships with a respect and seriousness which acknowledges more overtly the legitimacy of such aspirations; they are not afraid to take on the role of educator rather than entertainer.

Finally, the fear of engulfment that suffuses British literature of the 1930s and the rhetoric of the 'cultural terrorists', as Wynard Browne called the Leavises,[49] is replicated later in America, during the onset of the Cold War and the Red Scare of the 1950s. Dwight Macdonald, a scourge of the middlebrow and 'Midcult', whose violent rhetoric and anticipation of cultural apocalypse matches that of the Leavises, wrote: 'There is slowly emerging a tepid, flaccid Middlebrow culture that threatens to engulf everything in its spreading.'[50] Like the Leavises, Macdonald saw himself as alienated from the institutionalized intellectual elite and, because of his wavering but always leftist allegiances, was certainly vulnerable in the anti-communist climate of post-war United States.

The situation is different again in colonial and postcolonial countries. As the Australian David Carter and the New Zealander Terry Sturm have argued, in postcolonial societies the middlebrow is often identified with an emerging nationalist identity being asserted against the authority of the imperial centre.[51] Sturm demonstrates how great a pressure there was on Ngaio Marsh, for instance, to set her novels in a European context in order to open up a wider market for her books. Thus to write a popular novel set in New Zealand is an assertion of national identity which is more likely to be allied to a middlebrow readership than a highbrow readership, which would traditionally be associated with European cultural referents. David Carter makes the point that in the 1940s there was a high respect for middlebrow culture in Australia because it represented a national book culture independent of Britain. Carter offers the notion of 'middlebrow nationalism', which he argues is characterized by aspiration, 'virtuous citizenship and "nationed" modernity'.[52]

So, if our study of discourses about the middlebrow leads us to the conclusion that we must always attend to the ways in which they are inflected by their particular contexts, how generally applicable are available theories about formations of cultural hierarchy and notions of a middlebrow culture?

Theorizing the middlebrow

Pierre Bourdieu accounts for the violence of expressions of distaste as the product of tension between the illusory sense that taste is individual and the reality that it is determined. He judges it to be determined both by a 'habitus' or inherited predisposition to a set of tastes, and by the class trajectory of individuals seeking to reposition themselves by acquiring a cultural identity consonant with a desired class position. Bourdieu, like John Guillory, identifies the violence of expressions of taste as the over-assertion that accompanies a statement which we know to be irrational. However, while Guillory argues that it is precisely because we know our tastes to be merely personal that we assert their universality, Bourdieu's account is somewhat different: our tastes are determined but must carry the force of election if our sense of uniqueness is to be preserved.[53]

Bourdieu's critique, as that of any other cultural critic, must be read in the context of the culture of which he is a part, yet he was resistant to inscribing himself in the cultural map he draws. For example, in one of his last books, *The Weight of the World* (1999), Bourdieu collects a series of interviews designed to reveal 'Social Suffering in Contemporary Society'. Any interviewee who attempts to use the language of the professional sociologist is censored, the interview described as 'botched'.[54] The distance between the analyst and the analysed must be maintained. As this manoeuvre of Bourdieu demonstrates, the temptation to put oneself beyond the reach of scrutiny by commanding, inventing or policing the terms of debate is a strong one.

Caroline Pollentier, in her reading in this collection of Bourdieu in a cross-cultural context, stresses the importance of self-reflexivity on the part of the researcher. She demonstrates the essentialist bias of Bourdieu's own models of culture, despite his rejection of the perceived essentialism of his fellow anthropologist, Edgar Morin. Pollentier argues that in his adoption of a binary model of culture, legitimate and illegitimate, Bourdieu's construction of *l'art moyen* effectively removes any possibility that it might be assigned a positive value. Critiquing Bourdieu's construction of the middle, Pollentier suggests that 'it is perhaps by engaging in cross-cultural thinking that one can best map and criticize Bourdieu's *art moyen* – in a word, "make it strange" '. If we are to discuss processes of cultural transmission, then we need to temporarily become strangers to ourselves, to consider our own roles as transmitters of print culture and the values we seek to transmit.

The desire to avoid acknowledgement of the processes by which we have acquired 'cultural capital' is analogous to the modernist author's attempts to erase the professionalism of authorship from their texts. By contrast if there is one trope which pervades writing labelled middlebrow it is the representation of the act of writing itself. Desks clutter the pages of novels by Gilbert Frankau and Angela Thirkell, while in modernist novels the artistic sensibility is represented, but not the discarded drafts or the typewriter. Novels by both Joyce and Proust end with the protagonist's moment of epiphanic resolve to write the great work, but we never witness their return to the desk.[55] It is significant that the novelists closely associated, and respectably so, with representations of Grub Street were Balzac and Gissing, both writing in the nineteenth century when realism was the dominant literary mode. When modernism gained the critical ascendancy, romantic prejudices against the professional writer intensified. It is possible that this was not mere social snobbery but closely connected with fears that representing the act of writing would tip the narrative uncomfortably into the realms of realist representation and desacralize the text under construction.[56]

Anxieties about the middlebrow are linked with the uncertain class position of any kind of writer, ourselves included. Marx briefly debates whether or not an author should be classified as a 'productive worker' and therefore be assigned a class identity; his conclusion is that he cannot be so classified unless his works become marketable commodities. Because Milton, for example, only received £5 for *Paradise Lost*, Marx asserts that he cannot be classified as a productive worker and therefore has no class position. Marx compares Milton advantageously with hack writers in Leipzig whose works are marketable and who thereby have a class position. The implication is that texts of high cultural status will not be marketable and therefore the avant-garde author floats above class structures, free to choose whether to align himself with one class or another.[57] In contrast, the texts that insistently anchor the fictionalized author in the study and the marketplace thus invite dismissal as middlebrow.

The use of Bourdieu's paradigm of the popular as the doomed imitation of elite culture has tended, in the last few years, to replace discussion of Marxist attitudes to the popular as serving only the interests of 'the culture industry'. In the 1970s and 1980s, such attitudes served to stifle debate about the precise nature of print culture associated with the middlebrow because of the underpinning assumption that all such representations were 'ideology' and representative not of the cultural interests of their consumers but of the commercial and ideological interests of the producers and the hegemony they purportedly served. This set of assumptions temporarily eclipsed the value of the most comprehensive study of British interwar mass culture, Dan LeMahieu's *A Culture for Democracy: Mass Communication and the Cultivated Mind in Britain Between the Wars* (1988). LeMahieu's work, with that of Adrian Bingham, John Baxendale and Lawrence Napper, usefully counteracts any ideologically driven oversimplifications about the way cultural identity and status were negotiated on the pages and airwaves in Britain between the wars.[58]

When Joan Rubin's study, unapologetically entitled *The Making of Middlebrow Culture* (1992), came out in the United States four years after LeMahieu's book, its reception was initially uncritical. Equally magisterial and derived from original examination of primary sources, Rubin's study, like LeMahieu's, is not aligned with any theoretical model of class.[59] Yet unlike LeMahieu, she was not defined as a 'neoliberal' and was not required to produce her underpinning model of class.[60] This is in part because the moment of the New Left had passed and in part because Rubin's scholarship provided the growing number of feminist academics with an enabling and authoritative cultural map on which to locate texts which had, because of the dominance of modernist studies, been delegitimized in the academy. Rubin's work also heralded the rise of a new academic discipline, Book History, which draws attention to the material object of the book as a signifier within many diverse but intersecting evaluative systems. This has been a key agent of change in the way histories of taste are constructed. Numerous and diverse projects demonstrate the ways in which reading communities and cultural classifications have been shaped by publishing history, marketing and specific national contexts.[61]

Conclusion

The tone and nature of the critical enquiry represented by the essays in this collection contribute to a more accurate sense of the way cultural hierarchies have been established in the West during the last century, and the way, as scholars, we are a part of that process. Perhaps the reluctance of some modernist authors and scholars to acknowledge the extent to which their work is embedded in the wider culture is linked to a fear of being tainted by association. Even in a notional postmodern wonderland of intertextual play and freedom from rigid cultural categorization, perhaps there *is* a lumpen mass of texts irredeemably 'middlebrow' which might blunt any critical tools exercised upon them.[62] Yet no scholar of eighteenth-century literature would have to apologize for linking the work of the ubiquitous Colley Cibber with his mighty detractor, Alexander Pope.[63] As Janet Casey argues in this collection, 'Collectively, *all* literary works define and refine the meanings and positionings of all other works in the field, and in the aggregate they interact in complicated ways with other arts, and with the larger culture. This obliges us to make the middlebrow – the proverbial elephant in the room of literary history – a legitimate object of inquiry and analysis.' The structure of this collection draws attention to the endless modifications of the terms of the debate in response to the historical and geographical perspectives of its participants. If these essays are works of advocacy, it is not for new taxonomies of literary value or for the recuperation of individual texts. Each essay helps us to attend to the plurality of voices engaged in 'the brow wars' and their legacy. Collectively they help us chart the complex negotiations and diverse literary tastes which the term 'middlebrow' still threatens to obscure and homogenize.

Notes

1. Virginia Woolf (1942; 1947) 'Middlebrow: unpublished letter to the editor of the *New Statesman*', in *The Death of the Moth and Other Essays* (London: Hogarth Press), p. 115.
2. Graham Greene (1936) *Journey Without Maps* (London: Heinemann), pp. 14–15.
3. Q. D. Leavis (1932; 2000) *Fiction and the Reading Public* (London: Pimlico), p. 39.
4. Woolf, p. 117.
5. Dwight Macdonald (January, 1958; 1962) 'By Cozzens Possessed', *Commentary*, reprinted in *Against the American Grain: Essays on the Effects of Mass Culture* (New York: Vintage Books), pp. 187–212.
6. Woolf, p. 117; Dwight Macdonald (1957; 1964) 'A Theory of Mass Culture', in Bernard Rosenberg and David Manning White (eds) *Mass Culture: The Popular Arts in America* (New York: Macmillan; Free Press), p. 63.
7. Michael Hirschorn (July/August 2009) 'Last Stand: Why the Economist is Thriving While Time and Newsweek Fade', *The Atlantic*. We are indebted to Sharon Hamilton for drawing this article to our attention.
8. For analyses of the professional critic's conflicted feelings towards texts associated with pleasure, see: Janice A. Radway's *Reading the Romance: Women, Patriarchy and Popular Literature* (London and New York: Verso, 1987); *A Feeling for Books: The Book-of-the-month Club, Literary Taste, and Middle-Class Desire* (Chapel Hill and London: The University of North Carolina Press, 1997) and Alison Light's *Forever England: Femininity, Literature and Conservatism Between the Wars* (London: Routledge, 1991).
9. Pierre Bourdieu (1994; 1998) *Practical Reason* (Stanford, CA: Stanford University Press), p. 24.
10. Douglas Hewitt (1988) *English Fiction of the Early Modern Period 1890–1940* (Harlow: Addison Wesley Longman), pp. 170–171.
11. Geoffrey Crossick (ed.) (1977) *The Lower Middle Class in Britain: 1870–1914* (London: Croom Helm) and Arno J. Mayer (1975) 'Lower Middle Class as Historical Problem', *Journal of Modern History*, 47, 409–436.
12. Rita Felski (2000) 'Nothing to Declare: Identity, Shame, and the Lower Middle Class', *PMLA*, 115, 33–45.
13. Faye Hammill (2010) *Sophistication: A Literary and Cultural History* (Liverpool: Liverpool University Press).

14. This is the second identified use of the term 'middlebrow' in print; the first is in the Irish *Freeman's Journal*, 3 May 1924: 'Ireland's musical destiny, in spite of what the highbrows or middlebrows may say, is intimately bound up with the festivals.' *Oxford English Dictionary*, available at http://www.oed.com (accessed 23 July 2009).

15. Françoise Baillet (2006) 'Images de l'étrange: *Punch* ou la re-présentation du paradigme bourgeois', *Cahiers victoriens et édouardiens*, 64, 21–35.

16. This is borne out by Faye Hammill's research on the targets of disparagement in a wide range of magazines including *Punch*. As she notes in *Women, Celebrity, and Literary Culture Between the Wars* (Austin: University of Texas, 2007) to 'conform to one of these types is to fail in the struggle for distinction' (p. 8).

17. Adrian Bingham (2004) *Gender, Modernity, and the Popular Press in Inter-War Britain* (Oxford: Clarendon Press), for example pp. 10–11.

18. Virginia Woolf (1925; 1938) 'Modern Fiction', in *The Common Reader* (Harmondsworth: Penguin), p. 146.

19. John Baxendale (2007) *Priestley's England: J. B. Priestley and English Culture* (Manchester: Manchester University Press).

20. Q. D. Leavis, p. 67.

21. Ibid., pp. 23–24.

22. Jane Dowson (2003) 'Poetry and the Listener: The Myth of the Middlebrow', *Working Papers on the Web*, 6, available at http://extra.shu.ac.uk/wpw/ (accessed 16 June 2010).

23. *Saturday Review*, 20 February 1926, pp. 222–223.

24. Woolf (1942; 1947) 'Middlebrow'.

25. Virginia Woolf to Hugh Walpole, Sunday, 28 February 1932, in Nigel Nicholson (ed.) (1994) *The Sickle Side of the Moon: The Letters of Virginia Woolf, 1932–1935, vol. 5* (London: Hogarth Press), p. 25.

26. Christine Kenyon Jones and Anna Snaith (2010) ' "Tilting at Universities": Woolf At King's College London', *Woolf Studies Annual*, 16, 1–44.

27. Beth Rigal Daugherty (1997) 'Virginia Woolf's "How Should One Read a Book?" ', in Beth Carole Rosenberg and Jeanne Dubino (eds) *Virginia Woolf and the Essay* (Basingstoke: Macmillan), p. 161.

28. Woolf, *Three Guineas*, p. 379, quoted in Christine Kenyon Jones and Anna Snaith.

29. Virginia Woolf (1966) 'Mr. Bennett and Mrs. Brown', *Collected Essays, Volume I* (London: Hogarth Press) and Woolf (1925; 1968) 'Modern Fiction', *The Common Reader: First Series* (London: Hogarth Press).

30. Woolf, 'Modern Fiction', p. 190.

31. Nicola Humble (2001) *The Feminine Middlebrow Novel, 1920s to 1950s: Class, Domesticity and Bohemianism* (Oxford: Oxford University Press), p. 11.

32. Hammill (2007), p. 6.

33. Tom Harrisson, Humphrey Jennings and Charles Madge, letter, *New Statesman and Nation*, XIII, 310 (30 January 1937), p. 155.

34 George Orwell (1969) 'Bookshop Memories', (written 1936) in Sonia Orwell and Ian Angus (eds) *Collected Essays, Journalism and Letters* (London: Secker and Warburg), i, p. 244.

35. Q. D. Leavis, p. 7.

36. Humble, p. 11.

37. Light, p. 7. See also Lisa Botshon and Meredith Goldsmith (eds) (2003) *Middlebrow Moderns: Popular American Women Writers of the 1920s* (Boston, Northeastern University Press).
38. Q. D. Leavis, p. 39. See for example, the horror of Q. D. Leavis at the shoddy American fiction peddled to the working classes by 'the American firm, Messrs Woolworth' in *Fiction and the Reading Public*, p. 14.
39. Baxendale, pp. 121–122 and 128–129.
40. Lawrence Napper (2009) *British Cinema and the Middlebrow in the Interwar Years* (Exeter: Exeter University Press).
41. Montgomery Belgion (1928) 'British and American Taste', *English Journal*, 17. Repr. in Davison, Meyersohn, and Shills (eds) (1978) *Literary Taste, Culture and Mass Communication Vol 5* (Cambridge and Teaneck, NJ: Chadwyck-Healey) pp. 207–15.
42. Joan Shelley Rubin (1992) *The Making of Middlebrow Culture* (Chapel Hill: The University of North Carolina Press).
43. Van Wyck Brooks (1934) 'America's Coming of Age', in *Three Essays on America* (New York: E.P. Dutton), p. 57.
44. Gertrude Atherton (1999) 'Why Is American Literature Bourgeois?', in Gordon Hutner (ed.) *American Literature, American Culture* (New York: Oxford University Press) p. 194.
45. Michael Kammen (1996) *The Lively Arts: Gilbert Seldes and the Transformation of Cultural Criticism in the United States* (Oxford: Oxford University Press), p. 389.
46. Paul Hervey Fox (January 1917) 'The Pirates of Virtue', *Smart Set*, 169–174; Anthony Wharton (April 1917) 'Lady Marjory's Undies', *Smart Set*, 131–150.
47. Peter Swirski (2005) *From Lowbrow to Nobrow* (Montreal and London: McGill-Queen's University Press); Lawrence Levine (1988) *Highbrow/Lowbrow: The Emergence of Cultural Hierarchy in America* (Cambridge: Harvard University Press).
48. 'You're the Top', Cole Porter (1934) available at http://www.stlyrics.com (accessed 19 June 2010).
49. See Wynard Browne (September 1933) 'The Culture Brokers', *The London Mercury*, 436–45.
50. Dwight Macdonald, 'A Theory of Mass Culture', p. 63.
51. Terry Sturm (1998) 'Popular Fiction', in Terry Sturm (ed.) *The Oxford History of New Zealand Literature in English*, second edition (Auckland: Oxford University Press), pp. 591–595 and David Carter (2004) 'The Mystery of the Missing Middlebrow or The C(o)urse of Good Taste', in Judith Ryan and Chris Wallace-Crabbe (eds) *Imagining Australia: Literature and Culture in the New World* (Cambridge, MA: Harvard University Press), pp. 173–201.
52. Carter, p. 184.
53. Pierre Bourdieu (1986) *Distinction: A Social Critique of the Judgement of Taste*, trans. Richard Nice (London: Routledge and Kegan Paul), orig. published as (1979) *La Distinction, Critique sociale du judgement* (Paris: Les Editions de Minuit) and John Guillory (1993) *Cultural Capital: The Problem of Literary Canon Formation* (Chicago: University of Chicago Press), p. 272 and the whole of Chapter 5, 'The Discourse of Value: From Adam Smith to Barbara Hernstein Smith', pp. 269–340.

54. Pierre Bourdieu (1999) *The Weight of the World* (Cambridge: Polity Press), p. 617, footnote 1.
55. Marcel Proust (1949) *Cities of the Plain*, trans. C. K. Scott Moncrieff (London: Chatto Windus), orig. published as *Sodome et Gomorrhe* (1921 and 1922) the final part of *A la recherche du temps perdu*, and James Joyce (1916; 1992) *A Portrait of the Artist as a Young Man* (London: Minerva).
56. We are indebted to Leigh Wilson for this possible explanation of the absence of the desk in modernist novels.
57. Discussed in S. S. Prawer (1976) *Karl Marx and World Literature* (Oxford: Clarendon Press), p. 310.
58. Adrian Bingham (2004) *Gender, Modernity, and the Popular Press in Inter-War Britain* (Oxford: Clarendon Press); John Baxendale (2007) *Priestley's England: J. B. Priestley and English Culture* (Manchester: Manchester University Press) and Lawrence Napper (2009) *British Cinema and Middlebrow Culture in the Interwar Years* (Exeter: The University of Exeter Press).
59. Dan LeMahieu (1988) *A Culture for Democracy: Mass Communication and the Cultivated Mind in Britain Between the Wars* (Oxford: Oxford University Press) and Joan Rubin (1992) *The Making of Middlebrow Culture* (Chapel Hill and London: The University of North Carolina Press).
60. James Curran (2002) *Media and Power* (London: Routledge), p. 22. For further discussion of LeMahieu in Curran see also pp. 17, 20, 42 and 163.
61. For example, Robert Fraser and Mary Hammond (eds) (2008) *Books Without Borders: Vols 1 and 2* (Basingstoke: Palgrave Macmillan). These essays chart the shifts in cultural value that occur when a text is transferred from one culture to another, thus enabling us to read one kind of cultural hierarchy against another.
62. Dwight Macdonald, 'A Theory of Mass Culture', p. 63.
63. Amongst many, see for example, Donald T. Siebert, Jr. (Winter, 1976–1977) 'Cibber and Satan: The Dunciad and Civilization', *Eighteenth-Century Studies*, 10.2, pp. 203–221.

Part I
Cultural Contexts

1
Middlebrow Reading and Undergraduate Teaching: The Place of the Middlebrow in the Academy

Janet Galligani Casey

Numerous negative connotations adhere to the middlebrow, and my students are quick to sustain them. Typically they stress that middlebrow literature is the kind of literature that is *not* studied in college. More specifically, they tell me that the middlebrow is 'easy reading', that it attracts 'less educated audiences' and that it is inexplicably, sometimes maddeningly, 'popular'. They would agree, I think, with the unnamed *Dial* critic of the 1920s, who suggested, in characterizing the novels of best-selling American author Edna Ferber, that the middlebrow 'puts no strain on either the emotional or the intellectual equipment of [its] very gentle readers'.[1] That such severe and long-standing critical judgements, often unexamined, have filtered down to twenty-first-century undergraduates is easy to demonstrate: just ask them. Most students, by the time they reach college, have internalized the notion that the texts we teach in school are somehow different from the larger body of mainstream books, and the difference, as they understand it, can only be explained through appeals to ambiguous notions of literary 'quality'.

To be sure, it could hardly be otherwise. Students have been conditioned to abide by the values of the academy, which has long perpetuated its own status through privileging certain types of literature, namely the types that yield most richly to academic modes of reading and interpretation. The attitudes of the New Criticism linger, resulting in the pronounced valuation of texts that are formally and thematically challenging – those that, in a word, require 'teaching'. Literature that is dense or difficult appears to justify the need for higher education; students thus come to perceive literary learning as the revelation of textual mysteries that would be impossible, or at least less likely, without the intervention of a professor. It is no surprise, then, that those works that seem, on the surface, to be less complicated, less demanding of the reader, appear to students (and often their teachers) to be extraneous to college-level literary studies – even though such works may form the bulk of the reading that they do outside the classroom.

Yet I'd like to argue that teaching the middlebrow has become essential to the undergraduate English curriculum that it represents a final frontier of sorts in the consideration of literature's nuanced relations to society at large. In acknowledging that literature responds to, and is inflected by, social and aesthetic currents, and in conceiving of it as one element in a complex and ever-shifting set of power struggles within the field of cultural production more broadly, we have laid the groundwork for a serious and sustained consideration not just of some texts, but of all texts. Collectively, *all* literary works define and refine the meanings and positionings of all other works in the field, and in the aggregate they interact in complicated ways with other arts and with the larger culture.[2] This obliges us to make the middlebrow – the proverbial elephant in the room of literary history – a legitimate object of inquiry and analysis.

Of course, we have already added scores of newly appreciated texts by women and various minority groups to our syllabi and curricula, demonstrating that we *have* enlarged our conception of the literary field. Some of these works, including, for instance, regional texts by women or ethnic writers, overlap with the category of the middlebrow. Yet such texts have typically been recuperated through the efforts of feminist scholars or scholars of race/ethnicity, while the middlebrow as a concept unto itself remains largely an uninvestigated 'other', serving as a foil to serious literature rather than a location for genuine literary study. Curiously, though, its role as the implied backdrop against which great art distinguishes itself is precisely what makes the middlebrow so essential to a consideration of literature writ large. As Gordon Hutner has argued recently in his study of American middlebrow tastes, knowledge of 'average' literary preoccupations is the key to grasping the historical relations between artistic production and the nuances of social life.[3] Hence a meaningful exploration of 'middling' literature becomes crucial to an expressed goal of many contemporary literary studies educators: namely, a fuller understanding of the literary landscape in all of its gendered, classed and racialized complexity. This applies not only to United States literature, where my own work is located, but also to British and other European literatures as well.

I want to stress, however, that teaching middlebrow literature to undergraduates is not merely or even primarily a recovery project. Although work by scholars on both sides of the Atlantic has resulted in intriguing and significant reassessments of particular middlebrow texts and authors – including such best-sellers as Anita Loos's *Gentlemen Prefer Blondes* and Rose Wilder Lane's historical pioneer narratives, as well as the novels of Rosamond Lehmann[4] – it is the middlebrow's centrality to the entire enterprise of literary studies that demands our attention. This has been especially true in the last one hundred years or so, and particularly at the dawn of what we know as modernism. The enormous growth in the bookselling industry in the early twentieth century, together with such phenomena as the emergence of best-sellers' lists and the development of a literary prize culture, created new stratifications in the literary field; competition for the ever-expanding audience of readers, played out in part through fresh experiments in the art of advertising, lent an exciting dynamism, and a modern market sensibility, to the business of writing, promoting and consuming books. That novels were frequently the basis for moving pictures, feeding the public appetite for the new medium of cinema, only heightened the stakes. As scholars have amply demonstrated, these were exciting times indeed, and they altered permanently – and made far more complex – the relations between literature and the broader culture.[5] A literary pedagogy that confines itself to the canonical texts of this period (so often the works of high modernism), ignoring these cultural currents, not only flattens literary history, but also robs students of the opportunity to encounter cultural jockeying in action, to make applicable connections to their own cultural moment and to understand literary value as relative and situational rather than timeless and absolute.

But a consideration of modernism is only the beginning. Stretching from the middle of the nineteenth century (when Nathaniel Hawthorne famously complained of the 'damned mob of scribbling women' who threatened his own literary status) to the present time, the middlebrow should be integral to our conception of a literary canon. As a key term in undergraduate literary education, *canonicity* marks our efforts to make students more conscious of the politics of literary evaluation; hence it is logical that the middlebrow as a category should find a place in these discussions. But if the undergraduate literature classroom in the twenty-first century is the site of an increasingly sophisticated investigation into cultural hierarchies of all types, we have typically been more concerned with the extreme poles – that is, with 'high' versus 'low' culture – than with the large and amorphous ground of the middle. Why is it that this *middle* has largely eluded pointed interrogation, even within an academic literary culture that has broadened its horizons so greatly in recent times?

The reasons are varied. Owing to its sheer size and variety, for instance, the territory of the middlebrow is difficult to define, theorize or map; as my students suggest, we recognize it less by what it is than by what it is not. Moreover, its oft-cited status as 'aspirational' literature, allegedly pitched towards an audience of moderately educated readers who seek to become cultured through the (indiscriminate) consumption of books, surely makes it more genuinely threatening to academic standards than 'low' cultural artefacts might be. (Dwight MacDonald, notorious critic of what he called 'midcult', summarized this view when he sneered that the middlebrow 'pretends to respect the standards of high culture while in fact it waters them down and vulgarizes them'.[6]) Perhaps most obviously and most famously, the middlebrow is tainted by its close association with the consumer marketplace, wherein economic capital presumably trumps cultural capital.

But these reasons, when considered judiciously, only make the middlebrow more compelling as an area of study, since they throw into high relief the standards and practices of canon formation and preservation. In short, the middlebrow has largely enabled the very concept of hierarchy in the literary realm, and therefore warrants investigation by undergraduates, whose tasks as English majors include tracing the broad outlines of literary history as well as grappling with assessments of literary worth. As I see it, then, there are two main arguments for making this dimension of literary culture visible to students.

First, the middlebrow contextualizes canonical works and writers within the larger, mainstream arena through which they acquire much of their meaning and presumed authority. Indeed, when we merely present acknowledged 'masterpieces' as if their superiority is self-evident, we fail to give students experience in identifying and sifting the various indices of literary value. We can enrich the study of canonical literature by promoting an understanding of the dynamics through which it achieves that status; the surprise for students is that sometimes those dynamics have less to do with literariness than with social, political or even commercial interests. Plumbing the workings of the middle, then, goes a long way towards enabling a more subtle appreciation of the high.

The second argument for teaching the middlebrow is that it greatly expands the variety of texts through which students may learn about various literary-cultural phenomena, including not only issues of style, but also readerships, modes of production and dissemination and critical reception. Again, surprises abound. The relationship between literary prizes and academic acceptance, for instance, is quite unstable historically (many Pulitzer Prize winners, in particular, were middlebrow successes and are now largely unknown), a fact that can lead students to reconsider their own assumptions about honours and accolades as well as the bases for canonicity. High and middle texts of the same period often reveal similar thematic preoccupations, which open up more textured investigations into the role(s) of art in culture. And certain writers have spanned the middle and high domains (where would we place Ernest Hemingway or Willa Cather, e.g.?), a reality that complicates productively the academy's versions of literary history, which are often overly neat.

Of course, these arguments assume a conscious treatment of the middlebrow as such, rather than the unremarked insertion into a course of an occasional, token middlebrow text. This is not to downplay the importance of close readings of these texts (which, in many cases, richly reward such efforts) but to emphasize the significance of the middlebrow as both a collective material reality and a trope. What is clear, I think, is that teaching the middlebrow as a construct of literary history foregrounds questions of literary assessment and cultural power in a way that teaching canonical texts may not; this compels students to follow, and even engage in, subtle acts of discrimination that may not be required of them within a canon-based pedagogy. It also forces them to confront and evaluate cultural prejudices, both from historical and contemporary perspectives. Ideally, then, individual middlebrow works should be carefully contextualized so as to underscore their complex relations both to the academy and to a more broadly conceived literary history. Even better, when appropriate, would be a course unit dedicated to the exploration of the middlebrow as a cultural phenomenon.

But these comments beg the question of how, exactly, the middlebrow might be accommodated within the English literature curriculum. Certainly many, if not most, undergraduate departments lack the resources or the inclination to offer an entire course on middlebrow literatures, though such courses, I suspect, will eventually become more prevalent. More likely at present, however, is the introduction of middlebrow issues into more traditional literature syllabi – an approach that potentially leverages the middlebrow through juxtaposition with canonical texts. (My assumption, of course, is that such comparisons would be used not to reinforce traditional hierarchies, but to problematize them.) But what types of courses might be particularly hospitable to the middlebrow, and what approaches might help to highlight its politics?

As I have already suggested, the early twentieth century is a prime location for thinking through the emergence and influence of middlebrow literature. The flourishing of scholarship on the middlebrow in this period suggests as much; studies range from the comprehensive (Joan Shelley Rubin's work on the advent of the middlebrow; Janice Radway's monograph on the creation of the Book of the Month Club; Faye Hammill's consideration of the culture of literary celebrity between the wars) to the highly specific (tightly focused essays on individual texts and authors in collections such as *Middlebrow Moderns*).[7] These studies can assist college faculty in acquiring knowledge of literary trends and, perhaps more importantly, in tracing the outlines of the debate that erupted with particular virulence at this time concerning the middlebrow's supposed bastardization of the aesthetic. Courses on modernism, then, may be greatly enhanced by consideration of the middlebrow's role in the literary politics of the period – perhaps, but not necessarily, accompanied by the reading of a particularly provocative middlebrow text. In addition to enjoying middlebrow novels by writers such as Zane Grey and Dorothy Canfield Fisher, my students have been especially intrigued by certain fascinating moments in modern middlebrow history, such as when Sinclair Lewis famously turned down the Pulitzer Prize for *Arrowsmith* (1925) because he associated literary awards with sub-par literature that was, in his words, 'safe, polite, obedient, and sterile'.[8] Such moments bring alive for students the controversies that raged in the early twentieth century, inviting them not merely to stand back and admire accepted texts, but to dip into messy debates about what and how literature *signifies*.

One particular cultural location rewards investigation and is quite adaptable to undergraduate classroom work: namely, magazines. Mainstream periodicals literally brought together under a single cover highbrow and middlebrow texts and writers, dramatizing their coexistence and challenging the hierarchies imposed retrospectively by literary history. Since many novels, 'serious' as well as 'popular', were first serialized in magazines, additional questions arise about the presumed divisions among readerships. At what point, if any, can the line be drawn in this period between 'high' aesthetic enterprises and those intended for a less exclusive audience? This question can be explored through hands-on work with virtually any available mainstream magazine of the early twentieth century, from *Collier's Weekly* to *Ladies' Home Journal*. Students may be startled to find highbrow authors in these 'commercial' locations; even more important, they will encounter frequent and striking juxtapositions – as in, for example, the March 1913 edition of *Scribner's*, where an instalment of Edith Wharton's canonical novel, *The Custom of the Country*, is immediately preceded by a short story by Thomas Nelson Page, popularizer of southern plantation romances.[9] Such examples go further than any lecture in demonstrating the dynamic and ongoing interactions between high and middle cultures.

Periodicals are also the major site of book reviews and offer a chance to capture the contours of literary debate. Using the *Book Review Digest* as a starting point, I like to ask students to hunt down reviews of both canonical and popular works of the modernist period for two very different ends. First, they typically uncover discriminatory language that may have pre-ordained the eventual positions of certain works within or outside of the academy; together we consider those words that seem especially loaded, such as 'romantic', 'sentimental' and 'propagandistic', all of which could have negative connotations and often lasting impact within the machinery of literary evaluation. Second, and more surprisingly, students find through contemporary reviews that the critical assessments of canonical and popular works were sometimes quite similar, leading to further questions about the supposedly inherent superiority of academic texts. (Another way to make this same point is to expose students to evaluations of middlebrow works by highbrow writers; e.g., William Faulkner and Edith Wharton both admired *Gentlemen Prefer Blondes*, and Gertrude Stein was an avid reader of detective fiction.[10]) Utilizing the mainstream press in these ways not only addresses relevant pedagogical questions, but also gives students access to a wide world of print culture that is not usually explored in undergraduate English courses. Moreover, the use of magazines opens up interesting possibilities for course projects that further demonstrate patterns of influence between 'serious' and 'popular' writers, including comparisons of mass-disseminated commercial periodicals – which featured a great deal of poetry and fiction – with 'little' (i.e., literary) magazines.

An equally compelling but quite different way to accommodate study of the middlebrow is to organize a modernisms course or unit around a formal or thematic issue; I find the question of 'accessibility' to be a particularly provocative point of departure. In the context of modernism particularly, students have assumed that formally complex texts are somehow 'better' texts, which makes many middlebrow works seem, by default, inferior. But focusing on why writers might *choose* a more accessible aesthetic, rather than assuming that they are incapable of formalist experiment, widens considerably the ideological terrain. Indeed, as scholars of minority literatures have long argued, writers who wish to reach a large audience for social or political purposes are unlikely to embrace esoteric structures – an observation that helped to reframe many works of the Harlem Renaissance, for example. That many middlebrow authors have sought to reach large numbers of readers, then, hardly invalidates the often acute social critiques embedded in their works.

The literature and rhetoric of the organized Left in the 1920s and 1930s suggests itself as a useful site for considering questions of accessibility, since the Left regularly and quite publicly assaulted what it saw as the elitism of the highbrows. Of course, the political purposes of the Left gave it good reason to eschew recondite literary styles, but it went a step further by disparaging as 'bourgeois' any literature that excluded average readers. Mike Gold, the acknowledged literary theorist of the Communist Party USA, referred to Gertrude Stein as a 'literary idiot' and painted Proust as the 'master-masturbator of bourgeois literature', suggesting that such writers fetishized individual emotive states, thereby furthering the interests of capitalism.[11] My students are frequently astonished and sometimes delighted (though occasionally distressed) to discover that canonical works were not uniformly valorized from the moment of their creation. More to the point, the legitimate question, persistently raised by the Left, of whom or what art is *for* redirects in provocative ways the typical (i.e., negative) assessment of the middlebrow – a category that overlaps frequently with Leftist literature.[12] (Indeed, one of the great American middlebrow triumphs of the twentieth century was also a triumph for anti-capitalism: John Steinbeck's 1939 *The Grapes of Wrath*.) Linking middlebrow cultural production and its stylistic tendencies to the weighty socio-political concerns of groups such as the organized Left thus revises in fruitful ways our understanding of the middlebrow. In these contexts, the middlebrow becomes not merely lightweight entertainment, but rather a mode of artistic expression that intervenes in meaningful ways in social and cultural life.

I hasten to point out that while my own teaching and scholarship are generally in the modernist period, consideration of the middlebrow is not at all confined to that cultural moment. Feminist scholars of the United States, for example, have long studied the popular literature of temperance and domesticity in the nineteenth century, though the use of the term 'middlebrow' to describe this work would be anachronistic.[13] Yet this raises important questions about the temporal location of the middlebrow, and about its various manifestations. When, historically, do we begin to identify a genuine 'middle' culture? What differences come to light when we plot this culture over time? Across national and racial borders? Across genders? Can it be genuinely subversive? To what extent is the middlebrow necessarily connected to class aspirations? These questions will continue to be probed by scholars, but some of them are also appropriate as guiding questions for the undergraduate classroom. Once we dispense with the stale notion that the middlebrow is, by definition, inferior and thus unworthy of study, a host of investigative possibilities arises.

To my mind, however, the most exciting aspect of teaching middlebrow literature is that it reaches students where they live, so to speak: in the realm of their own 'guilty' textual pleasures. Thanks to Oprah Winfrey's Book Club and similar cultural vehicles – including the still-thriving Book of the Month Club – the middlebrow is alive and well in the twenty-first century, and students are acutely aware of it. The reading they do outside the classroom, in their free time, is often of the middlebrow variety; indeed, it is frequently this type of reading that got them interested in literature in the first place. Yet that reading has not been sanctioned by the academy and remains largely external to their studies; sometimes they are even ashamed of it. To introduce middlebrow literature as a valid object of inquiry is thus to bring to light the convergence of fears, desires and ambitions that colours students' interest in the literary. It bridges the gap between the scholarly and the mundane, and invites students to question what they study and why. Specifically, a consideration of the middlebrow presents opportunities to engage students in reflective consideration of their own roles as both readers and consumers of texts; it also licenses them to make their own assessments about the historical construction of literariness and their complicity in its ongoing stratifications. Ultimately, it encourages them to take control of their learning by deciding for themselves what kinds of academic categories matter, and why. The middlebrow, then, potentially makes the study of literature less precious and more relevant to everyday acts and concerns – a reinvigoration that has important ramifications in a world in which the arts and humanities disciplines are frequently accused of being out of touch.

Teaching the middlebrow also brings issues of power and disempowerment – a heady topic for students – into conversation with art. Typically we think of the aesthetic as somehow floating above the grosser struggles of day-to-day existence: if books portray and even critique social life, so we assume, then they must somehow be outside of that life rather than implicated in it. But studying the location of the middlebrow reminds us that art, too, is subject to the slings and arrows of fortune, and that its 'success' or 'failure' sometimes has as much to do with cultural manoeuvrings as with a transcendent literariness or lack of it. This awareness can help students to engage with increased confidence in the debates about art, literary, or otherwise, that rage in our own time: Who decides what constitutes it? What powers enable it? What are the consequences when society censors it?

What I am suggesting, ultimately, is that we are obligated not only to teach the middlebrow, but also to contextualize it in a manner that recognizes it as a meaningful cultural force and that enables productive, affirmative and even scholarly accounts of it.

And such a position is not as novel as we might think. Back in the early twentieth century, many claimed a positive role for middlebrow culture, though sometimes it took the backhanded form of disdain for more exclusive modes of expression. Editor Katherine Williams, for instance, in introducing the first edition of *The Colored American Magazine* in 1916, targeted her middlebrow audience pointedly and proudly:

> It will not be our ambition to make this magazine a 'literary gem' either for our own gratification or to suit the high-brows, but to present facts in plain, commonsense language, so that the masses may read and understand; or, in the words of Brother Taylor, we propose to call a 'spade a *spade*' and not an 'excavating instrument for manual manipulation.'[14]

More recently, in an article entitled 'Confessions of a Middlebrow Professor', W. A. Pannapacker narrated his graduate-school embarrassment about his lower-middle-class roots, but went on to champion middlebrow texts and postures. Specifically, he defended his classic middlebrow collection of Great Books of the Western World, a 'beloved' set of '54 leatherette volumes' published in 1952 that greatly influenced him in childhood and adolescence. Despite their parochialism, he argues, and despite their naked appeal to the pedestrian reader, such collections reflected a better world, one in which 'the liberal arts commanded more respect' and intellectual aspiration was valorized.[15] Such attempts to situate the middlebrow as a legitimate arena of intelligent exchange help to recuperate for us and our students a vast landscape of writing and thinking that is in no way external to our earnest and concentrated efforts to comprehend the relations between literature and culture. On the contrary, the middlebrow arguably stands at the very centre of that inquiry.

Notes

1. 'Briefer Mention' (December 1924) *Dial*, 77, 523.
2. Clearly I am indebted here to Pierre Bourdieu's 'The Field of Cultural Production', in Bourdieu (1993) *The Field of Cultural Production: Essays on Art and Literature* (Columbia University Press), pp. 29–73.
3. Gordon Hutner (2008) *What America Read: Taste, Class, and the Novel* (University of North Carolina Press).
4. On Loos, see Faye Hammill (2007) ' "Brains are really everything": Anita Loos's *Gentlemen Prefer Blondes*', in *Women, Celebrity, and Literary Culture Between the Wars* (Austin: University of Texas Press). On Lane, see Donna Campbell (2003) ' "Written with a Hard and Ruthless Purpose": Rose Wilder Lane, Edna Ferber, and Regional Middlebrow Fiction', in L. Botshon and M. Goldsmith (eds) *Middlebrow Moderns: Popular American Women Writers of the 1920s* (Boston: Northeastern University Press), pp. 25–44. On Lehmann, see Wendy Pollard (2004) *Rosamond Lehmann and Her Critics: The Vagaries of Literary Reception* (Aldershot: Ashgate).
5. In particular, the Modernist Studies Association, founded in 1998, has both highlighted and fostered new approaches to modernism that have stressed interdisciplinarity and have embraced the role of the middlebrow.
6. Dwight Macdonald (Spring 1960) 'Masscult and Midcult', *Partisan Review*, 27, 203–233 (Fall 1960) 27, 589–631.
7. Joan Shelley Rubin (1992) *The Making of Middlebrow Culture* (Chapel Hill: University of North Carolina Press); Janice Radway (1997) *A Feeling for Books: The Book-of-the-Month Club, Literary Taste, and Middle-Class Desire* (Chapel Hill: University of North Carolina Press); Faye Hammill (2007) *Women, Celebrity, and Literary Culture Between the Wars* (Austin: University of Texas Press); Lisa Botshon and Meredith Goldsmith (eds) (2003) *Middlebrow Moderns: Popular American Women Writers of the 1920s* (Boston: Northeastern University Press).
8. Quoted in 'Lewis Refuses Pulitzer Prize', *New York Times*, 6 May 1926, p. 1.
9. Thomas Nelson Page (1913) 'The Shepherd Who Watched by Night', *Scribner's*, 53(3), 365–373; Edith Wharton (1913) 'The Custom of the Country' (Book II, chapters XI–XIV), *Scribner's*, 53(3), 373–395.
10. On highbrow attitudes towards *Blondes*, see Sarah Churchwell (2003) ' "Lost Among the Ads": *Gentlemen Prefer Blondes* and the Politics of Imitation', in *Middlebrow Moderns*, pp. 135–164, 158. On Stein's reading, see Karen Leick (2009) *Gertrude Stein and the Making of an American Celebrity* (New York: Routledge), e.g. pp. 182, 184.
11. Michael Gold (1936) 'Gertrude Stein: A Literary Idiot', *Change the World!* (New York: International); Gold (1930; 1972) 'Proletarian Realism', in M. Folsom (ed.) *Mike Gold: A Literary Anthology* (New York: International), pp. 203–208.
12. For examples of this interaction in the American context, see Michael Denning (1998) *The Cultural Front: The Laboring of American Culture in the*

Twentieth Century (New York: Verso) and B. Mullen and S. Linkon (eds) (1996) *Radical Revisions: Rereading 1930s Culture* (Urbana: University of Illinois Press).

13. See the website of the Middlebrow Network, which indicates that the first use of the term appeared in the early twentieth century: www.middlebrownetwork.com, 'Defining the Middlebrow', date accessed 1 August 2011.

14. Quoted in Noliwe M. Rooks (2004) *Ladies' Pages: African American Women's Magazines and the Culture that Made Them* (New Brunswick: Rutgers University Press), pp. 69–70.

15. W. A. Pannapacker, 'Confessions of a Middlebrow Professor', *Chronicle Review*, 5 October 2009, available at http://chronicle.com/article/Confessions-of-a-Middlebrow/48644/, accessed 1 August 2011.

2
Configuring Middleness: Bourdieu, *l'Art Moyen* and the Broadbrow

Caroline Pollentier

In his preface to the English edition of *Distinction: A Social Critique of the Judgement of Taste* (1984),[1] Pierre Bourdieu started by addressing his American readership with a noteworthy disclaimer, allowing him to highlight, rather than resolve, the methodological difficulties resulting from the transference of his theoretical framework into a different national context: 'I have every reason to fear that this book will strike the reader as "very French" – which I know is not always a compliment' (p. xi). While raising the possibility of cross-cultural thinking, he alerted his readership to 'the dangers of a facile search for partial equivalences which cannot stand in for a methodological comparison between systems' (p. xii). However, Bourdieu did not clarify the grounds of this disclaimer, and, taking America as the test case for a problematic 'search for equivalents', he proceeded to suggest a few cross-cultural examples testifying to the presence of 'structural invariants' in every 'stratified society'. For instance, 'the undemanding entertainment which Parisians expect from boulevard theatre, New Yorkers will seek in Broadway musicals'. Inviting the American reader to above all 'reflec[t] onto his own society, onto his position within it', Bourdieu thereby foregrounded critical reflexivity as a founding sociological principle, constitutive of the potentially universal dimension of his critical approach to culture (p. xii).

The question of transferring Bourdieu's category of *art moyen* to an English context has not yet been raised as such by English or French critics, although several studies have fruitfully included discussions of his sociological model in their analysis of middlebrow writers.[2] If one is to try and think the middlebrow across borders, one may first engage in a similar 'search for equivalents' (p. xii): bearing in mind the cultural embeddedness of Bourdieu's sociology of taste, can we envision 'middlebrow culture' as an 'equivalent' for what Bourdieu refers to as *la culture moyenne*?[3] The fact that the translator Richard Nice took care to include Bourdieu's original phrase in parenthesis in the English edition signals a semantic and ideological slippage in the translation process. Importantly, his choice to quote the phrase in French exposes the original associations attached to Bourdieu's concept of *culture moyenne*, namely, its relevance as a class ethos practised by the *classe moyenne*, and its less clearly defined echoes of a widespread French stereotype, *le français moyen* – which, *de facto*, emerged as a pejorative cultural marker in the French cultural field of the 1960s.[4] Unlike its English translation, the adjective *moyen*, meaning average, does not function on its own as a cultural keyword in French, and rather points to an average standard, conceived in the vein of the statistician Adolphe Quételet's and the sociologist Maurice Halbwachs's understandings of *l'homme moyen*.[5] The concept of *culture moyenne* therefore retains a certain semantic fuzziness, all the more so as Bourdieu never reflects on its problematic pejorative connotations. Though he identifies the petit-bourgeois ethos as an intermediary position in the hierarchy of taste, he theorizes in *La distinction: critique sociale du jugement* (1979) as well as in his previous work on photography, *Un art moyen: essai sur les usages sociaux de la photographie* (1965),[6] his idea of *moyen*, which, as we shall see, remains partly undefined, so much so that the surface issue of its translation may in fact catalyze larger limitations in its conceptualization.[7]

Rather than simply considering *moyen* and middlebrow as possible cultural 'equivalents',[8] I therefore propose to develop a meta-theoretical questioning of Bourdieu's category: how does the sociological concept of *moyen* configure the social and symbolic values attached to this arguably national-based middle ground, and can this way of configuring middleness help us account for the emergence of the English middlebrow ethos?[9] I would like first to clarify how the category of *art moyen* functions in Bourdieu's analysis of symbolic struggles, which will lead me to highlight its limitations as a devaluative category. While acknowledging the capacity of Bourdieu's relational model to avoid essentialist reductions, I will show that his theoretical framework produces a restrictively negative assessment of middlebrow practices. By examining an earlier configuration of middleness rooted in an English context – namely, J. B. Priestley's ethical revaluation of the Broadbrow – I shall argue that the emergence of the middlebrow in England should ultimately be positioned outside Bourdieu's agonistic conception of culture. Paradoxically enough, it is perhaps by engaging in cross-cultural thinking that one can best map and criticize Bourdieu's *art moyen* – in a word, 'make it strange'.[10]

Bourdieu's idea of *moyen* is central to the logic of distinction he posits at the core of the cultural field. In *Distinction*, Bourdieu intends to move away from the 'pure' gaze established by Kantian aesthetics in order to expose the mechanisms of domination at work in cultural practices and representations. According to him, the elite wishes to differentiate itself from middle-class and working-class practices, while the petite bourgeoisie wishes to differentiate itself from working-class practices. Judgements of taste are thus caught up in a symbolic hierarchy dominated by legitimate culture, practised by the bourgeois elite and recognized as legitimate by the other classes. This hierarchy of taste is internalized by all cultural actors, so that the petit bourgeois, belonging to the middle class, reveres legitimate culture and aspires towards it, without possessing the knowledge of the elite. Understanding this aspiration as 'cultural goodwill' (*Distinction*, p. 321), Bourdieu therefore categorizes petit-bourgeois taste as an intermediary position within a tripartite model of culture. One the one hand, 'the petit bourgeois is filled with reverence for culture' (p. 321): '[t]his middlebrow culture (*culture moyenne*) owes some of its charm, in the eyes of the middle classes who are its main consumers, to the references to legitimate culture it contains' (p. 323). On the other hand, 'middle-brow culture is resolutely against vulgarity' (p. 326).

Bourdieu elaborated this double emphasis on differentiation and reverence in a previous collective work devoted to photography, *Photography: A Middle-brow Art* (1990), originally commissioned by the company Kodak. In his analysis of the distinctive attitudes held towards photography, which he understands as being always mediated by the individual's relationship to his own class and other classes, Bourdieu identifies photography as a 'middle-brow art', in the sense that it belongs to the 'sphere of the legitimizable', occupying an intermediary position between legitimate art and vulgar practices.[11] Beyond this contestable definition of 'photography', which remains rooted in a specific historical context,[12] it is worth understanding Bourdieu's analysis of the petit bourgeois' attitude to photography. Photography being a democratic, ordinary practice, the petit bourgeois endeavours to 'ennoble themselves culturally by attempting to ennoble photography':

> The meaning which *petits bourgeois* confer on photographic practice conveys or betrays the relationship of the *petite bourgeoisie* to culture, that is, to the upper classes (bourgeoisie) who retain the privilege of cultural practices which are held to be superior, and to the working classes from whom they wish to distinguish themselves at all costs

by manifesting, through the practices which are accessible to them, their cultural goodwill; it is in this way that members of photographic clubs seek to ennoble themselves culturally by attempting to ennoble photography.[13]

Thus, conceiving the whole cultural field within a general 'hierarchy of legitimacies',[14] Bourdieu foregrounded a structural link between an *art moyen* and the *petit bourgeois* who, dominated by legitimate culture, wished to ennoble it.

The future developments of photography having largely belied this model, what remains of Bourdieu's project is his explicit ambition to think the petit bourgeois outside an essentialist framework attached to subjective, universal judgements of taste. One may wonder whether this anti-essentialist project did not partly fail because of his very conception of *art moyen*, which, de facto, defines middlebrow practices as 'average' and thus duplicates uncritically the negative value judgements attached to an ordinary art form. Significantly, in *Distinction*, his later and more theorized project, Bourdieu refers to but does not develop extensively the notion of *moyen*, foregrounding rather the figure of the petit bourgeois as a central case of cultural goodwill.[15] When he explicitly defines the idea of *moyen*, Bourdieu does so in order to posit his relational model against an essentialist conception of 'average' culture. However, in doing so, he still resorts to the term 'average' and thus encodes the perspective of legitimate culture in his own concept:

> As is shown by the fact that the same object which is today typically middle-brow – 'average' (*moyen*) – may yesterday have figured in the most 'refined' constellations of tastes and may be put back there at any moment by one of those taste-maker's coups which are capable of rehabilitating the most discredited object, the notion of an 'average' culture (*culture moyenne*) is as fictitious as that of an 'average', universally acceptable language. What makes middle-brow culture is the middle-class relation to culture – mistaken identity, misplaced belief, allodoxia. (p. 327)

The English translation establishes a difference between 'average culture' and 'middle-brow culture', which is not present in the original ('il n'*existe* pas plus de culture moyenne que de langue moyenne. Ce qui *fait* la culture moyenne, c'est le rapport petit-bourgeois à la culture' ('the notion of average culture (*culture moyenne*) is as fictitious as that of an "average", universally acceptable language. What makes middle-brow culture is the middle-class relation to culture'.)).[16] Bourdieu's repetition of the phrase *culture moyenne* is allegedly predicated on the opposition between a 'substantialist' (p. 22) and a relational approach to *culture moyenne*, as performed by petits bourgeois. This semantic confusion creates conceptual uncertainty, all the more so as the phrase itself, while referring to the attitude of the *classe moyenne*, simultaneously echoes the depreciative figure of the *français moyen* – a stereotype encoding a dismissive view of middle-class practices. While purporting to relate middlebrow cultural practices to the middle-class attitude to culture, Bourdieu therefore grounds his sociological concept on the adjective's negative connotations, which he implicitly alludes to by using inverted commas. While aiming at criticizing a 'substantialist' approach to *culture moyenne*, Bourdieu therefore re-essentializes it as a pejorative sociological concept. Reiterating the hierarchy of legitimacies he supposedly reflects on, his infelicitous definition of *moyen* results in a theoretical double bind, betraying a problematic lack of reflexivity.

Bearing in mind these limitations, it is worth acknowledging what lies behind Bourdieu's anti-essentialist statement, namely, a critique of Edgar Morin's anthropological conception of *l'homme moyen*.[17] Going back to Morin's anthropology of the average is revealing, as Bourdieu developed his whole sociological project against the essentialist basis of Morin's method.[18] Against Morin, who considered the average as a classless instinct present in mass culture, Bourdieu rethought the middlebrow as produced by relationship to class. As a matter of fact, Morin takes an opposite approach to Bourdieu, as he questions any *a priori* emphasis on high culture: '[b]ut before asking ourselves whether mass culture is indeed how the cultured man sees it, we should ask ourselves whether the values attached to "high culture" are not dogmatic, formal, and fetishised'.[19] Indeed, he proceeds to praise the anthropological imaginary of *l'homme moyen*, which he understands in universal terms ('it is on these anthropological foundations that mass culture's tendency to universality is based').[20] The main virtue of this sociological essay is to reconfigure the devaluation of middlebrow practices. This essentialist conception of *l'homme moyen* may not give us a method to analyse the emergence of the English middlebrow, but it does invite us to refocus our attention on positive configurations of middleness, and value them as such, instead of exposing the logic of domination undermining them from within. The contrast between Morin's anthropological vision and Bourdieu's class-based model leads us to reassess both the relevance of Bourdieu's relational framework and his reductive emphasis on legitimate culture.

In opposition to Morin's 'substantialist' approach, Bourdieu defined the 'petit bourgeois' through his strategies of differentiation. This relational conception of the cultural field allows us to envision the emergence of the English term 'middlebrow' as a controversial category embedded in a struggle for legitimacy. The term 'middlebrow' appeared after the emergence of the highbrow/lowbrow division at the end of the nineteenth century, and thus took shape in relation to both labels, rather than as an essentialist category.[21] One of the first mentions of the term underlined the middlebrow's aspirations towards legitimate culture: 'The B.B.C. claim to have discovered a new type, the "middlebrow". It consists of people who are hoping that some day they will get used to the stuff they ought to like.'[22] Departing from this negative configuration of the middlebrow, which connoted its domination by highbrow culture, J. B. Priestley reconfigured middleness as a happy medium, by pitting the figure of the broadbrow against both highbrows and lowbrows: 'The Broadbrow, you must understand, is not some one who stands somewhere between the other two [...]. The difference between Broadbrowism and the other two is one not merely of degree but of kind, as the change of dimension would suggest.'[23] The 'difference' in 'kind' through which Priestley sought to define the broadbrow should be examined as a relational strategy of differentiation, whereby he aimed at discrediting the two other existing cultural categories. Similarly, in 'Middlebrow', an unsent letter to the *New Statesman and Nation*, Virginia Woolf essentialized the middlebrow in order to differentiate both the highbrow and the lowbrow from 'the go-betweens': 'They are neither one thing nor another. Their brows are betwixt and between.'[24] Within Bourdieu's conception of symbolic struggles, Priestley's and Woolf's opposing configurations of middleness can thus be envisioned as conflicting essentialist discourses. Rather than being reiterated by our own critical categories, the essentialist turn of their discourses should be historicized as such, and reinscribed within a debate over cultural legitimacy.

Developing the logic of distinction he identifies in cultural practices, Bourdieu elaborates a relational approach to the literary field, which can fruitfully allow us to reconsider middlebrow writers through their positionings. In *The Rules of Art* (*Les règles de l'art:* 1992), which focuses on the emergence of the French literary field at the end of the nineteenth century, Bourdieu identifies a central opposition between two subfields of production – 'pure' art and commercial art.[25] Against a strictly formalist, internal reading of texts, Bourdieu seeks to position authors in a struggle for legitimacy, dominated by 'pure art': 'to the extent that they occupy a position in a specific space, that is, in a field of forces [...] which is also a field of struggle seeking to preserve or transform the field of forces, authors [...] affirm the differential deviation which constitutes their position'.[26] As shown by Peter McDonald, this analysis of the author's positioning strategies in this polarized field allows us to reinscribe commercial art within the literary life of the time, rather than merely treat it as minor literature.[27] One could fruitfully analyse aesthetic controversies of the time in the light of this agonistic model. For instance, Virginia Woolf's defence of 'spiritualist' against 'materialist' writers in 'Modern Fiction' could be treated as an instance of 'pure art' positioning itself against commercial art.[28] While reintegrating 'pure art' as a positioning within a literary polemic, Bourdieu's perspective gives visibility to opposing claims to legitimacy. For instance, one can examine the argumentative discourses developed by middlebrow essayists in the first decades of the twentieth century, at a time when familiar essays were said to be in decline, and criticized for circulating in mass-market newspapers. Rather than devaluing the writings of these writers on formal grounds, one can retrace the debate from the popular essayists' side, as they claimed to form part of the essay tradition, against their highbrow critics, who denied them their very generic allegiances.[29]

Even though Bourdieu's model fruitfully allows us to reappraise middlebrow in relational terms, it is worth noting that it does not take up the idea of *art moyen*, since it in fact establishes a binary model of the literary field. By positing a structuring dichotomy between pure art and commercial art, Bourdieu establishes an alternative between legitimate art and non-legitimate art, eclipsing the very middle ground he previously tried to define in *Photography: A Middle-brow Art* and in *Distinction: a Social Critique of the Judgement of Taste*.[30] More than a revision of his previous model, the binary logic expounded in *The Rules of Art* and the eclipsing of the *moyen* category reveals *a posteriori* the intrinsic limitations of Bourdieu's emphasis on legitimate culture. Bourdieu theorizes the petit bourgeois through his lack of cultural capital and his reverence for legitimate art. Dominated by 'noble' cultural practices, he is caught up between 'two classes of goods, which, at the two ends of the social space, are mutually exclusive' (*Distinction*, pp. 326–327). This devaluative conception of the petit bourgeois is structurally produced by a negative configuration of middleness. The intermediary position of the *art moyen* is indeed that of a 'not-yet-legitimate' art (p. 326), an art 'in the process of legitimization'[31] – that is, an art falling short of cultural legitimacy, or, at best, constituting a transition towards it.

However useful Bourdieu's relational method may be in avoiding essentialist depreciations of middlebrow writers as minor writers, his theoretical framework results in a negative understanding of the middlebrow. If we treat Bourdieu's model as one possible configuration of taste, rather than a descriptive model of the French literary life, it is worth contrasting it with other understandings of middlebrow. As a matter of fact, it seems that the ethics of middleness configured by J. B. Priestley cannot be accommodated by this reductive alternative between legitimate and non-legitimate art. These conceptions of the middlebrow admittedly belong to two separate discursive levels – the scientific study and the ideological pamphlet – and one should not forget the fact that Bourdieu elaborates a sociological concept, while Priestley defends a cultural keyword, which should be historicized as such. However, Priestley's positive rethinking of the middlebrow precisely allows us to redefine it as a discursive category in the making, rather than a methodological tool. In the remainder of this chapter, I would like to contrast Bourdieu's implicit devaluation of *art moyen* with Priestley's ethical revaluation of the Broadbrow. In doing so, I wish to move away from Bourdieu's reference to class ethos as a class-based set of attitudes towards culture. Adapting Aristotle's rhetorical ethos to his own concept of *habitus*, Bourdieu's understanding of ethos postulates above all a strong mediation of cultural practice by class. By tracing the middlebrow back to the texts which configured its values in the social world, I would like to reappraise the rhetorical value of the concept of ethos, and thus consider it as a discursive production, rather than a set of acquired dispositions.

In 'High, Low, Broad', published in *The Saturday Review* in 1926 and reprinted in *Open House* a year later, Priestley elaborates a skilfully argued defence of the Broadbrow, based on an ethical revaluation of social inclusivity. Starting the essay with 'a new nursery rhyme' – 'Lowbrow,/ Highbrow,/ Broadbrow's My Brow', he proceeds to include himself in a positive middle ground: 'My friends and I are Broadbrows.'[32] According to him, the valuable category to be defended in the cultural tripartite model of the time is the Broadbrow, understood as a happy medium, both exclusively, against both lowbrows and highbrows, and inclusively, within a sphere of friendship. Devalued as negative terms, high and low are undermined through a cultural re-reading of Wordsworth's poem 'Mutability'[33] – echoing, through its allusion to musical notes, Priestley's opening nursery rhyme:[34]

'From low to high doth dissolution climb/ And sunk from high to low ...'

In the gloss that follows, Priestley gives a contemporary cultural twist to the poem's representation of mutability, by explaining that the absent core of the poem, middleness, is precisely that which remains 'untouched' by the passing of time. High and low are identified as mere 'slaves of fashion', falling prey to time's 'casual shout' – Priestley quotes the phrase without inverted commas, thus presenting it as shared knowledge.[35] From this culturally charged distinction between permanence and mutability, Priestley elaborates a contrast between reason and opinion – while highbrows and lowbrows have 'no minds and wills of their own', are 'hag-ridden by convictions', and follow 'one [...] fashion to the next', the Broadbrow 'exerci[ses] independent judgement' and 'looks at things simply and steadily and asks himself if they have any value'.[36] Through these neoplatonic distinctions between permanence and change, 'critical faculty' and opinion, Priestley develops a philosophically grounded defence of broadbrowism, thus elevated as a reflexive 'appreciation of the human scene'.[37] The Broadbrow's 'critical faculty', also defined as a 'balance between emotion and thought', is therefore conferred a direct ethical dimension, as it produces both discrimination and eclecticism in taste.[38] Conventionally associated with mass culture, the Broadbrow is thus revalued as a thinking subject, capable of founding, through his eclectic judgement, a truly democratic sphere.

This revaluation of critical thinking stands in sharp contrast with Bourdieu's conception of cultural goodwill. Ethical value, rather than cultural legitimacy, is the touchstone of Priestley's praise of middlebrow. This ethical emphasis is entirely absent from Bourdieu's model, which reduces ethics to the set of values encoded in the class ethos, which he does not examine as a moral category. In her critical renegotiation of Bourdieu, Michèle Lamont fruitfully pointed out that his model not only tends to 'downplay the importance of moral character as a status signal', it ultimately identifies 'moralism as a low status signal'.[39] While Bourdieu's configuration of middlebrow devalues the ethical, Priestley's foregrounds it. It is crucial to grasp the ethical grounds of Priestley's cultural thinking, if one is to map the inclusive democratic space he seeks to construct, against current devaluations of mass culture. In both 'High, Low, Broad' (1927) and 'To a Highbrow' (1932), which was originally broadcast on the BBC and subsequently reprinted in the *John O'London's Weekly*, Priestley related the broadbrow ethos to two main values of inclusiveness, namely friendship and eclecticism. Addressing either his imaginary broadbrow or highbrow addressee as a 'friend' through the use of the second person pronoun, Priestley developed an informal, conversational rhetoric, which he reflected on in 'Making

Writing Simple': 'Deliberately I aim at simplicity and not complexity in my writing. [...] I want to write something that at a pinch I could read aloud in a bar-parlour'.[40] His simple diction is part and parcel of this ethical emphasis on inclusiveness: 'I've spent years trying to make my writing simple. What you see as a fault, I regard as a virtue [...] I do not feel that there is a glass wall between me and the people in the nearest factories, shops and pubs.'[41] As a practitioner of the familiar essay form, Priestley also valued the inclusion of a wide range of topics, however trifling. As opposed to the narrow tastes of the two other cultural extremes, his praise of the broadbrow includes a classless blend of interests, accumulated through personal eclecticism rather than organized in a hierarchy: 'Russian dramas, variety shows, football matches, epic poems, grand opera, race meetings, old churches, new town halls, musical comedies, picture galleries, boxing booths, portfolios of etchings, bar parlours, film shows, symphony concerts.'[42] Friendship and eclecticism materialize as cultural values promoted and enacted by the text itself, as Priestley projects his own ethos within his pamphlet and simultaneously constructs a communal ethos, building an intersubjective bond with his reader: 'you are the salt of the earth, and, of course, one of us'.[43]

By configuring middleness as an inclusive stance, Priestley redefines a set of values rather than an in-between position; a happy medium, produced by a 'balance between emotion and thought'.[44] Middleness therefore emerges as a democratic value in itself, rather than a position 'somewhere between the other two'.[45] Significantly, Priestley also extends this ethic of middleness to his appreciation of literature. In 'Are Authors Human Beings?', he encouraged authors to remain 'ordinary human beings': 'The trouble about authors is that they extend themselves up and down but miss the common level of humanity. They become sub-human and super-human.'[46] Likewise, in his later book *Literature and Western Man* (1960), Priestley presented the humanist writers Montaigne and Rabelais through the image of a 'broad middle road', which he highlighted as a crucial democratic value: '[B]oth men move along the same broad middle road; they share a common dislike of pedants, intellectual bullies, bigots and fanatics.'[47] Referring again to 'the middle highway that Rabelais and Montaigne knew', he compared Shakespeare to Rabelais and Montaigne: 'Shakespeare can be said to be farther along that middle road where we found Rabelais and Montaigne.'[48] Deriving the central metaphor of the 'broad middle road' from his reading of Montaigne, Priestley renegotiated Montaigne's image as a memory of middleness, allowing him to revalue inclusiveness in the age of mass culture.[49] It is worth noting that Montaigne also served as an inspiration for Virginia Woolf, who, in her essay on Montaigne, also dwelt on the image of the road: 'It is best to keep in the middle of the road, in the common ruts.'[50] Woolf's essay, however, finally moved away from this image of middleness in order to successively examine withdrawal from and communication with the crowd, contempt for the rabble, and a search for a 'well-born soul'.[51] In her unsent letter 'Middlebrow', she pits the highbrow and the lowbrow against 'the middle party in the state', which, tellingly enough, she criticizes through a classical humanist phrase, connoting eclecticism – *Humani nihil a se alienum*: 'The tag "Nihil humanum" is often on his lips. But he takes care not to talk Latin often. Everybody is a good fellow at bottom he says.'[52] As opposed to this negative configuration of middleness associated with humanism, Priestley inscribes himself in the humanist praise of the golden mean. Priestley's image of the 'broad middle road' can be traced back to Montaigne's well-known ethical statements in 'Of experience': 'The people deceive themselves; a man goes much more easily indeed by the ends, where the extremity serves for a bound, a stop, and guide, than by the middle way, large and open; and according to art, more than according to nature: but withal much less nobly and commendably.'[53] In the vein of Montaigne's praise of the Aristotelian golden mean, Priestley reconfigured middleness as a valuable cultural positioning, enacting an ethical revaluation of mass culture. Choosing to align himself with the humanist tradition of thought, he reactivated a positive genealogy of middleness grounded in ethics, at a time when the middlebrow was becoming a pejorative cultural category.

Although Priestley does not quote this passage from Montaigne, whom he praises in his introduction to *Essayists Past and Present*, I would like to end with this excerpt from 'Of Vanities', where the ideal readership is figured as an exclusion of two extremes:[54]

> [W]ere these Essays of mine considerable of judgment, it might then, I think, fall out that they would not much take with common and vulgar capacities, nor be acceptable to the singular and excellent sort of men; the first would not understand them enough, and the last too much; and so they may hover in the middle region.[54]

This 'middle region' is a fitting image of the humanist ethical imaginary through which Priestley invited his contemporary readers to rethink the middlebrow ethos. As today's readers and critics of middlebrow writers, we should bear in mind the ethical turn of this defence, rather than understand cultural value in purely social terms, and, as Bourdieu's concept of *art moyen* may lead us to, reiterate uncritically its pejorative bias. As an ethical response to the cultural problems raised by mass culture, Priestley's positive assertion of middleness ultimately urges us to acknowledge the capacity of cultural agents to produce, displace and remodel symbolic constructs, beyond the social processes they were caught up in.

Notes

1. Except when I refer specifically to the French edition of the book (Pierre Bourdieu (1979) *La distinction: critique sociale du jugement* (Paris: Les Éditions de Minuit)), the following parenthetical references are from the English edition of Pierre Bourdieu's text, as translated by Richard Nice: (1984) *Distinction: A Social Critique of the Judgement of Taste* (New York and London: Routledge).
2. See in particular Peter McDonald (1997) *British Literary Culture and Publishing Practice 1880–1914* (Cambridge: Cambridge University Press) and Mary Grover (2009) *The Ordeal of Warwick Deeping: Middlebrow Authorship and Cultural Embarrassment* (Cranbury: Rosemont Publishing). I am indebted to Mary Grover for encouraging me to reflect on this question.
3. See Bourdieu's use of the phrase in *Distinction*, pp. 323, 326.
4. See François Provenzano and Sarah Sindaco (eds) (2009) *La Fabrique du Français moyen. Productions culturelles et imaginaire social dans la France gaullienne (1958–1981)* (Bruxelles: Le Cri). This collection of articles retraces the emergence of the imaginary of the *français moyen* in the 1960s, when Charles de Gaulle was in power. Surprisingly, the book does not mention earlier sociological conceptions of *l'homme moyen*. The book does not engage with the relevance of Bourdieu's category, but fruitfully historicizes it, by replacing it within a larger scientific context (see François Provenzano, 'Naissance d'une sociologie française du "moyen" ', pp. 19–34).
5. In *La théorie de l'homme moyen: essai sur Quetelet et la statistique morale* (1912), the sociologist Maurice Halbwachs examined the *homme moyen* as an average social type, in the light of Quételet's 'homme moyen' and Durkheim's 'type normal'. Maurice Halbwachs (1912) *Théorie de l'homme moyen: essai sur Quételet et la statistique morale* (Paris: Félix Alcan).
6. Pierre Bourdieu (1965) *Un art moyen: essai sur les usages sociaux de la photographie* (dir.) (Paris: Éditions de Minuit). The English translation of this early work came out much later, in 1990: *Photography: A Middle-brow Art*, trans. Shaun Whiteside (Cambridge: Polity Press). As the translator underlined, 'the translation is based on a text which was slightly modified by Pierre Bourdieu for the Italian edition of the work' (Preface to the English Language Edition).
7. Very few critics have developed a critique of the concept of *art moyen* as such. While the two-volume collection of articles edited by Florent Gaudez (2008) *Les arts moyens aujourd'hui* (Tomes 1 et 2. Paris: L'Harmattan) aims at assessing the relevance of Bourdieu's concept, very few articles actually expose the negative bias of the category, or even raise its theoretical limitations.

8. In spite of my theoretical questioning of Bourdieu's 'search for equivalents' (*Distinction*, p. xii), it should be acknowledged that they function as linguistic equivalents *de facto*, if one agrees with Ricoeur's definition of translation: 'an equivalence without identity' (my translation). Paul Ricoeur (2004) *Sur la traduction* (Paris: Bayard), pp. 39–40.

9. I am only going to examine the English context of the middlebrow by focusing on J. B. Priestley's conception of the broadbrow.

10. At the end of his preface to *Distinction*, Bourdieu himself drew on Victor Chklovski's concept of *ostranenie* (p. xiv), by renegotiating it as a means of cultural critique.

11. Bourdieu, *Photography: A Middle-brow Art*, p. 96.

12. For Bourdieu, however, the changing values attached to a cultural practice over time do not contradict the validity of his method (see Bourdieu (1994) *Raisons pratiques: sur la théorie de l'action* (Paris: Seuil), p. 19).

13. Bourdieu, *Photography*, p. 9.

14. Bourdieu, *Photography*, p. 95.

15. One may note that the French index does not include an entry on 'moyen', while the English edition included a 'middlebrow' entry.

16. Bourdieu, *La distinction: critique sociale du jugement*, p. 377, italics mine.

17. Edgar Morin (2008) *L'esprit du temps* (Paris: Armand Colin). On Morin's conception of 'l'homme moyen', see Eric Macé (2006) *Les imaginaires médiatiques: Une Sociologie postcritique des médias* (Paris: Amsterdam), pp. 52–73.

18. In a founding article of his sociological project, co-authored with Jean-Claude Passeron, Bourdieu harshly disqualified Morin's essentialist approach (Pierre Bourdieu and Jean-Claude Passeron, 1963) 'Sociologues des mythologies et mythologies de sociologues', *Les Temps Modernes*, 24 December 1963, 998–1021.

19. Edgar Morin, *L'esprit du temps*, p. 30, my translation.

20. Ibid., p. 56, my translation. See also Morin's conception of the average: 'The average trend triumphs and levels, blends and homogenises, taking with it both Van Gogh and Jean Nohain. It favours average aesthetics, average poetry, average talent, average audacity, average vulgarity, average intelligence, average stupidity. Mass culture is average in its inspiration and its aim, for it is the culture of the common denominator', p. 61, my translation.

21. On the emergence of the category 'middlebrow', see in particular John Baxendale (2007) *Priestley's England: J. B. Priestley and English Culture* (Manchester: Manchester University Press), Nicola Humble (2001) *The Feminine Middlebrow Novel 1920s to 1950s: Class, Domesticity and Bohemianism* (Oxford: Oxford University Press) and Joan Shelley Rubin (1992) *The Making of Middlebrow Culture* (University of North Carolina Press).

22. *Punch*, 23 December 1925, p. 673.

23. J. B. Priestley, 'High, Low, Broad', *Saturday Review* (February 1926), p. 222. Reprinted in Priestley (ed.) (1929) *Open House: A Book of Essays* (London: Heinemann) pp. 162–167, 162–163.

24. Virginia Woolf (1942) 'Middlebrow', in *The Death of the Moth and Other Essays* (London: Hogarth), pp. 113–119, 115. In the manuscript version of this letter, Woolf portrays 'three characters'. The 'Broad Brow' is presented as the essence of mediocrity: 'He is the middle party in the state. He is neither one thing nor the other. He goes to no extremes. He is hail fellow well

met with all.' (Woolf (1972) 'Three Characters', *Adam International Review*, 364(66), 24–29).

On Woolf's critique of middlebrowism, see Melba Cuddy-Keane (2003) *Virginia Woolf, the Intellectual, and the Public Sphere* (Cambridge: CUP), pp. 22–34.

25. Bourdieu (1996) *The Rules of Art: Genesis and Structure of the Literary Field*, trans. Susan Emanuel (Cambridge: Polity Press). The French original came out only a few years before: Bourdieu (1992) *Les règles de l'art: genèse et structure du champ littéraire* (Paris: Seuil). He elaborates this model in various other articles, including in 'Principles for a Sociology of Cultural Works', reprinted in Randal Johnson (ed.) (1993) *The Field of Cultural Production: Essays on Art and Literature* (Cambridge: Polity Press), pp. 176–191.

26. Bourdieu, 'Principles for a Sociology of Cultural Works', p. 184.

27. See Peter McDonald's analysis of the literary field in the 1890s in *British Literary Culture and Publishing Practice 1880–1914* (pp. 1–21).

28. Virginia Woolf (1925; 1994) 'Modern Fiction', in Andrew McNellie (ed.) *The Common Reader First Series* (San Diego: A Harvest Book), pp. 146–154.

29. I am writing at greater length on this topic in an article devoted to middlebrow essayists: ' "Everybody's Essayists": On Middles and Middlebrows', in Kate Macdonald (ed.) (2011) *The Masculine Middlebrow, 1880–1950, What Mr Miniver Read* (Basingstoke: Palgrave Macmillan).

30. This reductive alternative was pointed out by Nathalie Heinich, as part of a critical assessment of Bourdieu's sociology of art: (2008) 'Sociologie de l'art: avec et sans Bourdieu' in Louis-Jean Calvet, Pierre Chartier, Philippe Corcuff, Nathalie Heinich (eds) *Bourdieu: son œuvre, son héritage* (Paris: Sciences Humaines Editions).

31. Bourdieu, *Photography*, p. 98.

32. Priestley, 'High, Low, Broad', pp. 162, 167.

33. William Wordsworth (1847) 'Mutability', in *The Poems of William Wordsworth* (London: Edward Moxon), p. 332.

34. Priestley, 'High, Low, Broad', p. 163.

35. Ibid., p. 163.

36. Ibid., pp. 163–164.

37. Ibid., p. 166.

38. Ibid., p. 165.

39. See Michèle Lamont (2004) 'French Social Theory: The Contribution of Pierre Bourdieu', in Derek Robbins (ed.) *Pierre Bourdieu 2* (London: Sage) pp. 113–125, 117. Indeed, according to Bourdieu, the 'culturally most deprived' tend to perceive a moral meaning in works of art, as they are unable to see them in a pure aesthetic sense (*Distinction*, p. 44).

40. J. B. Priestley (1949) 'Making Writing Simple', in *Delight* (London: William Heinemann), pp. 42–45, 43.

41. Ibid., p. 43.

42. Priestley, 'High, Low, Broad', pp. 166–167.

43. Ibid., p. 167.

44. Priestley, 'High, Low, Broad,' p. 167; 'To a High-brow', Transcript (October 1932): 1–6, BBC Written Archive Centre. Published in *John O'London's Weekly* (December 1932): 354–356, 354.

45. Priestley, 'High, Low, Broad', p. 163.

46. Priestley (April 1931) 'Are Authors Human Beings?', *The Bookman: A Review of Books and Life*, 73(2), 137.
47. Priestley (1960) *Literature and Western Man* (London: Penguin Books), p. 32.
48. Ibid., pp. 60, 48.
49. See Priestley, *Literature and Western Man*, p. 34: 'But then the essayist does not claim to know too much outside himself [...]. All this there is in Montaigne, and in all those who have travelled, then and since, that broad road with him.'
50. Virginia Woolf (1925) 'Montaigne', in *The Common Reader First Series*, p. 61.
51. Ibid., p. 61.
52. Woolf, 'Three Characters', p. 26.
53. Michel de Montaigne (1588; 1913) 'Of Experience', in *The Essays of Michel de Montaigne*, Book 3, trans. Charles Cotton (London: G. Bell and Sons), p. 374.
54. Montaigne (1580; 1913) 'Of Vain Subtleties', in *The Essays of Michel de Montaigne*, Book 1, trans. Charles Cotton (London: G. Bell and Sons), p. 359. For a commentary on Montaigne's passage, see Richard Scholar (2005) *The Je-Ne-Sais-Quoi in Early Modern Europe, Encounters with a Certain Something* (Oxford: Oxford University Press), p. 250.

Part II

Taste-Makers and Print Cultures I: UK

3
Cultural Hierarchies and the Interwar British Press

Adrian Bingham

In the first half of the twentieth century, national newspapers became an inescapable and almost irresistible force in British culture. After Alfred Harmsworth[1] launched the *Daily Mail* in 1896, the habit of regularly reading a daily newspaper spread to the lower middle classes and then, from the 1930s, to the working classes. The market was soon dominated by a handful of London-based titles which achieved mammoth circulations: the *Daily Herald* broke the 2-million barrier in the early 1930s, while by the 1940s both the *Daily Express* and the *Daily Mirror* were selling over 4 million copies per day. Sunday papers were even more successful: the all-conquering *News of the World* sold around 8.5 million copies per week in the early 1950s, and was read by more than half of the adult population of Britain. At its peak in the early 1950s, the market was almost saturated, with some 85 per cent of the population regularly reading a daily paper, and almost everyone seeing a Sunday paper.[2] The British were, indeed, the world's most avid newspaper readers, consuming more than twice as many papers per head as the Americans, and four times as many as the French.[3]

The relentless spread of the newspaper throughout British society provoked an intense and anguished debate. Countless articles, essays and speeches explored the political, social and cultural ramifications of mass newspaper readership and examined the influence of the 'press barons' such as Lords Northcliffe, Rothermere and Beaverbrook; it was, as Patrick Collier has noted, almost impossible for a writer in this period to 'refrain from taking a position in the widespread discussion of the state of British journalism'.[4] More broadly, the newspaper became a key motif of fiction and art; a prime symbol of the emerging urban mass culture; and one of the most acute guides to the stratification of British society. An individual's choice of newspaper became a key signifier of his or her status and worldview. All of this was a testament to the sheer cultural power of the newspaper. Chris Baldick has correctly observed that 'almost everything' that was written, 'and most of what was read in this period, was in some way shaped by the overwhelming commercial and cultural dominance' of the newspaper.[5] A favourable review in a national newspaper could transform a book's fortunes, just as the opportunity to contribute articles or serialize works could significantly raise an author's profile. Books which escaped Fleet Street's notice, meanwhile, often struggled to generate attention outside literary circles.

The debates prompted by the rise of the newspaper, and more broadly by the emergence of mass culture, have received considerable scholarly attention. The lamentations of the Leavises are familiar in works on the interwar period, as are the anxieties of leading modernist authors.[6] The commercial influence of the press – and particularly of leading reviewers such as Arnold Bennett – is widely acknowledged. Yet in contrast to the various modernist magazines, or leading weeklies such as *Time and Tide* and the *Listener*, the precise manner in which the main national daily and Sunday newspapers helped to shape taste and define literary value has been remarkably neglected.[7] This chapter offers a brief overview of four of the main ways in which the national press sought to interpret the literary world for their readership, and in so doing circulated and moulded ideas about social and cultural hierarchies. First, it examines how newspapers acted as guides for the public by reviewing new books and plays. Secondly, it outlines how the press claimed the role of moral guardian, seeking to protect readers from 'inappropriate' or 'indecent' forms of cultural expression. Thirdly, it demonstrates how the press offered a platform for leading authors and playwrights to contribute articles on key issues of the day. Finally, it shows how newspapers also operated as suppliers of fiction by serializing books believed to be suitable for their audience. The chapter will focus largely on the most dynamic sector of the interwar market, namely the popular titles aimed at the suburban lower middle classes, such as the *Mail*, the *Express*, the *Mirror* and the *Weekly Dispatch*. I will argue that these papers provided a powerful cultural and commercial support for the middlebrow section of the market, not just by their overt interventions in literary matters, but also by serving as one of the most important channels of what could be described as 'middlebrow' attitudes. This overview will necessarily be sketchy and even speculative in places, partly due to constraints of space, but more fundamentally because of the paucity of research upon which to draw; it is offered in the hope that scholars will take forward the important task of exploring the content of national newspapers.

By the turn of the twentieth century, newspapers were publications which incorporated a spectacular diversity of material. Far more than just retailers of the latest news, they sought to entertain, provoke, educate and advise. Patrick Balfour, a high-profile society columnist, noted in 1933 that the 'immense' development and expansion of the modern newspaper had turned it into 'a mixed bag of tricks, providing sufficient material to occupy the whole of the average man's leisure time'.[8] Informing readers about contemporary culture, and guiding them to the best books, plays and films, was seen by this period as an important part of the press's mission. The Sunday papers, which based their appeal firmly on the quality of their feature material, took this cultural role particularly seriously: in some, literary reviews filled six or even eight pages. But most dailies also had weekly book review columns, often covering ten or more works a week. The style of these columns varied significantly. The elite press included weighty disquisitions on the most notable recent books, while at the popular end of the market columnists provided short, descriptive reviews, often with some focus on the personality of the author. Popular newspapers nevertheless attempted to create an impact by using their financial muscle to attract 'star' reviewers. It was a commonplace of interwar literary debate that the practice of book reviewing was in crisis, and popular newspapers in particular were accused of undermining the process of cultural evaluation with their brief, ill-informed or partial reviews.[9] T. S. Eliot was typical, for example, in his despair at the 'confused cries of newspaper critics and the susurrus of popular repetition that follows'.[10] Newspaper editors were inured to such attacks, however, and continued to meet what they perceived as the demands of their market.

The newspaper reviews which carried the greatest critical authority, at least in the 1920s, were those to be found in the *Sunday Times* and the *Observer*. Sir Edmund Gosse, a venerable pillar of the early twentieth-century literary establishment, was chief reviewer for the *Sunday Times* between 1919 and his death in 1928, while J. C. Squire combined editorship of the influential *The London Mercury* with reviewing duties at the *Observer*.[11] Looking back in 1939, Frank Swinnerton emphasized how much these two columns had shaped literary taste:

> [Gosse] wrote a chaste and polished article every week for the *Sunday Times*, and it was at one time the habit of literary-minded men to read

what he said in that paper before turning to see what J. C. Squire was saying in the *Observer*. The Sunday newspaper as an organ of literary opinion, and as a field for publishers' advertising, rose high above the horizon.[12]

The columns of Gosse and Squire – and indeed those of Desmond MacCarthy, Gosse's successor at the *Sunday Times* – were, as Julia Paolitto's thorough study has demonstrated, characterized by a defence of traditional literary values and a suspicion of modernist experimentation.[13] Gosse believed, for example, that Joyce was a 'literary charlatan of the highest order', and Squire did little to hide his dislike for 'modern novelists'; MacCarthy, meanwhile, was caustic in his reviews of Virginia Woolf's work.[14] The preference of the elite Sunday press for realist works which exhibited continuities with Victorian and Edwardian literary traditions undoubtedly served to limit the contemporary impact of the modernists; indeed, the conservatism of the *Sunday Times* and its competitors left plenty of space for specialist magazines like Eliot's *Criterion* to carve out their own niche.

The literary columns of the popular press may have been less substantial, but they carried far more commercial clout. Many of them were penned by key middlebrow figures and they became important sites for the elaboration of middlebrow values. The highest-paid, and perhaps the most influential, reviewer of the period was Arnold Bennett, who wrote a weekly article for the *Evening Standard* from 1926 until his death in 1931.[15] F. R. Leavis claimed that Bennett was 'the most powerful maker of literary reputations in England', and indeed booksellers often placed their orders after consulting Bennett's latest comments.[16] Bennett's column provided – much to the consternation of critics like Leavis – a staunch defence of 'middlebrow', realist writing for a broad public, while at the same time popularizing some notable modernist texts. Bennett was adamant that it was an essential part of the job of the artist to meet the demands of a market, and had little patience for 'highbrow' inaccessibility and 'This "Bosh" About Art for Art's Sake'.[17] Bennett was succeeded at the *Standard* by J. B. Priestley, another high-profile author dismissed in Bloomsbury circles as 'middlebrow'. Priestley – who preferred to describe himself as a 'broadbrow' – was critical of many aspects of Fleet Street's populism, but used the *Evening Standard*, and many other papers, as a platform to reach the general public. Priestley was a disciplined reviewer and was, like Bennett, supportive of serious writing that explored contemporary social trends.[18] Other influential 'middlebrow' reviewers in the popular press included

Robert Lynd, the literary editor of the *Daily News* (subsequently the *News Chronicle*) from 1912 to 1947;[19] Compton Mackenzie, who contributed to the *Daily News* before writing a high-profile weekly column for the *Daily Mail* between 1931 and 1934;[20] and Winifred Holtby, who reviewed regularly for the *News Chronicle* and the *Yorkshire Post* (as well as acting as *Good Housekeeping*'s literary critic).[21]

The literary columns of the popular press were, in general, brightly written and accessible, focusing on commercially palatable novels from mainstream publishers. The main exceptions were the rather more austere columns of the left-wing *Daily Herald* and *Reynolds's News*, which were aimed above all at the politically informed working-class autodidact, and which reviewed a wide range of non-fiction books as well as novels. In spring 1922, for example, the regular *Herald* reader would have found Wyndham Lewis's review of Clive Bell's *Since Cézanne* and G. D. H. Cole's assessment of Harold Laski's *Foundations of Sovereignty*. H. G. Wells, meanwhile, criticized the paper's penchant for reviewing obscure poetry.[22] *Reynolds's News* was similarly ambitious, although it tended to share the cultural conservatism of the more elite press and often had harsh words for modernists. In May 1936, for example, R. L. Megroz attacked the 'motley gang of pseudo-critics ... who have taken advantage of the deliberate obscurities of a narrow school of modern poetry to pose as oracles on genius, whereas they are only purveyors of Mumbo-Jumbo'.[23] Political differences certainly coloured the content of the review columns, but the whole spectrum of the popular press remained committed to works that were intelligible to lower middle-class and working-class readers without the benefits of an expensive education: 'deliberate obscurities' received short shrift from left and right.

One important element of the reviewing process for the popular press was to ensure that books, plays and films conformed to certain moral standards. The elite newspapers were concerned above all with their particular conceptions of artistic merit, and were rarely troubled by issues of obscenity; popular dailies and Sundays, by contrast, tended to assume the role of moral guardians and believed they had an important role to play in ensuring that the culture consumed by the mass of the population met what were essentially middle-class notions of decency and decorum.[24] The most notable example in the interwar period of this moral guardianship was James Douglas's denunciation of Radclyffe Hall's novel *The Well of Loneliness* in the *Sunday Express* in August 1928. For Douglas, this was 'A Book That Must Be Suppressed' because it addressed issues of 'sexual inversion and perversion' that were unsuitable for all but a specialist audience. 'Its theme is utterly inadmissible in the novel, because the novel is read by people of all ages [...] I would rather give a healthy boy or a healthy girl a phial of prussic acid than this novel. Poison kills the body, but moral poison kills the soul.'[25] Douglas's tirade demonstrated the power of popular journalism: three days later the book was withdrawn by the publisher, Jonathan Cape, on the advice of the Home Secretary, and in October, copies of the novel were seized and successfully prosecuted for obscenity. The details of this case are well-known, and need not be rehearsed here; more significant for the present purposes is the way in which Douglas's article fitted in with the broader patterns of press rhetoric.[26] It is rarely noted, for example, that the *Sunday Express* was not the only paper to denounce Hall's novel on that weekend in August. The *People* – which had a higher circulation than the *Sunday Express* – reported on the same day that Scotland Yard had an interest in a 'secret book' which described 'with astounding frankness a revolting aspect of modern life'. Despite acknowledging the 'brilliance of the writing', the paper argued that 'nothing could justify its publication': 'The book, unless action is taken, will inevitably get into the hands of unscrupulous persons who will exploit its sexual aspects for their own ends.'[27] Unlike Douglas, the *People* did not name the book in question, but it is important to note that Douglas was not a lone voice in Fleet Street, nor were his arguments particularly unusual. Some other popular papers – notably the *Daily Herald* and *Reynolds's News* – did provide a staunch defence of the novel, but the conservative press offered little sympathy, and recorded the subsequent prosecution with little comment.[28]

This was, moreover, by no means the first time that James Douglas had made moral interventions of this kind. Thirteen years earlier, he had used very similar language in an article in *The Star* to lambast D. H. Lawrence's novel, *The Rainbow*: 'It is a greater menace to our public health than any of the epidemic diseases which we pay our medical officers to fight inch by inch [...] They destroy the body, but it destroys the soul.'[29] And in November 1927, he had launched a more wide-ranging, but equally vehement, attack on 'sex novelists' who 'glorified lust and lechery' and had 'turned marriage into a mockery'.[30] Douglas may have been Fleet Street's the finest and the most prominent packager of moral outrage, but plenty of others adopted similar rhetorical poses. Sexual or social 'deviancy' were certainly not the only targets: novels, plays or films which addressed sexual themes with any degree of explicitness, or which contained overt depictions of sexual activity or violence, were liable to face censure in the popular press. In October 1921, for example, the *Daily Mail*'s (unnamed) drama critic invited the Lord Chamberlain to act against Oscar Asche's musical *Cairo* for a scene of 'stark sensuality' and 'erotic excess' in which 'dancing girls madden both themselves and the men present': 'I think he [Asche] has gone beyond the bounds of permissible realism in the theatre. I will even go as far as to say that the scene is indecent both in conception and execution.'[31] (Asche retaliated by declaring the scene no worse than newspaper 'pictures of men and women dancing and romping in the sea in nothing but a wet, clinging bathing costume'.)[32] Much of this moral outrage was aimed at supposedly corrupting influences from abroad, particularly the United States. In 1924, the *Daily Express*'s 'cinema correspondent' described the film version of Warner Fabian's 'disgusting American novel' *Flaming Youth*, as 'highly salacious and sinister': 'Flaming Youth will surely hasten the day [...] when there will be a revulsion of feeling against the flood of unpalatable American pictures, the most pestiferous affliction which this country has ever endured.'[33] Popular newspaper reviewers, in short, waged an ongoing battle to defend their idea of a chaste British culture, taking on challenges from 'decadent' artists (such as Oscar Wilde and D. H. Lawrence), 'neurotics' and 'deviants' (such as Radclyffe Hall) and foreign invaders, led above all by Hollywood and its associates.

In the short-term, these journalistic fulminations often served only to draw attention to controversial works. In the longer term, however, the popular press's vocal support of the attitudes and policies underpinning the British censorship regime helped to reinforce a moral conservatism in middlebrow and lowbrow culture. Authors and publishers seeking to make commercial returns were reluctant to run the risk of drawing unfavourable notices from the press or being withdrawn from libraries. This lesson was frequently underlined in commercial writing circles. In 1926, for example, an article in *The Writer* warned authors of the need to 'respect Mrs Grundy': not only was she 'far more easily offended than many of us suspect', but, more importantly, 'Her power over editors is wide.'[34] Handbooks for freelance writers offered similar advice.[35] Avoiding 'offence' became a hallmark of many forms of commercial writing, just as it was for middle-class sociability more generally.[36]

Leading authors and playwrights had a presence in the press far beyond the reviews columns, however. Newspapers required an almost endless supply of opinion pieces on the issues of the day, and prominent cultural figures were, alongside politicians and socialites, amongst the most sought-after contributors. If politicians offered proximity to power, and socialites exuded glamour, authors lent intellectual credibility to popular papers very conscious of the sneers of the elites; they enabled editors to flatter lower-middle-class readers that they were keeping up to date with cultivated opinion. Given the sums on offer – Fleet Street titles paid around £10–£15 for a casual essay in the early 1920s, and significantly more to celebrities[37] – it is unsurprising that many authors were tempted, and newspapers thereby became a significant platform from which leading writers could communicate ideas to a mass readership. The opinion pages of the popular press were studded with famous literary names, and unsurprisingly it was those writers keen to educate, engage or entertain a broad public – 'middlebrow', by most definitions – who were most prominent. H. G. Wells and J. B. Priestley were prolific commentators on social developments and global affairs; Rose Macaulay, Vera Brittain and Winifred Holtby wrote widely on the position of women and the evolution of feminism; E. M. Delafield and Beverley Nichols specialized in light or humorous pieces.[38] But other, less typically 'middlebrow', writers appeared too: Osbert and Edith Sitwell both featured regularly in the pages of popular Sunday papers such as the *Weekly Dispatch*, and D. H. Lawrence made a number of contributions on sexual issues.[39]

It is, of course, impossible to generalize about this extensive and diverse body of journalistic writing. Most opinion pieces were fairly short – often under 1000 words – and they were designed to be both accessible and thought-provoking: editors wanted, above all, to create 'talking-points' that would encourage readers to converse with friends and colleagues about the contents of their paper.[40] Some authors undoubtedly traded upon their reputation and submitted articles that were hurriedly written and trivial; many others, though, produced substantial and sincere pieces that were significant contributions to public debate. Rebecca West, for example, was struck by the amount of correspondence she received after publishing two lengthy and controversial pieces in the *Daily Express*.[41] Just as scholars have re-evaluated middlebrow novels in recent years, there is certainly a case for reassessing the worth and influence of mass-market journalism.[42] More broadly, though, the willingness of an author to contribute to the pages of the popular press had a significant impact on his or her cultural visibility; indeed, newspapers did much to turn some authors – like Wells and Bennett – into celebrities.[43] By the same token, this willingness did much to influence their designation as being 'middlebrow': it was not merely the nature or readership of an author's books and plays that dictated their cultural esteem, but also their wider participation in the commercial world of the mass media. Conversely, both the relative cultural marginality and the 'highbrow' reputation of authors such as Joyce, Eliot and Woolf was not just due to the (perceived) inaccessibility of their writing, but also their lack of interest in engaging with the popular press. Authors who accepted the popular press's gold inevitably risked a critical backlash.

For those who did want to reach a wide audience, even better than contributing opinion pieces was the serialization of one's work. Serialized fiction was a very important part of the popular newspaper package in the first half of the twentieth century, for both dailies and weeklies, but it has received very little scholarly attention (unlike the serials included in the Victorian press, admirably surveyed by Graham Law).[44] The serial was introduced by Northcliffe into the popular daily press in the first issue of the *Daily Mail*, largely as a way of enticing female readers: he hoped that it would encourage wives to remind commuting husbands to bring the paper back home.[45] Northcliffe's research consistently revealed the importance of the serial for female readers: a bulletin to the *Mail*'s staff in 1918 recalled 'how surprised Fleet Street was when it discovered that the majority of women readers started their perusal with the serial'.[46] Two years later, he went so far as to observe that 'Thirty years experience has taught me that more people read serials than anything else, provided they are good'; indeed, such was the competition, the serials needed to be 'very good'.[47] In order to maintain quality, he encouraged his journalists to 'get their womenfolk to read and criticise the Serials'.[48] The success of the serial in the *Mail* inevitably encouraged rivals to follow suit, and in the interwar period most newspapers carried fiction of some sort. Detailed market research conducted across the popular press in the early 1930s confirmed the continuing popularity of serials, finding that reader interest in them was 'above average', higher even than 'gossip articles'.[49]

A very diverse range of material was serialized. One survey of the press in 1937 concluded that 'Sex-romance appeared to be the most popular subject, followed by humour and crime.'[50] Some of this was 'low-brow' genre fiction, including, in papers like the *Mirror*, romances from the Mills and Boon stable. Plenty of more challenging books were serialized, too, including works from prominent 'middlebrow' authors such as Gilbert Frankau, Agatha Christie, Daphne du Maurier, Somerset Maugham and Noel Coward.[51] In the late 1920s, sections of significant war novels were serialized, including Remarque's *All Quiet on the Western Front*.[52] One middlebrow 'classic', Jan Struther's *Mrs Miniver*, started life as a series of articles for *The Times*. Struther was asked to brighten up the paper's Court Page by writing about 'an ordinary sort of woman who leads an ordinary sort of life'; the popularity of the series led to the publication of a book and subsequently a film.[53] Some serializations had a major impact on circulation: when the *Dispatch* serialized Kathleen Windsor's racy romance *Forever Amber* in 1946, its sales rose by over one hundred thousand copies a week.[54] Similarly, the *Evening Standard*'s 1949 serialization of *A Streetcar Named Desire* was responsible for a 'very big' increase in sales.[55] An interesting book could be just as much a draw for readers as the latest crime story or celebrity revelation.

Further research is required before conclusions can sensibly be drawn about the broader effects of newspaper serializations. The availability of fiction in the press may have satisfied some people's need for reading material; it is likely to have encouraged others to try new authors and to search out different books in libraries and bookshops. Major new serializations were accorded substantial publicity – reflecting the significant financial investment that went into securing them – and presented as important cultural events. 'Middlebrow' works – those which combined accessibility with a certain level of seriousness and 'literariness' – were highly prized by popular newspapers, and therefore their value was reinforced to a wider reading public.

For critics such as Queenie Leavis, the emergence of the popular press in the early twentieth century had disastrous effects on British culture. 'Northcliffe's interference with reading habits alone,' she contended in her influential work *Fiction and the Reading Public*, 'has effectively put literature out of the reach of the average man'. Literature demanded concentration and effort whereas the popular press provided a simply written and conveniently digestible 'collection of scraps' for tired minds. It was 'inevitable', Leavis suggested, 'that the cheaper gratification to be derived easily and immediately [from popular newspapers] should be preferred by the younger generation to the finer cumulative pleasure that literature gave their fathers'.[56] Equally damaging was the way in which the press had served to undermine the authority of literary critics: by working upon the 'herd instinct', Northcliffe was able 'to mobilise the people to outvote the minority, who had hitherto set the standard of taste without serious challenge'. Newspapers championed the work of derivative middlebrow writers whose writing was as bright and superficial as their own; the most interesting modern writing was rendered inaccessible to ordinary readers and the reading public was dangerously fragmented. The result, she concluded, was that the 'reading capacity of the general public [...] has never been so low as at the present time'.[57]

Leavis's interpretation rested on a narrow and tendentious conception of literary value, and a naïve belief in an earlier 'golden age' in which the common reader accepted standards dictated from above. In some senses, though, Leavis was correct to highlight the huge cultural impact made by the popular newspapers. With their review columns, opinion pages and serializations, the press did much to define and organize what Leavis regarded as middlebrow taste; their cultural centrality made them even more powerful than the book clubs and circulating libraries in this regard. Leavis was also right to highlight the ways in which the popular press helped to embed commercial and consumerist values into British culture. Fleet Street was driven by profit and circulation figures, and it encouraged a mindset in which sales and circulation became essential markers of value. The preoccupation with the bottom-line discouraged certain types of risk-taking, and especially the avoidance of moral controversy. Yet when interwar newspapers are viewed without Leavis's presumption of cultural decline – and, indeed, with a consciousness of the evolution of the popular press in the second half of the twentieth century – one is struck not by their philistinism but by their commitment to the world of books. Many lower-middle- and working-class readers with little knowledge of literature were exposed to reviews of the latest works, the opinions of leading authors and serializations of notable novels. By paying well for articles and reviews, moreover, the press enabled many young and upcoming writers to sustain themselves. It is perhaps revealing that as late as 1956, shortly after the introduction of ITV, Beaverbrook was encouraging the editorial team of the *Evening Standard* to increase the visibility of books in the paper: books 'should be news', and should outweigh television, he suggested, because there was 'more interest in books than television'.[58] The *Standard*'s editor, Percy Elland, perhaps aware of the immense popular enthusiasm for television, respectfully disagreed. That this debate even occurred, though, should signal to scholars that more needs to be done to explore the role of the press in shaping and sustaining literary values.

Notes

1. Alfred Harmsworth was ennobled as Lord Northcliffe in 1905; in this chapter he will be referred to as Northcliffe.
2. G. Harrison, F. Mitchell and M. Abrams (1939) *The Home Market*, revised edn, (London: G. Allen & Unwin), ch. 21; A. P. Wadsworth (1955) 'Newspaper Circulations 1800–1954', *Manchester Statistical Society Transactions*, 4; C. Seymour-Ure (1996) *The British Press and Broadcasting since 1945*, 2nd edn, (Oxford: Blackwell), ch. 3.
3. F. Williams (1958) *Dangerous Estate: The Anatomy of Newspapers* (London: Longmans, Green), pp. 1–2. See also Royal Commission on the Press 1974–1977 (1977) *Final Report* (London: HMSO), Cmd. 6810, Appendix C, p. 105.
4. P. Collier (2006) *Modernism on Fleet Street* (Aldershot: Ashgate), p. 3.

5. C. Baldick (2004) *The Oxford English Literary History, Vol. 10, 1910–40: The Modern Movement* (Oxford: Oxford University Press), p. 17.
6. D. LeMahieu (1988) *A Culture for Democracy: Mass Communication and the Cultivated Mind in Britain between the Wars* (Oxford: Clarendon Press); J. Carey (1992) *The Intellectuals and the Masses: Pride and Prejudice among the Literary Intelligentsia 1880–1939* (London: Faber & Faber); N. Humble (2001) *The Feminine Middlebrow Novel 1920s to 1950s: Class, Domesticity, and Bohemianism* (Oxford: Oxford University Press), ch. 1.
7. For example, P. Brooker and A. Thacker (2009) *The Oxford Critical and Cultural History of Modernist Magazines: Volume I* (Oxford: Oxford University Press); D. Spender (1984) *Time and Tide Wait For No Man* (London: Pandora Press); J. Dowson, 'Poetry and The Listener', *Working Papers on the Web: The Thirties Now*, http://extra.shu.ac.uk/wpw/thirties/thirties%20dowson.html, accessed 7 February 2010. One notable exception is the work of Julia Paolitto, and this chapter draws upon her PhD thesis in several places: J. Paolitto (2008) 'Guardians of British Culture: The British Sunday Press Between the Wars' (Oxford University, unpublished PhD thesis).
8. P. Balfour (1933) *Society Racket: A Critical Survey of Modern Social Life* (London: John Long Ltd.), p. 82.
9. Collier, *Modernism*, ch. 3; P. Waller (2006) *Writers, Readers and Reputations: Literary Life in Britain 1870–1918* (Oxford: Oxford University Press), ch. 4.
10. Collier, *Modernism*, p. 4.
11. Ann Thwaite (2004) 'Gosse, Sir Edmund William (1849–1928)', *Oxford Dictionary of National Biography* (Oxford University Press); online edn, 2009. http://www.oxforddnb.com/view/article/33481, accessed 2 February 2010.
12. Cited in Paolitto, 'Guardians', pp. 232–233.
13. Ibid., ch. 3.
14. Ibid., pp. 235–236.
15. Andrew Mylett (ed.) (1974) *Arnold Bennett: The 'Evening Standard' Years; Books and Persons 1926–1931* (London: Chatto & Windus).
16. F. R. Leavis (1930) *Mass Civilisation and Minority Culture* (Cambridge: Minority Press), p. 14; Baldick, *Modern Movement*, p. 17.
17. Mylett, *Arnold Bennett*, pp. 297–299.
18. On Priestley, see J. Baxendale (2007) *Priestley's England: J. B. Priestley and English Culture* (Manchester: Manchester University Press).
19. R. A. Scott-James (2004) 'Lynd, Robert Wilson (1879–1949)', rev. Sayoni Basu, *Oxford Dictionary of National Biography* (Oxford University Press) online edn, 2006, http://www.oxforddnb.com/view/article/34646, accessed 2 February 2010.
20. Collier, *Modernism*, p. 81.
21. P. Berry and A. Bishop (eds) (1985) *Testament of a Generation: The Journalism of Vera Brittain and Winifred Holtby* (London: Virago).
22. H. Richards (1997) *The Bloody Circus: The Daily Herald and the Left* (London: Pluto Press), pp. 42, 59.
23. Paolitto, 'Guardians', p. 252.
24. On the elite press's lack of concern for obscenity, see Paolitto, ch. 3. On the popular press's sense of morality, see A. Bingham (2009) *Family Newspapers? Sex, Private Life, and the British Popular Press 1918–78* (Oxford: Oxford University Press).

25. *Sunday Express*, 19 August 1928, p. 10.
26. See V. Brittain (1968) *Radclyffe Hall: A Case of Obscenity?* (London: Femina Books); D. Souhami (1999) *The Trials of Radclyffe Hall* (London: Virago), chs 20–25; L. Doan and J. Prosser (eds) (2001) *Palatable Poison: Critical Perspectives on 'The Well of Loneliness'* (New York: Columbia University Press).
27. *The People*, 19 August 1928, p. 2.
28. Bingham, *Family Newspapers?*, p. 179.
29. *The Star*, 2 October 1915, p. 4, cited in S. Hynes (1990) *A War Imagined: The First World War and English Culture* (London: Bodley Head), pp. 61–62.
30. B. Melman (1988) *Women and the Popular Imagination in the Twenties: Flappers and Nymphs* (Basingstoke: Macmillan), p. 44.
31. *Daily Mail*, 17 October 1921, p. 6.
32. *Daily Mirror*, 18 October 1921, p. 3.
33. *Daily Express*, 27 October 1924, p. 7. Warner Fabian was the pseudonym of Samuel Hopkins Adams.
34. *The Writer*, April 1926, p. 154.
35. S. Moseley (1926) *Short Story Writing and Freelance Journalism* (London: Pitman), Part 2, ch. VIII.
36. R. McKibbin (1998) *Classes and Cultures: England 1918–1951* (Oxford: Oxford University Press), ch. III.
37. Collier, *Modernism*, p. 3.
38. Paolitto, 'Guardians', ch. 3; Collier, *Modernism*, ch. 5; P. Berry and A. Bishop, *Testament*; A. Bingham (2004) *Gender, Modernity, and the Popular Press in Inter-War Britain* (Oxford: Oxford University Press).
39. Paolitto, 'Guardians', ch. 3.
40. T. Clarke (1931) *My Northcliffe Diary* (London: Hutchinson), pp. 195–205.
41. Collier, *Modernism*, p. 176.
42. See Bingham, *Family Newspapers?*
43. Baldick, *Modern Movement*, pp. 36–38.
44. Graham Law (2000) *Serializing Fiction in the Victorian Press* (Basingstoke: Palgrave Macmillan).
45. Clarke, *Northcliffe*, p. 136.
46. Bodleian Library, Oxford, MS.Eng.hist d.303-5, Northcliffe Bulletins to *Daily Mail*, 9 March 1918.
47. Northcliffe Bulletins, 17 January 1920.
48. Northcliffe Bulletins, 28 January 1921.
49. J. Curran, A. Douglas and G. Whannel (1980) 'The Political Economy of the Human Interest Story', in A. Smith (ed.) *Newspapers and Democracy: International Essays on a Changing Medium* (Cambridge, MA: MIT Press), p. 318.
50. Political and Economic Planning (1938) *Report on the British Press* (London: PEP), p. 253.
51. For example, Frankau: *Daily Mail*, 6 June 1923, p. 15; du Maurier: *Daily Express*, 14 September 1938; see also Baldick, *Modern Movement*, p. 18; Berry and Bishop, *Testament*, p. 76.
52. Richards, *Bloody Circus*, p. 135; R. Graves and A. Hodge (1940; 1971) *The Long Week-End: A Social History of Britain 1918–1939* (Harmondsworth: Penguin), p. 213.

53. Valerie Grove, 'Introduction', in Jan Struther (1939; 1989) *Mrs Miniver* (London: Virago).
54. House of Lords Record Office, Beaverbrook Papers, H/114, Max Aitken to Beaverbrook, 28 December 1946.
55. Beaverbrook Papers, H/136, E. J. Robertson to Beaverbrook, 28 October 1949.
56. Q. D. Leavis (1933; 1965) *Fiction and the Reading Public* (London: Chatto & Windus), pp. 224, 183, 117.
57. Ibid, pp. 185, 231.
58. Beaverbrook Papers, H/259, Elland to Beaverbrook, 3 July 1956.

4
Priestley and the Highbrows

John Baxendale

On 4 June 1930, a mock trial in aid of charity took place in the main lecture theatre of the London School of Economics. In the dock was J. B. Priestley, already a well-established critic and essayist, who had recently become famous and was becoming rich through his run-away best-selling novel *The Good Companions*.[1] Prosecuting Priestley was Harold Nicolson – former diplomat, writer and aesthete, currently slumming it somewhat as editor of the *Evening Standard*'s 'Londoner's Diary'. The charge was that Priestley had 'made a vast success with a healthy book'. Although he pleaded not guilty on the grounds that far from being healthy *The Good Companions* encouraged people to run away from home in search of adventure, Priestley was convicted and sentenced to write a better book – to which he replied that he had already done so: *Angel Pavement* would be published a few weeks later.

In 1930, Priestley was rapidly becoming a prime example of a familiar twentieth-century type: the author as celebrity. It was the latest of several versions of authorship which he was to live out during his long career. He constructed his first version of the writer's life while a teenager working as a clerk in a wool merchant's office in Edwardian Bradford, affecting a bohemian style with long hair, floppy bow ties, wideawake hats and brightly coloured jackets, scribbling epic poetry in his attic bedroom and writing a literary column for the local socialist paper (unpaid), while living a café lifestyle, albeit in Lyons Corner House on Market Street rather than the Café Royal.[2] This phase of his writing career peaked with the publication during the Great War of a proverbially slim volume of poems, *The Chapman of Rhymes*, which has not stood the test of time; indeed it was lucky to survive at all as after the War its author 'still alive and coming to my senses [...] destroyed every copy I could lay my hands on, now well aware of my folly'.[3] He then went to Cambridge, where by his own account he read his way through almost the entire body of English literature, and afterwards to London to seek his fortune as a writer.

Priestley had turned his back on academia, and as he lacked the family resources which kept Bloomsbury afloat, the flirtation with bohemia was also over. Now with a wife and child he needed to earn a living, and did so in the distinctly unromantic world of Grub Street, reading publishers' manuscripts, reviewing and essay-writing in newspapers and literary magazines such as *The London Mercury* and *The Saturday Review*, frequenting editors' offices and pubs in the vicinity of Fleet Street, where he conversed with the literary lions of his own and the previous generation.[4] This was hard work and it meant producing what the market demanded, so Priestley became the author as artisan, making a living with his pen, and at this he was prolific and successful. But he knew that the reviewing and essay-writing world was on the way out and that only a popular success as a novelist would release him from the Grub Street treadmill. After two well-received but not particularly successful novels, it was *The Good Companions*, published in 1929, which brought him fame and fortune, and made him just the kind of man-of-the-moment to undergo a mock trial for charity. After that, there was no looking back for Priestley: more best-selling novels and an alarming quantity of reviews, essays and newspaper columns. He became lead reviewer of the London *Evening Standard* in succession to Arnold Bennett, thereby ascending one of the country's most influential literary pulpits. He became a successful playwright, made radio broadcasts and wrote about the state of the nation in books such as *English Journey* (1934). By the end of the 1930s, he was well into the third phase of his career: a household name, a star of the celebrity culture which projected best-selling authors much as it did film stars – a phase which soon overlapped with another: the author as public figure and wartime national voice. Meanwhile, magazines would carry interviews with Priestley, gossip columns would report his theatre going, his house purchases and the christening of his son (godfather, J. M. Barrie).[5] Typical was a Pathé News item screened in November 1944 which showed the writer at work. In the opening shot, the camera pans across his extensive library, against a soundtrack of vaguely classical violin music. Priestley is shown typing, pipe in mouth. He crosses to the bookshelves and consults a weighty tome. Finally, he offers some equally weighty thoughts on the prospects of literature after the war and some kindly words of advice for young writers. The respectful voice-over commentary takes his status as a significant writer – of a different ilk from, say, Edgar Wallace – utterly for granted.[6] Some years earlier, Virginia Woolf had imagined Priestley at 50, complaining ' "why don't the highbrows like me? It isn't true that I write only for money". He will be enormously rich; but there will be that thorn in his shoe – or so I hope.'[7] Priestley was 50 when Pathé shot its newsreel, and certainly well off, but he showed no sign as yet of craving the plaudits of Bloomsbury or Cambridge.

The charge against Priestley of having written 'a healthy book' is a significant one, worth examination. This good-humoured event, like an earlier trial in which the critic James Agate had been charged with 'falsely pretending to be a Highbrow', made light of contemporary cultural conflicts and anxieties which were often felt, and expressed, more seriously.[8] A 'Battle of the Brows' had been flaring up throughout the 1920s, fanned from one direction by the rise of modernist literature, art and music, and from the other by the explosive growth of commercial popular culture. Each development was suspected of heralding the end of civilization, in a world knocked off its balance by the experience of the Great War. If some saw the power of Hollywood and the popular press as the surrender of culture to the lowest common denominator, others regarded the novels of James Joyce and Virginia Woolf, the music of Stravinsky, the sculpture of Jacob Epstein and the paintings of the post-Impressionists as a deliberate attack against decency and popular taste on the part of a snobbish and self-indulgent 'highbrow' elite; while yet others damned both *Ulysses* and the *Daily Express* as irrefutable evidence that the culture was going to the dogs.

During most of the 1920s, it was highbrowism which bore the brunt of the attacks. Populist highbrow-hunting could be glimpsed before the First World War in mainstream reactions to the exhibition of post-Impressionist paintings at the Grafton Gallery organized by Roger Fry in 1910, where the works of Cézanne, Van Gogh, Gauguin and others excited violent hostility from some critics and a vocal section of the general public.[9] There were similar responses to the arrival of modernist music, typified by Stravinsky's *Rite of Spring* in 1913, and to literary modernism, in the shape of *Ulysses* (1921, and banned for many years) and *The Waste Land* (1922, and much reviled – and probably a hoax, asserted *Time* magazine).[10] The sculptor Jacob Epstein became a perennial target, and his public work, in particular a modest and, to us, inoffensive memorial in London's Hyde Park, was attacked in the press and parliament and repeatedly vandalized.[11] Meanwhile, Sir Robert Baden Powell warned Boy Scouts against 'horses, wine, women, and highbrows', and the untimely death of a public schoolboy in Bristol was blamed on an excess of highbrow reading.[12] The state of the battle, and its familiarity to mainstream readers, was acknowledged in another piece of quasi-legal humour, one of A. P. Herbert's 'Misleading Cases' – fictional court cases usually appearing in *Punch* which satirized the eccentricities of the law or of human nature or both. In 'Trott v Tulip', written in 1927, a novelist sues a reviewer for calling her a 'highbrow'. The court hears from a parade of literary witnesses, including George Bernard Shaw and the popular novelist Gilbert Frankau, and most significantly from a proprietor of railway bookstalls, who declares that he can tell at a glance from the picture on the dust cover whether a book is 'healthy and suitable for the general public, on the one hand; or highbrow and not so, on the other'. After hearing damning testimony (from a witness who 'gave his evidence in a manly and straightforward way') about the gruesome details of the highbrow lifestyle – apparently 'incapable of cricket, unacquainted with golf, [and] wholly without patriotism or decent feeling' – the judge can only conclude that 'highbrow' carried 'even in literary circles the general force of an abusive term', and the plaintiff is awarded damages, though only in the sum of one penny.[13] Less fortunate than either Priestley or Miss Trott was the real-life, if somewhat improbable, Polish-New Zealand poet Geoffrey Potocki de Montalk, who in 1932 got six months in Wormwood Scrubs prison for publishing an obscene libel: three short bawdy verses and some translations from Rabelais and Verlaine. 'A man must not say he was a poet and be filthy', thundered the Recorder of London, 'He had to obey the law just the same as ordinary citizens, and the sooner the highbrow school learnt that the better for the morality of the country.'[14]

So we can see that the term 'healthy' in the indictment against Priestley, and in the testimony of Herbert's bookstall proprietor, was drawn from life. The health in question was, of course, moral rather than physical, and in this respect both Priestley's and de Montalk's indictments referenced the moralistic language of Victorian cultural reformers, now deemed in smart circles to be as hopelessly and comically outdated as everything else Victorian. Although poets and artists had always been morally suspect, the Victorian moral critique had been mainly directed at the culture of the masses rather than that of the intellectual elite. Popular pastimes such as cruel sports, vulgar music halls and sensational popular literature threatened to corrupt individual conduct and social values and, therefore, obstruct the progress of civilization among the working classes.[15] In the event, what prevailed was neither traditional vulgarity nor the 'rational recreation' favoured by the reformers, but new forms of commercial mass culture. Ironically it was one of these, the popular press, particularly the *Daily Mail* and the *Daily*

Express, which took over the role of public moralizer-in-chief, which it retains to this day. Combining Victorian criteria of beauty and healthiness with twentieth-century cultural democracy, the press turned its wrath on the 'highbrows' both for embracing the ugly and for rejecting the tastes of ordinary people: 'Their greatest contempt is for humanity at large,' declared the *Daily Express*, 'their greatest admiration – themselves'.[16] 'They consider that the book or play or picture that entertains and educates and pleases and uplifts 90 people out of every 100 cannot possibly have any artistic merit,' complained the popular novelist Gilbert Frankau in a 1927 radio talk. 'Humanity at large', or the uplifted 90 per cent of it, was now deemed the standard-bearer of a healthy culture, and the treasonous clerks of Bloomsbury, with their 'ugly statues [and] still uglier pictures', its chief enemies.[17]

Priestley himself would not have gone all the way with Frankau's dismissal of highbrow art, but like other popular writers he enjoyed caricaturing highbrow attitudes and lifestyle in his novels, essays and radio talks. In *The Good Companions*, we encounter the protagonist Miss Trant's absurd but rather likeable nephew Hilary, one of the 'Statics', who believes that 'life and Art have got absolutely choked up with filthy emotion', and should be rendered 'feelingless, all calm and clear', and wants her to finance a literary magazine.[18] Less sympathetically, in *Let the People Sing*, we encounter 'Mr Churton Talley, the great art critic and expert', who proves to be 'a slender, wavy-haired youth of about 55, with enamelled pink cheeks, a cherry lip, and the eyes of a dead codfish', who minces and hisses 'with those long drawn-out sibilants'.[19] Priestley had already described the typical highbrow as 'the thin sheep with the spectacles and the squeak from Oxford or Bloomsbury', and in a 1932 radio talk he returned to the theme: 'You decide – and God knows why – to over-emphasise your sibilants, so that you sound like a hissing serpent', he complained.[20] When we meet some highbrows at a cocktail party in *Wonder Hero*, they are, sure enough, 'hissing amiably at one another and smiling and swaying and waving their delicate little paws'.[21] Whether or not Bloomsburyites and their ilk really did squeak and hiss at each other like this, the widespread suggestion that they did carried intimations of effeminacy linked to upper-class affectation. This caricature implicitly connects highbrowism to ideas of post-war decadence, in which the moral bearings of the pre-war world have been lost and dividing lines of gender, race and culture have been blurred.

If there was a political and polemical force behind his depiction of highbrow lifestyles, when it came to highbrow literature – that is to say, modernism – Priestley, ever the professional critic, was more balanced and thoughtful in his judgements. Although he considered *Ulysses* stronger on 'verbal ingenuity' than 'sheer creative vitality', and doubted whether it was worth 'laborious days and nights wrestling with it', he regarded Proust as the greatest novelist of the century, and gave high praise to the novels of Virginia Woolf, a writer of 'innate genius' and 'a perceptive and delightful critic'.[22] *To the Lighthouse*, he told *Evening Standard* readers in 1932, 'has long seemed to me one of the most moving and beautiful pieces of fiction of our time. Nobody should fail to read it, and to read it with the loving care it deserves.' However – and as we shall see, it is a crucial however – he went on to ask why 'so good a critic should want to bully us all into writing the same kind of novel [...] Some novels, like hers, draw near to pure poetry. Others, equally valuable, draw near to social history. Why not recognise this fact?' Finally, and fatally, unable to restrain himself from a further dig at the highbrow manner and lifestyle, Priestley proceeded to refer to the 'poetic' school of novelists as 'terrifically sensitive, cultured, invalidish ladies with private means', by contrast with more active, if less sensitive, writers such as, presumably, himself; and, as if to make sure that real offence was caused, he pinned on Woolf the detested label 'high priestess' of Bloomsbury. Priestley's remarks began in good humour and with the best intentions, but these had been overwhelmed by the conflict of classes and lifestyles.[23] Just four days later, he broadcast a radio talk entitled 'To A Highbrow' which once again homed in on the cultural attitudes of the highbrows rather than on the kind of books they read or wrote, accusing them of bad faith in allowing cultural fashion to mould their tastes rather than their own authentic responses, and of rejecting out of hand anything that had become popular – by now a sore point with the author of *The Good Companions*.[24]

Mrs Woolf was not pleased. The review and the broadcast prompted her to write her celebrated, and at the time unpublished, letter to the *New Statesman*, which identified the main target of the highbrow fightback – not Tarzan nor Edgar Wallace nor even the *Daily Express* but the 'middlebrow'. Prominent among the alleged middlebrows was, of course, Priestley himself, whom the letter referred to repeatedly, scornfully, and without directly naming him, quoting several times from his notorious *Evening Standard* review, alluding to his latest novel and describing a visit to his house. The gist of the letter, which contained rather more verbal play and polemic than clear argument, was that middlebrows lacked both the 'thoroughbred intelligence' of the highbrow who pursued ideas, and the 'thoroughbred vitality' of the lowbrow who pursued life; middlebrows seek neither – or rather, both, 'mixed indistinguishably, and rather nastily, with money, fame, power, or prestige'. It was they who were responsible for spreading the idea that lowbrows and highbrows hated one another – in other words, for artificially creating the 'battle of the brows' which so 'troubles the evening air'. If lowbrows but knew it they had a natural affinity with highbrows and should join with them to exterminate the middlebrow pest; sadly, they seem to prefer the 'mixture of geniality and sentiment stuck together with a sticky slime of calves–foot jelly', with which the middlebrows seduce them.[25] Geniality, sentimentality, writing for money and poor taste in interior decor – these are the main points of the indictment; but Woolf had already laid down the foundations of a more serious critique in 1924 in her essay 'Mr Bennett and Mrs Brown'. The novels of the Edwardians, Wells, Bennett and Galsworthy, while necessary in their time, no longer sufficed. Human nature had changed, and if the novel was to move on, their realist approach, dealing with material externalities and social issues, had to give way before a focus on the inner life and consciousness itself. Apart from the dubious assertion about human nature, there is little in the piece to suggest why the externalities and social issues of post-war life are not worthy of the same attention given in their own time by the Edwardians or their Victorian predecessors.[26] In the 1932 letter – and not least in its personal attack on Priestley himself – we can perhaps detect Woolf's exasperation that her manifesto aims in 'Mrs Brown' had not been realized, and that most of the novels being written, and read, had more affinities with Wells, Bennett and Galsworthy than with Joyce, James or Woolf.

Also deploring, though for slightly different reasons, the direction modern culture had taken was Q. D. Leavis in *Fiction and the Reading Public* (1932). There was little love lost between Bloomsbury and *Scrutiny*,[27] but Woolf and Leavis agreed that the main problem was not the lowbrow but the middlebrow, prominent among whom was Priestley. Lowbrow novels, Leavis admitted in terms similar to Woolf's, could 'exude vital energy as richly as a manure heap', when their 'bad writing, false sentiment, sheer silliness and a preposterous narrative are all carried along by the magnificent vitality of their author'.[28] Further up the scale, in ' "middlebrow" read as "literature" ', was where the damage was done. The work of Galsworthy, Walpole, Bennett and Priestley himself, 'respected middling novelists of blameless intentions and indubitable skill', may have seemed thoughtful and cultured enough to the unwary reader, but really offered only 'commonplace sentiments and an outworn technique'. Written 'on the traditional model, and therefore easy to respond to', they were 'easily recognised by the uncritical as "literature" ', but dealt in 'soothing and not disturbing sentiments', like 'academy art' or magazine fiction. Worryingly, books like these were to be found not only in 'the average well-to-do home', but also on the shelves of such people as dons and schoolmasters.[29] Thus, unlike the popular entertainments of Edgar Wallace and his ilk they posed a direct threat to the standards of the educated minority on which the future health of the culture depended. For the *Scrutiny* group, the underlying cause of the cultural malaise was the steady growth from the eighteenth century onwards of the cultural marketplace, whose values had now infected writing which claimed to be, and was accepted as, proper literature. As a result, the general public knew nothing of 'the living interests of modern literature' and the 'critical minority' was, for the first time in history, threatened with extinction.[30]

It is not difficult to see why, seeking an object for their ire, both Woolf and Leavis should light upon Priestley. He was a best-selling novelist who was widely thought of as a serious writer. His novels appeared to owe nothing to modernism, but to continue the Victorian, or earlier, tradition of the novel as, in Priestley's words, 'a large mirror of life', peopled with 'vital figures in whose existence, no matter how wild and strange they may be, we are compelled to believe while we are reading'.[31] The language he used was straightforward and transparent – a tool for conveying thoughts, events and people, not an object of interest in itself. Most of his plots, with a few exceptions, had 'happy endings', in the sense that loose ends were tied up, and the characters we find sympathetic end up, roughly speaking, how we want them to.[32] Once he had gained a secure foothold in public taste, Priestley went on to write just the kind of novels which Woolf denounced in 'Mr Bennett and Mrs Brown', whose preoccupation with social issues and material externalities prompted the reader 'to do something – to join a society, or, more desperately, to write a cheque', instead of delving deeper into the novel itself in order to understand it better.[33] In *Angel Pavement* (1930), *Wonder Hero* (1933), *Let the People Sing* (1939) and *Daylight on Saturday* (1943) among others, Priestley sought not only to attack social problems in the reforming Victorian spirit of *Hard Times* or *North and South*, but also simply to present people in modern society, problems and all, within a believable and pleasurable context.

Although not hostile to modernism, Priestley was robust in the defence of his own, non-modernist, practice, arguing that 'the novel is a very loose, wide form; and the task of the novelist is to write as well as he can the kind of novel he wants to write', and if he wants to write about 'men in a particular society, and the character of that society', then Woolf's 'highly subjective, inner monologue' method will not do the job.[34] As he argued in his 1932 review, some novels were like poetry, others were like social history: why were both not equally valid?[35] Woolf, who thought novels should not encourage readers to sign cheques and join societies, was not averse to doing these things unprompted by fiction, when she could find herself politically on the same side as Priestley: as in 1936, when they met at a Bloomsbury gathering in support of the Spanish Republic: 'how we glared at each other', Woolf reported.[36] Priestley's view was that there were moments in history, and this was one of them, when literature must eschew perfect artistry and charge 'into the middle of life'.[37] In his social novels of the 1930s, in his prolific newspaper journalism, in *English Journey* and in his wartime broadcasts, and as a founder of the wartime Common Wealth Party and the post-war Campaign for Nuclear Disarmament, that is exactly what he did, and he was not the only so-called 'middlebrow' novelist to do so. Although Priestley regarded it as almost self-evident that his realist technique was the way to write politically progressive fiction – all the rest being a retreat into subjectivism – others on the left disagreed. Adorno in the 1930s, as well as later critics of realism in film and television, argued that only modernism could disrupt the established patterns of thought and perception sufficiently to get a radical message across, and all else was simply perpetuating the status quo, no matter how progressive its message appeared to be on the surface.[38] For Priestley – a visionary perhaps, but no revolutionary, rather a social-democratic reformist in day-to-day politics – such a view would seem harsh and excluding, turning its back on the very people whose support any radical politics must win.

Priestley's discontent with the state of literary culture is closely connected with his political and social stance. As D. L. LeMahieu has perceptively argued, Priestley was part of a process of cultural democratization which was more complex than the damning of 'mass culture' by the likes of F. R. Leavis or Theodor Adorno might lead us to believe.[39] The increasing divide between 'serious' and 'popular', 'high' and 'low' was widely observed, and widely deplored, though for widely differing reasons. Leavis himself regarded the term 'highbrow' as 'an ominous addition to the English language', because it signalled the fragmentation of a once-common culture under the impact of commercialization – 'there were no "highbrows" in Shakespeare's time'.[40] For Priestley, interwar highbrow intellectuals like Leavis were to blame for abandoning the Victorian and Edwardian promise of a steadily broadening culture. 'They wanted literature to be difficult [...] They did not want to share anything with the crowd', he wrote later, so general readers were made to feel that literature was not for them.[41] Literary critics were active in this process of exclusion: 'intolerant in manner, arrogant in tone [...] theological and absolutist [...] Only a small amount of writing, written by and for the elite, was Literature, all else was rubbish'.[42] Leavis had notoriously declared that life was too short to devote any of it to reading Priestley[43]: Priestley retaliated by putting Leavis in his 1951 novel *Festival at Farbridge*, thinly disguised as the Cambridge critic Leonard Mortory, whose critical works were entitled *Disavowals, Rejections, Exclusions* and *Refusals*, and who thought life was too short to read almost any of the 'so-called great novelists' – though Priestley would later give a favourable review to Leavis's book on D. H. Lawrence.[44]

Priestley, naturally enough, resented highbrows' dismissal of his own work – 'I was out of date before I even began' – but there is more depth than this to his critique of literary culture.[45] Priestley was a man of the people, growing up in Bradford in a family and an environment which straddled the lower middle and working classes, and with a strong dose of provincial socialism in his background. To echo Chekhov, he had peasant blood and could not be astonished by tales of peasant virtues, such as Virginia Woolf's good-hearted lowbrows, based largely, it seemed, on her own domestic servants. Faced with the rich and diverse spectacle of modern culture, his instinct was not to make fastidious discriminations, but to plunge in, judging each experience on its own merits, whether football, Russian drama, grand opera or detective stories. In his essay 'High, Low, Broad', written in 1926 before he became famous, and before the term 'middlebrow' had gained currency, he argued against cultural fragmentation, damned highbrows and lowbrows alike, and urged his readers to become 'broadbrows', engaging with the whole cultural spectrum, bringing to bear their own values and critical faculties, and not those dictated to them by fashion or the mass media.[46] The concept of 'broadbrow' was not, of course, fully theorized – this was, after all, *The Saturday Review* – but beneath it lay a well-considered response to the new conditions of modern culture: not fragmented, as pessimists argued, but richly diverse, but no longer lending itself to universal criteria of aesthetic value. His was the opposite reaction to those who would apply such criteria ever more rigorously, and perhaps a foretaste of postmodernism's relativistic response to the same cultural changes further along the line.

In the more immediate future, it seemed that highbrow fears were justified and the middlebrow was to hold the stage. It was the arrival of the 'People's War', with its ideology of democracy, equal shares and the heroism of the common people, that for some set the seal on the triumph of the middlebrow. George Orwell, who had begun his literary career in highbrow circles, writing a rather snooty review of *Angel Pavement* in *The Adelphi* in 1930, discovered ten years later that the 'Bloomsbury highbrow, with his mechanical snigger, is as out of date as a cavalry colonel.'[47] A *Times* leader in March 1941 celebrated the 'Eclipse of the Highbrow', sparking off a lengthy and furious correspondence. Highbrows, *The Times* maintained, had spurned the 'unspectacular virtues' of 'endurance, unselfishness, and discipline', preferring instead 'hasty brilliance' and 'clever triviality', leading to a 'deliberate obscurity or perversity' which bewildered and bored the public. But now, the public can at last breathe a sigh of relief:

> What changes of taste this war, and the reactions following it, may produce, no one can foresee. But at least it can hardly give rise to arts unintelligible outside a Bloomsbury drawing-room, and completely at variance with those stoic virtues which the whole nation is now called upon to practice.[48]

Whether or not he agreed with this robust philistinism, at that particular moment, it was Priestley, in his writing and broadcasts, who embodied more than anyone the populist spirit and common culture of wartime.[49]

Notes

1. 'Author "In the Dock" ', *Daily Mirror*, 5 June 1930, p. 11.
2. J. B. Priestley (1962) *Margin Released: A Writer's Reminiscences and Reflections* (London: Heinemann), Part One.
3. J. B. Priestley (1918) *The Chapman of Rhymes* (London: Alexander Moring Ltd); J. B. Priestley (1977) *Instead of the Trees: A Final Chapter of Autobiography* (London: Heinemann), p. 46; Alan Edwin Day (1980) *J. B. Priestley: An Annotated Bibliography* (New York & London: Garland Publishing Inc.), pp. 3–4.
4. Priestley, *Margin Released*, Part Three; John Baxendale (2007) *Priestley's England: J. B. Priestley and English Culture* (Manchester: Manchester University Press), pp. 10–12; John Lehmann (ed.) (1957) *Coming to London* (London: Phoenix House).
5. For example, 'Coleridge's Home: London House Bought by Author of "The Good Companions" ', *Daily Mirror*, 8 August 1931, p. 11; 'Novelists at a Play', *Daily Mirror*, 19 May 1932, p. 11.
6. Pathé News 1944: 'Personalities: J. B. Priestley', http://www.britishpathe.com/record.php?id= 47378, accessed 7 January 2010.

7. Virginia Woolf to Quentin Bell, 12 December 1933, in Nigel Nicolson (ed.) (1979) *The Sickle Side of the Moon: The Letters of Virginia Woolf Volume 5 1932–1935* (London: Hogarth Press).
8. *The Times*, 26 April 1930, p. 8.
9. Ian Dunlop (1972) *The Shock of the New* (New York: American Heritage Press), chapter 4.
10. 'Has the Reader Any Rights Before the Bar of Literature?', *Time*, 3 March 1923.
11. *The Times*, 10 October 1929, p. 16.
12. *The Times*, 6 January 1922, p. 5; *The Times*, 4 October 1934.
13. A. P. Herbert (1927) 'Trott v. Tulip: Is "Highbrow" Libellous?', *Misleading Cases in the Common Law* (London: Methuen).
14. *The Times*, 9 February 1932, p. 14.
15. Peter Bailey (1978) *Leisure and Class in Victorian England: Rational Recreation and the Contest for Control 1830–1885* (London: Routledge and Kegan Paul).
16. *Daily Express*, 6 January 1921.
17. Quoted in Leonard Woolf (1927) *Hunting the Highbrow* (London: Hogarth Press), p. 7.
18. J. B. Priestley (1929; 1962) *The Good Companions* (Harmondsworth: Penguin Books), pp. 64–67.
19. J. B. Priestley (1939) *Let The People Sing* (London: Heinemann), pp. 204–205.
20. J. B. Priestley (1926) 'High, Low, Broad', *Saturday Review*, 20 February, p. 165; J. B. Priestley (1932) 'To a Highbrow', *John O'London's Weekly*, 3 December, p. 354.
21. J. B. Priestley (1933) *Wonder Hero* (London: Heinemann), p. 168.
22. J. B. Priestley (1932) 'A Good Little Book for Shakespeare Week', *Evening Standard*, 21 April, p. 11; J. B. Priestley (1960) *Literature and Western Man* (London: Heinemann), pp. 419, 434.
23. J. B. Priestley (1932) 'Tell Us More About These Authors', *Evening Standard*, 13 October, p. 11.
24. Priestley, 'To a Highbrow', p. 354.
25. Virginia Woolf (1942) 'Middlebrow', in *The Death of the Moth and Other Essays* (London: Hogarth Press), pp. 113–119. For further discussion, see Baxendale, *Priestley's England*, pp. 24–26; Melba Cuddy Keane (2003) *Virginia Woolf, the Intellectual, and the Public Sphere* (Cambridge: Cambridge University Press), p. 25ff.
26. Virginia Woolf (1924; 1966) 'Mr Bennett and Mrs Brown', *Collected Essays*, vol. 1 (London: Hogarth Press).
27. *Scrutiny* was the quarterly journal published from 1932–1953 which was a vehicle for the opinions of F. R. Leavis, Q. D. Leavis and fellow academics who shared their literary values.
28. Q. D. Leavis (1932) *Fiction and the Reading Public* (London: Chatto and Windus), pp. 62–63.
29. Ibid., pp. 35–37.
30. F. R. Leavis (1930) *Mass Civilisation and Minority Culture* (Cambridge: Minority Press).
31. J. B. Priestley (1927) *The English Novel* (London: Ernest Benn), p. 3.
32. Holger Klein (2002) *J. B. Priestley's Fiction* (Frankfurt: Peter Lang), pp. 12–18.
33. Woolf, 'Mr Bennett'.
34. Priestley *Literature and Western Man*, pp. 434–435.

35. Priestley, 'Tell Us More'.
36. Virginia Woolf to Dorothy Bussey, 15 December 1936/1 January 1937, in Nigel Nicolson (ed.) (1980) *Leave the Letters till We're Dead: The Letters of Virginia Woolf 1936–41* (London: Chatto and Windus), p. 100.
37. J. B. Priestley, 'A Contrast in Two Great Writers', *Evening Standard*, 25 February 1932, p. 7.
38. Theodor Adorno (1991) *The Culture Industry* (London: Routledge); for the *Days of Hope* debate see Tony Bennett et al (eds) (1981) *Popular Television and Film* (London: BFI Publishing), Part IV.
39. D. L. LeMahieu (1988) *A Culture for Democracy: Mass Communication and the Cultivated Mind in Britain Between the Wars* (Oxford: Clarendon Press), pp. 317–333.
40. Leavis, *Mass Civilisation*, p. 25.
41. J. B. Priestley (1949) *Delight* (London: Heinemann), p. 70.
42. Priestley, *Margin Released*, p. 156.
43. F. R. Leavis (1948) *The Great Tradition* (London: Chatto and Windus), p. 11.
44. J. B. Priestley (1951) *Festival at Farbridge* (London: Heinemann), pp. 375–376; J. B. Priestley, 'Who Will Pass His Scrutiny?', *News Chronicle*, 6 October 1955, p. 8.
45. Priestley, *Margin Released*, p. 156.
46. Priestley, 'High, Low, Broad'.
47. George Orwell (1930) review in *Adelphi*, October 1930, and in Sonya Orwell and Ian Angus (1968) *The Collected Essays, Journalism and Letters of George Orwell, Volume 1* (London: Secker and Warburg), pp. 47–50; George Orwell (1940) *The Lion and the Unicorn: Socialism and the English Genius* in Sonya Orwell and Ian Angus (1968) *The Collected Essays, Journalism and Letters of George Orwell, Volume 2* (London: Secker and Warburg), p. 96.
48. *The Times*, 'Eclipse of the Highbrow', 25 March 1941, p. 5.
49. J. B. Priestley (1940) *Postscripts* (London: Heinemann); Baxendale, *Priestley's England*, pp. 140–165.

5
Aesthetics for Everyman: Arnold Bennett's *Evening Standard* Columns

John Shapcott

When Lord Beaverbrook bought the *Evening Standard* in 1923, Arnold Bennett was quick to write congratulating him and offering his advice. Bennett's assertion that the *Standard* is 'the only evening paper that appeals even a little to educated people, and it ought to be made to appeal a great deal more to them than it does' was the opinion of a successful journalist.[1] That same year Bennett, the successful novelist, acknowledged the commercial viability of the paper in his *Riceyman Steps*, when he has the Earlforwards's servant, Elsie, fail to buy a copy: ' "I couldn't get no paper, 'm" ', Elsie explained ' " ... it isn't the *Evening Standard* – it's the *Star*. They were all sold out, 'm" '.[2] Beaverbrook, for his part, welcomed Bennett's enthusiastic interest in his new venture. The two men's friendship had grown steadily since May 1918 when Beaverbrook appointed Bennett Director of British Propaganda in France. Bennett believed that his powerful friend should now use his money to create a paper able to appeal to, and influence the opinion of, a wide readership:

> I should have that whole paper well written [...] Books, pictures, theatres and music are none of them well done at present. There is a great interest springing up in architecture, but I don't know any London paper that attempts to touch it.
>
> I don't think it matters [...] what your policy is, if only it is adhered to and is brilliantly explained. I can see a *Standard* that every well-educated person would *have* to read, if only for pleasure, but it is not the present *Standard*.[3]

Bennett contributed occasional articles to Beaverbrook's *Standard* until, in November 1926, he finally agreed to write a regular column. Central to Bennett's conditions of employment was the stipulation that when he 'took on the job it was clearly understood that I should be absolutely free to review or not to review, just as I chose'.[4] The result was that in 'the late Twenties, booksellers would wait to see which books had been recommended by Arnold Bennett – the country's highest-paid book reviewer – in his regular Thursday literary column in the *Evening Standard* before placing their orders'.[5]

Yet within 30 years of Bennett's death James Hepburn was forced to concede that whilst in 1930 '[f]or the great middle-brow reading public, his [Bennett's] opinion was final' it was nevertheless 'also ephemeral. With his death in 1931 it was forgotten.'[6] Until 1974, it was difficult for the general reader to judge whether Bennett's columns merited relative obscurity, but the publication of Andrew Mylett's *Arnold Bennett: The Evening Standard Years, Books & Persons 1926–1931* (1974) prompted a short-lived reassessment of their value, both as literary criticism and as social documents. The immediate critical response to the collection's publication was overwhelmingly positive. *The Times Literary Supplement* considered them 'even better reading now than when they first appeared' and David Holloway in *The Bookman* saw them as 'important essays on such topics as literary history and censorship'.[7] Despite such acclaim, there has not been any subsequent exegesis of the *Evening Standard* columns. Their sheer bulk and the near overwhelming number of literary references to works old and new might in part account for their neglect. To read them closely, however, is to realize that Bennett both reflected and set the cultural agenda of the late 1920s in an authoritative, stylish and accessible format that has never subsequently been equalled in the pages of a popular newspaper. If Bennett's literary tastes are held to reflect the aesthetic and moral values of a supposedly 'middlebrow' readership, then such a readership was far less conservative than this derogatory label suggests.

Clearly defining Bennett's presumed community of readers is problematic and Bennett's own journalistic avoidance of the label 'middlebrow' in his critical writing may be evidence of his professional adroitness in not wishing to circumscribe either his popular commercial or his literary aesthetic appeal. Believing that 'the majority of people in every section of life are and must be middling',[8] Bennett adopts a tone of ironic self-deprecation, remarking that Virginia Woolf is 'the queen of the high-brows; and I am a low-brow' (p. 327). Despite his bravado, he remained personally vulnerable to criticism from his literary peers, finding it necessary to apologize to 'High-brows' for including detective fiction within his professional remit – 'I Read a "Thriller" – And

Startle My Friends' (pp. 176–178) – and relieved when E. M. Forster's *Aspects of the Novel* – 'Life and the Novel: Witty Author Laughs at the "Big Guns" and the public' – appears to validate his own critical stance, permitting him to 'state exultantly that I [too] am a pseudo-scholar' (pp. 100–102). As a former solicitor's clerk, Bennett knew the strengths and limitations of his target middle-class audience better than most and never denigrated these readers when personal fame and wealth placed him in a more privileged social and economic position. His journal entry for January 1897 records an evening spent in the company of the 'typical respectable Clerk and his wife' during which he noted their reading interests – the wife read the Brontës, George Eliot and Mrs Henry Wood, while her husband preferred Charles Lamb and Robert Louis Stevenson – remarking on their enthusiasm but stressing their evident lack of literary exploration beyond the familiar.[9] The clerk, for example, professed ignorance when Bennett mentioned *The Yellow Book*. Bennett's short story contribution to *The Yellow Book*, 'A Letter Home' (1895), and his 1898 novel *A Man From The North*, both published by John Lane, represented his own consciously calculated entry into the highbrow avant-garde segment of the literary marketplace. But Bennett never saw his contributions to highbrow publications as compromised by his engagement with more obviously commercial literary cultures. Instead he sought, from his earliest days to his *Evening Standard* years, to bridge the distance between high and low for a socially diverse readership, to make it possible for the clerk and his wife to read both *The Yellow Book* and Mrs Henry Wood without fear of embarrassment.

The difficulty with confining both Bennett and the texts he recommended within the often implied pejorative term 'middlebrow' is demonstrated from the very earliest days of his journalistic practice. In 1894, we find him publishing his own French translations of short stories by Remy de Gourmont and Georges d'Esparbès in *Woman*. That same year he laments in his 'Book Chat' column in *Woman* that whilst the names of 'Homer, Shakespeare, Dante, and Goethe, are all on men's tongues, but few there are that read them'.[10] To combat this ignorance he recommends a book, *A Shadow of Dante*: the beginning of a life-long commitment to introducing English readers to continental European literature that persists until his very last *Evening Standard* column.

From the start of his career, then, Bennett refused to withdraw into a modernist minority culture of which he was personally appreciative, but not exclusively so. Sean Latham's *'Am I A Snob?' Modernism and the Novel* (2003) recognizes Bennett's importance in attempting to free his readers from literary snobbery. Latham considers Bennett's 1909 study, *Literary Taste: How to Form It*, to be not only an 'intriguing guide to the formation of literary taste [offering] more than just an acute diagnosis of the problem of snobbery' but also a solution based on a 'most remarkable simplicity and its direct appeal to an audience grown familiar with the mass media and commodity culture'.[11] Latham maps a direct route from Bennett's 1909 position to his *Evening Standard* columns, arguing that though Bennett employs an Arnoldian argument, now associated with the Leavisite tradition, that, ' "taste has to pass before the bar of the classics", [yet he] also keeps before his readers the fact that the books he recommends are themselves commodities, objects that can command a certain cultural as well as economic capital'.[12]

It is perhaps appropriate that, as a successful novelist himself, Bennett's first column, 'Price of Novels Must Come Down' (18 November 1926), deals with the practical problem of book marketing. Adopting a friendly fireside chat persona, he addresses the reader directly: '*You* see...' (italics added). He also readily admits to sharing a fallibility with the population at large: 'And who knows a good book from a bad book within a year, or five years, from publication? Very few of us' (p. 1). Bennett then raises the topical issue of the formation of the National Book Council and considers its potential for influencing book buying. This is a subject he returns to at intervals throughout the columns. He suggests the Council extend its remit to negotiate with authors and publishers to market books in the then British Empire at affordable prices: 'Books are the great colonisers, the great penetrators, the great spreaders of ideas' (p. 66).

Bennett not only perceived that every text was an economic unit or marketable commodity but he was also highly conscious of the materiality of the book. His article 'Publishers Who Produce Bad Work' (6 January 1927) is devoted to persuading his readers of the importance of seeing the book as a total aesthetic object, involving the skills of the bookbinder, designer, illustrator, printer and the author. He claims that whilst contemporary reviewers and critics cannot with any certainty judge the enduring moral and artistic value of the latest books, they 'can, however, immediately judge the value of our books considered as physical objects' (p. 14). He then proceeds to castigate the general quality of book production in Britain:

> Most books, and especially most novels, are bad examples of the art and craft of making books. They are badly set up from bad founts of type in a badly designed page, printed on bad paper, badly bound,

and enveloped in bad dust-covers [...] They offend the eye of taste;
they offend an honest partiality for sound workmanship [...]

The 'book-makers' employed by some publishers seem to be mar-
vellously unaware that a page and a title-page can be designed with
beauty; that the question of margins is important; that paper can be
good or evil; that traditions of fine printing exist; that to produce a
beautiful book need cost no more than to produce an ugly book; that
book-making is an art and a craft – or should be. (pp. 14–15)

I have quoted at length both to give some idea of the uncompromising
stand that Bennett had evinced since youth on the desirability of combining utility with beauty in a publication, and also because it sets out
a credo that will be regularly invoked throughout his columns. At the
same time, he consistently argues for the growing importance of design
across industry in an increasingly competitive marketplace: 'If man-
ufacturers of biscuits, hosiery, shipping, and cakes can avail themselves of the latest efforts towards beauty in printing, surely publishers
can' (p. 15).

Bennett's remarks acquire an additional significance if we recall that
1927 saw the publication of the facsimile manuscript version of his
1908 masterpiece *The Old Wives' Tale*. Its publication saw Bennett's
journalistic strictures promoting books as aesthetic objects become a
personal commercial reality. Returning to the theme of 'The Craft of
Writing and Printing' in June 1928, he directs attention to a book that
might as well help us develop a more informed appreciation of the
layout and typographical accuracy of the 1927 *The Old Wives' Tale*.
In typical avuncular style, Bennett recommends Oliver Simon and Julius
Rodenberg's *Printing of Today* 'to all those who (like myself) can discover as much pleasure in a fine page as in a fine cigar' (p. 171).
More seriously, he looks back to the contribution made to the aesthetics of book production by William Morris's Kelmscott Press. Ever
aware of present circumstances, he then questions the near monopoly of
typography standards by the Linotype Corporation and the Monotype
Corporation and their responsibility to 'set artists to design a beautiful
type recognisably modern' (p. 171).[13]

Today the facsimile of *The Old Wives' Tale* has become a collector's
item. As Bennett advised his readers in 1929, 'There's Joy – And Money –
In Book Collecting' (30 May 1929). In recommending *Letters from George
Moore to Edward Dujardin, 1886–1922*, Bennett appeals jointly to the
acquisitive and the aesthetic interests of his readers: 'A volume *de luxe*.
Limited edition. Signed. It has a great literary interest as well as physical.

Already it is worth quite a lot' (p. 273). These credentials could be applied as equally to some of the productions of the small modernist presses as to Benn's printing of the 1927 *The Old Wives' Tale*. Bennett's columns consistently demand that printing and bookmaking acknowledge their debt to the Arts and Craft spirit of William Morris in an ideal synthesis of text, design and material. Mindful of the pockets of his readers, Bennett never neglects issues of production costs at the cheaper end of the market. In a 1928 column, he praises the Nonesuch Press for marketing practices aimed at stimulating 'public interest in fine books [...] Its complete Blake ([...] nearly 1200 beautiful pages for five half-crowns) makes about the best value in cheap editions ever offered' (p. 172). It is important to appreciate that from his earliest devotion to manuscript and bibliographic practices – his manuscript title pages and chapter headings for *The Old Wives' Tale* in 1908 bore a striking resemblance to Ezra Pound's ornately decorated illuminated capitals and two-colour printing suggestive of Pre-Raphaelite design – Bennett never wavered in his promotion of the book as beautiful artefact. His columns read as a popular manifesto, reinforcing the values inherent, but often overlooked, in the text of his novels. In his 1909 novel, *The Glimpse*, for example, Bennett appears as the thinly disguised hero whose extended two-page rapture on book production loses none of its intensity when transferred to the *Evening Standard* columns:

> Books not merely – and perhaps not chiefly – as vehicles of learning or knowledge, but books as books, books as entities, books as beautiful things, books as historical antiquities, books as repositories of memorable associations. Questions of type, ink, paper, margins, watermarks, paginations, bindings, were capable of really agitating me [...] Radiant, light-giving, immaculate! To touch it was to thrill.[14]

Bennett wanted his mass-circulation readership to experience this same thrill, irrespective of a book's genre.

This same sense of aesthetic epiphany extends to such an unexpected field as the design of silent film inter-titles. Bennett would have been very conscious of the importance of cinema as a major entertainment vehicle for a large proportion of his readers. He himself grossed large sums for film adaptations of his novels, beginning in 1914 with the Eclipse Film Company's version of *Grand Babylon Hotel*, and for writing film scenarios, culminating in one of the last great silent British films, *Piccadilly*, in 1929. He published very little comment on cinema, although a 1927 article 'The Film Story' appeared in the modernist film journal *Close Up*, alongside contributions from Dorothy Richardson and Bryher. In the *Evening Standard*, he restricts his commentary to the graphics of film production, encouraging his readers to note the introductory titling and subsequent inter-titling of film and to make informed comparisons with other forms of print culture. In his *Journal*, he writes of lunching with Beaverbrook to discuss his article before 'rush[ing] off to Wardour films, and [spending] a final $2^3/4$ hours on "Faust", finishing it except for passing proofs of titles and choosing some types'.[15] This is the F. W. Murnau 1926 German film for which Bennett wrote the English inter-titles and of which he wanted his *Evening Standard* readers to be critically appreciative. 'After various trials I failed to get the titles done in a style of lettering that I could conscientiously approve. At last I sent to the scribe a copy of the very lovely quarto edition of Terence printed in the original tongue by Charles Whittingham in MDCCCLIV. I said: "Imitate these characters" ' (Mylett, p. 15). Which they did.

Bennett's interest in graphic design was all-encompassing and he rarely let pass an opportunity to influence his readers' taste when contemplating their environment. As an early enthusiast of E. McKnight Kauffer's Underground Railway posters, fusing commercial and cultural authority, Bennett believed that they had mentally 'changed the face of London streets for a lot of people, including me'. Ever ready to massage his readers' egos where possible, Bennett continued: 'popular success of those posters proves that popular taste is on the up-grade' (p. 173). Bennett chose Kauffer as the illustrator for the limited edition of *Elsie and the Child* (1929). This volume is not only testament to the clear aesthetic agenda promulgated in Bennett's columns, but is also evidence of his ability to recognize and collaborate with talent from other artistic fields in the interests of ensuring that '[i]n the matter of artistic book production [popular taste] is assuredly on the up-grade' (p. 173).

Whilst directing attention to publishing standards, Bennett regularly voiced his opinion that 'it is easier to write books than to sell them' (p. 104). His 'The American Mind and the British' column evaluated possible marketing strategies in the light of what he considered to be the enlightened American approach of creating book clubs. 'In America selling books is a business, whereas in Britain it is too often a superior, lordly, and distinguished profession. In America men of business explore the possibilities of markets for books' (p. 104). Although Bennett foresees initial obstacles to persuading British readers who 'obstinately insist on thinking and choosing for themselves', he believes that with some small modifications similar schemes could be made to flourish in Britain (p. 106). His enthusiasm for the Book of the Month Club and the Literary Guild must have come as something of a surprise to many of his readers and certainly there was no early rush to emulate the American models. Indeed, some 30 months later Bennett returned to the subject, his 29 May 1930 column 'Young Authors Should Shock' reiterating the need for 'a Book-of-the-Month Club devised on similar lines' to the American club (p. 379). Bennett was left frustrated by 'the myopic frowning of certain booksellers in Britain' while envying the American culture that seemed able to combine commercial values with middlebrow cultural standards: 'The Book Clubs, I hear, are flourishing more and more mightily in the United States, and quite satisfactorily prospering' (p. 380). Bennett saw American marketing techniques as not merely a way of increasing sales but also of educating taste by 'send[ing] out books which as a rule only the keenly interested would have heard of' (p. 380).

Only the 'keenly interested' would have known of many of the American novelists and novels Bennett was to promote through his columns. The full range of his recommendations is certainly eclectic and remains challenging to critical categorization. An early example is his December 1926 column 'Two Great Imaginative Works', where he writes that '[a]t the end of the year I recall that the most important large works of imagination which I have read in 1926 are both American', Theodore Dreiser's *An American Tragedy* and Herman Melville's *Pierre* (p. 12). Bennett did not recommend *An American Tragedy* 'to all and sundry dilettante and plain people', due to its length and perceived infelicities of literary style (p. 12), but it remained a fairly safe recommendation, operating as it did in familiar Dreiser territory, playing out fantasies of upward mobility and success. The case of *Pierre* is quite different. Bennett acknowledges that it is 'difficult to read', that the 'basic idea of its plot is entitled to be called unpleasant', but that these defects are outweighed by its 'marked originality [...] the author essays feats which the most advanced novelists of to-day imagine to be quite new' (p. 13).

For the next three years, Bennett was in the vanguard of British taste-makers for American fiction, promoting new work by, for example, Sinclair Lewis, Ernest Hemingway, Thornton Wilder and William Faulkner. Alongside these (now) well-known names, Bennett was also able to offer his British readers the opportunity to share some of his excitement at discovering the wellspring of an American textual discourse that was to influence post-1930s writing and thinking. Two examples must suffice. Claude McKay now occupies an important place in the African-American literary canon, yet Bennett was recommending his 1929 novel *Banjo* well before such black working-class literary realism had penetrated British literary consciousness. Bennett recognizes the complexity of the text, acknowledges its 'fair propaganda' and praises McKay's 'psychology [which] is deep and startling' (p. 283). Fascinating, then, to see Bennett lined up with American intellectual Michael Gold who, in the late 1920s, was promoting a proletarian, neo-Stalinist view of literature's role in society. Even more fascinating to find Bennett in 1930 reviewing another American book from outside the literary mainstream, Edward Dahlberg's *Bottom Dogs*, which Edmund Wilson, in the course of his polemical dispute with Gold, praised for its 'revolutionary power'.[16] Bennett was in no doubt about the novel's powerful, relentless depiction of life in the lower depths: 'It takes you by the scruff of the neck and violently forces you to see, and to see afresh' (p. 338). He nevertheless feels it necessary to alert his column's readers to its extreme gloom: 'The repulsiveness of the book is not a particular repulsiveness. It is a general repulsiveness. It is strong meat for robust stomachs' (p. 336). Interesting, though, that Bennett considered his readers to have the stomach for a novel now recognized as having mapped the social and textual territory to be colonized by the Beats.

This is far from suggesting that Bennett ignored the more traditional mainstream books where there existed a shared ideology of taste between reviewer and reader. Many of these have fallen into near total critical neglect and there is a case to be made for reading Bennett's column as an archival treasure chest of precisely those texts that indicate the popular taste of the time and the contemporary social dynamic which they both reflected and helped create. Bennett's lengthy and considered review of, for example, H. M. Tomlinson's first novel, *Gallions Reach: A Romance* (1927), is conventional enough in praising its descriptive prose – 'In landscape and seascape Mr. Tomlinson has no superior' – but suggests the possibility of further analysis when he raises the 'problem of the influence of Joseph Conrad' (pp. 78–80). Its opening pages recreate the initial Thames setting of *Heart of Darkness* and later passages invoke Conrad to suggest a continuing colonial shadow: 'Cast your mind back to the Thames embankment at midnight, and get the horrors.'[17] Reappraising Tomlinson's text in the light of Bennett's comments, positions it alongside such modernist works as *Mrs Dalloway* and *The Waste Land*. In recommending *Gallion's Reach* and linking it to *Heart of Darkness*, Bennett prepares the ground for some of his readers to reach out to the more challenging texts of 1920s modernist writers. The book's publishers, Heinemann, attest to the promotional value of Bennett's columns by devoting the entire back panel of the dust jacket to an earlier review of his (23 June 1927) in which the recognizable brand name Arnold Bennett claims a larger typeface than that of the author himself on the front cover. Bennett's *Evening Standard* review of her work also took top billing on the dust jacket of Norah Hoult's 1930 novel, *Time Gentlemen! Time!* This novel uses the *Evening Standard* itself as a social indicator. In one of several references to the paper, Hoult suggests that its conspicuous display is a marker of taste and social standing: 'he was comforted by the feel of the newspaper under his arm [...] it helped him imagine that he was a perfectly respectable citizen'.[18] Throughout the novel, Hoult refers to popular culture, and indeed the hero admits: 'there's nothing I like better than a good movie, as they call them, myself. I'm not a highbrow.'[19]

Bennett was also willing to use the considerable influence of his column to enter the political arena in defence of novels threatened by censorship but which he thought to be of literary merit and demonstrating a 'courageous-discriminating' talent. Reviewing Radclyffe Hall's *The Well of Loneliness* (1928), he sympathetically drew attention to Havelock Ellis's introduction: 'He praises it for its fictional quality, its notable psychological and sociological significance, and its complete absence of offence. I cannot disagree with him' (p. 185). He then writes an extraordinary paragraph to appear in the popular press calling for tolerance in matters of sexual difference, whilst acknowledging that the constraints of the social status quo would almost certainly prevent this in the near future.

> Uncertain in touch at first, this novel is in the main fine. Disfigured by loose writing and marred by loose construction, it nevertheless does hold you. It is honest, convincing, and extremely courageous. What it amounts to is a cry for unprejudiced social recognition of the victims. The cry attains genuine tragic poignancy. The future may hide highly strange things, and therefore conservative prophecy is dangerous; nevertheless, I must say that I do not think the cry will be effectively heard. (p. 185)

Three months after publication the Chief Magistrate at Bow Street declared the novel obscene on the grounds that it made perversion seem attractive and unshameworthy, and on 16 November 1928, the novel was banned, not only in Britain but also throughout the British Empire. Bennett was one of the many prominent literary figures to offer public support in defence of the novel. What is significant is that once the case was lost he used his column to argue against the undiscriminating use of censorship whilst widening his remit beyond that of influencing public taste in novels to rousing an interest in social justice. In late November 1928, his 'Who Should Select Books for Censorship?' argued that books were incapable of debasing the moral character of children – 'Children, if they are to be influenced, require something more concrete than books' – recalling 'contemporary earnest students of Smiles's *Self-Help* whose later careers have besmirched the honour of the Five Towns' (p. 218). He goes further in his 'A Censorship By All Means, But –' column of March 1929 in excoriating the use of Victorian legislation to prosecute authors and publishers. In a passage which prefigures the 1960s debate on censorship and public mores, Bennett also attempts to expose the absurdity of excessive legislation which *creates* social problems:

> The definition of obscenity is so wide and so loose that hardly any book with any stuff in it could not be attacked under it [...] And any meddlesome idiot who chose to invoke the law might well obtain the suppression of 50 per cent. of the imaginative literature of the last hundred years. And yet we are threatened with a further 'strengthening' of the law [...] The results of such interference are sometimes truly astonishing. Thus to-night, after a certain hour, I am allowed by law to buy a copy of the *Evening Standard* from a boy exposed to damp and rheumatism outside a newspaper shop, but I am not allowed to buy the same esteemed sheet within the shop. (pp. 247–248)

There are interesting intertextual echoes of *The Well of Loneliness* in Bennett's 1930 novel *Imperial Palace*. Radclyffe Hall's description of the Parisian club scene in Chapter 47, for example, finds parallels in Bennett's 'Caligula' Parisian chapter:

> Then two girls extricated themselves from the thronged floor and approached the bar. One was tall and slim, in a close-fitting, high-necked gown which rendered the wearer conspicuous by its long trailing skirts. The other was short and plump in the scantiest possible flimsy frock. The demeanour of the tall girl was protective. They settled themselves at the bar, next to Evelyn and Gracie. The tall girl furtively, delicately, fondled her friend, with whom she had been dancing.
> 'Shall we go?' said Gracie, very abruptly. And in the doorway as Evelyn held aside the bead-curtain for her, she murmured harshly: 'I can't stand that kind.'[20]

There is a very real sense of Radclyffe Hall's novel having entered Bennett's literary consciousness and his using the *Evening Standard* columns, not only to defend her novel, but also to prepare public taste for his own venture into previously unexplored sexual territory in his last literary masterpiece.

In 1928, a young Norah James, working as a publicity manager for Radclyffe Hall's publisher Jonathan Cape, sat in the public gallery during the trial of *The Well of Loneliness* at Bow Street Magistrates' Court. Less than a year later James herself was in the same court, but this time defending her first novel, *Sleeveless Errand*, which was itself censored and suppressed.[21] In her memoir, *I Lived in a Democracy*, James writes 'it never occurred to me that it would be considered obscene to let the characters in it use the language they used in real life'.[22] Bennett launched a spirited defence of the novel in his column, detailing his appreciation of precisely this use of the vernacular: 'it records realistically the chatter of a familiar type of persons who cannot express themselves at any time on any subject without employing words beginning with "b" ' (p. 249). Banned in Britain, the novel was published in Paris in 1929 by the Obelisk Press, with a preface by Edward Garnett in which he quoted Bennett's *Evening Standard* review as evidence of the folly of censorship in suppressing precisely those books that, read in context, could influence the moral climate for the better:

> After the Prosecution had overwhelmed the novel and its author, with a flood of vulgar abuse – 'foul stuff... a terrible book... indecent situations... degrading muck', etc., Mr. Arnold Bennett (*Evening Standard*, March 7) declared *Sleeveless Errand* to be 'an absolutely merciless exposure of neurotics and decadence, and I should say that the effect of it on the young reader would have been to destroy in him all immoral and unconventional impulses for ever and ever'.[23]

Bennett's review was both fair and perceptive and perhaps not unsurprisingly the Obelisk Press incorporated quotations from it on the front flap of the first edition's dust jacket and then reset it to appear on the rear panel of the second issue. Today the British Library catalogue lists over 70 books by James, but none is in print. Reading *Sleeveless Errand* whilst researching Bennett's 1930 encounter with James in Lamorna, Cornwall, I readily concurred with his review's conclusion: 'it reveals a new talent for fiction' (p. 249).[24] The fact that Bennett's recognition of the novel's raw power has not been subsequently pursued is perhaps an indictment of the narrow focus of contemporary literary analysis. James's and Hoult's texts are early and now forgotten examples of what Hilary Hinds refers to as 'the so-called feminine middlebrow, a body of work in which domesticity is repeatedly an arena for feminine disappointment'.[25] Both novels engage with Hinds's description of a 'paradigm of subjectivity and sexuality that had only entered into the domain of popular middle-class culture in the early 1920s'[26] and to read them in tandem is to discover a feminist version of dirty realism prefiguring the advance of the masculine proletarian novel in the economically strained 1930s.

Unfortunately, Mylett's collection overlooks two reviews: 'A Year's War Books of Two Nations' (27 December 1929) and 'Young Man's Novel Slaps Your Cheek' (26 February 1931). The former omission is regrettable because it provides evidence of Bennett's continued admiration for *Sleeveless Errand*, recommending it as one of the best books of the year. The second omission is more serious. Printed whilst Bennett was dying of typhoid, it was to be his last ever column. It offers a rare contemporary portrait of the now largely forgotten writer Lionel Britton, who persuaded Bennett to accompany him to the Savoy Theatre for the first night of his play *Brain*. Bennett found the production terrible and 'though advertised for "the masses", was the highest-brow play I ever lived through'. He then proceeds, however, to recommend Britton's new novel, *Hunger and Love* 'It is not a book to be ignored' – but with reservations about the 'excessive zeal of [Britton's] reforming ardour' overpowering the narrative structure.[27] In his recent pioneering study of Britton, Tony Shaw judged Bennett's review as particularly insightful and worthy of resurrection in reassessing Britton's literary importance.[28] It is also noteworthy as vintage Bennett with its playful pastiche of Britton's style and self-referencing, reminding the reader that Bennett is one of them and shares their taste:

> Very long [...] All about the masses and the classes. I know a bit about the masses myself, both my grandfathers having been working men and myself a boy collector of rents from industrial cottages. The book imposed itself. I read and read [...] The day wore on. Curtains. Bourgeois electricity. The surface of the planet on which I sat moved several thousand miles [...] I didn't know where I was in space and time [...] Next day I resumed. Page after big page. I reached page 705. The last.[29]

Bennett's own 'last' page is a tribute to his ability to recognize an important literary talent in advance of critical acceptance. It also recalls his

major role in educating public taste towards reading European literature in translation. In the literally dying last words of this final column,
we find him recommending a study of 'Stendhal, Balzac, Flaubert, de
Concourt, de Maupassant, Proust'.[30] Beginning with his 1890 'Book
Chat' columns and his later *New Age* essays, it would be hard to over-
estimate Bennett's centrality in introducing continental writers to the
British Market. 'He taught the English to admire the Russian ballet [...]
and the Russian novel [...] He introduced his own favourite French
writers, such as Romain Roland, Gide, Valéry, and Claudel'.[31]

By 1931, Bennett had become, in Olga Broomfield's estimation, 'the
most powerful and important reviewer of books in England. With independence from all cliques and coteries, in a style succinct, thoughtful,
provocative, he achieved a rapport with his readers from all levels of
society which enabled him to move their perspective into the modern
age.'[32] Readers turned to Bennett's columns, secure in the knowledge that whilst they might find their literary taste challenged as
often as confirmed, they would not be patronized for occupying the
middlebrow ground. The secret was, as Frank Swinnerton reminisced,
Bennett 'always talked so that all might join in. He did this in *The
Evening Standard*.'[33]

Notes

1. James Hepburn (ed.) (1976) *Letters of Arnold Bennett III 1916–1931* (London:
   Oxford University Press), p. 203.
2. Arnold Bennett (1923) *Riceyman Steps* (London: Cassell), p. 160.
3. Hepburn, *Letters*, pp. 203–204.
4. Ibid., p. 290.
5. Chris Baldick (2004) *The Oxford English Literary History, Volume 10, 1910–
   1940: The Modern Movement* (Oxford: Oxford University Press), p. 17.
   Bennett's 'Books and Persons' column, printed every week until his death in
   1931, was in effect a continuation of his 1908–1911 *The New Age* weekly articles with the same title but appearing under the pseudonym Jacob Tonson.
   Even earlier in his journalistic career Bennett had contributed a regular 'Book
   Chat' column to *Woman* in which he drew attention to the merits of avant-
   garde fiction to be found in publications such as the *New Review* and the
   aesthetically important and influential *The Yellow Book*. Bennett's short story
   'A Letter Home' appeared in Volume VI of *The Yellow Book* in July 1895.
6. James Hepburn (1963) *The Art of Arnold Bennett* (Bloomington: Indiana
   University Press), p. 11.
7. *The Times Literary Supplement*, 9 August 1974; *The Bookman*, 27 July 1974,
   reviews quoted in Anita Miller (ed.) (June 1975) *The Arnold Bennett Newslet-
   ter*, 1.2.

8. Andrew Mylett (ed.) (1974) *Arnold Bennett: The Evening Standard Years, Books & Persons 1926–1931* (London: Chatto & Windus), p. 403. Subsequent references will be in parenthesis in the text.
9. Newman Flower (ed.) (1932) *The Journals of Arnold Bennett I 1896–1910* (London: Cassell), p. 31.
10. Arnold Bennett, *Woman*, 22 August 1894, p. 3.
11. Sean Latham (2003) *'Am I A Snob?' Modernism and the Novel* (Ithaca: Cornell University Press), p. 219.
12. Ibid., p. 220.
13. Kurt Koenigsberger's 'Fine Writing and Illuminated Industry: *The Old Wives' Tale* and Late Manuscript Culture' (unpublished Conference Paper, Modern Language Association Conference, 2007) concludes that it 'might well be that Bennett's reputation has suffered disproportionately because of the constriction of consideration to the linguistic component of his aesthetic production in a way that, for instance, William Morris's or Max Beerbohm's work has never been so constrained. If Bennett's works are to be re-historicized – their "auratic" character reconstructed – and their de-historicized character re-considered, then we ought [...] to consider the bibliographic code' (p. 8). A close reading of certain *Evening Standard* columns redirects attention to precisely the importance of the bibliographic code in an overall assessment of a writer's contribution to the formation of literary taste.
14. Arnold Bennett (1909) *The Glimpse: An Adventure of the Soul* (London: Chapman & Hall), pp. 152–153.
15. Newman Flower (ed.) (1933) *The Journals of Arnold Bennett III 1921–1928* (London: Cassell), p. 168.
16. Gordon Hutner (2009) *What America Read: Taste, Class, and the Novel 1920–1960* (Chapel Hill: University of North Carolina Press), p. 152.
17. H. M. Tomlinson (1927) *Gallion's Reach: A Romance* (London: William Heinemann), p. 226.
18. Norah Hoult (1930) *Time Gentlemen! Time!* (London: William Heinemann), p. 68.
19. Hoult, p. 107.
20. Arnold Bennett (1930) *Imperial Palace* (London: Cassell), p. 406.
21. Norah C. James (1929) *Sleeveless Errand* (Paris: Henry Babou & Jack Kahane).
22. Norah C. James (1939) *I Lived in a Democracy* (London: Longmans), p. 230.
23. Edward Garnett (1929) 'Preface', in Norah James, *Sleeveless Errand* (Paris: Henry Babou & Jack Kahane), p. 1.
24. Published as 'Bennett in Cornwall' in Pam Lomax (ed.) (2005) *The Flagstaff. The Lamorna Society Magazine*, 16, Winter 2005.
25. Hilary Hinds (2009) 'Ordinary Disappointments: Femininity, Domesticity, and Nation in British Middlebrow Fiction, 1920–1944', *Modern Fiction Studies*, 55(2), 300.
26. Ibid., p. 308.
27. Arnold Bennett, 'Young Man's Novel Slaps Your Cheek', *Evening Standard*, 26 February 1931, p. 4.
28. Tony Shaw (2006) *The Work of Lionel Britton* (unpublished doctoral thesis) available online at http://tonyshaw3.blogspot.com/2009/02/phdthesis-2006-work-of-lionel-britton_16.html, date accessed 15 February 2010.

29. Arnold Bennett, 'Young Man's Novel Slaps Your Cheek', *Evening Standard*, 26 February 1931, p. 4.
30. Ibid., p. 5.
31. Margaret Drabble (1974) *Arnold Bennett* (London: Weidenfeld and Nicolson), p. 165.
32. Olga Broomfield (1984) *Arnold Bennett* (Boston: Twayne), p. 136.
33. Frank Swinnerton (1963) *Figures in the Foreground: Literary Reminiscences 1917–1940* (London: Hutchinson), p. 176.

6

'A Strongly Felt Need': Wilfred Whitten/John O'London and the Rise of the New Reading Public

Jonathan Wild

Wilfred Whitten has a strong claim to be recognized as the most influential literary taste-maker during the first half of the twentieth century in Britain. Any attempt to justify this grand claim, however, needs to recognize Whitten's own reluctance to accept such a public role. For the whole of his career as a literary critic, Whitten's own name remained largely cloaked behind pseudonyms – the most prominent of these being John O'London – and this relative anonymity allowed him to craft a distinctive working relationship with his readers. While this relationship was certainly an intimate one, it was also one in which the employment of a pseudonym ensured a respectful distance between critic and reader. This distance enabled Whitten to play out the role of 'old guide and friend' that was claimed for him on the front cover of the first edition of *John O'London's Weekly* (*JOLW*) in April 1919. To better understand the importance and particular nature of the bond between Whitten and his readership, it is necessary to reconstruct some of the historical and cultural contexts in which the writer and his audience were located. These contexts, largely obscured for us in the twenty-first century, would have required little elucidation for readers during the first decades of the previous century. At this time, the relevance of literary criticism that provided explicit cultural guidance to its audience would have appeared entirely understandable and indeed necessary. Now, in the wake of widening opportunities for university training in the arts, the sorts of *ad hoc* tutorials that Whitten provided in his columns might appear merely patronizing attempts to educate the dull masses. But to the majority of Whitten's core readers, whose formal education had incorporated only a tantalizing glimpse of literary

was initially employed in white collar work in the metropolis, he was also able to develop his talents as a writer after his daytime office work. In Whitten's case, the initial rewards from nocturnal authorship were gained by writing 'turnovers' for the London papers such as the *Globe*. These 'turnovers' were articles on casual topics which overlapped their initial page and were a familiar feature in newspapers of the day.[6] During the 1890s, further publishing opportunities emerged for Whitten and his ilk as the literary marketplace continued to expand with fresh publishing ventures emerging on a weekly basis. These new publications are perhaps typified by *The New Budget*, an illustrated weekly founded in 1895 by the cartoonist Harry Furness and to which Whitten contributed from its inception.

But it was while working on the *Academy* that Whitten was able to develop the literary style and help craft the format of literary publication with which he would become popularly associated. The *Academy* was a well-established, respectable but arguably dated periodical when it was taken over in 1896 by John Morgan Richards, a wealthy American drug manufacturer. The new editor installed by Richards, Charles Lewis Hind, was charged with redesigning the publication to make it appealing to the tastes of a new generation of readers. Hind's revamping of the *Academy* included the incorporation of literary prizes and competitions for its readers, lists of best-selling books, columns of literary gossip, portrait supplements and short, often pithy, anonymous reviews. The resulting publication provided something of a landmark in broadening the appeal of the British literary magazines and in doing so anticipated much of the direction of this market in the ensuing decades. The scale and nature of Whitten's contribution to the *Academy* are, to a large extent, obscured by the journal's general policy of unsigned contributions, but those articles that can be attributed to him are revealing in their form and content. They range from articles signed 'John O'London' which convey Whitten's passion for the topography of the metropolis, to a review (unusually published under Whitten's own name) of his friend E. V. Lucas's latest volume in his collected works of the Lambs,[7] and other articles attributed to 'W.W.' which evoke the excitement of the rapidly changing book trade at the time. The latter include breezy interviews with the manager of the *Review of Reviews* Circulating Library[8] and with Grant Richards on the opening of his publishing firm in 1897.[9]

It is in an article entitled 'Some Child Critics of Browning. A Board School Experiment' that we can really observe Whitten's growing preoccupation with the broadening franchise of readers.[10] Here, Whitten follows up a newspaper report he had read about an essay-writing competition for board school children in the London Borough of Walworth, by visiting the local Methodist settlement which had sponsored the prize. The warden of this settlement, F. Herbert Stead (brother of the popular newspaper editor W. T. Stead), explained the rationale behind the prize: 'You are bound by the [board school] code [...] to give a certain amount of instruction in English Literature; why not take up Browning, who was born and bred in Walworth, and in whom, therefore, it will be easy to interest Walworth boys and girls?' The difficulty in providing the children with texts of Browning's work, Stead further remarks, was overcome by the recent publication of the poet's work in his brother W. T. Stead's 'Penny Poets' series.[11] The new opportunities for working class children to access literary culture in this way clearly excited Whitten and he invited the *Academy*'s readers to share his delight by incorporating sizeable chunks from the submitted essays into his article. He ends the piece by quoting from the essay of Nita Laurie Drake, a pupil in the Standard VII class at Victory Place School, who claimed that: 'It was while walking through the fields and leafy lanes of Dulwich that many of his [Browning's] best ideas came into his mind.' 'Thus,' Whitten concludes, 'Browning's child-critics are doing more to bring out this fact than all the Browning societies put together.' Whitten's article brings together a number of his preoccupations and looks forward to much of the work he would conduct in the twentieth century. On the one hand, it suggests the extent to which board schools were able to encourage literary interests and develop critical skills in children living in even the humblest areas of the city. On the other hand, it suggests a preferred method of critical engagement that was informed by an enthusiastic appreciation of the texts in question and a sound understanding of the biographical contexts in which these texts had emerged. Whitten's article, which might in other hands have become an indictment of the wisdom of giving Browning to 11-year-old pupils in solidly working-class London boroughs, ends instead as a celebration of the potential for cultural democracy brought about by board schools.

Whitten's experience at Walworth must have given him great confidence in helping to set up a new literary paper, *T.P.'s Weekly*, in 1902. Here, as acting editor under the well-known journalist and politician T. P. O'Connor, Whitten appears to have been offered much scope to devise a penny literary paper which would have a widespread popular appeal. The evident physical (and price) disparity between the threepenny *Academy* and the penny *T.P.'s* is revealing in suggesting the differing markets to which these publications were directed. Although the *Academy* had in many ways pioneered the popularization of the literary paper, it retained its focus on 'serious' culture and would probably have appeared forbidding for the average board school graduate. *T.P.'s*, by contrast, seems calculated to address the putative concerns of its culturally unsophisticated readers by appearing more like a newspaper than a learned review. This impression is immediately conveyed by the quality of its newsprint paper, by its illustrated advertisements for tobacco, bleach and biscuits, and most evidently by its short, enticingly subtitled paragraphs. In part, these elements of *T.P.'s* design and content were dictated by its modest penny cover price, but the latter decision to lighten the appearance of the paper by breaking up the text on its pages was evidently chosen to replicate the experience of reading a daily newspaper. Thus, the easy familiarity of *T.P.'s* textual format would permit a seamless shift for its readers from reading newspaper stories to reading Whitten's weekly cultural despatches. Accessed in this way, Whitten's lucid introductions to writers such as Shakespeare, Milton, Byron or indeed Browning, were made doubly accessible.

In terms of the content of *T.P.'s* more generally, these articles on higher literary culture were typically included alongside a number of lighter and/or more topical items. The issue dated 1 July 1904, for example, includes travel tips for those holidaying in the Lake District, a literary notes and queries section, an article for the budding writer entitled 'Why Short Stories are Rejected', a number of brief and largely descriptive reviews of new works, an instalment of the first publication of Conrad's *Nostromo*, an article by Ernest Rhys on Swinburne's lyric poems and a leading article signed by John O'London entitled 'Intellectual Honesty', which focused on the French critic and historian Hippolyte Taine. What should be evident from the content of this randomly selected edition of *T.P.'s* is that Whitten was given licence here to introduce his readers to a wide range of material while never losing sight of his desire to extend and challenge the nature of his audience's reading. The Taine article is particularly revealing in this respect in that it deals with a literary figure who, although almost certainly unfamiliar to *T.P.'s* core readership, is discussed in a way calculated to make his work appear relevant and appealing. The tone adopted in Whitten's introduction to this article perfectly captures his method of approach:

It has just been my fortune to spend a whole day alone. Under such circumstances the book in one's hand, if it be a good one, seems perfectly alive and intimate, and is certain to give a lasting impression.[12]

Following this companionable opening, Whitten goes on to establish Taine as a 'young man of fine intellect and lofty aspirations'. For those of *T.P.'s* readers with plans to graduate from their routine office jobs to become professional writers, Taine is posited by Whitten as an exemplary figure. The article backs up this inspirational theme with lengthy quotations from Taine's own work that demonstrate his 'exultant belief of the power of thought and investigation'. Finally, having established Taine's impressive credentials for his autodidact readers, Whitten concludes: 'I am content to point out that for the man who desires an exemplar of the intellectual life, at once strenuous and honest, this book waits.' The rhetorical flourish with which he signs off here is entirely characteristic of Whitten's work during this period. The lightness of an opening which serves to bait the hook is followed by an earnestness of purpose which seeks to push its readers on towards self-improvement.

One recognizes in much of Whitten's work on *T.P.'s* a strong sense of mission on behalf of his board school readers. This zeal, while utterly genuine and heartfelt, seems at times rather forced, suggesting that Whitten was rather too conscious here of the significance of his educative role. Whitten's consciousness of the weight of this role was probably exacerbated by the negotiations that he needed to conduct with T. P. O'Connor (who continued as editor on *T.P.'s* throughout Whitten's time on the paper) regarding the paper's level of 'literary' content. Whitten later remarked that in an early discussion about the content of the new paper, O'Connor had informed him in his distinctive Irish brogue that 'I see no reason in the wur-r-rl why every line in the paper should not thra-arb with human int'rist.'[13] Given O'Connor's single-minded desire regarding the populist direction of the paper's content (and the extent to which this desire might clash with Whitten's own ideas), we can better understand the singleness of purpose and earnestness with which Whitten employed the space licensed to him in the paper.

After 1919, however, when he was given control of the literary paper that incorporated his own pseudonym, *John O'London's Weekly*, Whitten had new freedom to craft a relationship with readers on his own terms. Unconstrained by those external forces which had hemmed in his contributions to *T.P.'s*, Whitten was now able to ease his way towards a mature style and in the process forge a new affiliation with his readers.

While *JOLW* clearly attracted the now middle-aged readership of the defunct *T.P.'s Weekly*, it also embraced a new generation of readers, many of whom were then returning to civilian life following the Great War. The potential importance of this new post-war reading public is recognized in the first sentence of Whitten's opening leading article in *JOLW*:

> Our young men can live a larger life than has ever been lived before. Nearly five years ago they were mobilised to enforce order and decency in the human family; they have done their part in that great business; and now they are called to the immense and perilous task of remoulding our normal life.[14]

Whitten clearly sensed the potential centrality of literary culture in this remoulding of normal life and evidently felt keenly the role that his new paper might have in this respect. But it is also clear that apart from books offering a vital civilizing mission here they might also, and perhaps more importantly, offer therapy and pleasure to a generation damaged and disillusioned by the war. Viewed in this way, Whitten's post-war reading public posed a complex challenge to his editorial skills. On the one hand, the 'old friends' of John O'London required more of those companionable literary causerie essays with which they were familiar from *T.P.'s* days. But on the other hand, a much younger and more restless readership looked for more directed forms of cultural guidance and advice.

Whitten's understanding of the differing needs of his variegated readership is embedded in those early editions of *JOLW*. We can recognize this, for example, in the two weekly columns which were to become a central feature of Whitten's paper over the next 20 years. In one of these columns entitled 'Passing Remarks' (which appeared under the pen name 'Jackdaw'), Whitten addressed miscellaneous literary matters but always retained his focus on issues of grammar and correct English; this latter focus was arguably addressed to the new generation of ambitious autodidacts. The other column, entitled 'Letters to Gog and Magog' (which was signed by 'John O'London'), offered a return to those leading articles on books and writers that had provided the centrepiece for *T.P.'s*. Apart from these new regular features, the content of *JOLW* in many ways resembled that of *T.P.'s*. The main differences between the two publications were the incorporation of photographic illustrations into *JOLW* (a technical development which served to further lighten the paper's appearance) and the accent on topicality foregrounded in the new paper. In the latter respect, the 'Book of the Week' article which appeared on the front page of *JOLW*, and which focused on a recently published work, established the paper's relevance for the post-war readership. While Whitten's editorial rationale with *JOLW* was to ensure the paper was recognized as up to date and relevant, he also ensured that significant space was devoted to what he saw as the canon of literary history. Rather than assuming that the readerships for ancient and modern material in his paper would be discrete, he clearly anticipated a healthy flexibility in his readers' literary tastes. Indeed, Whitten saw his role as one in which he might promote this sort of flexibility and in the process bring his apparently separate audiences together.

Something of Whitten's promotion of flexibility in his readers' tastes is captured in a regular column entitled 'After Hours: Study and Recreation', which featured from the first issue of *JOLW*. The very choice of title for the column appears to embrace Whitten's continuing role as *de facto* tutor to his ambitious new autodidact readership, while also recognizing the potential pleasure to be gained from reading 'good' books during leisure time. In the theme of the first 'After Hours' column, 'Book Shyness', Whitten provides further clues about the ways in which he was working and thinking at this time. Indeed, from its opening paragraph we can grasp much of Whitten's rationale in *JOLW*:

> Book Shyness. Many thousands of people suffer from it. They ask themselves vaguely and fearfully, 'ought I to read Ruskin?' 'ought I to read Balzac?' ... 'and Jane Austen's novels, and Hazlitt's essays?' and so on. There is, of course no *ought* about it. Right reading is self-chosen reading, and the bogeys of correctness and completeness are responsible for a great deal of shivering on the brink of literature.[15]

The cultural anxiety that Whitten anticipates in the readers of the new paper can, he assures us, be cured by simply taking 'up any book of entrancing interest and allow[ing] it to excite [that reader's] curiosity'. Whitten further anticipates here the likely connections between the reader's social class and their apparent book shyness: shy readers, he argues, regard books as they do formidable individuals who they imagine are 'a cut above them'. The clear aim of Whitten here and elsewhere through the paper is to act as a democratic broker between the shy working-class/lower-middle-class reader and those books of 'entrancing interest' which might appear out of reach.

Whitten's critical approach in this respect is usefully summarized at the end of this article:

I believe myself that a taste for good reading can be acquired by infection, that is by reading good criticism – by which term I do not mean, in this case the criticism which seeks to correct or classify literary works, but the kind which seeks to communicate the writer's enjoyment of them. When you see a man smacking his lips over a good dish, or raising his glass of wine to revel in its colour [...] you are apt to enjoy his enjoyment, and even by sympathy, to share it.[16]

This belletrist form of criticism, although distinctly unfashionable in wider critical circles by 1919, appears perfectly judged in this context to appeal to Whitten's putative readership. Rather than the cut and thrust of a more muscular style of combative criticism, *JOLW*'s readers arguably sought direction in the types of 'good' books which might appeal to them. In this way, they trusted John O'London, an established, wise and avuncular guide, to assist in the potentially hazardous business of taste formulation.

The 'Book Shyness' article offers further clues about the more specific models upon which Whitten honed his critical approach. Before offering a list of suggested inexpensive editions of the work of such critics as James Russell Lowell and Augustine Birrell, Whitten claims 'The supreme master in this gracious art ... [was] the great French critic Sainte-Beuve. His finest essays can now be had in English, and cheaply; to read them is to be at home with a man who was utterly at home with books.'[17] For Whitten, the causerie essay of Sainte-Beuve, with its air of informality, its desire to communicate the subjective effects of a text on its reader and its focus on the biographical detail of the text's author, provided the perfect engine of critical communication. Just as Sainte-Beuve himself was able to perfect his causerie style over a 20-year period in the mid-nineteenth century, Whitten was similarly able to refine the approach he took in his own articles over an extended period: from *Academy* days in the 1890s until his death in 1943, at which time he was still contributing weekly 'Letters to Gog and Magog' for *JOLW*, some seven years after he had retired from his position as editor of the paper. The eclectic subject matter chosen for the letters from December 1919 to April 1920 offers some sense of the ground that Whitten covered in his work. These include favoured literary topics such as Shakespeare, Lamb and Hazlitt; appreciations of newly published works by W. G. Bell, W. N. P. Barbellion and E. T. Raymond; a review of Wells's *Outline of History* (1919) following its recent appearance in a cheap edition; and early forays into cultural studies with accounts of the significance of the popular paper *Tit-Bits*, which had recently published its 2000th edition, and an investigation into the popularity of Charles Garvice, the best-selling and recently deceased novelist.[18] The last of these articles is worthy of scrutiny because it provides a model of the causerie style as Whitten had perfected it, and in terms of subject matter it offers an indication of Whitten's range as a critic. While one might expect an individual of Whitten's seemingly conventional and conservative literary tastes to use this opportunity to attack a prolific and arguably 'lowbrow' best-selling novelist, the essay instead turns into a measured attempt to understand and account for Garvice's popularity. Whitten challenged the evident book snobbery of a recent article in the *Nation*, which used Garvice's popularity as proof of 'the loss of that precious thing, a common national standard of good literature', by questioning the existence of that benchmark. Literature, Whitten responds, has historically worked on a number of different levels and the high and low forms of publication have tended to operate in healthy co-existence. While the work of Garvice may, Whitten concedes, have 'no literary importance', it clearly served a special purpose for its vast readership which is, he suggests, both 'half-educated and wholly alive'. Garvice, he continues:

> novelized the day-dreams of the daughters of the people. They were innocent, sentimental day-dreams, and he added nothing to them. He simply gave them shape as stories, invented details, found backgrounds, and presented his millions of readers with something in which they saw themselves in the sunlight of love and the starlight of luck. His stories were enormously popular, but they were read by a public which one does not take into account when discussing public taste.[19]

Most revealing aspect here is Whitten's generosity of vision. The public he identifies in the article is not *his* public, and Garvice is certainly not *his* writer, but the acknowledgement of the existence of these entities provokes in Whitten little sense of either snobbery or despair.

Whitten's democratic literary vision is similarly evident at what might be considered the highbrow end of the cultural scale. While one might assume that *JOLW* would avoid (or otherwise awkwardly satirize) those experimental texts which we now recognize as examples of literary modernism, this was simply not the case in practice. When texts of this nature are discussed in the paper they are acknowledged as challenging but readers are equally encouraged to rise to this challenge. The *JOLW* review of Virginia Woolf's second novel, *Night and Day* (1919), provides a case in point here. Although this unsigned critique is focused on plot detail rather than form, its conclusion recognizes the scale of Woolf's stylistic achievement:

> The story is told with individual humour and with a wealth of observation and knowledge of human nature, and it is really faint praise to say that 'Night and Day' is the novel of the season. It is an achievement of outstanding distinction, an important addition to modern imaginative literature.[20]

We can also recognize this openness to literary innovation in a 'Book of the Week' feature piece on Dorothy Richardson's stream of consciousness novel *Interim* (1919). Under the heading 'Something New and Strange', Richardson's work is described in terms that acknowledge its deliberate challenge to existing literary convention. But rather than setting up *Interim's* divergence from the norm as an implicit plea for a literature which conforms to conservative literary modes, the review recognizes the continual need for cultural change: 'Progress and development absolutely depend on experiment.' In accessible terms the piece goes on to set out the nature of Richardson's 'experiment' in capturing the 'human train of thought': 'Miss Richardson writes exactly as most of us think, one thing almost arbitrarily suggesting another.' The large chunks of text from *Interim* included in the review serve to let *JOLW* readers make up their own minds about the wisdom of tackling what is readily acknowledged to be 'a hard book'. But, like the Woolf review quoted above, the Richardson article concludes on a highly affirmative note: 'one feels as [Richardson] finished her last page that she said to herself [...] this is exactly what I meant to do and I have done it. And assuredly it was worth doing.'[21]

It would be misleading to claim that *JOLW* was in any way a particular champion of literary modernism under Whitten's editorship. But Whitten was certainly open to the whole cultural spectrum of his age and, unlike other contemporary editors of literary periodicals such as J. C. Squire (editor of *The London Mercury*), had no desire to enforce an anti-modernist agenda for his paper. While we might discover Charles Garvice, Florence Barclay and Berta Ruck in the pages of *JOLW*, we typically encounter these popular writers alongside 'high' cultural figures such as Wyndham Lewis, W. B. Yeats and Jacob Epstein. This variegated focus is perhaps more unexpected to us than it was to a readership unfamiliar with the strict literary demarcations of more recent years.

Whitten, at one level, simply delighted in the idea that literature might play an important part in the lives of its readers, and while he hoped that it might be a Lamb or a Hazlitt who provided those readers with literary enlightenment, he was commendably realistic in his aims for the reading public at large. While this realism tempered Whitten's desire to convert the millions of Garvice readers to share his own literary tastes, he equally understood that a proportion of that 'half-educated and wholly alive' market would always seek to broaden their literary horizons under his tutelage. Whitten instinctively knew which readers would make up this group, having addressed this audience from the *Academy* days in the last decade of the nineteenth century through to the new post-war readership of the 1920s. An intimate knowledge of this cohort's cultural needs, gathered over an extended period of time, allowed Whitten to measure and refine his style to suit his evolving audience. It is perhaps not surprising that the manifestations of this style have come to be so strongly associated with the term 'middlebrow'. Many of those commonly recognized core components of the literary 'middlebrow' are identifiable in Whitten's work: the belletrist criticism and the endorsement of an apparently conservative canon of English literature match the characteristic features of British literary 'middlebrow' culture. But the reduction of Whitten and his work to the single term 'middlebrow' has seemingly inhibited scholars from taking on the task of accounting for the important social and historical roles played by this large body of material. In the process, we have rapidly lost our ability to recognize the cultural environment in which literary papers such as *T.P.'s Weekly* and *John O'London's Weekly* flourished. In regaining some understanding of the contexts in which Whitten and his criticism operated, we can begin to recognize just how 'strongly felt' the need for cultural guidance was in the first half of the last century.

Notes

1. Jonathan Wild (2006) ' "Insects in Letters": *John O'London's Weekly* and the New Reading Public', *Literature and History*, 15(2), 50–62.
2. Patrick Collier's recent '*John O'London's Weekly* and the Modern Author' usefully situates Whitten's paper in relation to other print media of the period. See Ann L. Ardis and Patrick Collier (eds) (2008) *Transatlantic Print Culture, 1880–1940: Emerging Media, Emerging Modernisms* (Basingstoke: Palgrave).
3. Richard Hoggart (1957; 1977) *The Uses of Literacy* (Harmondsworth: Pelican Books) p. 309.

4. Q. D. Leavis (1932) *Fiction and the Reading Public* (London: Chatto and Windus), p. 10.
5. Bevis Hillier (2003) *John Betjeman: New Fame, New Love* (London: John Murray), p. 480. Kingsley Amis's reference to the paper as being of the 'Jack Squire-Jack Priestley persuasion' further nails *JOLW* as quintessentially 'middlebrow'. Amis (1991) *Memoirs* (London: Hutchinson), p. 21.
6. For more information on the 'turnover' see 'Bygone Guineas' in John O'London (Wilfred Whitten) (1944) The *Joy of London and Other Essays* (London: George Newnes).
7. *Academy*, 1640 (10 October 1903), p. 384.
8. *Academy*, 1329 (23 October 1897), p. 329.
9. *Academy*, 1289 (16 January 1897), p. 82.
10. *Academy*, 1309 (29 May 1897), p. 573.
11. The emergence of cheap versions of the classic texts of English literature played a crucial role in Whitten's print lectures to autodidact scholars. His essays tend to refer his readers to inexpensive editions of texts he is discussing, giving the sense that his readers should be book owners rather than book borrowers.
12. *T.P.'s Weekly*, IV, 86, 1 July 1904, p. 17.
13. John O'London (Wilfred Whitten) *The Joy of London*, p. 154.
14. *John O'London's Weekly*, 1/1, 12 April 1919, p. 17.
15. Ibid., p. 21.
16. Ibid.
17. Ibid.
18. See the following *JOLW* editions: W. G. Bell, 6 December 1919, p. 229; W. N. P. Barbellion, 7 February 1920, p. 515; E. T. Raymond, 20 December 1919, p. 319; Wells, 20 March 1920, p. 683; *Tit-Bits*, 28 February 1920, p. 599; Charles Garvice, 10 April 1920, p. 15.
19. *JOLW*, III, 53, 10 April 1920, p. 15.
20. *JOLW*, II, 51, 27 March 1920, p. 702.
21. *JOLW*, II, 47, 28 February 1920, p. 585.

II: US

7
The Excluded Middle: Cultural Polemics and Magazines in America, 1915–1933

Victoria Kingham

This article looks at some aspects of the idea of a 'middle way' in America in the 1910s and how it was viewed as undesirable even though at least one influential critic appears, initially, to have suggested the opposite. I use two seminal texts: ' "Highbrow" and "Lowbrow" ' by Van Wyck Brooks (1915) and *The Seven Lively Arts* by Gilbert Seldes (1924). Seldes's essay collection is commonly (but erroneously) held to be the first to attempt an extended serious critical evaluation of 'popular' culture, and in it Seldes protests very strongly against the taste of the 'middle class'. Between Brooks and Seldes, a number of 'little magazines' strongly positioned themselves against the middle ground, often associating it with puritan repression or the American 'genteel tradition'. These publications applied their critical ideas of taste to a wide cultural field of literature and the arts.

Brooks's essay, included in his 1915 collection *America's Coming-of-Age*, remarked on a cultural division that he expressed as follows:

> These two attitudes of mind have been phrased once for all in our vernacular as 'Highbrow' and 'Lowbrow' [...] What side of American life is not touched by this antithesis? [...] there is no community, no genial middle ground.
>
> The very accent of the words 'Highbrow' and 'Lowbrow' implies an instinctive perception that this is a very unsatisfactory state of affairs. For both are used in a derogatory sense. The 'Highbrow' is the superior person whose virtue is admitted but felt to be an inept unpalatable virtue; while the 'Lowbrow' is a good fellow one readily takes to, but with a certain scorn for him and all his works. And what is true of them as personal types is true of what they stand for. They

are equally undesirable, and they are incompatible, but they divide American life between them.[1]

This is, of course, a highly subjective – and as Brooks writes, an 'instinctive' – view, articulating and polemicizing a sociological and intellectual division with which Brooks was to become preoccupied for a number of years. His syntax, the use of the impersonal 'one' who has some 'scorn' for the lowbrow, necessarily includes his own observation and implicitly assumes an elite readership of university-educated Americans. Brooks goes on to describe how the idealistic ambitions of the Harvard undergraduate are subsumed, outside academia, to the economic conditions that necessitate 'his' pursuit of business interests. He uses as an example those writers who succumb to economic interests, who 'set themselves to the composition of richly rewarded trash'[2] and who by subjugating their own finer artistic impulses, represent the scorned lowbrow. Following de Tocqueville, he sees the 'pursuit of wealth' as an innate acculturation: the American, Brooks writes, 'has it embedded in his mind [...] that it is the prime and central end'.[3] In spite of this, Brooks would like to have admired the writers, if not their 'trash'. 'Has it ever been considered how great a knowledge of men, what psychological gifts of the first order their incomparable achievement of popularity implies?' he asks, though he does not expand on this statement, which follows rather oddly after his condemnation of economic success. Finally, though, the 'middle' was for Brooks definitely the solution rather than the problem: 'Where is all that is real, where is personality and all its works, if it is not essentially somewhere, somehow, in some not very vague way, between?'[4] He thus sought, at least rhetorically, cultural renewal via compromise; indeed, a 'genial middle ground'. Predominantly the pursuit of profit, and hence the production of any kind of art for profit, was a primary constituent of the group of items that Brooks labelled 'lowbrow'.

Nine years later, critic and essayist Gilbert Seldes published *The Seven Lively Arts*, an interesting (and lively) collection of essays, mostly about perpetrators of what might be called popular culture: actors, ballroom dancers, comic strip characters, vaudeville artists, music hall comics, Charlie Chaplin and popular satirist Ring Lardner.[5] The majority of Seldes's articles had in fact already appeared in print over the previous two years, some in the rather select, specialist magazine of the arts, *The Dial*, while some in the large-circulation, middlebrow-oriented *Vanity Fair*. In the course of a chapter involving discussion of the highbrow and the lowbrow, Seldes wrote of the 'middle class': '*be damned to these last and all their tribe!'*[6] By the word 'class' he believed he was not referring primarily to people's economic status, there being, in America, as he remarked, 'no recognized upper class to please'.[7] The *middle* people were those whose tastes he perceived as being largely dictated by the American genteel tradition.[8] Seldes thus sought to eliminate such tastes rather than to conciliate the people who held them, an aim which precluded Brooks's idea of a compromise.

Seldes does take what might be called an educated delight in the pleasures of the lowbrow. But to help his readers appreciate the satire of Ring Lardner, he validates it by comparing it to Mark Twain. The art of Charlie Chaplin, the cartoons of George Herriman and the baseball of Babe Ruth, though, are justified in what one might call the ultimate highbrow terms: their immanent, eternal classical beauty. Thus, he 'presents' lowbrow arts to an educated minority, using the criteria of a long-established aesthetic tradition and therefore placing them within an existing field of intellectual discourse. Of the then popular Ted Lewis jazz band he writes: 'he is merely callous to some beauties and afraid of others, and by dint of being in revolt against a serene and classic beauty pays it unconscious tribute.'[9]

Given that modernism is sometimes associated with a breakdown of cultural barriers, it may seem surprising that between the dates of Brooks's and Seldes's rhetoric, a significant number of small-circulation magazines made it their business to consolidate a culturally divisive ethic, a difference. One of these was *The Seven Arts*, to which Van Wyck Brooks was a frequent contributor.[10] *The Seven Arts* ran 12 issues between 1916 and 1917, and is now generally acknowledged as one of the more important minority publications of those years just before America entered the First World War. It arose as an eclectic offshoot of the liberal progressive journal *The New Republic* (1914), in that its founding editor, James Oppenheim, assembled from among *New Republic* writers an editorial team dedicated to the regeneration of American national identity through artistic culture. The magazine boasted an exceptional array of talent: besides Oppenheim and Brooks, contributors included novelists, poets and socialists; cultural critics and historians Randolph Bourne and Waldo Frank; art critic and collector Leo Stein; music connoisseur Paul Rosenfeld; and creative writers and poets among whom were Sherwood Anderson, Kahlil Gibran, Theodore Dreiser, Carl Sandburg and the prolific and much-published poet Maxwell Bodenheim. Works by D. H. Lawrence and Eugene O'Neill also made brief early appearances.

In spite of the magazine's democratic and nationalist fervour, its main contributors variously expressed a wish to set themselves apart from those they identified as the mainstream, middle-of-the-road, standard 'American'. In an article in the February 1917 edition, for instance, Theodore Dreiser attacks his own background for its inability to instil the intellectually 'correct'. He writes:

> To me, the average or somewhat standardized American is an odd, irregularly developed soul, wise and even forward in matters of mechanics, organizations, and anything that relates to technical skill in connection with material things, but absolutely devoid of any true spiritual insight, any *correct* knowledge of the history of literature or art.[11]

The 'standardized' American, from whom Dreiser would distance himself, sounds rather like the American lowbrow 'fellow' to whom we saw Brooks refer, particularly in relation to the love of commodities. The 'average American school', continues Dreiser, is against the development of the individual, and the 'iron band of convention' binds its pupils against the production of original thought. He attributes this partly to an 'idealistic constitution, which is largely a work of art and not a workable system' but also, like Brooks, emphasizes the point that a nation cannot be devoted to intellectual and spiritual freedom while actually 'devoted with an almost bee-like industry to the gathering and storing [...] of purely material things'.[12] He inveighs, too, against the repressive nature of American moral guardianship. Dreiser had had a running battle with the perpetrators of repression since 1900, as Anthony Comstock's New York Society for the Suppression of Vice had successively attempted to prohibit publication of his novels *Sister Carrie, Jennie Gerhardt* and the semi-autobiographical *The Genius*. Dreiser therefore writes against mediocrity, against convention and against compromise, and blames the state, its laws and its religion for what he sees as a dumbing down. 'Art,' he writes passionately, 'is the stored honey of the human soul, gathered on wings of misery and travail. Shall the dull and the self-seeking and the self-advertising close this store on the groping human mind?'[13] Unlike Brooks, therefore, Dreiser does not seek a middle ground of any kind but hopes for the emergence of the individual on to a higher intellectual and spiritual plane. By implication, he sets himself and his 'individual' colleagues apart, reinforcing substantially the division between art and commerce, highbrow and lowbrow, and definitely *ex*cluding the middle.

Another article in *The Seven Arts*, by music critic Hiram Moderwell, appears to be intended as an appreciation of the popular music of

Black Americans. Closer attention reveals that, in fact, Moderwell would like to modify this to suit the 'professional' [white] singer. He sets out a rather homogeneous and bland concert of 'acceptable' blues and ragtime tunes, assuring his readers that 'professionals' can learn to sing these 'correctly'. Moderwell thus 'justifies' the songs by removing them from their own cultural sphere and placing them against the background of the concert hall. This gentrified ragtime muzak looks at first as though it might be a 'middlebrow' compromise, but Moderwell uses highbrow criteria to justify its acceptance. The music is praised for its implicit Nietzschean qualities, its technical resourcefulness and its consequent appeal to 'one who was educated on Haydn, Beethoven and Mendelssohn'. 'Ragtime,' he writes, 'should stand being brought out of the café' – the café, with its plebeian connotations, not being de rigueur for musical performance.[14] He attempts in this way to bring it into the realm of the musically au fait, educated, discerning audience represented by *The Seven Arts*' readership. His proposal, then, is to 'raise' what he sees as low, on the basis of criteria that can be identified at the higher end of the artistic hierarchy, and appropriate it along with the cultural capital of an educated class.

As a relative contrast to *The Seven Arts*, there existed within the same time period an idiosyncratic little magazine, *The Soil*. Its editor, New York art dealer Robert Coady, published only five issues, which brought what might now be called 'popular culture' to the attention of a rather select audience.[15] Almost 10 years earlier than Gilbert Seldes, and just after Brooks had published ' "Highbrow" and "Lowbrow" ', *The Soil* printed articles on Chaplin, Bert Williams (a black vaudeville comedian) and Annette Kellerman (a popular 'artistic' swimmer). It praised the art of window-dressing and the skill of commercial building, displaying pictures of the then new Flat-Iron and Woolworth buildings in central Manhattan. It serialized a 'Nick Carter' dime novel and also featured legendary gonzo boxing reports by Robert Alden Sanborn. There were reproductions of city schoolchildren's art, printed alongside, and favourably compared with, pictures by contemporary American artists (Stanton MacDonald Wright and Marsden Hartley) whose work the editor did not admire. Coady preferred to print, as representative of American art, a number of admirable photographs of steam engines and heavy plant and machinery. These were sometimes accompanied by reproductions of pictures by Ingres and Poussin. In addition, the beauty of classical sculpture was used to ridicule the radical art of proto-Dadaist Jean Crotti.[16]

The magazine's presentation and ethos are singular and remarkable; what links it with *The Seven Arts* is its fervour for national urban culture:

> There is an American Art. Young, robust, energetic, naive, immature, daring and big spirited.
> Active in every conceivable field.
> The Panama Canal, the Sky-scraper and Colonial Architecture. The East River, the Battery and the 'Fish Theatre'. The Tug Boat and the Steam-shovel. The Steam Lighter. The Steel Plants, the Washing Plants and the Electrical Shops. The Bridges, the Docks, the Cutouts, the Viaducts, the 'Matt M. Shay' and the '3000'. Gary. The Polarine and the Portland Cement Works. Wright's and Curtiss's Aeroplanes and the Aeronauts. The Sail Boats, the Ore Cars. Indian Beadwork, Sculptures, Decorations, Music and Dances. Jack Johnson, Charlie Chaplin, and 'Spike' in 'The Girl in the Game'. Annette Kellerman, 'Neptune's Daughter'. Bert. Williams, Rag-time, the Buck and Wing and the Clog. Syncopation and the Cake-Walk [...] This is American Art.[17]

Nevertheless, despite its egalitarian presentation (wide margins, large font, single-column pages and full-page art plates and photographs) and topical diversity, the overall effect of *The Soil* was to package up 'the popular' for a minority educated readership. The article by Chaplin is well-considered, serious and informative; but by then, it must be remembered, mainstream publications and widely read journals and monthlies such as *Motion Picture Magazine* and *Motion Picture Classic* were also very thoroughly supplied with articles by and about Chaplin. Chaplin was in any case at that time busily cleaning up his image and, according to one biographer and historian, 'presenting a picture of his private life that would make him acceptable even to genteel Americans'.[18] Thus, in the same way that Moderwell, in *The Seven Arts*, attempts to infuse blues and ragtime into the repertoire of white professional singers, *The Soil* attempts to justify the new and popular by means of well-established criteria of taste. For the editor of *The Soil*, art continues to be validated by an individual appreciation of its beauty, a 'taste' which is held to be innate and unchanging – a bit like Dreiser's 'correct knowledge' of art history – according to Coady, artists were actually *hindered* by 'a struggle to be new'.[19] *The Soil*'s readership, who judging by its advertisements were expected to be interested in skiing holidays, real estate and stocks and bonds, thus needed to be 'introduced' to art and artefacts which were already well-known to the more plebeian section of the population. Far from searching for compromise, then, and in spite of its Whitmanesque homage to city buildings and phenomena and popular entertainment, *The Soil*'s exposition of the art of America has the effect of institutionalizing 'the popular' and imposing a traditional aesthetic. It demonstrates one form of a process that has been generalized by Pierre Bourdieu:

> The aim of inverting or *transgressing* [...] is necessarily contained within the limits assigned to it *a contrario* by the aesthetic conventions it denounces and by the need to secure recognition of the aesthetic nature of the transgression of the limits (i.e. recognition of its conformity to the norms of the transgressing group).[20]

In other words, the transgression of limits assumes knowledge of limits, and the act itself is a containment of the cultural power of the controlling group.

Other magazines of that time explicitly voiced their intentions to exclude the taste of the majority. *The Little Review*, subsequently well-known for being the first to publish parts of James Joyce's *Ulysses*, made 'no compromise with public taste' and in one issue famously preferred to publish blank pages rather than 'lower' its standards of literary discernment.[21] The left-wing organ, *The Masses*, aimed 'to conciliate no-one, not even its readers', a determinedly highbrow position which antagonized its readers and boldly advertised the antagonism as a reason for reading it, like a punk rocker used to spit on his or her own rapturous audience (or indeed, as the Futurist Filippo Marinetti regularly abused delighted Wigmore Hall audiences in the UK during a 1912 tour). *Rogue* (a pun on the newly launched *Vogue*), a brief and ephemeral publication, was largely set out as a fashionably highbrow gossip sheet and published the opinion that 'newspapers and magazines are both ruled by money, and money has yet to learn brains or expression', thus continuing to assume, like Dreiser and Brooks, and de Tocqueville before them, an irreconcilable art/commerce division.[22] 'Advertise in Rogue – It Doesn't Pay' reads an advertisement therein.[23] The publication of *Rogue* was largely financed by the wealth of private patrons, supplemented by advertisements for investment securities and life insurance.

Despite Brooks's optimistic search, then, most of these small-circulation, modernist or proto-modernist publications articulated views which were against the average or middle. Now in contrast, although the distinction between a 'little' magazine and any other magazine is contentious, I'd like briefly to turn to larger-circulation examples. While

The Seven Arts, The Soil, The Masses, The Little Review and many others pitched their various editorial manifestoes firmly towards a highbrow elite, forming from their collective readership a small but distinctive counterpublic, at least two magazines subsequently classified as 'mainstream' were carving out an intentionally middle-of-the-road audience. These were *The Smart Set* and *Vanity Fair*.

The small press magazines reached, at the most optimistic estimate, 5,000 readers, apart from *The Masses*, which has been estimated to have 14,000.[24] *The Smart Set*'s circulation was, at its lowest point, about 30,000. Under the joint editorship of Henry Mencken and George Nathan, it raged a vociferous editorial campaign against the bourgeoisie, identifying a particular section of the American population with a lack of artistic taste and a lack of sensitivity. Mencken was well-known for *not* making compromises; at least in his written editorials he has never been considered to be among the moderate. But in spite of this, he and George Nathan rejected works which they considered too radical for general distribution. These included some of Sherwood Anderson's early *Winesburg, Ohio* stories, which they considered were 'too frank' (but which were accepted by *The Seven Arts*). They also regularly published what they called 'escapist fiction'.[25] Despite their contempt for the bourgeoisie, then, they held definite publication policies based on pleasing a possible bourgeois audience. Though often satirical, their material usually remained within the limits of conventional 'taste': they veered towards at least some kind of middle-of-the-road readership by carefully interspersing the conventional with the untried.

The magazine had, however, a more experimental period between 1913 and 1914, under the editorship of the art critic Willard Huntington Wright. At the time, Wright was an important taste-maker for an American readership that was a numerical minority but, retrospectively, an intellectually influential minority. Already literary and art critic for *The Los Angeles Times*, he came to *The Smart Set* at the suggestion of Mencken (who was already on the staff). Wright's own concept of *The Smart Set* was unashamedly highbrow: he wanted a magazine which 'would succeed with the better class of readers'.[26] As noted above, 'class' in the United States was taken by many writers to mean something a little different from its equivalent in England; rather than a hierarchy of monarchic descent and social standing or even of wealth, perhaps a hierarchy of intellect, the 'right' choices. Wright's advanced interests ensured that *The Smart Set* for this period contained some of its most controversial and experimental art and articles: Yeats, Robert Bridges, D. H. Lawrence, James Joyce, Ford Madox Ford, Strindberg,

Schnitzler, Beerbohm and the ubiquitous Ezra Pound (briskly appointed as European editor) were all represented, along with stories that had been rejected by other magazines as risqué.[27] Wright's contract was shortly terminated by the magazine's conservative owner John Thayer, whose business club associates began to cancel their advertising contracts with the suddenly 'bohemian' *Smart Set*, and many established subscriptions were also withdrawn by outraged readers. During Wright's year *The Smart Set*'s circulation plummeted and the magazine finances went into deficit, thus offering at least one example of an inverse relation between artistic innovation and short- to medium-term commercial viability.

This warrants a brief look at the expensively produced New York 'slick', *Vanity Fair*. Michael Murphy has remarked on the sales pitch of this magazine, which was *exactly* towards the reader which the editor (Frank Crowninshield) had identified as the person acknowledged as less likely to be interested in original art and literature. A 1919 subscription advertisement, for instance, offers 'to keep the tired businessman [...] in touch with the newest and liveliest influences of modern life'.[28] Murphy shows how *Vanity Fair* intentionally offered what might now be called 'high modernist' aesthetics to a non-academic audience. In between glossy spreads of fashion collections, coming-out parties and automobile shows were various features designed to give 'high' modernism a popular appeal. A glance through its 1917 contents shows articles by 'occultist' Aleister Crowley, by critic and poet Floyd Dell and by music critic, poet and photographer Carl Van Vechten. There are drawings by well-known Greenwich Village bohemian artist Clara Tice; contributions by radical photographers and members of the Alfred Stieglitz circle, Baron de Meyer and Edward Steichen; a piece about James Joyce by modern art patron John Quinn; an essay by Gertrude Stein; photographs of Elie Nadelman sculptures and a critical article by Jean Cocteau about the production of the arch-modernist ballet 'Parade'. All of these writers were also contributors to various other small, radical reviews and magazines. This careful packaging of the highbrow into an 'acceptable' bundle was a key factor in the long survival of the Condé Nast *Vanity Fair* until 1936 (relaunched 1983).

There is a reductive position from which one might argue that any publication's movement at all away from the safety of a broad middle-ground target readership would be tempered by economic considerations. For *The Smart Set* and *Vanity Fair* and probably most other wide-circulation publications, economics were the major factor in the decision to publish. At the same time, the magazines endeavoured to put out what their editors judged to be high-quality art. For an insight into the economic process, we can return to the odd figure of *Smart Set* editor Willard Huntington Wright, who was perhaps a more significant, though indirect, critical influence on American arts and letters than has hitherto been acknowledged. Wright was well-respected as an art critic, producing *Modern Painting, Its Tendency and Meaning*, one of the first, and one of the more discerning, books on modern art after the influential New York Armory Show of 1913.[29] This included a section on the art movement Synchromism (condemned by *The Soil* as just another 'ism'), of which Wright's brother, the aforementioned Stanton MacDonald Wright, was one of two New York practitioners, and the young Thomas Hart Benton a pupil. There is, therefore, some irony in the fact that Willard Wright went on later to produce 12 best-selling detective novels under the name of S. S. Van Dine. At the height of his success, he published a wryly justificatory article, which eventually revealed his identity, called 'I used to be a Highbrow But Look at Me Now'.[30] As he remarks therein, he had envisaged the production of detective novels as a temporary economic measure but 'each one of my Philo Vance stories has made more money than all my nine serious books put together. My literary earnings for any six months during the past two and a half years have been more than were my entire literary earnings for the previous fifteen years.'[31] As Brooks would have put it, 'richly rewarded trash'. Yet the character of the detective Philo Vance was impossibly highbrow, modelled perhaps on Wright himself but certainly on Dorothy L. Sayers's Peter Wimsey but with more style, more erudition and less pretension.[32] Notwithstanding his decision to quit after his sixth detective novel, Wright went on producing these stories and supported his chosen lifestyle, that of an extravagant art collector, until his death in 1939. At the same time, he continued to write 'highbrow' art criticism and essays under his own name. It is a telling reflection on the nature of literary innovation that even the most aesthetically idealistic artists have been shown to moderate their art in order for it to be published, and one might nowadays associate this moderation, and all its connotations, with the middlebrow.[33]

Susan Hegeman's discussion of the emergence of a middlebrow culture in America in the early 1930s also involves the artist Thomas Hart Benton, whom I mentioned above as indirectly connected with Wright. To summarize Hegeman's view, the 'culture of the middle' was part of the regionalization of American art movements in the 1930s, and also developed from the work of the new anthropologists such as Edward Sapir and Ruth Benedict, and from 'folk' historians such as Constance

Rourke.[34] Van Wyck Brooks's original idea of there being some middle ground between idealism and materialism, as we have seen here, had by the 1920s become lost in the generally expressed wish to drive out the middle in favour of either end of the arts and entertainments spectrum: 'the best things in life', remarked George Santayana in 1927, 'are football, kindness, and jazz bands'.[35] One of the most enthusiastic proponents of regionalist art, and ultimately a supporter of a regionalist culture of 'middle' America, which has become associated with racism and xenophobia, was Benton. His prolific work in the early 1930s heralded the public art works encouraged and commissioned as a result of the New Deal politics of Franklin D. Roosevelt; projects like the Works Progress Administration were designed to encourage artists and also to stimulate proletarian interest in art.[36] Benton's own statement supports the idea that his work was deliberately anti-intellectual: public art, he decided, required 'a language that was plain, direct, and devoid of any of the fancy specialisms of Art'.[37] Benton's creations, therefore, also intentionally moved from the avant-garde towards the populist, though unlike Willard Wright, without cynicism. It is perhaps unfortunate that his work was supported by the critic Thomas Craven, whose anti-Semitic and racist articles made him one of the most hated critics of the 1930s. Thus, in spite of Brooks's original hope for a 'middle' way, that which did arise in the 1930s was one which, ideologically, he could not support.[38]

This is not to say that the explicit racism thus associated with American 1930s 'middle American' regionalism did not also have roots in the cultural distinctions of the 1910s which have been addressed here. While Seldes's 1924 collection poured scorn on what would become known later as the middlebrow, it was nevertheless suffused with an unacknowledged sidelining and denigration of black culture while claiming to be in support of it. In the same way that Moderwell's ragtime concert was carefully selected to be sung by white professionals, Seldes's judgements of black culture were almost a paradigm of the various social, psychological and political processes which, in 1920s America, at one and the same time embraced and castigated the idea of the black. *The Seven Lively Arts* has the running theme of the 'polished fake' which constitutes the 'bogus' art of the 'middle' that Seldes wishes to remove. At the same time, though, the jazz which he claims to be the authentic music of America is the white version:

Nowhere is the failure of the negro to exploit his gifts more obvious than in the use he has made of the jazz orchestra; for although nearly every negro jazz band is better than nearly every white band, no negro band has yet come up to the level of the best white ones, and the leader of the best of all, by a little joke, is called Whiteman.[39]

Seldes here not only denies the achievement of the best black musicians, but he also immediately afterwards trivializes this extraordinary declaration of white superiority by drawing attention to the 'little joke' about Paul Whiteman's name. Black culture, according to Seldes (and Moderwell earlier), is for white appropriation and 'improvement' – white people, in other words, polishing their own fake.[40] The suppression and 'primitivization' of the black American resident by the white critic became part of the general racial division evident by the end of the 1920s, when black culture and black writing was no longer 'fashionable' among the white intelligentsia faced with the Great Depression.[41] Michael North has remarked this reluctance among the American avant-garde:

Despite [...] its promises of a transnational America and a multi-ethnic American modernism, the avant-garde proved ill prepared to include within its conception of the new American writing any examples that actually stretched the old categories of race and ethnicity.[42]

Therefore, the extremes of highbrow and lowbrow which were emphasized and polemicized during the 1910s and 1920s in America also supported the exclusion of the work of Black Americans or sidelined them as 'primitive' and 'exotic' while falling short of the articulated racism of 1930s critics like Craven, who claimed to support the new, regionalist, American middlebrow.[43]

At the end of a careful analysis of the reading selections of the Book of the Month Club 'serious fiction' editors, Janice Radway comes to this conclusion about their activities:

It is, first of all, an aesthetic system that in its bow to cultural authority and artistic excellence affirms the validity of the traditional hierarchy of taste. The editors' choices and their justifications for those choices regularly underscore their identification with the *keepers of the dominant cultural traditions* of the West.[44]

The statement compares closely with that of Bourdieu on the transgression of known limits, which I cited earlier. The Book of the Month Club began in 1926, a little later than the magazines in question, but it looks almost as though its editors were deliberately choosing books which appealed to their readers for much the same reasons as *Vanity Fair* was designed to appeal: 'people caught up in the daily round of quotidian activities and responsibilities who have little time for leisurely intellectual contemplation or meditation'.[45] Both Wright and Benton made a deliberate choice to lower their brow, the one economic, while the other idealistic. Those magazines whose editorial controllers were conscious of their middle-of-the-road readership appear to have made sure that they kept that economically necessary readership at the expense of artistic freedom. In spite of the reputation of the 'little magazine' for avant-gardism, some little magazines, like *Poetry* (which is still in publication), and *Poetry Review of America*, displayed a carefully moderate editorial policy. Brooks, Seldes, Mencken, Dreiser and a number of others (including Ezra Pound) were of the opinion that America's artistic poverty was due to America's lack of an aristocracy who would have had the leisure to preserve and improve the general culture, like a European monarchy or 'line of titled idlers', as Dreiser called them. But the editors of the magazines documented above, at least, seem to have been acutely aware of their own position near the top of a white intellectual hierarchy, and in fact hyper-aware of their own position as taste-makers. What I have suggested is that early critical and editorial comment in America in the 1910s led to a cementing of the highbrow/lowbrow division and a squeezing out, by smaller magazines, of any idea that the middle had anything to offer as any kind of welcome compromise. Larger magazines sought a middle-of-the-road readership compromise for economic reasons, but all sizes and types of magazine painstakingly maintained control over their position in an intellectual aristocracy of refined taste.

Notes

1. Van Wyck Brooks (1915; 1958) *America's Coming-of-Age* (New York: Doubleday), pp. 3–4.
2. Ibid., p. 2.
3. Brooks, ' "Highbrow" and "Lowbrow" ', in Brooks, *America's Coming-of-Age*, p. 10; also see de Tocqueville (1835; 1998) *Democracy in America* (Ware: Wordsworth Editions), p. 188: 'the human mind, constantly diverted from the pleasures of imagination and the labours of the intellect, is there swayed by no impulse but the pursuit of wealth.'
4. Brooks, *America's Coming-of-Age*, p. 19.
5. Gilbert Seldes (1924; 2001) *The Seven Lively Arts* (New York: Dover Publications) reprint of Harper Brothers' 1924 edition.
6. Seldes, *7 Lively Arts*, p. 350.
7. Ibid., p. 355.

8. See George Santayana (1967) 'The Genteel Tradition in American Philosophy', in *The Genteel Tradition: Nine Essays by George Santayana* (Cambridge: Harvard University Press), for an originating view.
9. Seldes, *Seven Lively Arts*, p. 102.
10. *The Seven Arts* (November 1916–October 1917; all examples from the 1967 AMS reprint) (New York: Seven Arts Publishing Company).
11. Dreiser (February 1917) 'Life, Art, and America', *The Seven Arts*, 1(4), 363–389, 363.
12. Dreiser, ibid., p. 369–370.
13. Dreiser, ibid., p. 389.
14. Hiram K. Moderwell (July 1917) 'A Modest Proposal', *The Seven Arts*, 2(3), 368, 370–371.
15. Robert J. Coady (ed.) (December 1916–July 1917) *The Soil*, 1(1–1), 5.
16. R. J. Coady (December 1916) 'letter' to Jean Crotti, *The Soil*, 1(1), 32–34.
17. R. J. Coady (December 1916) from 'American Art', *The Soil*, 1(1), 3.
18. Charles J. Maland (1989) *Chaplin and American Culture: The Evolution of a Star Image* (Princeton: Princeton University Press).
19. R. J. Coady (July 1917) 'The Indeps', *The Soil*, 1(5), 207.
20. Pierre Bourdieu (1979; 1984) *Distinction: A Social Critique of the Judgement of Taste*, trans. Richard Nice (Cambridge, Mass.: Harvard University Press), p. 48.
21. *The Little Review* (September 1916) 3:6 features 13 blank pages.
22. Allan and Louise Norton (eds) (1915) *Rogue*, 1(1), 4.
23. *Rogue*, 1(1), inside front cover.
24. Hoffman, Allen, and Ulrich (1946) *The Little Magazine: A History and a Bibliography* (Princeton: Princeton University Press), p. 89 puts *The Masses*'s circulation at 14,000. Rebecca Zurier (1988) in *Art for the Masses: A Radical Magazine and Its Graphics, 1911–1917* (Philadelphia: Temple University Press) gives a figure of 20,000–40,000 copies.
25. Carl R. Dolmetsch (1966) *The Smart Set: A History and Anthology* (New York: Dial Press), p. 79.
26. Willard H. Wright (March 1913) 'Something Personal', *The Smart Set* 39(3), 159, quoted in Sharon Hamilton (1999) 'The First New Yorker? *The Smart Set Magazine*,1900–1924', *The Serials Librarian* 37(2), 92.
27. Dolmetsch, *The Smart Set*, p. 38.
28. Quoted in Michael Murphy (1996) ' "One Hundred Per Cent Bohemia": Pop Decadence and the Aestheticization of Commodity in the Rise of the Slicks', Kevin Dettmar and Stephen Watt (1996) *Marketing Modernisms: Self-Promotion, Canonization, and Rereading* (Ann Arbor: University of Michigan Press), pp. 61–89, 63.
29. Willard Huntington Wright (1915) *Modern Painting, Its Tendency and Meaning* (New York: John Lane).
30. (1928; 2000) 'I used to be a Highbrow But Look at Me Now: An Autobiographical Essay By the Creator of Philo Vance' (New York: The Mysterious Bookshop Limited Edition), originally published in *The American Magazine*.
31. Ibid., p. 21.
32. See discussion of Philo Vance in Julian Symons (1972) *Bloody Murder: From the Detective Story to the Crime Novel: A History* (London: Faber and Faber), pp. 110–113.

33. See Joyce Wexler (1997) *Who Paid For Modernism? Art, Money, and the Fiction of Conrad, Joyce, and Lawrence* (Fayetteville: University of Kansas Press), particularly the chapter on D. H. Lawrence.
34. See Susan Hegeman (1999) *Patterns For America: Modernism and the Concept of Culture* (Princeton: Princeton University Press), especially ch. 5, 'The Culture of the Middle', pp. 126–157.
35. George Santayana, letter to Van Wyck Brooks, 22 May 1927, in Daniel Cory (ed.) (1955) *The Letters of George Santayana* (New York: Scribner), pp. 225–226.
36. Alan Yentob (21 July 2009) radio programme 'Art in Troubled Times: A New Deal for Art' broadcast.
37. Thomas Hart Benton, 'The Thirties', Benton Papers, Archives of American Art (Smithsonian Institution, Washington), 12–18, quoted in Erika Doss (1991) *Benton, Pollock, and the Politics of Modernism: From Regionalism to Abstract Expressionism* (Chicago: University of Chicago Press), p. 112.
38. Hegeman, *Patterns for America*, pp. 142–143, also 132–133 in which she describes the opposition of the Popular Front League of American Writers (led by Brooks and Waldo Frank) to the culture of the middle.
39. Seldes, *7 Lively Arts*, p. 99.
40. See Kingham (2005) *'Seven Arts, 7 Lively Arts* and American Cultural Criticism' (unpublished M. Phil thesis), Cambridge University.
41. See Gilbert Osofsky (Summer 1965) 'Symbols of the Jazz Age: The New Negro and Harlem Discovered', *American Quarterly* 17(2), part 1, 229–238; Linda Mizejewski (1999) *Ziegfeld Girl* (Durham: Duke University Press); Ralph Ellison (1968) *Shadow and Act* (London: Secker & Warburg); James Weldon Johnson (1928) 'Dilemma of the Negro Author', *The American Mercury*; and the introductory comments of Jeffrey C. Stewart (1983) in *The Critical Temper of Alain Locke* (New York: Garland).
42. Michael North (1994) *The Dialect of Modernism: Race, Language & Twentieth-Century Literature* (New York: Oxford University Press), p. 150.
43. On the institutionalized racism in 1930s American art criticism, see Mary Ann Calo (September 1999) 'African American Art and Critical Discourse Between Two World Wars', *American Quarterly* 51(3), 580–621.
44. Janice Radway (Spring 1988) 'The Book-of-the-Month Club and the General Reader: On the Uses of "Serious" Fiction', *Critical Inquiry*, 14(3), 516–538, 538. My italics.
45. Radway, ibid., p. 538.

8
'Intellectual in Its Looser Sense': Reading Mencken's *Smart Set*

Sharon Hamilton

Gilbert Seldes almost single-handedly brought the highest of highbrow modernism into the United States by publishing T. S. Eliot's *The Waste Land* in the *Dial* magazine in November 1922, but when this critic looked back on American literary culture of the interwar years, he mainly remembered H. L. Mencken. As Seldes explained, 'Mencken influenced the minds of thousands of young people when they were in or recently out of college. In that sense, he took part in creating the climate of the time.'[1] While Seldes clearly associated H. L. Mencken with major cultural movements, he qualified this influence in an interesting way, adding, 'As far as ideas and the arts were concerned, he had an effect on the intellectual climate – here using intellectual in its looser sense.'[2]

Seldes's description of H. L. Mencken's work as intellectualism 'in its looser sense' highlights the kinds of distinctions being made by readers and critics in the 1920s and 1930s between highbrow and middlebrow magazines and the fluid manner in which middlebrow magazines often managed to be influential – owing to their popular readership – while also acting as venues that stayed abreast of some of the most avant-garde movements of their time. In the case of H. L. Mencken's *Smart Set*, its intellectualism did act in both a strict and a 'looser' sense, so that the same magazine that published early work by Ezra Pound, James Joyce, Eugene O'Neill, F. Scott Fitzgerald, Edna St. Vincent Millay and D. H. Lawrence also published bedroom fiction with titles like 'The Pirates of Virtue' and 'Lady Marjory's Undies'.[3] This magazine was both serious in its literary criticism and purposefully entertaining, publishing conventional short stories and comic epigrams alongside the work of writers who would go on to shape European and American modernism.

The *Smart Set's* 'looser' approach to intellectualism proved wildly attractive, especially to young readers. As a result of its popular approach, the *Smart Set* (published as a New York literary magazine from 1900 to 1923) attracted a generation of influential readers and critics, including Gilbert Seldes, Edmund Wilson, Richard Wright, Alfred Kazin, Dorothy Parker and Harold Ross. By approaching intellectualism in a way that remained accessible and decidedly a part of mass culture, Mencken's *Smart Set* influenced the tastes and opinions of America's university students and growing professional class and, in so doing, managed to attract a sizeable readership to the experimental work of modernist writers who might otherwise have remained relatively unknown.

The essays gathered in this volume collectively ask (and attempt to answer) the essential question, 'why does scholarly attention to the middlebrow matter?' The example of the *Smart Set* suggests that attention to American middlebrow magazines of the 1920s and 1930s should matter to anyone who cares about the future of the arts, because the histories of such middlebrow magazines tell us a great deal about the modes of cultural production: how great works of literature are produced, supported and reach the general public. We should not take such modes of production for granted. The example of Mencken's *Smart Set* connects to our own time; the history of this magazine reveals the importance to literary creation of paying popular venues for literary works – and especially for work by those just beginning their careers. The *Smart Set's* history illustrates the ways in which middlebrow venues can take great experimental works of literature and make them mainstream.

'Are we a nation of low brows?' – The *Smart Set* and cultural anxiety

If you open an issue of the *Smart Set* from September 1922 to the inside back cover, you will find an advertisement that asks in a bold headline 'Are We a Nation of Low Brows?' Underneath this headline, the advertisement reads, 'It is charged that the public is intellectually incompetent. Is this true?' This advertisement further asks, 'Are the People Ready to Read These 25 Books?' The following list of books (available for immediate order: 'Send No Money') included *Meditations of Marcus Aurelius*; *The Idea of God and Nature* by John Stuart Mill; *Life and Character* by Goethe; *Thoughts of Pascal*; and *Three Lectures on Evolution* by Ernst Haeckel. Mencken reveals in his memoir that he and George Jean Nathan (the magazine's co-editor, with Mencken, from 1914 to

1923) had nothing to do with the *Smart Set*'s advertising. Those duties belonged to the publisher Eltinge Warner, and it was Warner's advertising agents who were responsible for collecting advertisements for a 'Newsstand Group', which included the pulp magazines *Snappy Stories, Breezy Stories* and *Young's Magazine* so that, as a result, the *Smart Set* often ended up with advertisements out of keeping with its sophisticated intellectualism: advertisements for 'Diamond-Watches – Cash or Credit', or announcing 'Reduce Your Fat' and 'Your Face Is Your Fortune'.[4] Mencken later complained that the *Smart Set*'s advertisements included 'everything in the shabby line save lost manhood and bust developer ads'.[5] Sometimes, though – as in the case of this *Smart Set* advertisement – the magazine's advertisements inadvertently reflected its actual character. However coincidental its appearance in the magazine, this advertisement tapped into the same deep cultural anxiety that the *Smart Set* itself tapped into, and which was a significant part of its unique appeal and historical importance.

The *Smart Set* began publication in 1900 in Manhattan: a time and a place of particular cultural anxiety. When Colonel William D'Alton Mann founded the *Smart Set* as a New York literary magazine intended for the city's wealthiest classes – its 'smart set' – he did so when New York was rapidly expanding in wealth and establishing important cultural venues (such as the Metropolitan Opera and the Metropolitan Museum of Art) but when it was also, literally, a factory town. An industrial map of New York City from 1922 shows that in the 1910s and early 1920s, New York was home to 32,590 factories, which employed 825,056 workers and produced $5,260,707,577 in yearly product.[6] The largest industries were not in the cultural sector, although these were certainly growing, but in clothing manufacturing. Ironically, the same city that was actively nurturing the culture of the flapper and the speakeasy was thus rapidly undermining the sale of its own single-largest manufactured good: the corset.

During those early years of the new century, New York saw rapidly increasing numbers of employees who could read, and who worked in such sectors as marketing, advertising, publishing and business. New York's readers also tended to have more time to read, as many of them lived in the new American phenomenon of the suburb and commuted into the city on New York's subway, opened in 1904. In *Selling Culture: Magazines, Markets, and Class at the Turn-of-the-Century*, Richard Ohmann discusses the effect that the rise of a professional-managerial class had on the growth and popularity of the mass-market magazine industry, noting that the relationship between magazines and their new readers went two ways: if the new professional-managerial class gave mass-market magazines an audience, those magazines, in turn, played an important role in developing the tastes and interests of their readers.[7] The *Smart Set*, then, appeared in a city still figuring out its cultural identity and provided a popular reference point for a population anxious about the credentials necessary to move up in the world: to be seen as literate and educated. When H. L. Mencken began writing literary reviews for the magazine in 1908, he could not have been better positioned – or, with his bold, exuberant style, better suited – to provide literary advice to New Yorkers living in a changing city and determined, above all, not to appear 'low brow'. In his first review column, which appeared on New York newsstands in November 1908, when he was just 28 years of age, this unknown Baltimore journalist announced his presence on the New York literary scene by dismissing the widely esteemed work of Henry James. Of James's 'Views and Reviews', Mencken wrote, 'Early essays by Henry James – some in the English Language'.[8]

The kind of anxiety felt by New York readers who belonged to the emerging professional-managerial class was not, of course, limited to New York. Wherever urbanization was taking place, a similar phenomenon was occurring. One of the main 'middlebrow matters' this collection explores is precisely the establishment of new hierarchies of cultural value that were taking place on both sides of the Atlantic during an era of massive historical change. In America, as in England, readers unsure of their cultural and intellectual status were intent on finding their way into a completely new social structure and looked to the newly emergent products of the mass media to guide them – as appears, for example, in a remarkably frank letter printed in the American magazine *The New Republic* in November 1917, and headed simply, 'What Shall He Read?'[9]

In this letter, a correspondent who signs his name as 'T. G.' asks *The New Republic* for advice about what to read because he is 'ashamed of making naïve answers to questions of real moment'.[10] He explains that he is a civil engineer but is hoping to 'go into training for an executive position'; while he holds a 'degree from the leading American university', he considers himself 'wofully [sic] ignorant' and asks *The New Republic* to suggest some 'twenty or thirty books' that he might read to broaden his education, or to pass his letter on to 'some intelligent publishing firm or bookseller'.[11] T. G. was hardly alone in such anxiety. The popularity in England of such critics as Arnold Bennett and Wilfred Whitten (as noted elsewhere in this collection) indicates the hunger across the urbanizing world for guidance in matters of taste.

In America, members of the new professional-managerial class, eager to be taught, had similarly found a critic to follow. Even T. G., who felt so culturally lost, indicates in his letter to *The New Republic* that he was already reading the same critic to whom much of the rest of the nation had also turned for guidance: H. L. Mencken.[12]

The few articles in Mencken's scrapbooks that directly reveal the professions held by the *Smart Set*'s readers suggest that T. G. was not the only reader who possessed a university education, but who nevertheless required reassurance about what he should know in order to avoid appearing culturally 'naïve'. The magazine's largest appeal, however, seems to have been among precisely those readers who were not *yet* members of America's professional-managerial class, but who one day would be: students in American high schools and universities. The American literary critic Edmund Wilson later recalled that he had first encountered the *Smart Set* in 1912, when he was in high school,[13] and that at the time the magazine served as a 'sort of central bureau to which the young looked for tips to guide them in the cultural confusion'.[14] *New York Post* theatre critic John Mason Brown similarly recalled that 'all of us who were young' had adored the magazine's 'audacities',[15] and the Hollywood screenwriter Ben Hecht (*Gone With The Wind, His Girl Friday*) similarly began reading the magazine as a teenager, when it served as a 'sort of monthly Gospel'.[16] The soon-to-be modernist poet Hart Crane was only 18 when he wrote to his mother to say that he was 'busy thinking up plots for Smart Set stories',[17] and Sherwood Anderson summed up the feelings of many of the magazine's young readers when he recalled that 'Henry Mencken was our great hero'.[18]

The *Smart Set* also attracted female readers and writers. When Dorothy Parker wished to experiment with writing darkly-comic short fiction, she sent her work to the *Smart Set* and Anita Loos similarly submitted her work to the *Smart Set* when she began to write fiction. Willa Cather sent the *Smart Set* her only erotic work of short fiction, 'Coming, Aphrodite!', and Mencken published – and positively reviewed – work by Amy Lowell, Thyra Samter Winslow, Ruth Suckow and Helen Woljeska. The *Smart Set* was also very supportive of female dramatists: Mencken and Nathan published plays by Djuna Barnes and Zoë Akins, and helped Akins secure her first Broadway appearance. An American literature professor of the era, Stuart P. Sherman, was particularly alarmed by the magazine's appeal to female readers, devoting a chapter of *Americans* (1922) to this issue. Sherman was concerned with the magazine's establishment of a kind of 'Menckenian academy' which, he felt, would destroy the British-influenced standards in American taste, and predicted that Mencken would lead young female readers away from Emerson, Howells and Arnold Bennett to embrace, instead, the 'new literature'.[19] He had reason to be concerned. Writing about the impression Mencken made on his female readers, Anita Loos recalled that 'Menck's writings had caused him to be a "matinee idol" on every college campus'.[20]

Mencken's iconoclastic appeal crossed lines of race as well as gender. In his memoir, *Black Boy*, Richard Wright remembered that as a 19-year-old he forged a note from a white library patron to read collections of H. L. Mencken's *Smart Set* criticism,[21] and Claude McKay admired Mencken's *Smart Set* editorials so much that, despite their very different politics, he tried to commission articles from Mencken for *The Liberator*.[22] James Weldon Johnson also followed the *Smart Set*, and in his memoir he notes that after moving to New York, 'the first new contact I made was with H. L. Mencken, then one of the editors of *Smart Set*' because Mencken had 'made a sharper impression on my mind than any other American then writing, and I wanted to know him'.[23]

Ultimately, the magazine was a magnet for readers who wished to establish their cultural credentials – in the same way, and for the same reasons, that *The New Yorker* magazine still attracts such readers today. As John Leonard recalled, by the mid-1970s, *The New Yorker* had become 'the weekly magazine most educated Americans grew up on'. As Leonard explained, 'Whether we read it or refused to read it – which depended, of course, on the sort of people we wanted to be – it was as much a part of our class conditioning as clean fingernails, college, a checking account, and good intentions.'[24] In New York during the 1910s and early 1920s, reading the *Smart Set* was a move similarly intended to reinforce others' appreciation of your cultural and intellectual sophistication. Just being *seen* with the magazine was an act designed to confer immediate intellectual standing. John Dos Passos captured this social reality in the 'Nineteen Nineteen' section of *U.S.A.* One of the novel's characters is a 15-year-old student involved in an affair with a young married woman 'with a thin aquiline nose and bangs, who smoked cigarettes' and who was 'a great reader of the *Smart Set* and *The Black Cat* and books that were advanced'.[25] She introduces her lover to the *Smart Set*, which he reads as publicly as possible: 'He sat there a long time reading *The Smart Set* and drinking the sherry feeling like a man of the world.'[26]

Mencken's guidance to such readers was followed and appreciated. A 1917 *Knickerbocker Press* review commented, for example, on the fact that Mencken and Nathan were among America's 'best critics' and observed that they wrote about their subjects 'with authority'.[27] It was this posture of unassailable authority to which their readers responded, changing their reading habits in accordance with what Mencken suggested. In 1919, reporters at the *New York Tribune* stated they had begun to 'fill in one of the gaps in the list of books we ought to know' by reading Willa Cather's *My Ántonia* because 'H. L. Mencken seldom mentions May Sinclair without remarking that Willa Sibert Cather is more capable in work of the same character.'[28] F. Scott Fitzgerald similarly noted in his 1921 review of Charles Norris's *Brass* that he was reading American realist works because of Mencken and that, in contrast, none of his 'English professors in college ever suggested to his class that books were being written in America'.[29]

It was not only Mencken's critical opinions that were followed, but also his writing style. In the 1920s, the University of California student newspaper *The Laughing Horse* employed obvious Menckenisms (including hyperbole, lists and elaborate insults) in announcing that 'our aim is frankly destructive, regardless of the attitude of The English Club on that kind of criticism. We are not reformers; we are not architects. We are the wrecking gang, hurlers of brickbats, shooters of barbs, tossers of custard pie.'[30] Mencken's popular style and rebellious attitude contributed to his wide cultural impact – owing especially to his effect on readers who would later themselves become communicators. As Ben Hecht remembered, 'there was a Mencken underground, not only of writers who cribbed his attitudes, but of university professors, statesmen, and bachelor girls. And young newspaper men like myself.'[31]

Cultural omnivores: the *Smart Set* and taste beyond category

When I teach my students about *Smart Set* fiction, I always begin by showing them the cover of the magazine from March 1922, with its depiction of a rebellious flapper (see Figure 8.1). I ask them what sorts of things readers in the 1920s would have found shocking or surprising about what they saw. It doesn't take long for them to start calling out answers: 'The bobbed hair (bright red!)'; 'The cigarette'; 'The heavy blue eyeshadow.' 'Hey,' some student inevitably calls out, 'is she actually wearing any clothes?' The *Smart Set* was, essentially, streetwise. It was willing to appear hip, even trashy, on its cover – and in its contents – as a means of achieving wide popularity while simultaneously promoting literary work by some of Europe's and America's most innovative artists. The *Smart Set*'s flexible cultural posture – especially when compared to

Figure 8.1 Front cover, H. L. Mencken and George Jean Nathan's *The Smart Set* magazine, March 1922

Permission to publish this image provided by the George H. Thompson Collection of H. L. Mencken, the Sheridan Libraries, Johns Hopkins University.

that of the 'little magazines' (as explored by Victoria Kingham else-where in this collection) – was an approach to intellectual authority that depended on what sociologists describe as the stance of the cultural omnivore.

The magazine intentionally assumed a particularly urbane and expansive attitude. As Mencken explained in a 1923 editorial, *'Criticism Again'*, the best critic is the one who doesn't preach but, rather, begins with the assumption that what the critic 'finds interesting is very apt to seem interesting to all persons of taste and education'.[32] As Mencken and Nathan recognized, educated readers would not 'want to be told precisely what to think about the thing discussed'.[33] Mencken and Nathan's refusal to make what they said or published in the *Smart Set* fit within neat boundaries implied the compliment that their readers were worldly enough to appreciate material not designed to fit into a single form – an approach they adopted in conscious reaction to American universities. As Mencken showed in his review of Upton Sinclair's *The Goose-Step: A Study of American Education*, he agreed with Sinclair's thesis that the thing the American university 'combats most ardently is not ignorance, but free inquiry; it is devoted to forcing the whole youth of the land into one rigid mold'.[34] That Mencken and Nathan adopted an entertaining (often belligerent) prose style, and offered their readers a wide variety of material, without patronizing them, acted in intentional contrast to the situation in such university classrooms. Mencken and Nathan especially wanted to appeal to the intellectual needs of students and their innate tendency to be 'aspiring, rebellious, inquisitive, iconoclastic, [and] a bit romantic'.[35]

Sociologists have only recently begun to understand the sociological basis of the particular appeal offered by cultural products like the *Smart Set*. Building on the work of such scholars as Pierre Bourdieu, Nicola Beisel and Paul DiMaggio concerning the sociological grounds for stated cultural preferences, Shin-Kap Han suggests in his article 'Unraveling the Brow: What and How of Choice in Musical Preference' that in addition to considering *who* (i.e. what class of people) chooses *what* (i.e. what kind of cultural products), it is also important to consider 'the question of *how*'.[36] Han observes that most sociological studies in the past limited themselves to either/or scenarios in which people were asked if they liked or didn't like a particular cultural product (opera, heavy metal, rap, etc.). Han's assumption was that greater understanding of how cultural distinctions are formed would be revealed by examining data 'to show that it is not only what type of music the respondents choose' but also 'how they choose'.[37]

As with previous sociological research, Han's study confirmed a strong correlation between taste in musical forms and socio-economic status – but what was different about his study was his additional realization that 'the notion of tolerance and the presumption of its linear relationship with education should be reconsidered'.[38] In short, Han found that people establish their level of social and cultural distinction through something he refers to as the *dual basis of taste*.[39] Han argues that sociologists are increasingly coming to recognize the importance of an 'omnivore-univore axis' of taste and the ways in which this axis operates in contrast to cultural distinctions based simply on 'snobbish exclusion' or the 'elite-mass' (i.e. highbrow-lowbrow).[40] The creation of social and cultural distinctions can depend, in other words, not just on choosing the 'right' musical form, but in demonstrating an acceptance of a wide variety of musical genres, by being a cultural omnivore: someone who likes opera, but who also appreciates rap. Even poor T. G., who had to write a letter to a magazine to find out what he should read, recognized the importance of pointing out the range of his reading: 'In my own defense I will say I like to read good English composition and am rather catholic in my tastes.'[41] Recognition of the link between catholicity in taste and cultural sophistication probably always existed in some form, and this *particular* appeal to cultural sophistication was the one the *Smart Set* cultivated.

Although the *Smart Set* could be accurately described as 'middlebrow', the magazine was also, in significant ways, able to situate itself outside strict divisions between the 'brows' by aligning itself with omnivorous taste. The *Smart Set*'s eclectic contents appeared in a magazine that successfully based its main appeal directly – just as *The New Yorker* does today – on a snobbishness tinged with knowing humour. In Mencken and Nathan's first jointly edited issue of the magazine, they waggishly announced that 'One Civilized Reader is Worth a Thousand Boneheads' (see Figure 8.2). Such a proclamation *was* certainly intended as a method of exclusion: a distinction based on the elite against the mass. In this respect, the *Smart Set* employed some of the same tactics as the 'little magazines', which so actively aligned themselves with 'highbrow' tastes (like the *Little Magazine* with its slogan 'make no compromise with the public taste'[42]). The *Smart Set* used similar slogans, such as 'The Magazine for the Civilized Minority', 'The Magazine of Fifth Avenue' and 'The Only American Magazine with an European Air'.[43] But in contrast to the 'little magazines', the *Smart Set* also used irony to undermine its own stated exclusivity, and, in so doing, created an urbane, welcoming attitude that we still recognize as a form of cultural sophistication.

Figure 8.2 Front cover, H. L. Mencken and George Jean Nathan's *The Smart Set* magazine, October 1914

Permission to publish this image provided by the George H. Thompson Collection of H. L. Mencken, the Sheridan Libraries, Johns Hopkins University.

The *Smart Set's* formula for appealing to a large readership while simultaneously adopting the posture of an 'elite' was essential to the significant cultural achievements of each of the 'smart magazines'[44] that followed: *Vanity Fair, The American Mercury, The New Yorker* and *Esquire*. As Faye Hammill and Karen Leick have observed of the 'smart' magazines, 'their circulations, advertising revenues, content and readership all located them in a middle space between the author-centred production model of the avant-garde magazines and the market-driven arena of the daily papers and mass-circulation weeklies. In their ambivalent relationships to the literary marketplace, these magazines disrupted stratified cultural organisation and negotiated continually between aesthetic and commercial considerations.'[45] The conditions that combined to make the *Smart Set* both middlebrow *and* intellectual gave it the freedom to publish a wide variety of different styles of literature for an audience that had been flattered into a willing reception of new ideas: literature without boundaries.

As a result, although the *Smart Set* published a number of the authors we now associate with the difficulty of 'high modernism' (especially under the brief editorship of Willard Huntington Wright in 1913), it was a particularly supportive venue for those modernist authors writing works that were in some ways conventionally accessible, yet in others radical and new: the psychology-based drama and stories of Eugene O'Neill, Sherwood Anderson and Djuna Barnes; the social realism of Theodore Dreiser and Sinclair Lewis; urban sex satire by Dorothy Parker, Anita Loos and Zoë Akins; the realism spliced with myth of F. Scott Fitzgerald; and stories of female erotic desire by Willa Cather and Edna St. Vincent Millay. In short, the *Smart Set* proved particularly capable of nurturing and promoting an eclectic array of modern American writing precisely because its brand of cultural distinction wasn't a self-proclaimed 'highbrow' status but rather a 'middlebrow' humour-based catholicity. At the same time as Mencken and Nathan were getting this formula right at the *Smart Set, Vanity Fair* began publishing and it, too, would find the right balance between intellectualism and fun. The fact that we can, today, pick up issues of *The New Yorker, Vanity Fair* and *Esquire* and expect in-depth reporting, quality writing and popular entertainment is, in no small measure, owing to the changes that began in the *Smart Set* as it shifted its appeal away from entertainment for New York's wealthy classes to contents that privileged cleverness: literature for a different kind of 'smart set'. The magazine ultimately offered its writers and readers the literary equivalent of doing opera with a touch of rap.

The attractive combination Mencken's *Smart Set* offered of accessible and intelligent fiction and criticism continued to appeal to important readers and critics even after the magazine had ceased publication. In his memoir, *New York Jew*, Alfred Kazin recalled the years he spent doing research at the New York Public Library for what would become *On Native Grounds* (1942). 'I was my own staff researcher,' Kazin remembered, 'a totally unaffiliated free lance [*sic*] and occasional evening college instructor who was educating himself in the mind of modern America by writing, in the middle of the Great Depression, a wildly ambitious literary and intellectual history'.[46] As he worked, he picked up old issues of the *Smart Set* because, as he fondly recalled, it was 'not for the boneheads'.[47] The magazine's posture of self-congratulation (tinged with just the right amount of ironic self-criticism) made the *Smart Set* an ideal 'middlebrow' venue: a magazine that managed to be both popular and avant-garde and, through this unusual status, to serve the needs of art beyond boundaries by cultivating a readership willing to think of *itself* as amenable to cultural change, and thus able to position important new works before a wide audience made ready to receive them.

The future of the middlebrow: smartset.com?

The *Smart Set*'s history suggests that 'high' culture needs the 'middle', not just as a mode of rejection and self-definition, but also to survive. Middlebrow taste-makers such as H. L. Mencken were essential to establishing the grounds for the positive reception of much of what we now take for granted as canonical American literature.[48] The kind of intellectual middlebrow platform that Mencken enjoyed in the *Smart Set* is, however, rapidly disappearing. In the 1910s and early 1920s, Mencken used his *Smart Set* book review columns to declare the importance of such writers as Ezra Pound, James Joyce, Scott Fitzgerald, Willa Cather and Sherwood Anderson. Today, the book review is an endangered species. Only recently, in a move necessitated by the urgent need to ensure its own survival, *The Washington Post* eliminated its stand-alone book review section, leaving an even smaller number of American venues for in-depth reviews. Regular readers of the *Post*'s excellent 'Book World' learned in an announcement that book reviews would now be scattered through the other sections of the newspaper, throughout the week. The kind of reviews that Mencken provided to his readers – reviews that played such an essential role in the establishment of American literary culture – have been replaced today by

Figure 8.3   Homepage, www.thesmartset.com, 22 November 2010
Image provided courtesy of *The Smart Set* from Drexel University.

itinerant book reviews that can be hunted down only by the truly diligent reader.

The internet offers hope, however, that middlebrow venues attuned to bringing sophisticated cultural criticism to a wide audience may survive in new forms, as evinced through the surprising new incarnation of the *Smart Set* itself – as an internet magazine: thesmartset.com. This online forum covers 'everything from literature to shopping, medicine to food, philosophy to sports' – an eclectic mandate similar to the original *Smart Set* and, like the original, also aspires to be 'intelligent' but not necessarily 'written specifically for the academic crowd'[49] (see Figure 8.3). And, indeed, in this spirit, recent issues of the magazine have included articles on everything from William Blake, Søren Kierkegaard and Marcel Duchamp, to columns on new poetry and cooking turducken.[50] This electronic magazine has even resurrected Mencken's old *Smart Set* pseudonym, 'Owen Hatteras'. In the inaugural edition, 'Hatteras' explained that he was chosen as the magazine's ombudsman because he was 'the last living contributor to the original *Smart Set*'.[51] In the iconoclastic spirit of the original, in this opening column Hatteras wrote, '[Mencken] was always a real bastard. I'm still waiting for the $15 for my last contribution. [...] He told me the check was in the mail. This was 1922. Haven't heard from him since. Is he still alive?'[52]

Is he still alive? Well, no. But as the new Drexel University online version of the *Smart Set* shows, Mencken has never stopped attracting the attention of students, scholars and writers; and the resurrection of his Owen Hatteras pseudonym demonstrates that while the sage of Baltimore may be gone, the Mencken underground Ben Hecht once wrote about – which had the power to change American literature and to transform New York life – is still very much alive. And that is good news, because the extent to which middlebrow cultural venues are attuned to bringing in-depth reviews and new works of art to popular audiences in *this* century will affect how much literature of exceptional quality will emerge to become canonical in the next.

Notes

1. Gilbert Seldes, typescript, qtd. in Michael Kammen (1996) *The Lively Arts: Gilbert Seldes and the Transformation of Cultural Criticism in the United States* (Oxford: Oxford University Press), p. 389.
2. Ibid.
3. Paul Hervey Fox (January 1917) 'The Pirates of Virtue', *Smart Set*, 169–174; Anthony Wharton (April 1917) 'Lady Marjory's Undies', *Smart Set*, 131–150.

4. H. L. Mencken (1993) *My Life as Author and Editor* ed. and with an introduction by Jonathan Yardley (New York: Knopf), p. 381. Quotations from the writings of H. L. Mencken used by permission of the Enoch Pratt Free Library, Baltimore, in accordance with the terms of Mr Mencken's bequest.
5. Ibid., p. 382.
6. 'Industrial Map of New York City Showing Manufacturing Industries' (1922) Merchants' Association of New York, The Lionel Pincus and Princess Firyal Map Division, New York Public Library.
7. Richard Ohmann (1996) *Selling Culture: Magazines, Markets, and Class at the Turn-of-the-Century* (London and New York: Verso).
8. H. L. Mencken (November 1908) 'The Good, The Bad, and the Best Sellers', *Smart Set*, 159.
9. 'What Shall He Read?' (10 November 1917) *New Republic* in H. L. Mencken Scrapbooks, Enoch Pratt Free Library, Baltimore.
10. Ibid.
11. Ibid.
12. Ibid.
13. Edmund Wilson ([1968] 1973) 'The Aftermath of Mencken', *The Devils and Canon Barham* (New York: Farrar, Straus and Giroux), p. 94.
14. Edmund Wilson (1947) 'H. L. Mencken', in Edmund Wilson (ed.) *The Shock of Recognition: The Development of Literature in the United States Recorded by the Men Who Made It* (New York: Doubleday), p. 1156.
15. John Mason Brown (13 April 1958) 'Critic's View of A Critic', *New York Times*, Sec. 2, 3.
16. Ben Hecht (1965) 'About Mencken', *Letters from Bohemia* (London: Hammond, Hammond, and Co.), p. 71.
17. John Unterecker ((1969) 1970) *Voyager: A Life of Hart Crane* (New York: Anthony Blond), p. 91.
18. Sherwood Anderson ((1942) 1969) in Ray Lewis White (ed.) *Sherwood Anderson's Memoirs: A Critical Edition* (Chapel Hill: University of North Carolina Press), p. 369.
19. Stuart P. Sherman (1922) 'Mr. Mencken, the Jeune Fille, and the New Spirit in Letters', *Americans* (New York: Scribner's), pp. 7, 1.
20. Anita Loos (1966) *A Girl Like I* (New York: Viking), p. 213.
21. Richard Wright (1945) *Black Boy* (New York: Harper & Row), pp. 270–272 qtd. in Fred Hobson (1994) *Mencken: A Life* (New York: Random House), p. 250.
22. Wayne F. Cooper (1987) *Claude McKay: Rebel Sojourner in the Harlem Renaissance* (New York: Schocken Books), p. 159.
23. James Weldon Johnson (1973) *Along This Way: The Autobiography of James Weldon Johnson* (New York: Da Capo Press), p. 305. For more on Mencken's relationships with African-American writers see Charles Scruggs (1984) *The Sage in Harlem: H. L. Mencken and the Black Writers of the 1920s* (Baltimore: Johns Hopkins University Press).
24. John Leonard (2000) *New York Times Book Review* qtd in Ben Yagoda (2001) *About Town: The New Yorker and the World It Made* (New York: Da Capo Press), p. 12.
25. John Dos Passos (1932; 1960) *U.S.A.* (Harmondsworth: Penguin), p. 405.
26. Ibid., p. 410.

27. George Guest (11 November 1917) 'Pistols for Two', *Knickerbocker Press*, H. L. Mencken Scrapbooks, Enoch Pratt Free Library, Baltimore.
28. (No title) (5 December 1919) *New York Tribune* in H. L. Mencken Scrapbooks, Enoch Pratt Free Library, Baltimore.
29. F. Scott Fitzgerald (November 1921) ' "Poor Old Marriage": Review of Charles G. Norris' *Brass*' in *The Bookman* 54, 253–254 repr. in Matthew J. Bruccoli and Jackson R. Bryer (eds) (1971) *F. Scott Fitzgerald in His Own Time* (Toronto: Popular Library), p. 126.
30. The Editors (1922) 'Apologia', *The Laughing Horse* (Berkeley: University of California), p. 2.
31. Hecht, *Bohemia*, p. 72.
32. (H. L. Mencken) (June 1923) 'Criticism Again', *Smart Set*, 33.
33. Ibid.
34. H. L. Mencken (May 1923) 'Nordic Blond Art', *Smart Set*, 143.
35. Ibid., p. 144.
36. Shin-Kap Han (Winter 2003) 'Unraveling the Brow: What and How of Choice in Musical Preference', *Sociological Perspectives*, 46, 435–459.
37. Ibid., p. 436.
38. Ibid., p. 452.
39. Ibid.
40. Ibid., p. 438.
41. 'What Shall He Read?', *New Republic*.
42. Mark S. Morrisson (2001) *The Public Face of Modernism: Little Magazines, Audiences, and Reception, 1905–1920* (Madison: University of Wisconsin Press), p. 133.
43. *Smart Set* (April 1916), 1; *Smart Set* (May 1916), front cover; *Smart Set* (June 1916), front cover.
44. George Douglas (1991) *The Smart Magazines* (Hamden: Archon).
45. Faye Hammill and Karen Leick 'Modernism and the Quality Magazines: *Vanity Fair* (1914–1936); *The American Mercury* (1924–1981); *The New Yorker* (1925–); *Esquire* (1933–)', in Peter Brooker and Andrew Thacker (eds) *Modernist Magazines: A Critical and Cultural History Volume Two: North America, 1880–1960* (Oxford: OUP, forthcoming).
46. Alfred Kazin (1978) *New York Jew* (New York: Knopf), p. 6.
47. Ibid., p. 5.
48. For the need to reconsider Mencken's importance within the transatlantic development of literary modernism, and for some of the reasons why Mencken has been generally sidelined from such discussions, see David M. Earle (2009) *Re-Covering Modernism: Pulps, Paperbacks, and the Prejudice of Form* (Burlington: Ashgate).
49. Jim Benning (9 August 2007) 'Drexel University Launches "The Smart Set" ', http://www.worldhum.com, date accessed 11 December 2010.
50. Morgan Meis (6 November 2009) 'Noncanonical Line Reading: William Blake's "A Sunshine Holiday" ', *The Smart Set*, http://www.thesmartset.com, date accessed 11 December 2010; M. G. Piety (2 November 2009) 'Ideas: The Prose of Kierkegaard. A new translation of Søren Kierkegaard's Repetition', *The Smart Set*, http://www.thesmartset.com, date accessed 11 December 2010; Morgan Meis (7 October 2009) 'Noncanonical Peep Show: Marcel Duchamp's "Étant donnés" ', *The Smart Set*, http://thesmartset.com, date

accessed 11 December 2010; Kristen Hoggatt (26 October 2009) 'Ask a Poet: Sad Sack', *The Smart Set*, http://www.thesmartset.com, date accessed 11 December 2010; Stefany Anne Golberg (20 November 2009) 'Pertinent & Impertinent: Turducken, Meet Your Match. Vegetarian excess? Soy inside soy inside soy!', *The Smart Set*, http://www.thesmartset.com, date accessed 11 December 2010.

51. Owen Hatteras (6 August 2007) 'Pertinent and Impertinent: Letter from the Ombudsman', *The Smart Set*, http://thesmartset.com, date accessed 11 December 2010.

52. Ibid.

9
Middlebrow Authorship, Critical Authority and Autonomous Readers in Post-war America: James Gould Cozzens, Dwight Macdonald and *By Love Possessed*

Joan Shelley Rubin

Dwight Macdonald's trenchant essay 'Masscult and Midcult' (1960) is the most sweeping – and the most famous – formulation by an American of the post-war animus against middlebrow culture. Yet 'Masscult and Midcult' was not the opening shot in Macdonald's war against the pernicious products of the entertainment and publishing industries but, rather, the culminating episode in a campaign the writer had been waging for some time. By the early 1950s, Macdonald was already condemning particular works that, in his view, represented philistine assaults on art and language, including Colin Wilson's British best-seller *The Outsider*. In 1958, he issued his most inflammatory such piece, a review in *Commentary* excoriating James Gould Cozzens's widely praised novel *By Love Possessed*.[1]

More pointed and (hard as it may be to believe) more vitriolic than 'Masscult and Midcult', Macdonald's review, which he titled 'By Cozzens Possessed', is also possibly more interesting than the later essay because it provoked an equally vehement (although largely private) response from Cozzens. An inquiry into the assumptions of both parties to the discussion is especially useful in connecting the mid-century attack on middlebrow culture to the ongoing tensions surrounding the relationships among authors, readers and critics in modern America. If blogs and Amazon.com have empowered ordinary readers in the digital age, the Macdonald-Cozzens affair suggests that, along with other literary tempests in the immediate post-war period, the episode helped prepare the

way for the challenges to professional criticism that technology acceler-
ated. A look at the circumstances that shaped the novel's popularity and
at the values and reading practices that Cozzens and his public exemplified demonstrates as well how designating an author and his audience as
'middlebrow' had as much to do with literary politics and institutions
as with standards of taste. More generally, Cozzens's and Macdonald's
shared tendency to misgauge the power of the opposition is an instruc-
tive reminder that cultural authority, while it may appear entrenched,
is often precarious and always open to renegotiation on the basis of the
anxieties in play at a given historical moment.[2]

Given American academics' penchant for enshrining alienated intellectuals, Macdonald's is a far more familiar name than his adversary's.
Born in 1903, James Gould Cozzens was a graduate of the Kent School
and completed two years at Harvard before taking what turned out to be
a permanent leave of absence in 1924 in order to write fiction.[3] By the
early 1930s, Cozzens had discovered the subject that became his signa-
ture: the lives of white, middle-class men who grapple with issues of
duty to others. In 1949, he won the Pulitzer Prize for *Guard of Honor*, a
story of military discipline and race relations that Malcolm Cowley and
others called the best novel of the war.[4]

The accolades the book received heightened the expectations of both
the publishing business and the reading public when, after a nine-year
hiatus, Cozzens produced *By Love Possessed*, which appeared in September 1957. Its middle-aged hero, Arthur Winner, is an attorney in a small
city between New York and Washington. Following law school, Winner had joined the firm his father and Noah Tuttle had founded; after
Arthur Winner Sr.'s death, his son has come to regard him as the exemplary 'Man of Reason'. But the son's professional and personal life has
repeatedly drawn him into the realm of passion, where impulse, rather
than law, holds sway. In the course of the novel, Winner must assist his
prim, conscientious secretary Helen Detweiler by stepping in as coun-
sel when her brother Ralph is charged with rape. Ralph flees without
knowing that he is about to be exonerated; Helen commits suicide.
Simultaneously, Winner learns that Tuttle has embezzled money from
trust funds in order to compensate investors for their losses. Winner's
own defections from reason have involved him in an affair with the
wife of another partner in the firm, Julius Penrose. (The wife's attraction to Catholicism serves as an additional example of unreason, which
prompted numerous complaints from readers, as did Cozzens's patronizing portrayal of a Jew-turned-Episcopalian.) At the end of the book,
Cozzens positions Winner as a man caught between his allegiance to

principle and his appreciation for practical realities. Aware that allowing Tuttle's illegal practices to continue in order to square the accounts would involve him in 'a whole life of lies',[5] Winner nevertheless apparently chooses to countenance wrongdoing for the greater good, a moral compromise he has always abhorred.

The initial reviews of *By Love Possessed* were uniformly positive, albeit with some demurrals regarding Cozzens's prose style. In *The New Yorker*, Brendan Gill called the book a 'masterpiece' and 'an immense achievement'.[6] Cowley, in the *New York Times*, termed Cozzens an astute observer of 'human nature and human institutions'.[7] The book sold 170,000 copies in the first six weeks after publication. It was first on the *New York Times* best-seller list from late September 1957 to early March 1958, staying on the list for a total of 34 weeks. Hardcover sales (including Book of the Month Club distribution) reached 500,000 copies before the novel brought a record price for paperback rights. A 240-page *Reader's Digest Condensed Books* edition sold more than 3 million copies.[8] *The New Yorker* captured the instant cachet the novel acquired in a cartoon depicting one older woman remarking to another, 'I was looking forward to a few weeks of just doing nothing after Labor Day when along came James Gould Cozzens.'[9]

Macdonald's review in *Commentary* for January 1958 burst this bubble of enthusiasm. Macdonald had recently made the transition from his earlier career as political radical to a role as freelance critic, and brought to the table, so to speak, the personal anxieties attending that transition. Born in 1906, Macdonald shared Cozzens's prep school, Ivy League education and familiarity with Arthur Winner's milieu. Those commonalities make the Cozzens–Macdonald episode not a story of how class interests shape cultural hierarchy but, rather, one of competition within a fractured elite. Well before graduating from Yale in 1928, however, Macdonald had developed what his biographer, Michael Wreszin, has called his 'lifelong suspicion of wealth'.[10] In the mid-1930s, Macdonald had channelled his critique of capitalism into support for the Communist Party and, later, the Trotskyist, non-Communist left. By 1945, though, Macdonald was increasingly dismissive of Marxism. The arrival of the cold war further diminished Macdonald's prospects for effecting social change. In those circumstances, Macdonald decided to cast aside political radicalism and to concentrate on cultural matters.[11]

Macdonald's long history of insecurity about his intellectual abilities influenced how he managed the shift. Defensively, he imported into the cultural arena the role of gadfly he had played on the left and made crankiness the defining feature of his style. His need for distinctiveness and legitimacy accounts, more than anything, for the tone he brought to the Cozzens review. Yet, as formerly alienated intellectuals took up academic posts to teach the expanding university population of the 1950s, doubts about the 'hegemony' of the oppositional critic added a more general urgency to literary discussion.[12] The same winter that Macdonald's piece appeared, Geoffrey Wagner published an essay in the *American Scholar* decrying 'The Decline of Book Reviewing'. Accusing the media of failing to differentiate 'serious fiction' from 'trash' and of pandering to popular appeal, Wagner anticipated the position that Elizabeth Hardwick, writing in *Harper's* two years later, would take in her own article entitled 'The Decline of Book Reviewing'.

In 'By Cozzens Possessed', Macdonald joined that jeremiad tradition, which he inflected with his newly reconstituted hostility ('such reviews, such enthusiasm, such unanimity, such nonsense!').[13] Much of Macdonald's attack revolved around Cozzens's deficiencies as a stylist. *By Love Possessed* contained passages that were, in Macdonald's view, 'as bad as prose can get'.[14] Macdonald traced Cozzens's tin ear to his isolation from a cosmopolitan literary tradition, as well as from a vibrant intellectual community. Those long-standing problems of American writers, exacerbated by the author's reclusiveness (Cozzens lived in rural New Jersey and rarely socialized with anyone other than his wife) explained but did not excuse Cozzens's 'grotesque' effort to produce 'Literature'. In addition, Macdonald faulted Cozzens for his insensitivity to actual human behaviour and for formulaic sex scenes designed merely to sell books.[15]

These defects were less troubling to Macdonald, however, than the critical acclaim and large audience the book achieved, because both developments reflected the sorry state of American culture. The reception of Cozzens's novel, Macdonald declared in the final section of the review, was an 'episode' in what he called 'The Middlebrow Counter-Revolution'. Spurred by writings in the early 1940s of Archibald MacLeish and Van Wyck Brooks, the critics who embraced Cozzens did so, Macdonald thought, in order to strike a blow against the 'fashionable' assumption that great literature could emanate only from a modernist avant-garde. Quoting reviewers whom he saw as bent on giving Cozzens his due despite his exclusion from the community of the alienated, Macdonald sarcastically detected 'a highbrow conspiracy of paranoiac dimensions'. In reality, he argued, power lay not in the hands of the disaffected artist, whose sceptical stance was a 'luxury' the Cold War could not afford, but, rather, in the producers and consumers of middlebrow culture to whom the reviewers of *By Love*

Possessed were shamelessly pandering. For Macdonald's money, the critics who proclaimed themselves Cozzens's admirers were as guilty as Cozzens of lowering aesthetic standards and eroding the quality of American literature.[16] It may be helpful to stipulate at this point that Macdonald was right about Cozzens in several respects. Although Cozzens never employed the word 'middlebrow' himself, and while part of the purpose of this essay is to emphasize the instability of the category, Cozzens can justifiably be called a middlebrow writer because of the wide distribution of his novels to what the Book of the Month Club called 'average intelligent readers'. And, yes, the prose seems overwritten, as Cozzens later partially admitted. Moreover, Cozzens's religious prejudices cannot be denied. Though Macdonald attributed the success of *By Love Possessed* to the reviewers' 'counter-revolutionary' decision to redress the snobbery of the avant-garde, his explanation misses a host of other factors that contributed to the book's success.

Crucially, Cozzens added to and profited from the post-war vogue of the novel as magnum opus. The hefty hardcover edition of *By Love Possessed* ran close to six hundred pages. As such, it joined other lengthy best-sellers of the 1950s that announced the end of wartime paper shortages and, perhaps, the reading public's attention span before television became ubiquitous. The sheer bulk of the text suggests publishers' eagerness to capitalize on their perception that audiences equated a book's significance (or at least value received) with its size.[17] This was not a new phenomenon. But in the post-war years, the popularity of the long novel may have reflected readers' aspirations to certify themselves as beneficiaries of the ample leisure and educational advantages that middle-class affluence made possible. For authors whose view of their craft coincided with prevailing taste and economics, the form offered built-in benefits. If Hemingway's fiction had exemplified the possibility that the 'great American novel' could take shape in relatively few spare sentences, Cozzens's alternative choice invited judgements of greatness before readers even cracked the book's spine.

Cozzens's location in the New York literary world also conditioned the reception of *By Love Possessed*. His marriage in 1927 to the agent Sylvia Bernice Baumgarten, who represented the firm of Carl Brandt, gave him both access to and protection from the power of publishers and other mediators to make or break a book. Baumgarten was determined that Cozzens become a 'major writer', and used her knowledge of taste hierarchies within the publishing industry to realize that goal.[18] The fact that she was Jewish is not incidental to the story: the

1920s was precisely the period when new Jewish publishers unafraid of treating books as business propositions emerged to compete with older, genteel houses, and Baumgarten seemed to move easily between both milieus. (In addition, she was a ready-made rebuttal to accusations about Cozzens's anti-Semitism.) In the first three years of their acquaintance, Baumgarten extricated Cozzens from two contracts and moved him first to the Boni brothers' firm (a house with high culture aspirations) and then to William Morrow. In 1930, after Morrow pressured Cozzens to 'write in a more popular vein', Baumgarten placed her husband's work-in-progress, *S. S. San Pedro*, with Harcourt, Brace, thereby enhancing his status as a literary writer. *S. S. San Pedro* became the first of Cozzens's works to become a Book of the Month Club selection.[19]

For the rest of his career, Cozzens remained a Harcourt author – managed by Baumgarten. Her influence on the reception of *By Love Possessed* resulted not only from the cumulative effect of her efforts to position Cozzens as a 'major writer', but also from her direct intervention in the distribution of the novel. Because the Book of the Month Club's failure to choose *Guard of Honor* as a 'main selection' had so distressed Cozzens, when his next manuscript was ready for Club evaluation Baumgarten traded on her Brandt & Brandt connections to smooth the way: through Carol Brandt, she asked Club judge John Marquand (Brandt's lover) to identify in advance passages that might have to be altered to make the work acceptable to the entire Club board. Marquand found no such obstacles and *By Love Possessed* became the 'book-of-the-month' for September 1957. By 1959, the Club had mailed out 270,000 copies.[20] At the same time, Baumgarten apparently did not hesitate to let Cozzens take advantage of other distribution opportunities that, while they risked marking him as popular, as opposed to middlebrow, offered financial benefits too lucrative to pass up. Presumably she was involved in Harcourt's $100,000 sale of *By Love Possessed* to *Reader's Digest Condensed Books*. In 1958, Leona Nevler, a Fawcett/Crest editor keen to exploit the potential of the burgeoning paperback industry, bought the book as a mass-market – rather than a trade title for the record price of $101,505.[21]

For all of his reclusive tendencies, Cozzens's appreciation for – or at least his acquiescence in – the mechanisms of publicity likewise operated to shape critics' and readers' reactions. The week the novel was published, *Time* carried a cover story about Cozzens. The story depicted Cozzens as 'classical, dry, cerebral' and deeply inimical to sentimentality, concluding: 'An unstinting professional, he has never written a shoddy line or truckled to popular fancies or cliquish fads.' That judgement, with its implicit pitch to readers who thought of themselves as superior to consumers of best-sellers, arguably offset the liability to Cozzens's reputation for seriousness that appearing on the cover of a mass-market magazine could pose. Cozzens and Baumgarten nevertheless considered the article a disaster because Serrell Hillman had given the writer of the piece his notes of Cozzens's ironic 'jokes' about women, Jews and blacks – remarks the writer then quoted. Yet the celebrity *Time* conferred accounted for the sale of 'thousands of copies' of *By Love Possessed* and contributed to the need for three re-printings, at 50,000 books apiece, during September 1957.[22]

The other source of publicity for the novel was the almost unprecedented advertising campaign Harcourt, Brace mounted in collaboration with the firm of Franklin Spier. The 'heavy advertising program' for *By Love Possessed* consisted of unusually early and extensive pre-publication activity. As a result, 'upon publication', Harcourt's director of publicity, Julian Muller, reported, 'the book commanded the top review spot in practically every important publication in the nation'. What is more, Harcourt anticipated the success of the campaign by printing enough copies to satisfy the initial demand. Then came a barrage of articles and advertisements in newspapers, including a centrefold in the *New York Times Book Review* the Sunday following publication. As *By Love Possessed* climbed to the top of the best-seller list, the publisher placed ads in newspapers throughout the country calling attention to the novel's popularity. The campaign – in the press and through mail to booksellers – continued until the end of the year.[23]

Cozzens's sensitivity to the implications of formal choices, his network of personal connections, Baumgarten's astute negotiation of the basis on which readers encountered him and the access to publicity such negotiation facilitated all operated to create the positive reception of *By Love Possessed*. But Baumgarten's role also enabled Cozzens to stake out a position above the market that, paradoxically, contributed as well to his commercial success. His self-conception depended on distancing himself from the institutions of American literary culture that conferred authorial stature. Upon winning the Pulitzer Prize for *Guard of Honor*, Cozzens wrote to his mother that he 'certainly had it fixed in my mind that the fiction award was contemptible', because it typically went to 'pseudo-serious tripe'; his consolation came in Baumgarten's observation (as Cozzens put it) that the selection committee 'gave me free in the boob market perhaps half a million dollars worth of advertising'.[24] In 1960, Malcolm Cowley accepted the Howells Medal (which honoured *By Love Possessed* as the best work in American fiction published during the previous five years) from the American Academy of Arts and Letters on the author's behalf, Cozzens having decided not to attend the ceremony. He also refused to serve on juries for the National Book Award and the Harper Prize Novel Contest. His official reason for declining, which he offered in turning down invitations to teach and lecture as well, was that he was out of step with prevailing critical standards. Moreover, Matthew Bruccoli has explained, Cozzens was 'utterly contemptuous of the literary life of self-promotion and reciprocal back-scratching'.[25] Yet Cozzens coupled those aesthetic and moral objections with a pervasive desire to achieve the distinction of unpopularity. 'I confess I've always held a snide view of prizes and medals as mostly meaningless and often insulting,' he wrote to John Fischer of *Harper's* in the wake of the Howells Medal. In that respect, Cozzens conforms perfectly to the figures James English has discussed in *The Economy of Prestige* who, 'linking autonomy with truth', enhance their status within high culture precisely by disdaining the tokens of literary achievement devised to signify that location.[26]

Along with 'boobs' edition', which Cozzens used to describe the *Reader's Digest Condensed* version of *By Love Possessed*, the phrase 'boob market' suggests as well Cozzens's fraught relationship with the readers who made him a best-selling author. As Cozzens told several correspondents, the sales of the book had gotten 'out of hand' by late 1957, motivating perhaps 'tens of thousands' of 'people who would never normally think of trying to read a book of mine' to buy it. Although, on some occasions, Cozzens refuted directly the charges of obscurity, intolerance and obscenity that *By Love Possessed* provoked, the idea that he had only written the book for the limited number of readers who could understand him became his stock reply to much of the fan mail he received – flattering the intelligence and bolstering the support of his admirers in the process.[27]

Finally, Cozzens embraced high culture in his own aesthetic standards. His notebooks are replete with comments chastising writers for 'shoddiness', falsity and failure to respect the nuances of language. 'There's an apparent feeling', he complained in 1963 about a new novel by Hortense Calisher, 'that exactness is narrow and confining and truth and life can't be fitted into it. There is a resulting resort to similie [sic] and generalization. Naturally, I think they [Calisher and likeminded writers] couldn't be more mistaken.'[28] Cozzens's devotion to clarity and precision extended to non-fiction: recording his opinion of Frank Harris's memoir, he averred, 'There's a false-sounding turn of phrase here, an unconvincing detail there.'[29] Cozzens's small pantheon of figures to emulate consisted of Somerset Maugham, John O'Hara and certain inspirations from the past: Milton, Pope, Shakespeare and Thoreau.[30]

It is easy to recognize in Cozzens's judgements the same criteria that Macdonald invoked in assailing *By Love Possessed*. To be sure, Macdonald championed avant-garde experimentation while Cozzens repudiated it.[31] Yet Cozzens's pronouncements mirrored those of his adversary in their modernist allegiance to the quest for a language adequate to represent reality, their rejection of what Cozzens identified as 'sentimentality'[32] and their presumption that great literature entailed difficulty. In both its slightly mocking tone and its content, Cozzens's missive to the head of the Guggenheim Foundation in 1950 could be mistaken for a pronouncement by Macdonald: 'I think our writing age – that is, our so-called Serious Writing and nearly all our more talented writers – is infected beyond precedent with a poison of sentimentality; with [...] childish thinking and cheap feeling.' Similarly, Cozzens declared in 1962, 'It seems impossible to write a book so bad that quite a few reviewers won't say it's good' – a sentence Macdonald might have penned four years earlier.[33]

In light of that shared sensibility, Macdonald's famous epithet in 'Masscult and Midcult' that middlebrow culture 'pretends to respect the values of High Culture while it waters them down and vulgarizes them' – a statement which itself reflects a preoccupation with falsity – seems off the mark, if the measure is authorial intention. While Cozzens's appeals to a status-hungry public align him with Macdonald's portrait of the middlebrow as a bogus highbrow, as a writer and reader Cozzens's high culture commitments were genuine. Instead, Cozzens may be said to have mastered the institutions of middlebrow culture while dissociating himself from some of their consequences. This adroit balance explains more fully than marketing savvy alone reviewers' receptivity to *By Love Possessed*. Yet Cozzens's effort to achieve distance from the 'boob market' by affirming his investment in textual difficulty and the representation of reality must have made the sting of Macdonald's attack all the more painful. By the same token, for Macdonald the fact that his and Cozzens's aesthetic criteria might be confused with one another (although he regarded Cozzens as 'pretending') was among the most galling aspects of the novel's success.

Cozzens retaliated against Macdonald's *Commentary* review in terms that reveal additional common ground between the two antagonists, while illuminating some of the larger social tensions that attended his 'middle' location. The most troubling form of Cozzens's response (although it has its ridiculous side) is his depiction of himself as the victim of Jews. In journal entries from the 1960s, he repeatedly mustered that image, referring to 'that spew-out of Jewish fury that *By Love Possessed* provoked',[34] the 'venomous hatchet jobs the Jewish critics gave me',[35] the 'jew-boy line about me',[36] 'my poor Jew-Boys[,] and even perhaps that poorest of those poor [...], Dwight Macdonald'.[37] In Cozzens's view, the affiliation of *Commentary* with the American Jewish Committee made Macdonald's review a Jewish attack. Jews were reprehensible, he indicated, because of their ideas: they were 'liberals' given to sentimentality in art and politics. But they were also pernicious because they enjoyed control over the 'little magazine' and the New York literary scene.[38]

Cozzens's 'spew-out' of anti-Jewish 'fury' was not entirely paranoid: most New York intellectuals *were* Jews and had promoted socialism and modernism in the pages of the influential *Partisan Review*; by the 1950s, Jewish intellectuals were enjoying an increasingly central role at magazines such as *The New Yorker*. Yet calling Macdonald and his other opponents Jews was ironic on several levels. Of course, Macdonald was not only not Jewish but, especially early in his life, given to anti-Semitic remarks of his own. Secondly and more importantly, as a white Anglo-Saxon Protestant, Cozzens was a member of what was, at mid-century, still the most powerful social group in the United States and had gained access to authorship in part because of the opportunities thus afforded him. Yet (for all his self-imposed isolation) he experienced the blow to his literary reputation as a form of social exclusion. Cozzens's response reversed the traditional motif of the Jew as outsider, underscoring his felt status as unwilling exile. But, paradoxically, from Cozzens's standpoint, reducing his critics to 'Jews' also accomplished a number of retaliatory moves: the label marked Macdonald and his ilk as his social inferiors, as arrivistes, as individuals who held erroneous beliefs, and as figures whose judgements, rooted as they were in clannishness, need not be taken seriously as literary commentary.[39]

It should be noted that 'Jew' was not the only reference to presumptive inferiors with which Cozzens tagged his detractors, and that Macdonald joined him in additional variants of this unsavoury strategy. Like other writers of the period, including John Ciardi and Bernard DeVoto, Cozzens employed a variety of misogynistic tough talk that certified him as masculine. For example, when Serrell Hillman reported to him that a woman interviewed for the *Time* article had said Cozzens 'used to look like an Aubrey Beardsley drawing', Cozzens replied that she 'used to look like a cow in skirts'. Truculence was one of his trademarks: after recording in his journal that the novelist Terry Southern had called Arthur Winner a 'copy' rather than an 'original' character, Cozzens spouted, 'Look, Stupid. It's a copy, all right. [...] The copy is from life.' That stance – the novelist as streetfighter – bespeaks the struggle of mid-twentieth-century American men to differentiate themselves from what they understood as the feminizing consequences of both mass and elite culture.[40] During the Macdonald imbroglio, Cozzens was quick to adopt the specifically literary version of that attack; he repeatedly called Macdonald and his circle 'critical queers' or 'literary queers, the critical odd-balls, the pretentious pseudointellectuals and cockeyed communists'. In so doing, he buttressed his own status as a real man.[41]

But gender categories furnished ammunition to Macdonald as well. In his *Commentary* review, after referring to *The New Yorker* cartoon, he wrote with characteristic acerbity, 'How do those matrons cope with it, I wonder. Perhaps their very innocence in literary matters is a help – an Australian aboriginal would probably find *Riders of the Purple Sage* as hard to read as *The Golden Bowl.*'[42] That comment, which implicated Macdonald as much as Cozzens in misogyny, cast aspersions on Cozzens's masculinity by imagining the consumers of middlebrow culture as an audience of ignorant, unsophisticated women. Furthermore, Macdonald's determination to set himself up as a no-holds-barred cultural critic (a 'world-class demolition expert'[43]) has a masculinist flavour. The biggest tip-off to Macdonald's equation of Cozzens's deficiencies with failures of manhood, however, is his insistence on calling Winner both a 'prig' and a 'brute' – the latter quality epitomized in Cozzens's misguided 'idea of manly straight-from the shoulder talk'. Macdonald deserves some credit for his observation that Cozzens created male characters who treat women badly, yet his intimation that Cozzens misunderstood true masculine behaviour – that he, on the other hand, has gotten masculinity right – implicates Macdonald in the same anxiety about encroaching emasculation that Cozzens displayed.[44]

Cozzens's and Macdonald's reduction of each other to a subordinate social category – Jew, queer, feminized 'middlebrow' – exposes the struggle for power at the core of their dispute. That point is even clearer with respect to an additional marker of inferiority both writers invoked – the designation 'child' – because the post-war discourse about the nature of adulthood allowed for consolidating power over readers as well as critics. One locus of this discourse is H. A. Overstreet's *The Mature Mind* (1949). True (one might say real) adults, Overstreet explained, readily assumed responsibility for their actions, accepted the necessity of work, exhibited self-discipline, engaged in a long-term heterosexual relationship and exhibited a capacity for empathy. Behaviour that ill-served either the individual or society was not so much 'bad' or 'ignorant' as 'immature'.[45] Why this outlook (and a related preoccupation with innocence) assumed such significance in the post-war era is a matter for speculation: lingering questions about moral responsibilities in wartime and a spate of cold war anxieties come to mind. In any event, as Americans in the 1950s confronted youthful rebellion, whether in the form of juvenile delinquency or Beat poetry, insisting that people act like adults became a stock prescription for maintaining social order.[46]

Both Macdonald and Cozzens were caught up in those concerns. Macdonald had wrestled with questions of personal and collective obligation during the Second World War, but in 1953, reworking his 'Theory of Popular Culture', he applied the vocabulary of maturity to cultural critique. One result of *kitsch*, he argued, was that it created 'adultised children and infantile adults' – the latter 'unable to cope with the strains and complexities of modern life'. At the conclusion of his *By Love Possessed* review, Macdonald faulted Cozzens for contributing to that problem by conflating adulthood with the 'wholesale acceptance' of the status quo.[47]

Macdonald's reliance on the discourse of maturity to deprecate *By Love Possessed* anticipated Cozzens's rejoinder in the same terms. The opposition between childish and adult qualities had been part of Cozzens's aesthetic for a long time ('childish sentimentality'). The imperative to weigh passion against reason can be read as an alternate formulation of the responsibility to delay gratification. In that respect, adulthood was what *By Love Possessed* was *about*. Furthermore, the contributors to the book's marketing campaign seemed to recognize the sales potential of that theme. The headline for Clifton Fadiman's report in the Book of the Month Club *News* declared, 'The maturest and most readable piece of American fiction we have been privileged to offer our membership for many years.' Harcourt's two-page advertising spread quoted Fadiman's text: 'A grown-up novel by a grown-up man for a grown-up audience.' In part, that strategy was a way to signal, and to legitimate, the steamy sex in the book. But it also embellished Cozzens's persona as a serious writer, while potentially wooing readers eager to allay their fears about whether they were adult enough to cope with ethical dilemmas in their own lives.[48]

Thus, for Cozzens, the vocabulary of adulthood was readily at hand in the aftermath of the *Commentary* article. In the only direct reply Cozzens made to Macdonald, a letter of 5 March 1958, he exclaimed that 'your imperceptiveness is, for an educated adult, quite remarkable. Which, I suppose, is why the stylistic claptrap, the crypto-sentimentality, and the just plain childishness in so many of the books you indicate you admire can seem to you better "art" than a Somerset Maugham's lucid thinking and perfect writing.'[49] But the greater utility of the adult-hood defence was in structuring Cozzens's view of his audience. As he explained to a Berkeley student, 'I make many demands on my reader. He is expected, first of all, to be grown up. He is expected to have seen something of life and men. [...] He is expected to have read a good deal. He is also expected to pay close attention. Those who can't or won't meet such demands aren't going to be able to follow me.'[50] Adult readers, as Cozzens envisioned them, could handle the novel's sexual explicitness and occasional profanity. If they encountered a word they did not understand, they had the patience to look it up, thereby negating Macdonald's complaint about Cozzens's esoteric lan-guage. Most important, they possessed the competences (to use Richard Brodhead's term) to comprehend works of fiction without depending on the interventions of critics.[51]

Cozzens linked that construct to his rejection of certain elements of modernism: in the absence of what he called 'the literary rubbish of symbolism, of "levels of meaning"', interpretation became super-fluous. Somerset Maugham provided a case in point: 'The thing most held against Maugham,' Cozzens insisted, 'is obviously that he made critics and criticism unnecessary. [...] Any adult reader takes his mean-ings at a glance: he writes to be instantly understood.' But Cozzens's champion Bernard DeVoto had applied the same observation to Cozzens himself. Critics 'avoid Cozzens,' DeVoto averred, 'because his novels are so carefully written 'that they leave criticism practically nothing to do'. Stripping critics of their function as mediators concentrated power in authors, who need not fear that a third party would remove readers from their influence by distorting or misrepresenting their work. In this liter-ary utopia, recognizing that it could grasp the message and artistry of a text unaided led the audience, which was smarter than the critical estab-lishment, towards a heightened appreciation of the author's command over simple truth. At the same time, Cozzens made personal responsi-bility and self-discipline as germane to the act of reading as they were to love and work.[52]

While it is possible – even likely – that the correspondents who wrote to Cozzens to praise *By Love Possessed* chose the book on the basis of reviews, as readers some of them comported with Cozzens's fantasy. The most striking feature of their encounters with the novel is the extent of re-reading in which they engaged. 'I had to read it slowly and reread parts to grasp it,' a Brooklyn woman remarked, 'and it truly was an experience I wouldn't have wanted to miss.'[53] Another woman, who described herself as not a college graduate, reported, 'I got up at four – the moon was so bright and I had slept my six hours – When I finished your book I kept going back to the beginning to read this or that and I found myself reading the book over again.'[54] A 64-year-old Pennsylvania woman wrote in 1959 to tell Cozzens she had read part of the book four times. Those individuals made clear that re-reading furnished pleasure, but they also willingly shouldered the obligation to read closely, with an eye to literary craft, in order to discern the author's meaning.[55]

Furthermore, like Cozzens himself, his correspondents repeatedly invoked lack of 'falsity' as a key aesthetic standard: 'One can envy not only your mastery of the language and the extent of your erudition, but also the skilful, penetrating delineation of characters and philosophies, so that, although [...] one is more or less continually conscious of the fact that he is reading a novel put together by a master craftsman, the printed people none-the-less [sic] come vividly and stingingly alive.'[56] A Minnesota woman who read *By Love Possessed* in the condensed format wrote, 'I was deeply touched with respect for an author who seemed to have such an understanding of people. All of the characters were so REAL – so genuine I felt I knew them.'[57] Such individuals were also actively engaged in reshaping the text: as a Colorado man put it, 'You have given us another 500-odd pages to be written in our own minds, out of our own experiences, and that's another mark of greatness.'[58]

These disciplined, patient, standard-conscious, active readers, while only a segment of Cozzens's audience, may be considered middlebrow ('I am not a scholar,' the Minnesota woman stated). The individuals who chose the condensed format, one might argue, exhibited a lack of seriousness or respect for the author. Yet, in terms of their approach to the page, Cozzens's 'plodding' readers (as the Minnesotan described herself) read in a high culture way: or, rather, there was no distinction between the way they read and what the proponents of high culture valued. As Cozzens rightly intuited, their autonomy, coupled with the homage their letters paid to authorial skill, were a central aspect of the threat the 'Middlebrow Counter-Revolution' posed for Macdonald. To be sure, Macdonald's imagined middlebrow reader was sometimes a passive figure; what made the reviewers and advertisers who had commended Cozzens so dangerous was that the 'matrons' were all too ready to follow their advice. Yet Macdonald was equally worried about readers who exercised their own power rather than deferring to critical expertise.[59]

In 'Masscult and Midcult', he asserted that 'the demands of the audience, which has changed from a small body of connoisseurs into a large body of ignoramuses, have become the chief criteria of success'.[60] Macdonald's position was inherently contradictory: he claimed, at the end of 'MassCult and MidCult', to want 'an audience that can appreciate and discriminate on its own,' but only if it were 'sophisticated' enough to listen to him; his famous prescription 'So let the masses have their Masscult, let the few who care about good writing [...] have their High culture, and don't fuzz up the distinction with Midcult' represented a denial that the critic had a responsibility to 'raise the level of our culture in general'. Be that as it may, the shared competition for readers animating the reception of *By Love Possessed* suggests that, for Macdonald, 'the scandal of the middlebrow' was the diametric opposite of the phenomenon Janice Radway identified in characterizing the controversy surrounding the Book of the Month Club in the late 1920s. The observers who impugned the Club, Radway showed, did so because the creation of a Board of Judges who picked the 'best' books destroyed the myth that great literature emerged in the unmediated exercise of taste. Here the 'scandal' was the prospect that the autonomous middlebrow public, grown confident as the post-war expansion of higher education proceeded apace, would make an alliance with the author alone, bypassing the critic entirely. And here, again, was irony: Cozzens, the denouncer of liberalism, articulated a populist vision of the reader–author relationship rooted in a democratic 'right' to 'Culture', while Macdonald, the old socialist, reaffirmed cultural hierarchy.[61]

Yet there is the final commonality that both Macdonald and Cozzens tended to project onto the other greater power than their antagonist actually experienced, and that, conversely, 'By Cozzens Possessed' and the novel that prompted it are elegies for eras that each writer sensed was passing. Macdonald was transparent in this regard. In his 'Theory of Mass Culture' (1953), Macdonald had declared 'the Avantgarde is now dying'; in the Cozzens piece, he repeated the point and implicated middlebrow critics in its demise. By the 1960s, the context for Macdonald's vigil at the bedside of high culture included not only lamentations about the 'decline of book reviewing' but also increasingly frequent pronouncements about the 'death of the novel'.[62] At the same time, Macdonald was himself bridging high and popular culture by writing film criticism for *Esquire*. Thus, for all the energy he put into classification, when Macdonald finally refined his analyses of the 1950s in 'Masscult and Midcult' his intervention was not so much about establishing cultural hierarchies as about memorializing them.[63]

As for Cozzens, his protagonist would prefer to stop the antique French clock featured in the book so that he and his colleagues could go through their routines – days in office and courtroom, evenings at their lakeside summer homes – in charge of their environments, buoyed by the prestige and assurance to which their social class ostensibly entitles them.[64] Tellingly, in Winner's surroundings, American mass culture almost never intrudes. But change is on the way, and Winner knows it. The revelation of Noah Tuttle's embezzlement is, for Winner, merely the most tangible evidence that the ground is shifting underfoot. In the end, however, all that Winner can do is to carry on as an adult, to assume the burden of painful knowledge that he must shoulder indefinitely.[65] For this reason, Macdonald disapprovingly called *By Love Possessed* a 'Novel of Resignation'.[66]

And Cozzens's own position was shifting. In 1963, when *Esquire*'s cheeky 'Structure of the American Literary Establishment, with Shaded Heraldic Tree' placed him well outside the 'red hot center', Cozzens protested to the chart's author, L. Rust Hills, 'Granted I'm not really out; but still this is outrageous'. Yet Cozzens's complaint amounted to wishful thinking. His diminished position cannot be attributed to Macdonald's attack alone. Probable alcoholism, depression and a serious car accident in 1971 also contributed to Cozzens's decline, while his increasing identification with conservatives as the 1960s wore on made him decidedly unfashionable. Yet Macdonald's critique did irrevocable damage to Cozzens's stature (as he and others perceived it) because Macdonald so effectively used Cozzens's own values against him, while striking a tone and pose that masked the two antagonists' shared convictions. Within a few years of *By Love Possessed* he had become what Bruccoli called 'America's best unread novelist'. He died, bitter and obscure, in 1978.[67]

As several observers have pointed out, since the 1960s the real threat to high art has come not from a 'Middlebrow Counter-Revolution' but, rather, from mass culture and postmodern relativism. ('Masscult, midcult – who cares anymore?', James Wolcott wrote in a recent essay on Macdonald, who died in 1988. 'It's all one big postmodern mishmash.') If a long novel like *By Love Possessed* became a best-seller in part because of the promotional techniques the marketplace rewarded, at least it found a large audience, whereas today most Americans are reading fewer books of any size. But mass culture has cut both ways, creating new opportunities for the remaining middlebrow public to achieve the autonomy Cozzens's democratic fantasy sanctioned. As Rachel Donadio concluded in a recent essay on 1958 that discussed the *By Love Possessed* episode, 'In today's blog-crazy culture, everyone's a critic. What would Dwight Macdonald say?'

Still, one need not fall completely into Cozzens's and Macdonald's elegiac pose. The investigations of canon formation over the last several decades, although sometimes misguided in positing a unitary taste-making 'elite', have thoroughly undermined the fixity of what counts as high culture. The task is now to bring an awareness of the provisional nature of cultural authority, the impact of material conditions, the mediations of institutions and individuals and the responses of readers to the entire range of literary production, including the post-war American middlebrow, so that the historical factors that gave works such as *By Love Possessed* their status and significance come fully into view.[68]

Notes

*A fuller version of this essay appeared in *Modern Intellectual History*, 7 (2010). Excerpts are reprinted by permission of Cambridge University Press.

1. D. Macdonald (Spring 1960) 'Masscult and Midcult, I', *Partisan Review* 27, 203–233 and (Fall 1960) 'Masscult and Midcult: II', *Partisan Review* 27: 589–631, reprinted in Macdonald (1962) *Against the American Grain: Essays on the Effects of Mass Culture* (New York), pp. 3–75; M. Wreszin (1994) *A Rebel in Defense of Tradition: The Life and Politics of Dwight Macdonald* (New York), pp. 284–287; D. Macdonald (January 1958) 'By Cozzens Possessed', *Commentary*, reprinted in *Against the American Grain*, pp. 187–212. Citations to 'Masscult and Midcult' and 'By Cozzens Possessed' are to the reprinted versions.
2. Other contributory episodes include the 1949 Bollingen Prize controversy and John Ciardi's attack on Anne Morrow Lindbergh's poetry. I have written about the latter in 'The Genteel Tradition at Large', *Raritan*, Winter 2006, 70–91. David D. Hall underscored the point about continual renegotiation in 'Between Cultural History and Book Trades History: A Necessary Awkwardness?', presented at the Society for the History of Authorship, Reading, and Publishing 2009 annual meeting.
3. M. J. Bruccoli (1983) *James Gould Cozzens: A Life Apart* (New York: Harcourt Brace Jovanovich).
4. A. Kazin (1973) *Bright Book of Life: American Novelists and Storytellers from Hemingway to Mailer* (Boston), pp. 97, 102; M. Cowley (August 1957) 'The World of Arthur Winner, Jr.: Amid Neighbors Swayed by Passion He Tries to be the Man of Reason', *New York Times Book Review*, 25, 1.
5. J. G. Cozzens (1957) *By Love Possessed* (New York: Harcourt Brace), p. 562.
6. B. Gill (24 August 1957) 'Summa cum Laude', *The New Yorker*, 106.
7. Cowley, 'World of Arthur Winner Jr', 1. Other reviews are reprinted in *James Gould Cozzens: A Documentary Volume, Dictionary of Literary Biography* 294, ed. M. J. Bruccoli (Gale, 2004), pp. 292–313. Hereafter *DLB*.

8. Sales data are from Macdonald, 'By Cozzens Possessed', p. 187; *DLB*, p. 257 and Bruccoli, *A Life Apart*, p. 221.
9. The cartoon is reprinted in *DLB*, p. 301.
10. Wreszin, p. 4.
11. Ibid., pp. 62, 106, 143.
12. G. Cotkin (2003) *Existential America* (Baltimore), p. 120.
13. Macdonald, 'By Cozzens Possessed', p. 188.
14. Ibid., p. 201.
15. D. Macdonald (February 1958) response to A. Yarmolinsky, *Commentary*, 164; Macdonald, 'By Cozzens Possessed', pp. 195, 199–205.
16. Ibid., pp. 208–209.
17. Thus, for example, an advertisement for Jessamyn West's *South of the Angels* (Harcourt, Brace, 1960), which highlighted the work's 564 pages, credited West for devising 'a story worth every page of its telling'. *New York Times Book Review*, 17 April 1960, 13.
18. Bruccoli, *A Life Apart*, p. 89.
19. Ibid., pp. 93, 101.
20. John Marquand to Sylvia Bernice Baumgarten, 22 March 1957, Box 7, James Gould Cozzens Papers, Princeton University Library, Princeton, NJ. Hereafter cited as Cozzens Papers. Quotations from the Cozzens Papers are used by permission of the President and Fellows of Harvard College and the Princeton University Library. See also Bruccoli, *A Life Apart*, p. 221.
21. J. Tebbel (1981) *A History of Book Publishing in the United States, IV: The Great Change*, 1940–1980 (New York: Bowker), p. 388.
22. 'The Hermit of Lambertville', *Time*, 2 September 1957, pp. 72–78; Bruccoli, *A Life Apart*, pp. 215, 218.
23. Carl Spielvogel, 'Advertising: How They Sold a Best Seller: Why Harcourt Won't Turn to Making Sausages', *New York Times*, 20 October 1957, F10; *New York Times Book Review*, 8 September 1957, BR 11 and 12 September 1957, BR23.
24. *DLB*, p. 233.
25. Bruccoli, *A Life Apart*, pp. 189, 201.
26. James Gould Cozzens to John Fischer, 28 March 1960, Box 23, Cozzens Papers; J. English (2005) *The Economy of Prestige: Prizes, Awards, and the Circulation of Cultural Value* (Cambridge, MA: Harvard University Press), p. 220.
27. James Gould Cozzens to Shirley Covington, 23 November 1957, Box 7, Cozzens Papers; James Gould Cozzens to Buss Hall, 14 May 1958, Box 7, Cozzens Papers; James Gould Cozzens to Ben Heller, 9 January 1957, Box 7, Cozzens Papers. Apparently Cozzens did not save most of the negative letters.
28. J. G. Cozzens (1984) *Selected Notebooks 1960–1967*, ed. M. J. Bruccoli (Columbia, SC: Bruccoli-Clark), p. 56.
29. Ibid., pp. 73–74.
30. Ibid., pp. 73, 81, 83, 90.
31. Cozzens, *Notebooks*, p. 1.
32. Ibid., p. 52.
33. James Gould Cozzens to Henry Allen Moe, 22 April 1959, Box 26, Cozzens Papers; Cozzens, *Notebooks*, p. 29. On modernist commitments to the

representation of reality, see M. Orvell (1989) *The Real Thing: Imitation and Authenticity in American Culture, 1880–1940* (Chapel Hill: The University of North Carolina Press), p. 245.

34. Cozzens, *Notebooks*, p. 33.
35. Ibid., p. 63.
36. Ibid., p. 69.
37. Ibid., p. 78.
38. Ibid., pp. 17–18, 52–3.
39. Ibid., pp. 9–10; A. Bloom (1986) *Prodigal Sons: The New York Intellectuals and Their World* (New York: Oxford University Press), pp. 310–311; Wrezin, pp. 10–11, 228–32.
40. James Gould Cozzens to Serrell Hillman, c. 1 July 1957, Box 24, Cozzens Papers; J. Gilbert (2005) *Men in the Middle: Searching for Masculinity in the 1950s* (Chicago: University of Chicago Press), p. 191; Cozzens, *Notebooks*, p. 5.
41. Cozzens, *Notebooks*, pp. 36, 68.
42. Macdonald, 'By Cozzens Possessed', p. 188.
43. Wreszin, p. 275.
44. Macdonald, 'By Cozzens Possessed', p. 193.
45. H. A. Overstreet (1949) *The Mature Mind* (New York: W. W. Norton), pp. 42–75, 82, 122.
46. R. Donadio (11 May 2008) '1958: The War of the Intellectuals', *New York Times Book Review*, 39.
47. D. Macdonald (Summer 1953) 'A Theory of Mass Culture', *Diogenes* I: 3, 9–10; Macdonald, 'By Cozzens Possessed', p. 211.
48. C. Fadiman, 'BOMC Report', *Book of the Month Club News*, August 1957, 2–3; advertisement, *New York Times Book Review*, 8 September 1957.
49. *DLB*, pp. 316–317.
50. James Gould Cozzens to David Kiel, 14 June 1960, Box 7, Cozzens Papers.
51. R. Brodhead (1993) *Cultures of Letters: Scenes of Reading and Writing in Nineteenth-Century America* (Chicago: The University of Chicago Press), p. 113.
52. Cozzens, *Notebooks*, p. 16; B. DeVoto, 'The Easy Chair', *Harper's*, February 1949, p. 72.
53. Mrs. H. H. Hoenigsberg to James Gould Cozzens, 16 September 1957, Box 7, Cozzens Papers.
54. Karen Lindsay to James Gould Cozzens, 7 February 1958, Box 7, Cozzens Papers.
55. Emilie Case to James Gould Cozzens, 30 September 1959, Box 7, Cozzens Papers.
56. Orlando K. Cellucci to James Gould Cozzens, 17 June 1958, Box 7, Cozzens Papers.
57. Barbara Blanchard to James Gould Cozzens, 30 December 1957, Box 7, Cozzens Papers.
58. Tom Burnam to James Gould Cozzens, 28 October 1957, Box 7, Cozzens Papers.
59. Macdonald, 'By Cozzens Possessed', p. 196.
60. Macdonald, 'Masscult and Midcult', pp. 18–19.

61. Macdonald, 'Masscult and Midcult', p. 73; J. Radway (1997) *A Feeling for Books: The Book-of-the-Month Club, Literary Taste, and Middle-Class Desire* (Chapel Hill: The University of North Carolina Press), pp. 221–260.

62. Macdonald, 'A Theory of Mass Culture', 15; G. Hutner (2009) *What America Read: Taste, Class, and the Novel, 1920–1960* (Chapel Hill: The University of North Carolina Press), p. 312.

63. Wreszin, p. 361.

64. Cozzens, *By Love Possessed*, pp. 69, 190, 362.

65. Gill, 'Summa cum Laude', p. 109.

66. Macdonald, 'By Cozzens Possessed', p. 210.

67. L. R. Hills, 'Structure of the American Literary Establishment, with Shaded Heraldic Tree', *Esquire*, July, 1963, 41–43; James Gould Cozzens to L. Rust Hills, nd, Box 24, Cozzens Papers; Bruccoli, *A Life Apart*, p. 242.

68. J. Wolcott, 'Dwight Macdonald at 100', *New York Times Book Review*, 16 April 2006, F27; Donadio, '1958', 39. British scholars, notably John Baxendale, whose unpublished paper on J. B. Priestley delivered at the Society for the History of Authorship, Reading, and Publishing 2009 annual meeting, has influenced this essay, are starting to carry out this task for interwar Britain; see J. Baxendale (2007), *Priestley's England: J. B. Priestley and English Culture* (Manchester: Manchester University Press). Hutner's attention in *What America Read* (2009) to the expectations that critics brought to 'middle-class' fiction between 1920 and 1960 is also very useful.

Part III
Categorization and Valuation

10
The Returning Reader: Canadian Serial Fiction and Mazo de la Roche's Jalna Novels

Candida Rifkind

There is still much work to be done on the dynamics of middlebrow fiction in English-Canadian literature, especially that from the early twentieth century. The majority of studies focus on either popular or modernist fiction, pointing out the often-blurred line between these two positions in the English-Canadian field of cultural production. Landmark studies of women writers include Carole Gerson's work, Clarence Karr's *Authors and Audiences: Popular Fiction in the Early Twentieth Century* (2000) and Glenn Willmott's *Unreal Country: Modernity in the Canadian Novel in English* (2002).[1] Such discussions of highbrow aspirations and popular achievements in the Canadian fiction market tend to neglect the mediating term, 'the middlebrow'. Examination of the use of this term in a Canadian context provokes debate about distinctions of taste, the dynamics of gender, real and imagined audiences, popular and critical reception, ephemeral celebrity and canonical endurance. I propose that one starting point for an investigation of the middlebrow as a distinct phenomenon in Canadian literature is serial fiction from the first half of the twentieth century, more specifically from the modern period that spans 1920–1960. Recent British and American studies of the middlebrow open up a conceptual terrain for the study of Canadian serial fiction from this period that understands it as part of an international phenomenon with its own peculiar national inflections. There are many best-selling series from the modern period produced by Canadian authors, and still others set in Canada yet produced elsewhere. Here I focus on the Jalna series by Mazo de la Roche as an example in Canadian literature of the ways in which serial fiction is part of Canadian middlebrow culture. There are 16 novels in the Jalna series, published from 1927 to 1960, which follow the fortunes of the

Whiteoak family and their eponymous rural Ontario estate over a 100-year period.[2] These novels can best be understood as a family saga in the genre of domestic melodrama, and they are serial in the sense that the Whiteoaks and their house, Jalna, remain the central organizing function of the larger genealogy to which each book contributes.

Although some book historians parse the distinctions between serial, sequel and sequential novels quite closely, I share Laurie Langbauer's view that we can use the term 'serial fiction' with deliberate looseness to mean 'quite simply successive novels or stories that are linked together, usually by recurrent characters or settings'.[3] These novels are generally self-contained – they achieve narrative closure – but they can also be read as a set with a central organizing feature, such as the house of Jalna that grounds every one of de la Roche's novels, over the course of which there is either chronological extension or some spatial expansion.[4] One reason serial fiction has languished in critical obscurity is that it appears to be, in Pierre Bourdieu's terms, an interested and industrial format motivated by profit realized through the repetition of an original market success. Terry Castle labels the inaugural book of a series the 'charismatic text', arguing that sequels generally disappoint readers because they cannot reproduce the extraordinary qualities of the first book. Numerous scholars have problematized this privileging of a foundational text, however, using a variety of case studies to question the oversimplification that pure profit motive drives the writing of serial fiction and that the subsequent volumes are always disappointing repetitions of the first.[5] Still, Castle's assumption that serial novels are never as good as their originals has numerous precedents in literary and cultural theory and persists today. There is a long tradition of disdain for the serial shared by high modernists and Marxists alike over much of the twentieth century. Most famously, in the 1940s, Theodor Adorno and Max Horkheimer condemned the endless and sterile repetitions of 'the culture industry'; for them, the 'idiotic women's serial' exemplified the lure of mass culture's unsatisfied promises in an endless stream of stereotypes and illusions.[6] As Langbauer discusses in detail, the serial has frequently been associated with women and the banalities of their everyday lives; after all, its contemporary form is the television soap opera.[7] In their recent studies of de la Roche, both Lorraine York and Ruth Panofsky quote scathing newspaper reviews of the final Jalna novels. The most vicious is *The Times Literary Supplement*'s 1960 attack on the 16th novel (mistakenly and tellingly numbered the 17th) as the sign that 'the Jalna marathon has, indeed, moved outside the range of literary criteria'.[8] While Panofsky interprets these attacks as the ostracization of a writer because of her enormous popularity and market success, York adds 'that it is the very fact of the sequel itself – the publishing format – and the ridiculous extent to which de la Roche took it, that makes the saga seem less like a literary event and more like a sporting one'.[9] This interpretation explains the widespread description of the Jalna series as a marathon, but instead of conveying hard-won endurance this sporting metaphor, at least in York's assessment, conveyed an 'overwhelming sense [...] of a writer losing control of her publishing career' as a result of her stardom.[10] Despite harsh reviews and her own publishers' attempts to convince her to move on to something else, de la Roche persisted in writing Jalna novels until her death in 1960.

When he damned her as 'the dispensable de la Roche', novelist Mordecai Richler summed up the general attitude towards the Jalna series in Canadian critical and literary circles after her death.[11] In her lifetime, however, de la Roche was a much-celebrated and powerful author. After winning the prestigious $10,000 *Atlantic Monthly* prize for fiction in 1927 for *Jalna*, the first novel in the series, she enjoyed decades of the kind of international celebrity that authors today experience after winning a major prize or being featured in Oprah's Book Club.[12] Her fame had consequences for her fate in the field of Canadian literature, however, which was beginning to harden around canonical forms and movements in precisely the same decades that de la Roche published her 16 Jalna novels. On the one hand, as Joan Givner and Faye Hammill argue, de la Roche's 1927 American magazine prize allowed *Jalna*, her third published novel (her first two would languish in obscurity as juvenilia compared with the distribution powerhouse of the Jalna series) to be embraced by a Canadian public looking for a recognizably Canadian novel and writer to celebrate.[13] Yet, on the other hand, the contemporary critical response was far more ambivalent. As a *Canadian Forum* magazine reviewer put it in 1932, 'The flurry caused by a new book of hers comes from people who though they may neither enjoy nor approve her work, yet feel that what she may be doing next is a thing of definite importance to Canadian literature.'[14] This ambivalence has shaped the terms of her more recent critical recuperation and, because of her prolific output and fame, there has been less attention paid to the novels as texts than to the author as persona. Critics attempting to re-insert de la Roche into the narrative of English-Canadian literature, most notably Panofsky, tend to focus on either her mysterious personal life and self-fashioning through celebrity culture or the relationship between the author, her legions of fans, and her American and Canadian publishers.[15]

York's recent study, *Literary Celebrity in Canada*, continues Panofsky's interest in de la Roche as a cultural figure and focuses on the dynamics of celebrity and fame that shaped her life narrative and critical reception. York draws on Bourdieu's theories of the field of cultural production to argue that the position of the Jalna series in the field of Canadian literature exemplifies the struggle for dominance between small-scale production, the kind of literary and prize-winning print production with which the first Jalna novel was associated, and the sphere of large-scale industrial or mechanical popular print production to which the whole Jalna series would be relegated, precisely because it became a series. This is a common fate of sequel or sequential novels that follow on an initial critical success; they are often treated with disdain, seen as being commercial enterprises motivated solely by economics. York helpfully steers the critical discussion of de la Roche away from the prevalent rise and fall narrative of earlier critics to conclude that 'her career presents us with a portrait of overlapping, competing spheres of cultural production' namely the literary and the popular.[16] Building on York's productive analysis, I seek to examine the qualities that lead serial fiction to be identified with an emergent middlebrow culture in mid-century Canada. This culture, while it has some distinct national features, can also be understood in relation to a generic identity that emerges in British middlebrow fiction between the two World Wars, and which Nicola Humble argues is 'established through a complex interplay between texts and the desires and self-images of their readers'.[17] Just as Humble argues that textual pleasure is crucial to understanding middlebrow writing, so is serial fiction oriented towards the reader and the pleasures of reading, including the anticipation of the subsequent volume. Serial fiction also has a significant affective dimension that taps into readers' emotional investments in fictional characters, events, and experiences, but also in books themselves as mediators between individual and social identities.

The Jalna book sales declined in the later years of the series, but one of de la Roche's justifications to her publishers for continuing to write the novels was the loyalty of her fans and their requests for more stories about the Whiteoak family. In ways frequently identified as middlebrow, the serial intrinsically links writers and books to their readers' desires for fulfilment, both narrative and cultural. And, like constructions of the 'middlebrow', serial forms proliferated in the first decades of the twentieth century. Although long established, serial fiction burgeoned at the turn of the century due to increased market demand for reading material, changes in printing technologies and distribution systems, and reorganized relations between audiences and authors.[18] Popular and pulp serial fiction expanded in Canada (including fiction written about Canada), especially in the 1920s and 1930s. Much of this material is aspirational, expressing in popular form the desires and contradictions of modernity. Numerous critics have shown that international best-selling Canadian series of this period, such as L. M. Montgomery's *Anne of Green Gables* and Mazo de la Roche's Jalna series, appeal to a sentimentalized and anti-modern fantasy of a Canadian locale, whether Prince Edward Island or rural Loyalist Ontario. Such fantasies gloss over the real problems of modernity experienced in these regions and write out the very commercial modes of cultural production and consumption that made these texts possible. This disjunction between content and form, or more properly between content and the conditions of possibility for the serial form to succeed, is only one of many ironies of the Jalna series.

The serial form pervaded Canadian cultural production, with middlebrow institutions such as the Canadian Broadcasting Company (CBC, founded 1936) and National Film Board of Canada (NFB, founded 1939) relying on series and serials to fulfil their mandates to educate and entertain. However, it was its content as well as its cultural contexts that led the Jalna series to be considered middlebrow. It focuses on the turbulent Whiteoak family: its sexual jealousies, illicit affairs and legal wrangles over inheritance. This focus on familial disturbance led to frequent comparison, in de la Roche's lifetime, with John Galsworthy's *Forsyte Saga*. One such comparison by an American critic also reveals what makes the Jalna series middlebrow rather than more generally popular. In his 1934 article, 'The Mystery of the Best Seller', Granville Hicks observes:

> Galsworthy's Canadian disciple, Mazo de la Roche, is less pretentious than her master, speaks less solemnly and frequently of justice and tolerance, but she has the same slightly specious way of suggesting that her readers are being confronted with the solid realities of life and death. Very cleverly evocative in description, she is not above resorting to tricks of characterization, and she is ruthless in bringing each of the four volumes of the Jalna saga, despite the incompetence, misunderstanding, and neuroticism she has portrayed, to a happy ending. One comes to feel that, like Galsworthy, she would not be so popular if she either seemed less serious or were more so.[19]

Compared with Galsworthy, and based on only the first four novels in the series, de la Roche is neither too earnest nor too frivolous, neither too escapist nor too realist. Here, then, is a middlebrow author described in an echo of Virginia Woolf's widely quoted censure of the middlebrow as 'betwixt and between', neither fully one thing nor the other.[20] Yet it is precisely this middle location that Hicks identifies as the source of de la Roche's popularity and that is part of his larger argument about best-selling novels: they are not, as he had previously assumed, ridiculous and poorly written romances and adventures, which is to say the 'worst' kinds of books, but nor are they the 'best' because they depend upon formulaic characters and plots and tend towards didacticism.[21] Although he does not single out the Jalna novels for being particularly preachy or pious, there is in the above summary a tone of displeasure at de la Roche's insistence on happy endings that seem contrived out of thin material, given the emotional turmoil and familial strife that drives the series. The artificiality of such endings, then, is part of the middlebrow work of the novels. They neither paint an unrealistic portrait of the hot-house environment of an isolated family under financial stress, nor do they leave readers dissatisfied with inconclusive narratives, despite the promise of another volume to come. De la Roche satisfactorily concludes each instalment in a way that anticipates its continuation; the novels can be read alone or in sequence. The pleasures of conclusion and anticipation accompany a sense that something has been gained, and one has been improved in the reading itself. The middlebrow reader often returns because she feels that the book has yielded cultural returns and the price she has paid literally for the novels has also exacted an emotional toll for, as Hicks puts it, 'confront[ing] the solid realities of life and death'. This middlebrow reader of serial fiction pays for affect, but affect is the price she pays for the cultivation she gains from observing the social dynamics of modernization as they melodramatically play out in the domestic setting of the series.

An important ideological force in the field of Canadian cultural production that worked to discredit the aesthetic value of the Jalna series is middlebrow nationalism, a term I borrow from David Carter's discussion of the middlebrow in Australia. Carter suggests that, in 1930s Australia, the two categories of the nation and the middlebrow absorbed each other to produce a cultural formation characterized by aspiration but also by representations of 'virtuous citizenship and "nationed" modernity'.[22] Carter argues that the national and the middlebrow performed the same role 'in drawing boundaries around mass-commercial culture on one side and modernist culture on the other. Like the middlebrow, a modern national culture offered to reunite individuality, class aspiration, and democratic community; and to mediate between modernity, populism, and tradition.'[23] Serial fiction plays a particular role in Canadian middlebrow nationalism, one that is akin to the centrality of the newspaper to organizing the 'imagined community' of the nation as defined by Benedict Anderson. Like the newspaper, it organizes a public 'into a specific imagined world of vernacular readers'.[24] Initially, the Jalna novels filled this function for a middlebrow Canadian reading public, as well as critics, in search of books they could use as signs that the national literature had achieved maturity and autonomy from Britain and the United States. Yet, as time went on and subsequent volumes made the enterprise seem more economic than artistic, as well as more international than Canadian, their power to bind together the reading nation diminished.

The international success of the series' popularity is evident in the 1966 authorized biography of de la Roche by Ronald Hambleton, who notes that there were at that point 193 different English editions of the 16 Jalna novels, 92 foreign editions in other languages and 41 in Braille.[25] Moreover, the series was enormously popular in Europe during and immediately after the Second World War, a fact borne out by the fan letters de la Roche received from former Polish prisoners, members of the Dutch underground and French resistance, and clandestine readers from wartime Germany and occupied countries who, according to her editor Edward Weeks, felt that 'Mazo's writing carried a heartening assurance to those living in exile or under domination'.[26] It was less the setting of free Canada than the genre of family saga that offered this assurance, however, as Weeks concludes that 'for family fealty there is one tongue and universal sympathy'.[27] Indeed, even Canadian Prime Minister Mackenzie King recognized, in a letter to her, that de la Roche was more popular in Britain than Canada. He praised her for representing a Canadian scene, even though 'the first great mass of readers [of new Jalna novels] will be citizens of a country other than our own'.[28] Despite, or perhaps because of, this overseas popularity, de la Roche did not receive commensurate adulation at home and felt particularly wronged when she was passed over for a Governor-General's Award for Literature in the 1940s.[29]

Because de la Roche's later Jalna novels were not received as fully Canadian, they were also dismissed as aesthetic objects by Canadian critics and judged unsuitable for a literary canon serving nationalist interests. York sees this critical devaluation and nationalist agenda at work in the irony that the series' subsequent instalments were received as less Canadian than the first volume, not least because her financial success allowed de la Roche to move, with her partner Caroline Clement, to Britain in the 1930s.[30] According to Hambleton, it was not just her wealth and celebrity but also the real or imagined censure by Canadian literary critics that influenced her desire to relocate.[31] It appears that de la Roche faced a double bind: on the one hand, she left Canada because she felt underappreciated by the Canadian literati, but, on the other hand, her departure fuelled that depreciation, proving to her critics that she was more interested in commercial success and her own celebrity than in literary quality. The 'charisma' of the initial text in this case depended upon its identification with markers of Canadianness, and the author's own relocation was read by Canadian critics into the series' decline in quality.[32] Though she returned to Ontario before the Second World War broke out, by then her novels had been tainted by her apparent rejection of Canada as a suitable residence for famous writers. York summarizes the manifold ironies in this situation: 'By the time she returned, in 1939, the impression of her world as one manufactured elsewhere, in England, was firmly established among critics, and, as interest in promoting Canadian content grew in the 1950s, her cultural capital in the developing discourse of Canadian literary nationalism declined dramatically.'[33] As the series went on, the value of de la Roche's novels as middlebrow texts began to decline with the narratives' and their author's perceived distance from specifically Canadian content and contexts.

This critical devaluation of the series once it stops signifying Canadianness testifies to a desire for serial fiction to perform as national allegory, and there are indeed elements throughout the early novels that invite this reading. Another grounds for criticism of the series, especially after de la Roche's death, is its ideological conservatism in representing twentieth-century Canada as a rural Ontario backwater of British colonial tradition, where authentic leadership is rooted in rugged masculinity and the rewards reaped by hard work. There is no place more real, down-to-earth and powerful for this family than their magnificent home, even as it becomes anomalous within the changing modern world around it. In this way, the Jalna series offers the family as an allegory for a nation enthralled to its British heritage and resistant to the perceived encroachment on its territory by an upstart Americanism symbolic of all that is crass and disruptive about modern capitalism. The elderly matriarch Adeline, whose remarkable longevity is the pride and bane of all the younger members of the family, is at once ridiculous and revered, a colonial hold-over who stands for an admirable strength of character that is lacking in her prodigy, even if she is out of step with modern life. She is the wellspring of the family and the reminder of their mettle in earlier times of adversity. Her two sons, the elderly uncles Ernest and Nicholas, map two versions of masculinity that are inherited by their nephews: Ernest, with his farcical amateur Shakespeare scholarship is succeeded by the literary-minded Eden and the music-loving Finch; and Nicholas, the ribald horseman, is succeeded by the horse-mad Renny and the rugged outdoorsman Piers. If there is a national allegory in these masculinities, it is in the competition between culture and nature, aesthetic sensitivity and natural sympathy. As a late colonial nation, de la Roche seems to suggest, interwar Canada has a proud British Loyalist heritage that continues to cultivate the land it settled, but this cultural and geographic periphery is not without an aesthetic sensibility that appreciates the arts, in at least some quarters, as much as it does the verdant landscape. These two kinds of cultivation, artistic and natural, that shape the masculinities of the series perform an allegory of de la Roche's conservative vision of a nation rooted in inherited authority but susceptible to the individual subversions of those who stray from the family territory, both literally and figuratively. It is a white settler colony but its rough origins have been tempered over the generations by highly individual characters and their artistic aspirations.

Although it is possible to read at least the early Jalna novels as national allegory along these lines, the competing masculinities of the family also point to de la Roche's participation in transnational generic features of middlebrow writing. The Whiteoaks are marked as Canadian in numerous specific ways, including their Anglo-Irish Loyalist roots, prior colonial experience (the house is named after the Indian military station where Philip and Adeline met before emigrating to Canada), and anti-American sentiments; it is a form of Canadianness that embraces Britishness as the pinnacle of morally enlightened 'white civility' in the Dominion.[34] However, at the same time, they are an eccentric family of loners, recluses, and oddballs who find solace in each other more than any social world beyond the borders of their estate. Thus, they fit Humble's description of eccentric families in British feminine middlebrow novels between the wars, not just because the characters are unusual and the family dysfunctional, but also because the series is interested in the very idea of the family itself. From the beginning of the first novel, the series represents the family as a closed social unit, a noisy and fractious 'tribe' over which Renny is the 'Chieftain' who takes 'a very primitive, direct, and simple pleasure in lording it over them, caring for them, being badgered, harried, and importuned by them'.[35] Mealtimes, when the family gets together in a room full of heavy furniture to eat heavy food in enormous portions, offer the narrator opportunities to comment on their excitements and eccentricities. In the first of such descriptions, the narrator notes that the dining room's shutters and curtains 'seemed definitely to shut out the rest of the world from the world of the Whiteoaks, where they squabbled, ate, drank, and indulged in their peculiar occupations'.[36] Yet they are a compelling family, each with their idiosyncratic hobbies and passions – from grandmother Adeline's beloved swearing parrot to young Wakefield's illicit desire for sweets and cakes – and they have what Humble describes in relation to other middlebrow family novels, the 'shared and normative family identity' that both marks them off as different and pulls them towards each other with the 'psychological rewards of feeling oneself to be unusual'.[37] The Jalna series shares with British interwar eccentric family novels, such as Rosamond Lehmann's *Dusty Answer* (1927) and Nancy Mitford's *The Pursuit of Love* (1945), the perspective of an outsider who can register for the reader the attraction and repugnance of the family.[38] In the early Jalna novels, this figure is Alayne, an independent New York woman who gives up her publishing job to marry Eden and move to the estate. After enduring her first heavy lunch with the full family (she 'thought of little salad lunches in New York with mild regret'[39]), Alayne reflects on the Whiteoak's difference from everyone else: 'Would she ever get used to them, Alayne wondered. Would they ever seem near to her – like relatives? As they rose from the table and moved in different directions, she felt a little oppressed, she did not quite know whether by the weight of the dinner or by the family, which was so unexpectedly foreign to her.'[40]

Alayne is an important figure at the beginning of the series, both because she is the primary focalization of the family outsider and because she is a female interloper who disrupts the masculine hierarchies of the family tribe. She also supplements the generic identity of the series as family saga with aspects of domestic melodrama to heighten the affective register of the novels. Indeed, the overwrought emotionalism of de la Roche's characters, and her prose itself, has often been used as another way to devalue the novels. Almost all the contemporary reviews of Jalna note that the family is highly strung and agree with Jocelyn Moore that 'the whole complex group is passing from one emotional crisis to another – or rather through that state of constant emotional tension which is for them normality (for their emotions are as big and thorough-going as their puddings)'.[41] As early as 1929, however, a reviewer of *Whiteoaks of Jalna* shifted commentary on the affective charge from characterization to literary style in the veiled praise that 'the prose is forceful, straightforward, honest prose. Once or twice it gets hysterical but recovers its balance again before it is too late.'[42] Later reviewers were less kind, although even the landmark 1965 reference work, *Literary History of Canada*, had to acknowledge the popular appeal of de la Roche's seemingly outmoded style: 'The plot [of the series] is ingenious and continuously exciting, and the style, if a little too precious for our austere modern taste, is fresh and beguiling.'[43] In both style and characterization, de la Roche has overwhelmingly been accused of excessive emotionalism of the sort usually associated with melodrama. If melodrama can be understood as a genre that examines family tensions, between both sexes and generations, in which women play a central part but within a dominantly patriarchal ideology, then de la Roche's series clearly falls within this domain.[44]

In the introduction to *America the Middlebrow*, Jaime Harker traces a genealogy for interwar middlebrow novels by women back to the American 1850s novels frequently described as 'sentimental' because of their inspirational plots based in social reform ideals. These writers made emotional appeals to readers to advocate various causes, and as a result fell into critical disfavour in later decades because 'of their appeal to readers' pleasure and their investment in the marketplace'.[45] This theme of the affective register of middlebrow novels appears in many of the landmark studies of middlebrow culture because definitions of this field frequently note the importance of readers' emotional attachments to their books. Janice Radway's *A Feeling for Books* asserts that the Book of the Month Club can be understood as middlebrow not only because it combined literature with marketing and reading with social improvement, but also because it valued a heightened empathy produced through rich characterization and readerly identification with fictional people and problems which counteracted the alienating and isolating experiences of modern life. Not surprisingly, given the voluminous and international fan mail de la Roche received in the 1930s and 1940s, *The Building of Jalna*, published in 1944, was the Book of the Month Club selection for November 1944.[46] Radway's study of the club's selection criteria sees in their values a reaction against the perceived asceticism and cold intellectualism of literary modernism, evident in their preference for books that engaged with readers' sentiments:

> Whatever else the club succeeded in dispensing in its early years, it seems clear that it communicated to its subscribers a deep respect for something that might be called middlebrow personalism. That is, the club constructed a picture of the world that, for all its modern chaos, domination by abstract and incomprehensible forces, and

worries about standardization and massification, was still the home of the individual, idiosyncratic selves. Those selves, the club's selections seemed to say, experienced the excitement and pain of the new in extraordinarily intense ways and responded to its conundrums with highly complex, even contradictory emotions. [...] The individualism of the middlebrow subject, it seems to me, at least as he or she was constructed at the Book-of-the-Month Club, was an individualism of both affect and empathy. People felt – and they felt for others.[47]

This middlebrow personalism, to use Radway's term, made reading a transformative experience in the sense that readers of the club's selections would ideally both escape their own mundane everyday lives and respond so deeply to the emotional experiences of the selected books that they would feel a profound affiliation, even identification, with the fictional events and characters. As Radway concludes, drawing on Bourdieu's terminology, this produced a contradictory 'middlebrow habitus' among club readers who, on the one hand, felt a deep connection to something beyond themselves while, on the other hand, this very affiliation separated them from 'those persons marked by even greater difference, that is, by their *lack* of expertise' in reading books selected by professional experts.[48] The habits of reading encouraged by the Book of the Month Club at once constructed an empathetic and even sentimental subject whose deep feelings for fictional others could be at odds with real social constraints and hierarchies.

Given middlebrow culture's emphasis on deep feeling, and even sentiment, it would be easy to assume that a series such as Jalna is gendered feminine and was the literary equivalent of mid-century cinema's 'women's weepies'. However, I want to resist the assumption that the affective overcharge of this series must have appealed mostly to female readers. Indeed, the archival collection of fan mail de la Roche received over several decades suggests quite the opposite: male readers, across the class spectrum found affective release in her exploration of multiple types of masculinity and waited anxiously for the next instalment to see what would happen to their favourite male characters.[49] Ultimately, however, de la Roche does not commit to one gender ideology over another, just as her other ideological positions remain unstable. Whereas the 1850s American sentimental novels Harker sees as one precursor of interwar middlebrow fiction often advocated a specific cause, in the Jalna series social relations and political ideologies are always subsumed within the institution of the family. This is not to say that de la Roche ignores social change, but rather that she refracts public life through the private realm of the family and often narrows it further to the internal feelings of individual characters. In this sense, she produced a 16-volume domestic melodrama in which political structures are reorganized as affective ones always open to the extension and supplementation of the serial form. As Thomas Elsaesser notes:

> The persistence of the melodrama might indicate the ways in which popular culture has not only taken note of social crises and the fact that the losers are not always those who deserve it most, but has also resolutely refused to understand social change in other than private contexts and emotional terms. In this, there is obviously a healthy distrust of intellectualisation and abstract social theory – insisting that other structures of experience (those of suffering, for instance) are more in keeping with reality.[50]

Elsaesser's object of study is popular rather than middlebrow culture, yet his point is nevertheless applicable to the Jalna series. Indeed, it allows me to conclude that de la Roche's market success and fan loyalty are a consequence of the gentrification of the popular forms of domestic melodrama and family saga to the middlebrow and the infusion of aspiration into the act of reading these genres. As such, this series is formulated as a space in which the dynamics of history can be analysed and mapped through genealogical narrative. While the Jalna series invites a reading of it as national allegory, an invitation extended not least because of its serial form, this does not exhaust its power and affective force, as its international popularity attests. The problems and tensions of legacy and inheritance, ancestry and allegiance, belonging and ostracization are those of domestic melodrama that allow the Jalna series to stage for Canadian and non-Canadian readers alike a lesson in succession and historical change in all their inequalities and injustices. The affective power of this serial staging suggests that these middlebrow fictions draw on the wellspring of the emotional for their force, but the pleasures of feeling are experienced as pedagogical, lessons learned from, to draw on Hicks once again, 'the sordid realities of life and death'.

Notes

1. See Carole Gerson (1994) 'Canadian Women Writers and American Markets, 1880–1940', in Camille La Bossiére (ed.) *Context North America: Canadian/U.S. Literary Relations* (Ottawa: University of Ottawa Press), pp. 107–118;

(1991) 'The Canon between the Wars: Field-Notes of a Feminist Literary Archaeologist', in Robert Lecker (ed.) *Canadian Canons: Essays in Literary Value* (Toronto: University of Toronto Press), pp. 46–56.

2. The 16 Jalna novels are usually listed in chronological order according to historical setting, rather than publication date, because this is how readers were encouraged to encounter them by de la Roche and her publishers once she started to move back in time from the present setting of the first four published books. Following this convention, the novels in the series, beginning with the founding of the Jalna estate in the 1850s, are: *Building of Jalna* (1944); *Morning at Jalna* (1960); *Mary Wakefield* (1949); *Young Renny* (1935); *Whiteoak Heritage* (1940); *Whiteoak Brothers* (1953); *Jalna* (1927); *Whiteoaks of Jalna* (1929); *Finch's Fortune* (1931); *The Master of Jalna* (1933); *Whiteoak Harvest* (1936); *Wakefield's Course* (1941); *Return to Jalna* (1946); *Renny's Daughter* (1951); *Variable Winds at Jalna* (1954); *Centenary at Jalna* (1958).

3. Laurie Langbauer (1999) *Novels of Everyday Life: The Series in English Fiction, 1850–1930* (Ithaca: Cornell University Press), p. 8.

4. Paul Budra and Betty A. Schellenberg (1998) *Reflections on the Sequel* (Toronto: University of Toronto Press), p. 8.

5. See Terry Castle (1986) *Masquerade and Civilization: The Carnivalesque in Eighteenth-Century English Culture and Fiction* (Stanford: Stanford University Press). For challenges to Castle's theory of the charismatic text, see the Introduction to Budra and Schellenberg.

6. Langbauer, p. 53 and Theodor W. Adorno and Max Horkheimer (1972) 'The Culture Industry: Enlightenment as Mass Deception', in John Cumming (trans.) *Dialectic of Enlightenment* (New York: Herder and Herder), p. 152.

7. To this, I would add that there is a classed and racialized dimension to the disdain for serial fiction since it has long been viewed as a degraded literary form for working class, immigrant, and juvenile readers.

8. (29 July1960) 'Such Darling Dodos' *The Times Literary Supplement*, 477. See also York, p. 72 and Panofsky, p. 61.

9. York, p. 73.

10. York, p. 73.

11. Richler qtd in Lorraine York (2007) *Literary Celebrity in Canada* (Toronto: University of Toronto Press), p. 58.

12. York, p. 60.

13. In contrast to another female prize-winning novelist of the 1920s, the Norwegian-born American citizen Martha Ostenso, de la Roche's pro-British, late colonial representation of the descendents of Ontario Loyalists was a more favourable entry into a national literature seeking to define itself against American mass culture and influence. See Joan Givner (1989) *Mazo de la Roche: The Hidden Life.* (Toronto: Oxford University Press) and Faye Hammill (Summer 2003) 'The Sensations of the 1930s: Martha Ostenso's *Wild Geese* and Mazo de la Roche's *Jalna*' *Studies in Canadian Literature* 28(2), 74–97.

14. Jocelyn Moore (July 1932) 'Canadian Writers of Today VII. Mazo de la Roche', *The Canadian Forum*, 380.

15. Ruth Panofsky (2000) 'At Odds: Reviewers and Readers of the Jalna Novels', *Studies in Canadian Literature* 25(1), 57–67; (Spring 1995) ' "Don't let me

do it!'": Mazo de la Roche and Her Publishers', in *International Journal of Canadian Studies* 11, 171–184.

16. York, p. 75. See also Pierre Bourdieu (1993) *The Field of Cultural Production*, in Randal Johnson (ed.) (New York: Columbia University Press).

17. Nicola Humble (2001) *The Feminine Middlebrow Novel, 1920s to 1950s* (New York: Oxford University Press).

18. Mary Ann Gillies 'The Literary Agent and the Sequel', in Budra and Schellenberg, p. 133.

19. Granville Hicks (October 1934) 'The Mystery of the Best Seller', *The English Journal* 23(8), 625.

20. Virginia Woolf (1942) 'Middlebrow', in *The Death of the Moth and Other Essays* (London: Hogarth), pp. 113–119.

21. Hicks, p. 626.

22. David Carter (2004) 'The Mystery of the Missing Middlebrow or The C(o)urse of Good Taste', in Judith Ryan and Chris Wallace-Crabbe (eds) *Imagining Australia: Literature and Culture in the New New World* (Cambridge, Mass.: Harvard University Press), p. 184.

23. Carter, p. 193.

24. Benedict Anderson (1983) *Imagined Communities: Reflections on the Origin and Spread of Nationalism* (London: Verso), p. 63.

25. Ronald Hambleton (1966), *Mazo de la Roche of Jalna* (Toronto: General Publishing), p. 50.

26. Weeks qtd in Hambleton, p. 52.

27. Weeks qtd in Hambleton, p. 52.

28. Mackenzie King qtd in Hambleton, p. 52.

29. Hambleton, p. 55.

30. York, p. 62.

31. Hambleton, p. 55.

32. Castle, pp. 133–134.

33. York, p. 63.

34. Daniel Coleman uses the term 'white civility' in his analysis of Canadian literature between 1820 and 1950 to argue that a series of allegorical figures, including the Loyalist brother and muscular Christian, 'gradually reified the privileged, normative status of British whiteness in English Canada'. See Daniel Coleman (2006) *White Civility: The Literary Project of English Canada* (Toronto: University of Toronto Press), p. 6.

35. de la Roche, *Jalna*, p. 97.

36. de la Roche, *Jalna*, p. 17.

37. Humble, pp. 161–162.

38. Humble, p. 158.

39. de la Roche, *Jalna*, p. 157.

40. de la Roche, *Jalna*, pp. 159–160.

41. Moore, p. 381.

42. S. E. Read (December 1929) 'Old Lady Whiteoak', Review of Mazo de la Roche's *Whiteoaks of Jalna*, in *The Canadian Forum*, 95.

43. Desmond Pacey (1965) 'Fiction 1920–1940', in Carl F. Klinck (ed.) *Literary History of Canada: Canadian Literature in English* (Toronto: University of Toronto Press), p. 669.

44. This general definition of 'melodrama' is taken from Laura Mulvey (1987) 'Notes on Sirk and Melodrama', in Christine Gledhill (ed.) *Home is Where the Heart Is: Studies in Melodrama and Women's Film* (London: British Film Institute), p. 76.

45. Jaime Harker (2007) *America the Middlebrow: Women's Novels, Progressivism, and Middlebrow Authorship between the Wars* (Amherst: University of Massachusetts Press), p. 5.

46. 'Borden's Canadian Cavalcade' (8 September 1944) in *The Coaticook Observer*, 5.

47. Janice Radway (1997) *A Feeling for Books: The Book-of-the-Month Club, Literary Taste, and Middle-Class Desire* (Chapel Hill: University of North Carolina Press), p. 283.

48. Radway, p. 285.

49. See Panofsky, 'At Odds: Reviewers and Readers of the Jalna novels'.

50. Thomas Elsaesser (1987) 'Tales of Sound and Fury: Observations on Family Melodrama', in Christine Gledhill (ed.) *Home is Where the Heart Is* (London: British Film Institute), p. 47.

11
Illustrating *Mary Poppins*: Visual Culture and the Middlebrow

Kristin Bluemel

In 1934, the English publisher Gerald Howe brought out an illustrated children's novel by a relatively unknown Australian author, P. L. Travers, then living in London. The book, *Mary Poppins*, was an immediate success with readers, and not only with the children who were its ostensible market.[1] A protégé of AE (George Russell), Travers had always wanted to be a great poet; in her endless self-regard, she imagined herself a peer of the modernists, at least one of whom, T. S. Eliot, as editor of Faber and Faber, had expressed interest in the book. The illustrator she picked was a young woman named Mary Shepard, whose pedigree as a children's book illustrator was assured by the success of her father, Ernest H. Shepard, the illustrator of the 'Winnie-the-Pooh' books and cartoonist for *Punch*.

This chapter uses P. L. Travers as a case study for a larger theoretical investigation into three seemingly unrelated concerns: the ambiguous form of the book Travers wrote and Shepard illustrated, a 'lesser' (because children's) book that to a large extent achieved literary greatness; interwar cultural hierarchies that depressed realistic women's novels associated with domestic spaces and domestics (Mary Poppins is a nanny, after all); and more recent theories of visual–verbal relations that try to explain how we read illustrated texts and what that process means for our understanding of representation as such.[2]

While there are all kinds of fascinating things to say about Travers's self-image as a 'Bright Young Person' and her completely conventional ambition to join the ranks of the 'best' writers of her day by publishing what she viewed as avant-garde poetry, I aim to focus instead on Travers and Shepard's shared role as architects of a domestic verbal–visual space that challenges the dominant literary culture. The special focus of my study is *Mary Poppins*'s black-and-white illustrations and their relations to the surrounding words. I ask how *Mary Poppins* teaches us to look for new values in the border between statuses or 'brows' (modernist/middlebrow), textual forms (verbal/visual) and audiences (adults/children) in order to frame theoretically the meaning of *Mary Poppins*'s generically determined disparagement. I do not argue that such disparagement is a result of contemporary critics describing Travers as a middlebrow writer or criticizing her decision to turn from poetry to children's fiction. Rather, I contend that Travers was always in a position of low cultural value relative to the Great Male Poets who she admired; I take as given that children's literature is devalued by taste-makers and academics in ways that are consistent with the devaluing of women's novels, commercial fiction, advertising and other genres and forms labelled 'middlebrow'.

In what follows, I treat *Mary Poppins*'s devalued position within literary hierarchies as a problem of the literary elites and taste-makers whose critical choices exclude illustration – in particular the pen-and-ink illustration associated with the period's popular, low-cost magazines – from consideration of the meaning and importance of literary texts. In other words, my aim is to establish a theoretical paradigm for reading and valuing the forms of a disparaged genre, illustrated children's literature, and to provide a supporting case study. In the process of examining and celebrating what I might call the rhetoric of mixture characteristic of illustrated children's books, the chapter promotes future cross-disciplinary conversation among scholars of children's literature and scholars of the 'middlebrow matters' this volume aims to examine.

To understand how attention to relations between *Mary Poppins*'s words and pictures can enrich understanding of the mixed up history of interwar middlebrow and children's book publishing in Britain, it is helpful to consider the work of someone who has nothing at stake in the modernist/middlebrow debate but who is an expert on image–text relations in children's literature. In *Words about Pictures*, Perry Nodelman describes the temporal, physical and mental processes that come into play when readers try to make narrative sense of children's illustrated texts.[3] Although Nodelman is depicting the process of reading children's picture books in which half or more of the story is told by images, his understanding of process, of how we read words and pictures in terms of each other, also describes what happens when we read illustrated novels like *Mary Poppins*.

When a story is told in words as well as pictures, we first understand both the words and the pictures by means of the schemata we have already established for them – at first, our general understanding about how pictures communicate. Then, the words correct and particularize our understanding of the pictures they accompany, and the pictures provide information that causes us to reinterpret and particularize the meanings of the words. Then all of that becomes a schema for each new page of words and each new picture as we continue throughout a book. [...] Our simultaneous or almost-simultaneous experience of both words and pictures allows us to use each to correct our understanding of the other.[4]

An attempt to translate into everyday language what some image/text theorists would call 'the dialectic of discourse and vision',[5] this passage defines the complex interpretive processes put into play by illustrated children's literature. In the context of literary institutions that regard illustration as the discredited second sister of the book arts – as childish visual forms that supplement the primary verbal text – Nodelman's insistence on the narrative value of illustration is provocative. His understanding of the dialectic of discourse and vision legitimizes texts that draw on verbal and visual forms because they make obvious the inherently mixed forms of *all* books. Illustrated 'verbal' literature like *Mary Poppins* makes this inherent confusion of forms blatant and thus may disturb ideologies extolling verbal purity – the myth of textual singularity – more forcefully than other kinds of literature.[6] For many ambitious writers, and perhaps especially women writers, the label 'middlebrow' was an encoded and efficient way of containing the threat their mixed textual forms posed to these dominant literary ideologies.

Once Nodelman and other scholars of image–text relations are seen as suitable guides for middlebrow research, texts with illustrations, cartoons and marginal decorations come to have a special role in scholarly reconstruction and analysis of the battles over mixed media that shaped academic and literary culture during the twentieth century. These visual–verbal battles are exactly the kinds of messy conflicts that tend to evaporate in literary histories that idealize a purified modernism. Like scholars of mixed visual–verbal texts, scholars of the rhetoric of middlebrow have been hard at work revising such limited histories and from the first have recognized children's literature as a constitutive genre. Nicola Humble includes children's literature in her list of genres composing the 'hybrid form' of the feminine middlebrow[7] and judges children's literature and adult literature read by children (such as that by Jane Austen) to be fairly high up within the middlebrow hierarchy by virtue of their 'cultish, quirky associations'.[8] More daringly, Faye Hammill treats L. M. Montgomery, author of the *Anne of Green Gables* series and one of the most widely read authors of all time, as a central figure in her study of *Women, Celebrity, and Literary Culture Between the Wars*.[9] I say 'daring' because Hammill assumes a writer of children's popular fiction can be grouped with adult writers of popular fiction without explanation or apology. Scholars of children's literature are not so sanguine, and typically feel called upon to define and defend their approach to children's literature in terms of its relation to adult literature. In these accounts, children's literature emerges either as a variation of adult literature, different in degree but not in kind (and thus worthy of serious study), or as a genre of literature distinct from adult literature (and thus worthy of serious study).

One of the most ambitious recent studies to attempt to theorize children's literature as a distinct genre is Nodelman's *The Hidden Adult: Defining Children's Literature*.[10] Building on the theoretical explorations of *Words About Pictures*, *The Hidden Adult* begins by establishing a special relationship between children's and middlebrow literature even as its final goal is to distinguish children's literature as autonomous. Nodelman writes that 'the children in the phrase "children's literature" are most usefully understood as the child readers that writers, responding to the assumptions of adult purchasers, imagine and imply in their works'.[11] In other words, the children in children's literature are not those depicted in the books. They are the child readers imagined by the producers of children's literature. Nodelman muses, 'The only other literary category identifier I can think of that defines an audience rather than a time or a place or a specific type of writing like romance or tragedy is what is often called "popular literature" ' or 'the books Pierre Bourdieu identifies as "middle-brow literature" '.[12] While recognizing the parallels between literary taste-makers' tendencies to define middlebrow literature 'as those texts produced in the hope of appealing to a middlebrow audience' and 'children's literature [...] as those texts produced in the hope of attracting an audience of children',[13] Nodelman still distinguishes what he regards as unique conditions bearing upon the production of children's literature:

> [A]dults make their purchases [of children's books] on the basis of their ideas about what the children they purchase for like to and need to read – so it is those ideas that writers must appeal to in order

to be successful. This makes the production of children's literature a more complex variation of the situation of 'middlebrow literature' as Bourdieu outlines it.[14]

While I might argue that buying books for oneself or one's aunt is just as much a mediated act of fantasy building as buying a book for one's son or niece, I am persuaded that children's literature can be seen as a 'variation of the situation of "middlebrow literature"'. Certainly resistance to children's literature in the academy has been energized by variations of the same moral arguments used to resist middlebrow literature. W. J. T. Mitchell, author of *Iconology* and *Picture Theory*, acknowledges the long history of objections to mixed media such as illustrated books, but argues that these objections are not empirically grounded. Rather, he discovers in critics' pronouncements the moral belief that mixed media are 'bad for us and must be resisted in the name of higher aesthetic values'.[15] In the years that P. L. Travers was writing her first Mary Poppins books, intellectuals defended their criticism of what they considered aesthetically base writing with this kind of moral thinking. Travers herself believed that 'mixtures are bad for us' and to the great discomfort of her collaborator and illustrator, Mary Shepard, did everything she could to resist the dual forms of her own art in the name of 'higher aesthetic values'.

Ironically, it is René Magritte, an artist almost universally recognized as promoting these 'higher aesthetic values', who has proven most useful to theorists attempting to discredit the morality-based modernist logic that trapped Travers and other authors of children's literature in a devalued cultural category. Mitchell turns to Magritte's famous painting, *Les trahison des images* (1929), which features a realistic image of a pipe with the painted caption in script, 'Ceci n'est pas une pipe,' to help his readers picture theory about image–text relations. For Mitchell, this painting is particularly significant for the study of images and text because its real aim 'is to show what cannot be pictured or made readable, the fissure in representation itself, the bands, layers, and fault-lines of discourse, the blank space between the text and the image'.[16] Mitchell cites Foucault approvingly, for he, too, finds Magritte's pipe a 'metapicture' that 'shows everything that can be shown'.[17] Magritte's pipe leads Foucault to claim a special status for illustrated books, and within them, the white borders around pictures: 'It is there, on these few millimetres of white, the calm sand of the page, that are established all the relations of designation, nomination, description, classification.'[18] Such excitement, such certainty about a totalizing figure ('*all* the relations of designation') in the text of a poststructuralist philosopher is hard to resist and Mitchell, bewitched, exclaims in his turn:

> The double-coding of the illustrated book, its suturing of discourse and representation, the sayable and the seeable, across an unobtrusive, invisible frontier, exemplifies the conditions that make it possible to say 'this is that' (designation), to assign proper names, to describe, to place in grids, strata, or genealogies. The dialectic of discourse and vision, in short, is a fundamental figure of knowledge as such.[19]

While I will have more to say about Mitchell's discovery of a 'fundamental figure of knowledge as such' within the pages of illustrated books, for now I want to emphasize the importance of his theory to the material gap or white 'frontier' between the words and pictures in illustrated books. Although we typically think of those white spaces inside books as invisible, if we look at them through Mitchell's eyes we see how they define relations between words and images. And once we can see (instead of see beyond) the internal borders or white gaps within texts, the value for literary history of illustrated books, including children's illustrated books, rises dramatically.

To claim that the illustrations embedded in books emphasize an inherent contradiction and conflict between images and texts is to go against the common sense of most historians of children's book design and illustration. For example, the authors of *A History of Children's Book Illustration*, Joyce Irene Whalley and Tessa Rose Chester, assume that 'For most children the picture book precedes the story-book and for them these early forms of communication often become interpreters of the world which they have yet to discover for themselves' (p. 11). Here, pictures in books are bridges between self and world, not indicators of the distance between them. Whalley and Chester assert that:

> 'Pictures' are independent works. [...] Book illustration is something quite different [than pictures] and cannot properly exist outside its text – artists who forget this do so at their peril. Good book illustration should continue or enhance the narrative or verse that it accompanies. It should not overwhelm it, or contradict it.[20]

For these authors, the moral or aesthetic imperative ('good book illustration') is measured by the continuity or similarity between text and image; narrative and the images 'inside' narrative can aspire to a seamless synthesis.

Nodelman contradicts this view of image–text relations, arguing that the words of the text do not 'mirror' the images in the pictures. Like Mitchell, he insists that there is no pure or singular verbal form on the one hand, and no pure or singular visual form on the other.[21] If Nodelman is right, the twentieth-century fiction esteemed most highly for its pure verbal forms (say, *Ulysses*) has been read by modernism's critics as though the real relations between their mixed media didn't exist; in fact, these texts require readers to employ the same strategies, the same 'dialectic of discourse and vision', associated with readings of illustrated children's books. Nodelman's claims about the relation of words and pictures, which are based in part on theories of representation, perception and language developed by E. H. Gombrich, Roland Barthes, Rudolf Arnheim and Norman Bryson, refute the notion that a book's illustrations are secondary and inferior to the book's type – that they are the text's metaphorical servant or nanny, silently ministering to the demanding, noisy words of the story. They are, like Mary Poppins, strangely powerful, changing everything.

Mary Poppins: a middlebrow matter

Contrary to late-twentieth century audiences' association of Mary Poppins with the dulcet sounds of Julie Andrews's voice, contemporary readers of Travers's first novel would have encountered a heroine who was bossy, vain, rarely compassionate, occasionally cruel and usually silent. When she speaks, it is almost always to express disapproval of others. About her origins or purposes, we know practically nothing. The narrator tells us that '[N]obody ever knew what Mary Poppins felt [...] for Mary Poppins never told anybody anything...' (p. 15).

This description of an idealized English nanny ends the first chapter of *Mary Poppins*. At this point in the narrative, Mary Poppins has been blown by the east wind into the house of Mr and Mrs Banks, whereupon she condescends to look after the Banks's four children, Jane, Michael, and the infant twins, John and Barbara. She has already performed five magic tricks, including riding up the banister behind an unknowing Mrs Banks. She has spoken only a few dozen words, among them her pronouncement to the inquiring Mrs Banks, 'I make it a rule never to give references' (p. 8). Mostly, Mary Poppins sniffs. A sniff is the first sound that we hear from her and sniffs characterize her communication in the five Mary Poppins chapter books that follow the first.

When she isn't sniffing in the Banks's household, she's ordering the children around, issuing instructions, threats, criticism and warnings. She delivers information in the most concise form possible. Upon meeting her for the first time and noticing her curious luggage, the impetuous Michael exclaims 'What a funny bag!' 'Carpet', she replies. Confused, he asks, 'To carry carpets in, you mean?' 'No. Made of' (pp. 10–11). Like the modernist purists described by Mitchell and Foucault, she devotes herself to 'designation, nomination, description, classification'.[22]

The novel asks us to believe that Mary Poppins is uniquely elite, despite her status as a 'lower' class domestic servant and despite her appearance in a 'low' form of literature – illustrated children's books. Her refusal to explain anything, her silence about her origins, purposes and identity, stands as a metaphor for Travers's aesthetic allegiances and illusions. Travers was already a confirmed literary snob by the time she left Australia for London in 1924. She identified herself with her byline, P. L. Travers, hoping its two androgynous initials would promote her quest for highbrow fame as a poet.[23] Without wealth or specialized education, however, Travers had to support herself as a foreign correspondent for the Sydney *Triad* and for the 'Women's World' section of the Christchurch *Sun*, decidedly middlebrow (and unfashionably colonial) publications. Taught a romantic love of Eire by her dissolute father, Travers sent her poems to the Dublin literary celebrity, AE, who quickly became a doting mentor. Introduced to members of AE's circle, she earned the admiration of Oliver St John Goharty and the conversation of James Stephens and W. B. Yeats. This exhilarating contact confirmed for her that the only serious literature of her age was the supposedly autonomous productions of the male modernists that she idolized. A lifelong victim of what we would now call 'the myth of modernist singularity', Travers was trapped by a dominant literary ideology into scorning the readers, genres and markets that determined the enthusiastic reception of her own work.

For example, in the mid-1960s, after the release of the phenomenally successful Disney movie 'Mary Poppins', she told an audience of Radcliffe College students, 'I wouldn't say *Mary Poppins* is a children's book for one moment. It's certainly not written for children.'[24] Continuing her effort to dissociate *Mary Poppins* from children's literature, she protested, 'I never know why *Mary Poppins* is thought of as a children's book. Indeed I don't think there are such things. There are simply books and some of them children read. [...] I dislike the distinction very much. People say, "tell us the secret, how do you write for children?" I have to say that I don't know because I don't write for children.'[25] In a radio interview conducted in Boston around the same time, she told listeners that she definitely didn't want to be 'one more silly woman writing silly books. That's the idea, among publishers: "Oh yes, these curly headed women, they do it very nicely." It's never respected as literature, it's never given a high place in that sense.'[26]

Travers's gendered anxieties about her own and her books' frivolousness resonate with the terms of the modernist/middlebrow debates that have been a part of literary culture since the 1920s. These anxieties seem to be cause and symptom of Travers's efforts to dictate how her books would *look* in order to control how they would be received. In particular, she sought to control the books' illustrations, necessary but troubling indicators of the texts' status as children's literature. In the course of doing archival research, Travers's biographer, the Australian journalist Valerie Lawson, found her letters to her illustrator, Mary Shepard. She concludes from these that Travers 'insisted that her rules applied from the start. She told Howe [her English publisher] [that] she wanted a major role in the publication, suggested that she would find an illustrator and would even choose the type – in consultation with him.'[27] Though Travers never admitted it, Mary Shepard recounts in an unpublished autobiography that Travers had tried to persuade E. H. Shepard to illustrate *Mary Poppins*. He declined the invitation and Travers settled instead on his 24-year-old daughter Mary, stumbling upon her work by chance in December 1932.[28] Travers admired a hand-designed, pen-and-ink drawing on a Christmas card that Mary Shepard had sent to Travers's long-term roommate, Madge Burnand. Burnand set up an introduction between the young writer and younger artist and Shepard, who was a recent graduate of the Slade School of Art, agreed to work with Travers, little knowing that the relationship would last well into the 1980s.[29]

By all accounts, both women struggled with the process of representing Mary Poppins visually. Travers claimed that Mary Shepard's first drawings were 'impossible'. She showed them to her male mentors, who advised her to jettison Shepard and find another illustrator. But Travers persisted, supporting her protégée, taking her for long walks in Hyde Park in order to point out suitable children as models for Jane, Michael and the twins, and various young ladies as models for Mary Poppins. But it was not until Travers gave Shepard a Dutch doll that, in Travers's words, 'suddenly it seemed as though [Mary Poppins] [...] came to life; tentatively, very imperfect, but some of the atmosphere of the book came through'.[30]

Reflecting in later years on her choice of Shepard as illustrator, Travers described Mary's work rather disdainfully, saying, 'Of course it wasn't

Leonardo, but I didn't need Leonardo. [...] I was after a happy imperfection, innocence without naiveté, and as well, a sense of wonder.'[31] The reduction of Shepard to a second-rate artist, one who inevitably takes on the childish 'imperfection' and 'innocence' Travers ascribes to her art, is condescension worthy of Mary Poppins herself. Once measured against the extended history of Travers's exploitation of Shepard, however, condescension becomes something more ominous: signs of Travers's stifling impulse towards control not only of her art, but also of the people who were the necessary support and producers of it. Only Travers's biographer would have the generosity to describe the relationship between author and illustrator as that of 'teacher and pupil';[32] mistress and servant would be a better description. Tellingly, Shepard described herself in private papers as 'Eeyore'.[33] The material records that testify to the relationship between these two women (who were only 10 years apart in age and both members of the first generation to come of age in a post-suffrage Britain) suggest that Shepard never did get full credit or fair compensation for her work, despite her mastery of the same techniques that had sustained her father's career as illustrator and cartoonist for *Punch* magazine. *Punch* not only fostered the Travers–Shepard connection (it was regarded as 'essential reading' at Pound Cottage, the seventeenth-century house that Travers shared with Burnand),[34] but arguably defined the critical fate of middlebrow and children's literature more generally.[35]

Associations with *Punch* may have helped depress the stature of certain kinds of illustrated books within the cultural hierarchies maintained by literary critics. Certainly in literary criticism treating *Mary Poppins*, the verbal authority of Travers's words trumps the visual authority of Shepard's images every time. However, the 'de-disciplinary' crisis of representation described by Mitchell and Foucault throws into doubt such imagined verbal dominance. We can see the way visual authority extends over the words of a text if we pay close attention to the everyday practice of decoding illustrations, starting with analysis of our encounter with Shepard's illustration of Mary Poppins's arrival at 17 Cherry Tree Lane. The text reads, 'Jane and Michael could see that the newcomer had shiny black hair – "Rather like a wooden Dutch doll," whispered Jane. And that she was thin, with large feet and hands, and small, rather peering blue eyes.' This description is on the bottom of page 6. Facing it, on page 7 is Shepard's image of Mary Poppins with the typeset caption, 'Holding her hat on with one hand and carrying a bag in the other[.]' In the picture, Mary Poppins does indeed hold onto her hat with one hand and carry her bag with the other. But Shepard's details exceed the limits of both caption and adjacent text. For example, the general quality of 'thinness' mentioned by Travers becomes the *specific* thinness we associate with Mary Poppins in Shepard's image. Similarly, Mary Poppins's 'big feet' mentioned in Travers's first physical description of her heroine take on additional detail and meaning through their appearance in Mary Shepard's *specific* kind of working-woman's shoes. And while it is true that we encounter this image of Mary Poppins arriving at the Banks's home *after* we encounter Travers's brief description of her, it is also true that we encounter Travers's first description of Mary Poppins *after* we encounter Shepard's image of Mary Poppins in the frontispiece. Questions of precedence ('Which representation of Mary Poppins do we first encounter in the book?') lead to questions of dominance ('Which media – verbal or visual – provides the most authoritative representation of Mary Poppins?').

Shepard's frontispiece, which faces the book's title page, is a bust-length portrait of Mary Poppins. It is different from just about every other image of Mary Poppins because Mary looks cheerful instead of vexed or distracted or disgusted. Beneath the frame that surrounds the image is an inscription in Shepard's writing: 'Mary Poppins by Bert.' And beneath these words is the typeset caption, 'Inside a little curly frame was a painting of Mary Poppins.' So here we have a black-and-white reproduction of Shepard's original black-and-white ink drawing that pretends to be a copy of an original painting by Bert, a sidewalk artist who, like his art, really exists only as a string of words, as black marks on white paper. As readers cross and recross that unobtrusive, invisible white frontier between image and text, the seeable and the sayable, Shepard's frontispiece becomes a metapicture. 'Mary Poppins by Bert', within the context of the novel, functions in ways similar to Magritte's pipe, posing as a 'fundamental figure of knowledge as such'. Shepard's illustration performs the work of Magritte's elite contemporary paintings, helping us see the absurdity of cultural devaluation of children's literature and women's domestic fiction (not to mention fiction about women domestics). If Magritte's paintings and *Mary Poppins's* illustrations can serve in similar ways as period metapictures, figures of knowledge as such, the cultural elevation of one picture at the cost of the disparagement of the other seems more and more absurd.

Of course, *Mary Poppins's* ordinary readers would hardly find in Shepard's frontispiece a metapicture or figure of knowledge as such. It appears as a rather mysterious image, unfixed from the narrative and thus somewhat empty of meaning until the very end of the book. There readers discover that Mary Poppins has left the portrait of herself, by Bert, to Jane before she floats away on the west wind. It turns out that Shepard's frontispiece has prepared readers from the very outset of the book to limit Travers's inherently general, verbal descriptions of her heroine. According to Nodelman, this paradox – that additional visual information from pictures does not extend but rather limits a text – also works the other way around. The additional information provided by the words of the text – that Mary's eyes are blue, for example – limits the possible meanings of Shepard's black-and-white pictures.[36] Nodelman explains the implications of this dynamic. 'By limiting each other, words and pictures together take on meaning that neither possesses without the other':

> Because they communicate different kinds of information, and because they work together by limiting each other's meanings, words and pictures necessarily have a combative relationship.[37]

Nodelman confirms what Mitchell and Foucault have theorized: the rhetorically mixed and potentially oppositional effects and relations conducted by words and images across the white frontier or gaps of the page.

If Shepard's images do indeed talk back to Travers's words in ways that the gentle Mary Shepard never did to the domineering P. L. Travers, then the metaphorical 'combat' conducted in the pages of *Mary Poppins* might lead us to ask how do we resolve the battle between the text's mixed representational forms? Where does the dialectic of discourse and vision take us (or leave us) at the end of *Mary Poppins*? Turning to the pages of the book itself, we discover that *Mary Poppins* ends with a picture – a picture of illegible words, to be more exact (p. 209). Here is a drawing of a crumpled piece of paper that represents the goodbye note that Mary Poppins has left Jane and Michael. We know from Travers's text that the note reads:

> Dear Jane,
>   Michael had the compass so the picture is for you. Au revoir.
> MARY POPPINS (p. 208)

There are several things missing here, several things lost in the gap. One is love; Mary Poppins signs her note and leaves without ever saying she loves Jane or will miss her when she's gone. Another is the picture itself. Only those readers who remember Shepard's frontispiece will be able to find a visual representation of the picture we only learn about in the book's final pages. Thus, at what feels and looks like the end of the novel, the battle between Travers's words and Shepard's drawings continues.[38] We are left suspended, trapped in the reading-effects of what Mitchell calls the 'double-coding of the illustrated book'.

Mitchell, trained as a Blake scholar to read between the sayable and the seeable, turns the dubious, culturally suspect activity of reading illustrated books into a top priority for theorists of representation and reading. I would like to do the same for scholars investigating so-called middlebrow tastes and values. Perhaps those of us eager to promote study of middlebrow matters will take heart from Mitchell's declaration that:

> the interaction of pictures and texts is constitutive of representation as such; all media are mixed media, and all representations are heterogeneous; there are no 'purely' visual or verbal arts, though the impulse to purify media is one of the central utopian gestures of modernism.[39]

This claim not only supports my choice of *Mary Poppins* as a subject for investigation under the banner of middlebrow, it also suggests that scholars of twentieth-century literature and art should prioritize study of illustrated children's books produced in the years Magritte was working away at his stunning pipes. If 'all media are mixed media', illustrated books are not only the beginning points for study of image–text relations in books labelled 'middlebrow' they may also be the high points for study of 'representation as such'.

Notes

1. P. L. Travers (1934; 1981) *Mary Poppins* (New York: Harcourt). Subsequent references will be in parentheses in the text.
2. See for example, W. J. T. Mitchell's (1986) *Iconology: Image, Text, Ideology* (Chicago: University of Chicago Press) and (1994) *Picture Theory: Essays on Verbal and Visual Representation* (Chicago: University of Chicago Press), two foundational texts in this field of word–image relations.
3. P. Nodelman (1988) *Words about Pictures: The Narrative Art of Children's Books* (Athens: University of Georgia Press).
4. Ibid., pp. 217–218.
5. Mitchell, *Picture*, p. 69.
6. Limitations of space preclude full description of the cultural, formal and technical forces leading to distinctions between the turn-of-the-century high priced books esteemed by book collectors (e.g., those illustrated by Arthur Rackham and Aubrey Beardsley); the highbrow or modernist books

esteemed by taste-making academics (e.g., *The Tower, The Autobiography of Alice B. Toklas*); and the contemporary illustrated, non-collectable but eventually 'classic' illustrated books that are the subject of this essay (e.g., *Winnie-the-Pooh, The Wind in the Willows, Mary Poppins*). A thoroughgoing investigation of such distinctions might start with Stephen Prickett's brief outline of English illustration (2001) 'From Babylonian Railway Stations to Manic Toads: Children's Book Illustration in the Early Twentieth Century', in D. Carpi (ed.) *Literature and the Visual Arts in the Twentieth Century* (Bologna: Re Enzo), pp. 139–146, and move to Joyce Irene Whalley and Tessa Rose Chester's more detailed history, (1988) *A History of Children's Book Illustration* (London: John Murray with the Victoria and Albert Museum).

7. N. Humble (2001) *The Feminine Middlebrow Novel, 1920s to 1950s: Class, Domesticity and Bohemianism* (Oxford: Oxford University Press), p. 4.

8. Ibid., p. 14.

9. F. Hammill (2007) *Women, Celebrity, and Literary Culture Between the Wars* (Austin: University of Texas Press) makes a point of including children's literature and naming women authors of children's books in her description of the 'rich legacy of work in all genres' left by early twentieth-century women writers (p. 21). Humble's similar list of diverse middlebrow genres supports her different focus on women as readers rather than producers of middlebrow novels.

10. P. Nodelman (2008) *The Hidden Adult: Defining Children's Literature* (Baltimore: Johns Hopkins University Press).

11. Ibid., p. 5.

12. Ibid., pp. 3, 4.

13. Ibid., p. 5.

14. Ibid. p. 5. See Hammill on Pierre Bourdieu, who she describes as a 'hostile critic' of middlebrow culture, guilty of extending Virginia Woolf's and Q. D. Leavis's 'limiting definitions' of middlebrow into late twentieth-century critical discourse (p. 6). Mary Grover (2009) *The Ordeal of Warwick Deeping: Middlebrow Authorship and Cultural Embarrassment* (Madison and Teaneck, NJ: Fairleigh Dickinson University Press) is less critical of Bourdieu, engaging with his notion of cultural taste as a class strategy throughout her study of Warwick Deeping, but she also acknowledges that Bourdieu 'does not challenge the values and tastes exhibited by the dominant hegemony. His is essentially a determinist model' (p. 21).

15. Mitchell, *Picture*, pp. 96–97. Although *Mary Poppins* is popularly regarded as a 'classic', due in part to the enduring attractions of Walt Disney's movie based on the novel, the book has been excluded from scholars' rankings of 'good' children's literature according to a similar formalist logic. For example, see Humphrey Carpenter (1985) *Secret Gardens: A Study of the Golden Age of Children's Literature* (Boston: Houghton Mifflin), which dismisses Travers's achievement (along with that of Hugh Lofting, the author–illustrator of *Dr Doolittle*, and Arthur Ransome, creator of the 'Swallows and Amazons' series), because 'it is really a mediocre story strung round one good idea (a nanny with magical powers)' (p. 210).

16. Mitchell, *Picture*, p. 69.

17. Ibid.

18. Ibid.

19. Ibid., pp. 69–70.
20. Whalley and Chester, p. 11.
21. Nodelman, *Words*, p. 199.
22. Quoted in Mitchell, *Picture*, p. 69.
23. Travers was born on 9 August 1899 in Maryborough, Queensland, Australia, as Helen Lyndon Goff.
24. Lawson, p. 165.
25. Ibid., p. 165.
26. V. Lawson (1999) *Mary Poppins She Wrote* (New York: Simon and Schuster), p. 162.
27. Ibid., p. 161.
28. Ibid., p. 162.
29. Ibid., p. 163.
30. Ibid., p. 163. Travers kept changing the story about where she found the Dutch doll so Shepard's contradictory story, that it was *she* who bought the Dutch doll and thus paved the way to the Mary Poppins's look, may very well be true (Lawson, p. 164).
31. Lawson, p. 163.
32. Ibid., p. 163.
33. Ibid., p. 163.
34. Ibid., p. 162.
35. Erica Brown notes that *Punch* gets most credit for first identifying in print the use of the word 'middlebrow' (E. Brown (2008) 'Introduction' to 'Investigating the Middlebrow' issue of *Working Papers on the Web*, Vol. 11, n. p., accessed 5 August 2009), while Prickett cites *Punch* as one of two crucial influences on the 'sketchy, suggestive and sometimes fantastic' illustrations of E. H. Shepard and Golden Age children's book illustration (the other influence he mentions is Beardsley) (p. 143).
36. Nodelman, *Words*, p. 220.
37. Ibid., p. 221.
38. Given Mary Poppins's extended life as a protagonist in series fiction, this battle between Shepard's images and Travers's words is sustained diachronically through a prolonged publication history, as well as synchronically through the dialectics of form. Disney's transformation of the books into film in 1964 invites entirely new kinds of visual–verbal, biographical and institutional analysis for scholars of mid-century middlebrow. See L. Kenshaft (1999) 'Just a Spoonful of Sugar? Anxieties of Gender and Class in "Mary Poppins" ', in B. Lyon Clark and M. Higonnet (eds) *Girls, Boys, Books, Toys: Gender in Children's Literature and Culture* (Baltimore: Johns Hopkins University Press), pp. 227–242, for an astute analysis of the unpredictable ideological effects of the 'Mary Poppins' film and viewing conditions that recalls Mitchell's and Foucault's analysis of illustrated texts.
39. Mitchell, p. 5.

12
Imagism, Realism, Surrealism: Middlebrow Transformations in the Mass-Observation Project

Nick Hubble

In January 1937, Mass-Observation was launched in the letters columns of the *New Statesman* with an appeal for voluntary observers to take part in 'an anthropology of our own people'.[1] Similar appeals in higher-circulation newspapers such as the *News Chronicle* and the *Daily Express* attracted responses from across society but, as Tom Jeffery notes, far and away the largest identifiable distinct social grouping in the project's original membership was from the lower middle class.[2] This chapter investigates the dissemination of the ideas of imagism and surrealism by the Mass-Observation founders to its lower-middle-class membership as an example of the interaction between modernist techniques and middlebrow culture, which transformed that culture in the late 1930s and contributed to the wider socio-cultural changes that took place in mid-twentieth-century Britain. Following the work of Kristin Bluemel, this interaction, by which individual modernist consciousness accommodated itself to the modern mass values of the twentieth-century world and thereby both expressed and became part of the realization of those values, may be described as intermodern.[3] Therefore, this chapter will also seek to map out the relationship between the critical terms 'middlebrow', 'modernism' and 'intermodernism'.

The advent of modernism, as a movement that originated in or about December 1910 and then gained high cultural ascendancy after the First World War, led to the demarcation of middlebrow from highbrow culture. As Ross McKibbin notes, despite its supersession in elite literary circles, the neo-realist writing that had characterized the late Victorian and Edwardian periods remained widely read: 'Arnold Bennett, therefore, continued to be very popular in the 1920s for the same reasons that Dickens would have been considered middlebrow had he written in the 1920s or 1930s.'[4] This readership comprised the middle and lower middle classes and, therefore, middlebrow literature may be classified generally as realist writing 'read by the middle-class public – and particularly by the lower middle class'.[5] The tone in which the term 'middlebrow' was used by the literary elite was derogatory, as epitomized by Q. D. Leavis's *Fiction and the Reading Public* (1932). Middlebrow culture in general, and middlebrow literature in particular, came to be seen as superficial, shallow and lacking in lasting value. While middlebrow culture has become a subject of serious academic study in recent years, the academic canonization of 'modernism' since the Second World War seemingly leaves little space to accord value to a cultural category that is chiefly distinguished by its lack of the formal, experimental features often identified as the sole arbiters of artistic worth.

The example of Mass-Observation opens up a different perspective on this set of cultural processes. As discussed in more detail below, recent essays by James Hinton and Mike Savage both analyse how the Mass-Observers sought to create an intellectual space independent of existing class relations. However, while Hinton understands this as a process of cultural distinction in which the aesthetic resources of modernism were used to disembed individual Mass-Observers from their social spheres, Savage claims that the process of distinction that took place was a social one by which Mass-Observers embraced the techniques of social research in order to distance themselves from the cultural categories of high-, middle- and lowbrow.

Compatibility between Savage's and Hinton's positions can be re-established by hypothesizing that the 'modernism' that Hinton defines in relation to the cultural distinction of Mass-Observers is different from the 'modernism' implied by the highbrow which Savage suggests was one of the cultural categories that Mass-Observers sought to define themselves against. Such a perspective distinguishes between the fluid 'modernism' that actually existed in the first half of the twentieth century and a more fixed canonical construction of that 'modernism', which solidified in the second half of the century. If cultural history is understood in this way, then there is the potential for middlebrow culture to emerge as more than simply modernism's other. The following discussion of the interaction between that actually existing modernism and middlebrow culture in the Mass-Observation project is intended as a contribution to this process of reappraising how the term 'middlebrow' can best be employed to aid the understanding of cultural processes in twentieth-century Britain.

The wider transformation of middlebrow culture

McKibbin's *Classes and Cultures: England 1918–1951* (1998) discusses the transformation in interwar middlebrow culture represented by the difference between Warwick Deeping's *Sorrell and Son* (1925) and A. J. Cronin's *The Citadel* (1937):

In February 1938 Gallup asked its sample which book of all had impressed them most. Only a minority felt able to answer; but of that minority two books alone (other than the bible) had any significant number of votes: *Sorrell and Son* and *The Citadel*. Although these two books are not polar opposites – both believe in the predominance of an individualist middle class – the enormous popularity of *Sorrell and Son* in the 1920s and *The Citadel* in the 1930s is suggestive of the altered mood of the 'broad' middle class. In the 1920s the mood is resentful, defensive, and primarily anti-working class. In the 1930s it is self-confident and, if anything, primarily anti-traditional upper middle class. Above all, the working class is no longer seen as menacing. In Cronin the middle-class hero is now not a warrior or man of destiny, nor a retiring gardener or crossword-puzzler, but a socially and technically progressive proponent of modernity. The idiom is not 'feminine' and reticent but 'masculine' and public.[6]

McKibbin goes on to argue that the emergence of this individualist, but progressive, modern middle class, as reflected in the difference between these middlebrow novels, accounts for the extraordinary success of such late 1930s phenomena as the Penguin Specials and Gollancz's Left Book Club, which can be seen as the manifestation of a middlebrow politics. Mass-Observation was a part of this cultural constellation; not only was it initially funded with advances from Victor Gollancz but its numerous publications also included two Penguin Specials: *Britain by Mass-Observation* (1939) and *People in Production* (1942).

Mass-Observation set out to be an inclusive mass movement as an early statement by its three co-founders – the ornithologist and anthropologist, Tom Harrisson; the surrealist and documentary film-maker, Humphrey Jennings; and the communist and poet, Charles Madge – makes clear:

Mass Observation develops out of anthropology, psychology, and the sciences which study man – but it plans to work with a mass of observers. Already we have fifty observers at work on two sample problems. We are further working out a complete plan of campaign, which will be possible when we have not fifty but 5,000 observers [...] all human types can and must assist in this work. The artist and the scientist, each compelled by historical necessity out of their artificial exclusiveness, are at last joining forces and turning back towards the mass from which they had detached themselves.

It does not set out in quest of truth or facts for their own sake, or for the sake of an intellectual minority, but aims at exposing them in simple terms to all observers, so that their environment may be understood, and thus constantly transformed. Whatever the political methods called upon to effect the transformation, the knowledge of what is to be transformed is indispensable. The foisting on the mass of ideals or ideas developed by men apart from it, irrespective of its capacities, causes mass misery, intellectual despair and an international shambles.[7]

As can be seen, the three Cambridge-educated founders were profoundly concerned by the gap that had opened up in the modern, mechanized society of the 1930s between the masses and the intellectual and cultural elite. In particular, they were concerned about the threat of these conditions leading to fascism, as they had in Italy, Germany and Spain.[8] The characteristics defined by Jeffrey as shared by the Mass-Observers, such as secondary education, living with their parents through their twenties and employment in clerical or technical jobs, which were sometimes boring but not fundamentally unsatisfactory and which left plenty of time for other pursuits, would be equally descriptive of many of the adherents of continental fascism.[9] However, unlike much of the rest of Europe, Britain remained unique in that its black-coated (clerical) workforce had moved to the left politically during the 1930s.[10] A look at the shared generational relationship of these Mass-Observers to the key historical antecedents of the late 1930s suggests that it was not historical circumstances that distinguished the British from their continental counterparts:

Many had had childhoods interrupted by the crisis of the early years of the century: a number of fathers had been killed in the First World War, some families lost their savings in the inflation which followed the First World War, some had been ruined by the slump. Many of the diarists had themselves had problems finding work in the 1930s and there are many accounts of unemployment. [...] The homes of the lower middle class diarists tended to be in the suburbs of large cities, often in streets which were just beginning to go noticeably down in the world, streets which would have been eminently respectable when the twenty-five year old diarist was born.[11]

Such a history might be seen as providing the perfect breeding grounds for a shift into reaction but, nevertheless, it is also compatible with the transformation in interwar middlebrow culture identified by McKibbin, in which a defensive stance gave way to a progressive one. While in the 1920s the dominant concerns of the British middle class and its culture were with what had been lost and what could further be lost, the worst had happened to some by the late 1930s and turned out to 'not be so dreadful as [...] feared', as George Orwell suggested in *The Road to Wigan Pier* (1937).[12] Here, it is necessary to consider that the clerical classes in Britain, especially in London, had a long history stretching back deep into the nineteenth century and a well-established literary culture originating with Dickens – the forebear of the interwar middlebrow writers. With education, employment and spare time restored, there was room for the gradual return of a lower-middle-class optimism that had run from Dickens to the Edwardian heyday of H. G. Wells. Mass-Observation's pitch to a constituency beyond the 'intellectual minority' was perfectly weighted to gain approval from a younger fraction of that class ready to relive that heyday.

In this context, the sociologist Mike Savage has argued that the link between the 'popular social science' focus of Penguin paperbacks and the mobilization of several thousand Mass-Observers in 'the projects of diary keeping, letter writing and other forms of observation' testifies to:

> the dramatic emergence of a new kind of social body, one which saw the act of writing, research and reflection as central to its self-identity. This assertion of intellectual engagement broke in subtle ways from existing conceptions of the intellectual, which had previously been mobilised within a status-based discourse of 'high'-, 'middle'- and 'low'-brows.[13]

This cultural revolution was cemented by the wartime expansion of the civil service and local government, in which lower-middle-class clerical workers and the British intelligentsia were brought together. The emergent public-sector middle-class identity, which was to spread rapidly through post-war nationalization, was further reinforced in the late 1940s by the effects of status anxiety in the face of the welfare state's progressive erasure of old informal privileges and the relative rise in working-class income. Any attempt to reclaim former status was problematic in an era in which social legitimacy was defined in terms of democratic equality: 'To be blunt, for the "cultured middle classes" to overtly define their own privileges in terms of their innate cultural superiority struck the wrong tone. It was necessary to find an alternative way of explaining and justifying their social position.'[14] Large numbers of the more well-to-do middle class found compromise with the post-war welfare state by following the pre-war example of lower-middle-class participation in the Left Book Club and Mass-Observation, and positioning themselves as the enablers and managers of national progress. As Savage notes, this was still a claim to social distinction – albeit not located in aesthetic and cultural values but in the assumption of more practical and technical identities.

Modernist complications

This social and cultural evolution of the middle class from the resentful and anti-working-class individualists of the 1920s to the willing and pro-welfare-state technocrats of the 1950s and 1960s was not, however, as straightforward and unmediated as the above account suggests. As Jonathan Rose's *The Intellectual Life of the British Working Classes* (2001) cannot help highlighting in spite of itself, this middle-class evolution was the result of not only the change in middlebrow cultural values but also the widespread adoption of the apparently opposed values of modernism. Rose describes the origin of modernism as a reactionary consequence of the income of clerks beginning to overtake that of 'rentier intellectuals' such as Virginia Woolf and E. M. Forster: 'The latter could only preserve their cultural prestige by creating a new literature inaccessible to Board school graduates.'[15] He goes on to argue that the resultant entrenched division between rival modernist and middlebrow camps dominated British literary culture during the first half of the twentieth century before becoming distorted by the canonization of the modernists in the university curriculum since 1950. However, the rigidity of his claim is not supported by the examples he provides. For instance, the single source he cites as proof of his assertion that 'if academic specialists [...] treat middlebrow culture at all, they usually dismiss it as superficial and middle-class', is the account by McKibbin quoted earlier in this chapter which is clearly not dismissive in tone.[16] Moreover, the process by which he alleges 'modernists used difficulty to fence off and protect literary property' is clearly unworkable by his own account:

> [Ezra] Pound coined the term 'Imagist' as a kind of brand name for modern poetry, but he soon saw a problem in his marketing strategy: if the point of Imagist poetry was to overawe the masses, what was to prevent them from learning the trick of it and producing their own? Amy Lowell considered copyrighting the name 'Imagist' to keep out inferior imitators, but intellectual property law has never permitted a poet to register his movement as a trademark. Sure enough by 1917 Eliot was complaining that 'now it is possible to print free verse (second, third, or tenth-rate) in almost any American magazine'.[17]

Not only was nothing stopping the masses from learning the trick of imagist poetry and producing their own, but also renegade highbrows such as Jennings and Madge actively sought to promote the process. Together with fellow intellectuals and poets, including William Empson, David Gascoyne and Kathleen Raine, they met in the autumn of 1936 to discuss 'Popular Poetry', the working title for what was to become Mass-Observation. One of the ideas discussed was the possibility of issuing 'images' in the form of packs of cards with which suggested exercises could be played. As soon as Mass-Observers were recruited in the following year, they were invited to complete their day diaries (which were kept on the 12th day of each month from February 1937 to January 1938) by recording the dominant image of the day. Whereas Pound had wanted to make the image rather than the word the unit of signification so that poems generated their own meanings separate from dominant narrative associations, the aim of Mass-Observation was to enable its observers to liberate their perceptions from externally imposed associations and so create the possibility of social change.[18] Mass-Observation can, therefore, be seen as a paradigmatic example of the manner in which the 1930s middlebrow transformation from a defensive anti-working-class culture to a confident progressive one was due in part to the extension and incorporation of modernist techniques.

This insight can be productively compared with James Hinton's argument, based on his analysis of responses to the June 1939 Mass-Observation directive, that 'A highbrow like Virginia Woolf, we might argue, did more to construct modern selfhood than a far more widely read writer like J. B. Priestley, despite the latter's mastery of the means of mass communication.'[19] The assertion here is deliberately provocative to counter what Hinton sees as a bias in works such as John Carey's *The*

Intellectual and the Masses (1992). He goes on to acknowledge Priestley's importance to the nation in 1940, but suggests that the key area for identity formation was the private rather than the public sphere:

> Individual selfhoods were constructed around more intimate, private and internalised narratives of class, gender, family and personal history. For those liberated by education, leisure and the widening availability of high culture via the paperback, gramophone record and radio, access to the classics of British and international fiction, or even to Virginia Woolf (published by Penguin from the late 1930s), offered routes to self-invention, ways of freeing the self from the closure of predetermined roles. [...] It is likely that engagement with high culture helped people [...] to disembed themselves from 'the stock notions and habits' of their class.[20]

Hinton argues, contra Bourdieu, that rather than cultural distinction underwriting social class, the example of Mass-Observation respondents shows 'a quest for identity in which class was being downgraded in favour of culture'.[21] However, because Mass-Observation was a collective and participatory movement, the result of this social 'disembedding' was not narcissistic individualism but the evolution of 'a structure of feeling in which a readiness to participate in public affairs coexisted with a self-reflexive individualism and [...] an engagement with high culture'.[22]

The intermodern significance of mass-observation

Hinton's account provides an interesting contrast with Savage's analysis of substantially the same data. Their points of agreement and disagreement are highlighted in what are arguably the key sentences of each article:

> Most of those claiming cultural distinction or classifying themselves as intellectuals, from the working-class autodidacts to the upper-middle-class bohemians, were aspiring to inhabit a social space existing independently from the structures of social class.[23]
> [...] we can see many of these accounts of the 1939 Mass-Observers seeking to create an intellectual space, which did not reproduce existing class divisions, but which creatively sought to use Mass-Observation to distance itself from gentlemanly, artistic, highbrow motifs in favour of a more 'technical', scientific intellectual vision.[24]

Rather than declare one right and one wrong – the material can be plausibly presented either way – it makes more sense to consider these statements as descriptions of different aspects of a wider multifaceted process by which a new social and intellectual space was produced. On the one hand, it is hardly surprising that modernist techniques could contribute to social disembedding with the aim of creating a space of social and intellectual freedom as they were originally developed by much more socially marginalized writers than Woolf such as Dorothy Richardson, Katherine Mansfield and D. H. Lawrence, who had exactly such an end in mind. This urge for individual liberation was the essence of modernism before the First World War. However, it was an urge that could only be fulfilled culturally given the still relatively static nature of British society at that time. On the other hand, it is clear that by the 1930s a whole range of opportunities, which hadn't existed in the Edwardian period, had emerged in fields such as technology and social and scientific research. These opportunities provided the possibility for the liberation of many more lower-middle-class individuals than was afforded by the purely cultural sphere. The subsequent extension of these opportunities, as part of the wartime expansion of the state, established the support conditions for the new forms of technocratic middle-class identities that Savage identifies. Perhaps the mistake is to see either cultural or technocratic values as the sole possible basis of the desired classless identity; both were means to the same end and could perfectly well be combined in the same individual.

The significance of Mass-Observation to the wider transformation in middlebrow culture was as an organization that recruited the type of younger lower-middle-class progressive individuals that were attracted to Penguins and the Left Book Club, while promoting examples of modernist imagism, and, as the letter to the *New Statesman* shows, deliberately seeking to bring art and science together. By calling for an anthropology of British life, it invited its respondents to think about the extent to which they were both part of, and part outside, that society. It thereby reconciled individualism to the collective without subsuming it, diminishing potential feelings of isolation and alienation while supporting self-reflection and promoting its development into a conscious self-reflexivity. The popular poetry of Mass-Observation can, therefore, be seen as providing something similar to what was being demanded at the time by Christopher Caudwell in his call for a communist poetry which, instead of realizing bourgeois freedom through expressing individual needs, would express a consciousness of social necessity and thus meet the challenge of 'refashioning the categories and technique of art so that it expresses the new world coming into being and is part of its realisation'.[25]

Caudwell was cutting in his dismissal of the two contemporary movements which made claims to be fulfilling this function. On the one hand, he argues that the tendency of Auden group poets to accept proletarian values in any aspect of life except art itself was creating a distorted vision: 'His proletarian living bursts into his art in the form of crude and grotesque scraps of Marxist phraseology and the mechanical application of the living proletarian theory – this is very clearly seen in the three English poets [W. H. Auden, Stephen Spender and C. Day Lewis] most closely associated with the revolutionary movement.'[26] On the other hand, he castigates surrealism as 'the final bourgeois position': a last attempt of a dying culture to haul itself up by its own bootlaces through a positivist process of recording everyday phenomena, which are then treated as the key to the unconscious and the possibility of a dream state where 'men float into air, cut loose from both subject and object'.[27] With their respective strong connections to the first and second of these groupings, Mass-Observation founders Madge and Jennings might well have been expected to combine the worst of both positions. However, in their respective day jobs as a *Daily Mirror* reporter and documentary film-maker, they fitted Orwell's definition of those technical workers 'who are most at home in and most definitely *of* the modern world'.[28] Therefore, it is perhaps not so surprising that they had a very modern, technocratic attitude to poetry, as in this still shocking declaration:

> [Observers] produce a poetry which is, not at present, restricted to a handful of esoteric performers. The immediate effect of MASS-OBSERVATION is to devalue considerably the status of the 'poet.' It makes the term 'poet' apply, not to his performance, but to his profession, like 'footballer'.[29]

As noted at the beginning of this essay, a new critical term, 'intermodernism', has recently emerged to describe exactly this process, demanded by Caudwell, by which poetic consciousness 'expresses the new world coming into being and is part of its realisation'. Bluemel defines intermodernism as 'a category that alludes to both period and style'.[30] However, aside from referring to a period between 1930 and 1950 and a style between modernism and postmodernism, it also signifies a cultural politics both part of and not part of modernism. Indeed, on one level, it is the harnessing of modernist techniques to political ends. Elsewhere, I have described Mass-Observation as 'an exemplary intermodern project'[31] and what its history suggests is that intermodernism provides a much-needed critical term which can be used to describe the interaction that took place in the 1930s and 1940s between actually existing modernism and middlebrow culture, which has become retrospectively obscured by the post-war canonical construction of modernism. Middlebrow culture provided the social formation on which modernist techniques could find political purchase in the case of Mass-Observation in particular and intermodern interventions in general.

For example, a quintessentially intermodern novel such as George Orwell's *Keep the Aspidistra Flying* (1936) is profoundly concerned with effecting the transformation of middlebrow culture through modernist consciousness in order to celebrate the suburban values of a life of marriage and work and children: 'small clerks, shop-assistants, commercial travellers, insurance touts, tram conductors [...] it mightn't be a bad thing, if you could manage it, to feel yourself one of them, one of the ruck of men.'[32] Unlike Caudwell, Orwell could see that mass media advertising was doing a better job of expressing social needs than traditional poetry. While Caudwell cites Milton's line, 'Thick as autumnal leaves that strow the brooks/ In Vallombrosa', as evidence of poetry's musical resistance to external associations, Orwell highlights the absurdity of such misplaced romanticism: 'Thick as the Breakfast Crisps that strow the plates/ In Welwyn Garden City!'[33] It is only when his antihero, Gordon Comstock, finally rejects poetry and returns to his job in advertising that he truly finds himself. The copy he produces for a foot odour product turns out to be the best stuff he has ever written in his life:

> harrowing little stories, each a realistic novel in a hundred words, about despairing virgins of thirty, and lonely bachelors whose girls had unaccountably thrown them over, and overworked wives who could only afford to change their stockings once a week and who saw their husbands subsiding into the clutches of 'the other woman'.[34]

This 'happy ending' can be interpreted in various ways but the warmth and joy of the final scenes between Comstock and his girlfriend Rosemary suggest that it should be taken as genuine. One way of reading it as an earned happy ending would be to see Orwell as dialectically resolving the shortcomings of the antithetical poetical positions of the Auden group and the surrealists, as outlined by Caudwell above. In abandoning his highbrow conception of poetry as art, Comstock does not abandon the poetic vision which allows him to identify constituent fragments of everyday experience – similar to the images of the day that Mass-Observation collected from their respondents – and recombine them into personally and collectively meaningful narratives. Orwell's insight was that the importance of such micro-narratives of desire – 'being born, being married, begetting, working, dying' – to the suburban masses lay in the potential they provided for people to take on a form of poetic agency for themselves. It was because the lower middle classes believed in their own narratives of 'ke[eping] themselves respectable – ke[eping] the aspidistra flying' – that they were able to resist imposed political narratives and remain *alive*.[35] The novel, therefore, illustrates the wider transition in mid-twentieth-century British culture that is the subject of this chapter. One of the joys of reading *Aspidistra* is the even-handedness with which Orwell/Comstock expresses his contempt for the literary culture of the earlier part of the century; he might be scathing about Warwick Deeping, Ethel M. Dell and the interchange-able trio of Galsworthy, Walpole and Priestley, but he is equally blunt in his dismissal of the highbrows: 'Eliot, Pound, Auden, Campbell, Day Lewis, Spender. Very damp squibs, that lot.'[36] The only forms of litera-ture that Comstock is finally able to bear reading are twopenny weekly papers: '*Tit Bits, Answers, Peg's Paper, The Gem, The Magnet, Home Notes, The Girl's Own Paper*'.[37] It is knowledge of this popular culture in con-junction with his poetic vision that underwrites Comstock's skills in advertising. Orwell, himself, utilized the same skills in his pioneer-ing of what was to become cultural studies in essays such as 'Boys' Weeklies' from *Inside the Whale* (1940). But for a contemporary collective expression of those changing cultural values, it is more than conceiv-able that Gordon and Rosemary, who we last see happily together in their suburban flat sometime in the mid-1930s, would be exactly the kind of people to join Mass-Observation when it started shortly afterwards.

Rethinking surrealism

As we have seen, Caudwell denounced surrealism as 'the final bour-geois position'; a position that was retrospectively endorsed by another Marxist critic, Fredric Jameson, 70 years later:

> The stunning and depressing historical irony of the surrealist move-ment was that this pre-eminent anti-aesthetic vanguard movement,

which despised Literature and aimed at the radical transformation of daily life itself, became the very paradigm of Literature and literary production in the Western mainstream high-cultural tradition. To grasp the movement of a [...] narrative as a virtual dream, as the logic of fantasy, as unconscious free association and projection, as sheer subjectivity, is in other words to 'contain' those narratives and reduce them to a manageable literary option already classified and catalogued in advance. In this sense, the very category of the 'irrational' or the 'subjective-unconscious' is a category in the service of instrumental reason itself, and a way of defusing and marginalising otherwise aberrant, dangerous and subversive cultural phenomena.[38]

Jameson's argument can be extended to all forms of cultural modernism: what else have the techniques of Joyce and Woolf become but the very signifiers of 'Literature'? Of course, this problem is a product of the post-war canonical construction of modernism which, as discussed above, obscures the more fluid interaction between modernism and middlebrow culture that occurred before the war. The final part of this chapter considers how one branch of modernism, surrealism, can be rescued from its canonical dead end and re-energized by linking it to wider intermodern and middlebrow contexts as exemplified by Mass-Observation.

A third Marxist critic, Walter Benjamin, points the way here in his 1929 essay 'Surrealism: The Last Snapshot of the European Intelligentsia'. While the title might suggest an attitude similar to Caudwell's, Benjamin argues that surrealism is poised to supersede itself by moving beyond *l'art pour l'art* to a more 'materialistic, anthropological' orientation.[39] The key aspect of surrealism is, therefore, not the hallucinatory confusion of intoxication which has come to be seen as its defining characteristic, but the clarity by which experience suddenly crystallizes into the possibility of constructing new forms of social meaning: a process Benjamin defines as one of 'profane illumination'.[40] Surrealism's potential for this form of anthropology is revealed for Benjamin in works such as André Breton's semi-autobiographical novel, *Nadja* (1928):

Breton and Nadja are the lovers who convert everything that we have experienced on mournful railway journeys (railways are beginning to age), on Godforsaken Sunday afternoons in the proletarian quarters of great cities, in the first glance through the rain-blurred window of a new apartment, into revolutionary experience, if not action.[41]

Reviewers of Mass-Observation's first book, *May the Twelfth* (1937), felt the same way about what they were reading: 'One really seems to hear the people speaking, and to look into their lives – like passing back-yards in a train.'[42] Benjamin concludes his essay by suggesting that one further step is necessary for any surrealist to realize the full potential of this method: 'Indeed, might not perhaps the interruption of his "artistic career" be an essential part of his new function?'[43] Jennings, one of the leading lights of the English Surrealist Group, member of the organizing committee of the 1936 International Surrealist Exhibition in London, and friend of Breton and Paul Eluard, took this step.

With Madge, he set out to co-ordinate, and then edit into a montage, hundreds of mass observations of the Coronation of George VI on 12 May 1937 in the hope of discovering what effect Edward VIII's sexually motivated choice of Mrs Simpson over public duty had had on the widespread repression of desire in Britain. The result was similar to the fictional experience of Gordon Comstock returning to advertising and writing better than ever before; they produced a stunning sequence of micro-narratives of desire that eclipsed all their previous attempts at avant-garde prose poetry, such as this 'climax of a series of stories involving policemen and young women':

> At Hyde Park Corner Rovers are hurriedly putting up a metal barrier in the centre of the street where a lot of cardboard boxes (left by periscope and chocolate sellers) are lying on the ground in the rain. They are now as slippery as banana peels. A girl is lying on the ground in the arms of a policeman. [. . .]
> Along the East Carriage Drive the side of the road is actually an inch deep in sodden newspapers, cigarette packs, rubber mats and filth. Seat holders in covered stands are waiting for the rain to stop. The open stands are empty. The statue of Byron shines in the rain. The police are reforming their units.[44]

What we see in such passages is nothing less than the historical goal of surrealism realized: everyday experience transfigured into a vivid sequence of moments of being no longer restricted to a modernist minority but spread across British society to reflect all areas of experience. Mass-Observation's profane illumination did not just cast light for its intellectual founders and their immediate circle but also lit up the wider middlebrow culture of the late 1930s, turning it into a site of social transformation. To adapt Laura Marcus's argument about the intermodern character of British documentary cinema,

Mass-Observation 'offers one of the most significant and complex constellations for intermodernism, in its intertwinings of a [surrealist] aesthetic and a realist imperative': a modernist poetics and a middlebrow politics.[45]

Notes

1. Charles Madge (2 January 1937) letter, *New Statesman and Nation* XIII, 306, p. 12. For the history of Mass-Observation, see Nick Hubble (2006) *Mass-Observation, and Everyday Life* (Basingstoke and New York: Palgrave Macmillan).
2. Tom Jeffery (1978) 'Mass-Observation: A Short History', occasional papers, Centre for Contemporary Cultural Studies, University of Birmingham, p. 29.
3. Kristin Bluemel (2004) *George Orwell and the Radical Eccentrics: Intermodernism in Literary London* (New York and Basingstoke: Palgrave Macmillan) and Bluemel, ed. (2009) *Intermodernism: Literary Culture in Mid-Twentieth-Century Britain* (Edinburgh: Edinburgh University Press).
4. Ross McKibbin (1998) *Classes and Cultures: England 1918–1951* (Oxford and New York: Oxford University Press), p. 478.
5. Nicola Humble (2001) *The Feminine Middlebrow Novel, 1920s to 1950s: Class, Domesticity and Bohemianism* (Oxford: Oxford University Press), p. 13.
6. McKibbin, *Classes and Cultures*, p. 485.
7. Tom Harrisson, Humphrey Jennings and Charles Madge (30 January 1937) letter, *New Statesman and Nation*, XIII, 310, p. 155.
8. For examples of Mass-Observation's anti-Fascist alignment and strategies, see Hubble, *Mass-Observation and Everyday Life*, pp. 150–164.
9. See Rudy Koshar, ed. (1990) *Splintered Classes: Politics and the Lower Middle Classes in Interwar Europe* (New York: Holmes & Meier).
10. See Jeffrey, 'A Place in the Nation: The Lower Middle Class in England' and Susan Pennybacker, 'Changing Convictions: London County Council Blackcoated Activism between the Wars', in Koshar, ed., *Splintered Classes*, pp. 70–96; 97–120.
11. Jeffery, 'Mass-Observation: A Short History', p. 29.
12. George Orwell (1937; 1962) *The Road to Wigan Pier* (Harmondsworth: Penguin), p. 204.
13. Mike Savage (2008) 'Affluence and Social Change in the Making of Technocratic Middle-Class Identities: Britain, 1939–1955', *Contemporary British History*, 22: 4, 461.
14. Ibid., p. 470.
15. Jonathan Rose (2001) *The Intellectual Life of the British Working Classes* (New Haven and London: Yale University Press), p. 434.
16. Ibid., pp. 431, 514.
17. Ibid., p. 435.
18. See Hubble, *Mass-Observation and Everyday Life*, pp. 5–7, 119.
19. James Hinton (2008) ' "The 'Class' Complex": Mass-Observation and Cultural Distinction in Pre-War Britain', *Past and Present*, 199, pp. 207, 219.
20. Ibid., pp. 219–220.
21. Ibid., p. 222.

22. Ibid.
23. Ibid., p. 229.
24. Savage, p. 466. Somewhat misleadingly, Savage begins this sentence 'As Hubble argues' despite the fact that I do not explicitly make this argument in *Mass-Observation and Everyday Life* beyond claiming that Mass-Observation was part of a wider movement in the late 1930s seeking the advent of a classless society; see Hubble, *Mass-Observation and Everyday Life*, p. 227.
25. Christopher Caudwell (1937; 1977) *Illusion and Reality: A Study of the Sources of Poetry* (London: Lawrence & Wishart), p. 319.
26. Ibid., pp. 314–315.
27. Ibid., pp. 265, 280.
28. Orwell (1941; 1982) *The Lion and the Unicorn* (Harmondsworth: Penguin), p. 69.
29. Humphrey Jennings and Charles Madge (1937) 'Poetic Description and Mass-Observation', *New Verse*, 24, p. 3.
30. Bluemel, *Intermodernism*, p. 5.
31. Hubble, 'The Intermodern Assumption of the Future: William Empson, Charles Madge and Mass-Observation', in Bluemel, *Intermodernism*, p. 176.
32. Orwell (1936; 1989) *Keep the Aspidistra Flying* (Harmondsworth: Penguin), p. 267.
33. Caudwell, *Illusion and Reality*, p. 238; Orwell, *Aspidistra*, p. 142.
34. Orwell, *Aspidistra*, p. 272.
35. Ibid., pp. 267–268.
36. Ibid., p. 12.
37. Ibid., p. 249.
38. Fredric Jameson (2005) *Archaeologies of the Future* (London: Verso), p. 317.
39. Walter Benjamin (1979) 'Surrealism: The Last Snapshot of the European Intelligentsia', in *One-Way Street and Other Writings*, trans. Edmund Jephcott and Kingsley Shorter (London: New Left Books), pp. 227, 231.
40. Ibid., pp. 227, 236–237.
41. Ibid., p. 229.
42. L.A.Z. (A woman reader) (1937; 1967) *Life and Letters*, 17: 10 (New York: Kraus Reprint), p. 167.
43. Benjamin, 'Surrealism', p. 238.
44. Jennings and Madge, eds (1937) *May the Twelfth: Mass-Observation Day Surveys 1937* (London: Faber and Faber), pp. 144–145.
45. Laura Marcus, ' "The Creative Treatment of Actuality": John Grierson, Documentary Cinema and "Fact" in the 1930s', in Bluemel, *Intermodernism*, p. 205.

13
The Queer Pleasures of Reading: Camp and the Middlebrow

Nicola Humble

In 2001, I had published a book with a rather horrible title – *The Feminine Middlebrow Novel, 1920s to 1950s: Class, Domesticity and Bohemianism*. In the preface, I talked about my experience of reading the middlebrow women's fiction of this period with my friends at university. If I might self-indulgently quote myself, I said the following:

> Studying English – and a great deal of literary theory – at Oxford in the mid-1980s, my circle of female friends developed a cultish taste for what we called 'girly books' – those women's novels of the first half of the century discovered in second-hand bookshops, and just beginning to be reissued by Virago. The generic 'girly book' combined an enjoyable feminine 'trivia' of clothes, food, family, manners, romance, and so on, with an element of wry self-consciousness that allowed the reader to drift between ironic and complicit readings. A classic of the type would also reveal a maelstrom of thwarted impulse struggling beneath the surface of the text, even a hint of psychosis beneath its ebullient fripperies. We read these books not in a spirit of analysis but of pure self-indulgence: they were at one with the bright red lipstick we decided offered no contradiction to our radical feminist principles. I think we saw them as a form of camp – revelling in their detailing of a mode of feminine existence that seemed eons away from our own. They certainly had no direct bearing on the model of English literature we constructed for the benefit of our finals examiners. Fifteen years later, I no longer see these novels as camp: their concerns seem both more serious and less safely distant, and the world of the women who wrote them and the women who read them is central to the way I now understand the first half of the twentieth century.[1]

I have thought again about this statement – and decided I was wrong. I *do* still think these novels are camp. So I started wondering why; what camp really *is*; and whether perhaps their early readers might have found them camp too. And if so, what that might tell us about the middlebrow and its cultural place.

So what is camp? It is one of those things that seems to shift and re-form when you get too close to it. We all think we know what we mean by the term, but it seems to evade clear definition, playing in the murky waters between 'kitsch' and 'queer'. Susan Sontag teases out some of these issues in her 'Notes on Camp', published in 1964:

> Many things in the world have not been named; and many things, even if they have been named, have never been described. One of these is the sensibility – unmistakably modern, a variant of sophistication but hardly identical with it – that goes by the cult name of 'Camp'.
>
> A sensibility (as distinct from an idea) is one of the hardest things to talk about; but there are special reasons why Camp, in particular, has never been discussed. It is not a natural mode of sensibility, if there be any such. Indeed the essence of Camp is its love of the unnatural: of artifice and exaggeration. And Camp is esoteric – something of a private code, a badge of identity even, among small urban cliques.[2]

Nonetheless, Sontag does offer a range of defining characteristics of the camp sensibility: it is a mode of aestheticism; it emphasizes style over content; it converts the serious into the frivolous. 'It is the love of the exaggerated, the "off," of things-being-what-they-are-not' (p. 56). Camp is primarily a way of seeing, but it is not only that: it is also a quality discoverable in objects, in people, and although the camp eye has the power to transform experience, not everything can be seen as camp: 'It's not *all* in the eye of the beholder' (p. 54). Camp can be a way of transforming the artefacts of the past – a looking back with tongue in cheek, an enjoyment of the failed seriousness of the past object – and it is this sense that I intended in my dismissal of my early sense of middlebrow fiction as camp: I wanted to suggest that these novels are more than just ridiculous. But there is also the camp which speaks to its own moment, which is an integral part of the object, and it is this notion that I want to pursue, in suggesting that there is a camp sensibility *inherent* in middlebrow fiction and the reading culture that surrounds it.[3]

Sontag offers 58 separate 'notes' on the subject of camp – I want to deal with just a few of them. One of the most useful for my purposes has to do with the issue of character:

> What Camp taste responds to is 'instant character' (this is, of course, very 18th century); and, conversely, what it is not stirred by is the sense of the development of character. Character is understood as a state of continual incandescence – a person being one, very intense thing. This attitude toward character is a key element of the theatricalization of experience embodied in the Camp sensibility. (p. 61)

So many middlebrow texts can be described in these terms – the Provincial Lady novels, and those by Nancy Mitford; the works of Margery Allingham and Agatha Christie (in fact, detective fiction in general, which has no real interest in character development); *Cold Comfort Farm*, with its ludicrous character 'types'; the weirdly static world of Ivy Compton Burnett, and, of course, the campest of all interwar novels – those by E. F. Benson. Benson's Mapp and Lucia novels offer an immediate riposte to Sontag's contention that the truest form of camp is unconscious, since their campness is surely entirely within the control of their author. In terms of character, his novels overflow with outrageously one-dimensional stereotypes: bossy Miss Mapp, always ultimately routed by the endlessly pretentious Lucia; effeminate Georgie, with his piano duets and his embroidery; the snobbish Wyses; and so on. Many of the characters are themselves camp: the lisping Lucia, a vulnerable dominatrix as appealing to the queer sensibility as any Judy Garland or Bette Davies; the barely closeted Georgie; and Quaint Irene, an artist who dresses as a man and harbours an openly acknowledged 'schwarm' for Lucia. But more than this, the novels fulfil virtually all of Sontag's criteria: the camp sensibility, she suggests,

> is one that is alive to a double sense in which some things can be taken. But this is not the familiar split-level construction of a literal meaning, on the one hand, and a symbolic meaning, on the other. It is the difference, rather, between the thing as meaning something, anything, and the thing as pure artifice. (p. 57)

It is precisely this sensibility that animates Benson's novels. I have suggested elsewhere that his fiction functions as a sort of condensed pastiche of the women's middlebrow novel, in which the day-to-day minutiae of domestic details, social trivia and servant problems tip over into surrealism, with the refusal of a recipe leading to Mapp and Lucia being washed out to sea on an upturned kitchen table, and exclusions from dinner parties leading to revenge schemes as elaborate as those in a Jacobean tragedy. The small concerns of the women's middlebrow mean simultaneously everything and nothing in this fiction. It is not straightforward parody, which dismisses the thing it mocks, but a double vision which treats with profound affection the thing it reveals so clearly as ridiculous. Or as Sontag says, in a description that absolutely sums up the tone of Benson's fiction:

> Camp taste is a kind of love, love for human nature. It relishes, rather than judges, the little triumphs and awkward intensities of 'character'. [...] Camp taste identifies with what it is enjoying. [...] Camp is a *tender* feeling. (p. 65)

It is not just in E. F. Benson's fiction that we find this doubleness of vision, though his is the most marked case. It is, as seems to me, a key element in the sophisticated wryness which characterizes the tone and attitudes of much middlebrow fiction. Rachel Ferguson's wonderfully loopy *The Brontës Went to Woolworths* (1931), for instance, begins with a mocking dismissal of exactly the sort of novel – familial, bohemian, self-consciously modern – that it itself is:

> How I loathe that kind of novel which is about a lot of sisters. It is usually called *They Were Seven*, or *Three – Not Out*, and one spends one's entire time trying to sort them all, and muttering, 'Was it Isobel who drank, or Gertie? And which was it who ran away with the gigolo, Amy or Pauline? And which of their separated husbands was Lionel, Isobel's or Amy's?'
> Katrine and I often grin over that sort of book, and choose which sister we'd be, and Katrine always tries to bag the drink one.[4]

Or the ending of Nancy Mitford's *The Pursuit of Love* (1945), which offers us high romance (the death of Linda in childbirth; the death of her true love in war), only to simultaneously snatch it away by giving the last word to the cynical Bolter:

> 'But I think she would have been happy with Fabrice,' I said. 'He was the great love of her life, you know.'
> 'Oh, dulling,' said my mother, sadly. 'One always thinks that. Every, every time.'[5]

The double lens of this camp vision is one of the key ways, I would suggest, in which middlebrow fiction manages to negotiate the prickly terrain between high and low culture; the way in which it wrong-foots those who would seek to dismiss it; how it gets to have it both ways. Indeed, I would go further, and suggest that this sensibility is one that animates much of the culture of the interwar years. We find it in the strangest places – in the archness of address in women's magazines and cookbooks, for example and, most gratifyingly, in the writings of the plain-speaking George Orwell, who wonderfully remarks in his 1936 essay 'Bookshop Memories' that:

> For casual reading – in your bath, for instance, or late at night when you are too tired to go to bed, or in the odd quarter of an hour before lunch – there is nothing to touch a back number of the *Girls' Own Paper*.[6]

Camp because of its apparent straight-facedness, because of its playful gender-bending, and because of the supremely ridiculous image it conjures up of Orwell in his bath, this acknowledgement of decadent reading pleasure comes in the middle of an essay decrying the poverty of the public's reading tastes. This is a key element of the mindset of the cultural arbiters of the interwar years: if *you* read trash you are trashy, but if *I* read it I am sophisticated, because I get the joke. A paradoxical hauteur that transforms the icons of popular culture into the badge of membership of an exclusive coterie: this is camp – but it is also, I think, an apt summation of the game played by the interwar middlebrow. Or, as Sontag puts it:

> Camp is the answer to the problem: how to be a dandy in the age of mass culture. Camp [...] makes no distinction between the unique object and the mass-produced object. Camp taste transcends the nausea of the replica. (p. 63)

I could go on offering examples of the overlap between camp and the middlebrow, but instead I want to move on to a related issue: that of queerness. Sontag spends some time attempting to tease out the relationship between camp and homosexuality. She concludes that camp taste and homosexual taste are not the same thing, but that 'homosexuals, by and large, constitute the vanguard – and the most articulate audience – of Camp' (p. 64). It is this formulation of the relationship between homosexuality and camp that has led many queer theorists to reject Sontag's model. She is charged with having depoliticized camp, removing it from its original (queer) creators, and redefining it as something much closer to a kitsch aesthetic. Seen in this light, her assertion that the 'truest' form of camp is unconscious seems specifically designed to exclude the various camp modes of self-expression that characterized pre-Stonewall homosexual subcultures.[7] In asserting that there is a form of camp operating in the feminine middlebrow, I am moving beyond Sontag's depoliticized model of camp. These texts, I would argue, are camp in both Sontag's wider cultural sense, and also in the very specific sense reclaimed by recent queer theorists: they are interested in representing and considering the identity of homosexuality, and in the process they offer a model of gender identity as shifting, constructed, and somewhat arbitrary.

Homosexuality seems to become suddenly visible in literary culture after the First World War. Students on my courses on literature from the 1930s to the 1960s are always surprised by how many of the major writers of the period had same-sex relationships; by how many gay characters appear in the literature. Traditionally, literary criticism has tended to see this emergence of queer culture as a feature of the bohemianism of key high-cultural literary groupings – the Auden generation, the Bloomsberries – seeing it, in other words, as an eccentricity of genius. But it seems to me that this presence is in fact the sign of a much more general visibility of homosexuality, and an increasing cultural interest in it. The work of sexologists at the turn of the century and the public dissemination of Freudian ideas led to a more general openness about sexuality, and the trauma of the First World War created a more fluid sense of gender identities, allowing concepts of androgyny to feed into the public understanding of homosexuality. All of these features are apparent in the middlebrow treatment of the homosexual.

In considering homosexuality in the middlebrow, we need to think of two issues – the visibility of homosexuals and the attitudes the literature expresses towards them. I want to think about a few novels in which homosexual characters play a central role. The first is Rosamond Lehmann's *Dusty Answer* (1927), in which there are a number of significant homosexual characters and encounters. Judith, the protagonist, falls successively in love with the members of a family of cousins, and with her beautiful college friend Jennifer. The relationship with Jennifer is presented as a welcome relief after the awful betrayals of heterosexual love in her experiences with the most enigmatic of the cousins, Roddy. At first it is figured in terms of a tradition of romantic friendship that descends from the Victorians – less transgressive than relationships with the opposite sex – but as the book progresses, Jennifer's feelings are revealed in more and more clarity as incontrovertibly sapphic. The text's handling of these issues is a masterpiece of delicate encoding (and this in the year before the publication of *The Well of Loneliness*). The reader, like Judith, is allowed to both know and not know exactly what Jennifer feels – and what she gets up to with the masculine-looking Geraldine Manners: 'Now she would leave her with Geraldine and not trouble to ask herself what profound and secret intimacies would be restored by her withdrawal.'[8] So too in the novel's treatment of male homosexuality, both Judith and the reader know everything and nothing simultaneously. The description of Tony Baring, who Judith immediately recognizes as a threat to her hoped-for relationship with Roddy, makes no bones about his homosexuality, or his effeminacy – but only for those who know the codes (it is possible to conceive of an 'innocent' reader, for whom the following is not transparent):

He had a sensitive face, changing all the time, a wide mouth with beautiful sensuous lips, thick black hair and a broad white forehead with the eyebrows meeting above the nose, strongly marked and mobile. When he spoke he moved them, singly or together. His voice was soft and precious, and he had a slight lisp. He looked like a young poet. Suddenly she noticed his hands, – thin unmasculine hands, – queer hands – making nervous appealing ineffectual gestures that contradicted the nobility of his head. She heard him call Roddy 'my dear', and once 'darling'; and had a passing shock. (pp. 95–96)

Roddy's own sexuality is not clarified – but the strong implication is that he has dalliances with both men and women. What is interesting is the assumption – both the text's and Judith's – that the masculine bonds that may or may not include sexual relationships are the primary ones. Judith sees herself as a threat to those same-sex bonds, formed by Roddy at school and university:

Supposing she were to take Roddy from Tony, from all his friends and lovers, from all his idle Parisian and English life, and attach him to herself, tie him and possess him: that would mean giving him cares, responsibilities, it might mean changing him from his free and secret self into something ordinary, domesticated, resentful. Perhaps his lovers and friends would be well advised to gather round him jealously and guard him from the female. She saw herself for one moment as a creature of evil design, dangerous to him, and took her hand away from his that held it lightly. (p. 150)

A number of cultural commentators and historians of sexuality have noted that in the decades after the war there was what amounted to a cult of homosexuality at the ancient universities (John Betjeman in a radio interview exclaiming 'But everybody was queer at Oxford in those days!').[9] Jeffrey Weeks put it more circumspectly:

In certain strata (the ancient universities, literature, the higher echelons of the state) there was possibly a greater openness than previously; and for many homosexuals, reflecting in old age, the 1930s may have seemed a golden age. [...] [Some] managed to develop relationships, and integration into the (largely secretive) subcultures.[10]

It is exactly this world, of course, that Charles Ryder is drawn into as an undergraduate of the interwar years in the 1945 *Brideshead Revisited* – a world of romantic male-to-male passions and heightened aesthetic sensibilities, presided over by the Wilde-like Anthony Blanche. In *Dusty Answer*, both lesbians and gay men are visible, at least for the sophisticated reader, but the attitudes expressed towards them are very different. Lesbianism is largely safe, almost cosy, while male homosexuality is dark and secretive – the hostility towards Tony Baring and an almost physical revulsion is very close to the surface. This distinction is played out in most middlebrow fiction – lesbianism is easily accepted, male homosexuality is much more problematic. So in Benson's Mapp and Lucia novels, there is a key distinction between Quaint Irene and Georgie. The sexuality and the gender ambiguity of the former is unthreatening, though directly addressed:

Outside in the garden Irene, dancing hornpipes, was surrounded by both sexes of the enraptured youth of Tilling, for the boys knew she was a girl, and the girls thought she looked so like a boy.[11]

Poor Georgie, however, is kept firmly emasculated – effeminate, but never seen in sexual terms. His sexuality is so irrelevant that in *Lucia's Progress* (1935) he is annexed in marriage to the commanding Lucia. The fact that Benson was himself gay (as – fascinatingly – were all his siblings, and his mother) suggests that this distinction in attitudes is a function not of prejudice but of what seemed expressible at this historical moment.[12] (Male homosexual acts were, of course, illegal until 1967, while lesbian acts were not.)

Josephine Tey's *To Love and Be Wise* (1950) has at its centre the disappearance of Leslie Searle, a mysteriously beautiful young man. Searle, a photographer, has charmed the self-consciously bohemian inhabitants of the small village to which he has recently moved, but they all report an air of fascinating wrongness about him. A middle-aged romantic novelist declares that Searle makes her feel abandoned: 'I'm sure he was something very wicked in Ancient Greece'; others see him as demonic.[13] Tey's series detective Grant, responsible, through a series of coincidences, for introducing Searle into the hot-house environment of the artistic village, is thrown at their initial meeting when Searle laughs up at him as they are pressed together by the crush of bodies at a literary party. The implication of Searle's homosexuality is presented in the most highly coded terms, with Grant and his Sergeant raising and dismissing the possibility only through tone of voice:

> 'What was he like, sir?'
> 'A very good-looking young man indeed.'
> 'Oh,' Williams said, in a thoughtful way.
> 'No,' said Grant.
> 'No?' (p. 75)

When the mystery is solved, it turns out that Searle is in fact a woman, who has lived as a man for years for career purposes. It is testament to the relative shock value of various queer identities at this date that the transvestism and hints of lesbianism (Searle has pursued relationships with women) are considerably less worrying to the text than Searle as a male homosexual.

The most 'out' of middlebrow texts is probably Mary Renault's *The Friendly Young Ladies* (1944), which centres on Leo, a boyish writer of popular cowboy yarns, who lives on a houseboat with her ultra-feminine lover Helen. Their relationship is presented to us through the gaze of Leo's naive, much younger sister, who fails to understand its nature, while at the same time laying all the necessary clues for the reader. This is very much a text of the mid-century, with the representation of lesbianism poised precisely between Havelock Ellis's inverts and the self-assertion of the gay rights movement to come. The lesbianism is encoded, but pretty transparently – it is only the naive Elsie who does not see it. It is absolutely accepted by the other characters – and many of the men they meet seem to find it positively titillating. This is not lesbianism as desexualized romantic friendship, and yet it is so cosy as to seem somehow less than sex. Leo, at least, has chosen the relationship as a retreat from the scariness of penetrative sex with men, and both women continue to have dalliances with men as well. By the end of the novel, Leo has left Helen for her best friend Joe, who has managed to 'cure' her of her fear of heterosexual sex. It is a curious ending for a lesbian writer. The resolution of the novel's contradictions can be found, I think, not in its responses to femininity but to masculinity. Leo wants to be a boy, and it is as a boy that she relates to Joe. He makes this explicit in the letter he writes to her after they have had sex:

> There are two people in you. One of them I have known much longer than the other. I am missing him, already, as much as I have ever missed a friend. I should like him back – sometimes. But you know, now, how much he counted for when he came between my woman and me. [...] I can't tell how much he means to you. Perhaps, ultimately, he is you, and has the immortal part of you in his keeping.[14]

On the level of romantic fantasy, the book valorizes this relationship – but not as a retreat from homosexuality. The ultimate fantasy is of Joe and Leo as two *men*. It is no coincidence that for the rest of her career Renault wrote historical fantasies focused on the male-centred homoerotic culture of Ancient Greece and Asia Minor.[15]

If such an overtly gay-identified writer as Renault found it necessary to so heavily encode a romance between two men, it is interesting that a much more frivolous writer, Nancy Mitford, did not. My final example is *Love in a Cold Climate* (1949), the second of Mitford's brittle comedies of social snobbery, and a sort of sequel to *The Pursuit of Love*. The novel centres on the fortunes of two toadies and their rival methods of ingratiation. It is a device that, characteristically (and campily) allows her to ridicule snobbery while also indulging in it. Boy Dougdale, who has married into the very grand and very rich Hampton family, is the first of the toadies, passionately interested in the aristocracy: 'his great talent for snobbishness and small talent for literature have produced three detailed studies of his wife's forebears'.[16] His rival is the flamboyant Cedric, a distant cousin from the colonies in favour of whom the furious Lord Montdore disinherits his daughter Polly when she marries the ageing Boy. Cedric's power of fascination lies in his passionate appreciation of the beauty and luxury of Hampton, and his ability to transform the Montdores into creatures of cosmopolitan glamour. Cedric's gayness is completely apparent from the first moment he sashays into the novel: 'A glitter of blue and gold crossed the parquet, and a human dragonfly was kneeling on the fur rug in front of the Montdores, one long white hand extended towards each' (p. 274), but his is not the effete sexless camp of Benson's Georgie. Cedric has had many lovers, and drops tantalizing references to their indulgences and brutalities. One of his first acts on moving to Hampton is to pick up a young lorry driver and install him as an odd job man. Mitford absolutely expects the reader to understand what she is saying about Cedric's sexuality, and indeed, makes sly use of him as a device to 'out' other characters, such as Davey, Fanny's health-obsessed gossipy uncle, who remarks that 'in the course of his own wild cosmopolitan wanderings, before he had met and settled down with Aunt Emily, he had known too many Cedrics' (p. 289). The novel is completely on Cedric's side, his transformation of the stuffy Montdores offering the same sort of narrative gratification as does Flora's re-making of the inhabitants of Cold Comfort Farm.[17] It ends triumphantly, with Cedric bearing off to Paris not just Lady Montdore, but also Boy, with whom he has fallen in love:

> I went into the garden to find Cedric. He was sitting on the church-yard wall, the pale sunshine on his golden hair, which I perceived to be tightly curled, an aftermath of the ball, no doubt, and plucking away with intense concentration at the petals of a daisy.
>
> He loves me he loves me not he loves me he loves me not, don't interrupt my angel, he loves me he loves me not, oh, heaven! He loves me! I may as well tell you, my darling, that the second big thing in my life has begun.
>
> A most sinister ray of light suddenly fell upon the future.
>
> 'Oh, Cedric,' I said. 'Do be careful!'
>
> I need not have felt any alarm, however, Cedric managed the whole thing quite beautifully. As soon as Polly had completely recovered her health and looks, he put Lady Montdore and Boy into the big Daimler and rolled away with them to France. [...]
>
> So here we all are, my darling, having our lovely cake and eating it too, *One's* great aim in life.
>
> 'Yes, I know,' I said, 'the Boreleys think it's simply terrible.' (p. 320)

To shock the ghastly Boreleys, the representative of tedious middle-class respectability, simply confirms the perfection of it all. So why is it that Mitford can get away so easily with that which Renault feels the need to hide? One answer is simply – camp. The endlessly evasive playfulness of the camp mode makes all things acceptable. It is a point Sontag makes very clearly:

> Homosexuals have pinned their integration into society on promoting the aesthetic sense. Camp is a solvent of morality. It neutralizes moral indignation, sponsors playfulness. (p. 64)

Seen in these terms, camp functions as a spearhead for gay rights, insinuating 'queerness' into mainstream culture.

In suggesting that we read the middlebrow through the lens of camp, I do not want to offer yet another way in which it can be dismissed. On the contrary, I would suggest that the concept of camp provides one more way of understanding that elaborate dance whereby the middlebrow novel manages to be both populist and snobbish, conservative and radical, inclusive and excluding, sophisticated yet playful – all at the same time.

Notes

1. Nicola Humble (2001) *The Feminine Middlebrow Novel, 1920s to 1950s: Class, Domesticity and Bohemianism* (Oxford: Oxford University Press), pp. 5–6.
2. Susan Sontag (Fall 1964) 'Notes on Camp', first published in *Partisan Review* 31(4): 515–530; reproduced in Fabio Cleto (ed.) (1999) *Camp: Queer Aesthetics and the Performing Subject: A Reader* (Edinburgh: Edinburgh University Press), pp. 53–65, p. 53. Sontag's article propelled both the idea of camp and Sontag herself into the media spotlight, with articles in major US and British periodicals (the *New Statesman*, *Time*, *Holiday*, the *Observer*, and the *New York Times* among others) examining this 'new taste'. 'Camp' became a marketing buzz-word, and by the end of the decade, 'camp' and 'pop' had become synonymous.
3. There have been many other formulations of camp since Sontag's groundbreaking essay. One of the most compelling is that of Philip Core: '[a] working definition of camp is essential before we can pinpoint camp retrospectively and contemporarily. Camouflage, bravura, moral anarchy, the hysteria of despair, a celebration of frustration, skittishness, revenge [...] the possible descriptions are countless. I would opt for one basic prerequisite however: camp is a lie that tells the truth.' (Philip Core (1984), 'Camp: The Lie That Tells the Truth', reproduced in Cleto, p. 81). I am using Sontag's definitions as my model for two reasons: firstly, hers was the initiatory attempt to define this essentially indefinable sensibility, and, secondly, her interest in camp as a phenomenon of wider applicability than gay subculture offers a frame for my application of the concept to the women's middlebrow fiction of the interwar years.
4. Rachel Ferguson (1931; 1988) *The Brontës Went to Woolworths* (London: Virago), p. 7.

5. Nancy Mitford (1945; 1970) *The Pursuit of Love* (Harmondsworth: Penguin), p. 192.

6. George Orwell (1936; 1968) 'Bookshop Memories', in *The Collected Essays, Journalism and Letters*, ed. Sonia Orwell and Ian Angus, vol I: *An Age Like This, 1920–1940* (London: Secker & Warburg), p. 246.

7. 'Sontag's (non-)definition of camp as an elusive sensibility is charged with consenting its appropriation and reorientation by dominant culture, indulging in a nostalgia paradoxically eliding the historical existence of the object of nostalgic desire itself, just as it elides camp's alleged origins within the homosexual subculture.' (Cleto, p. 10).

8. Rosamond Lehmann (1927; 1986) *Dusty Answer* (Harmondsworth: Penguin), p. 162.

9. Cate Haste (1994) *Rules of Desire: Sex in Britain World War I to the Present* (London: Pimlico), p. 87.

10. Jeffrey Weeks (1981; rev. edn 1989) *Sex, Politics and Society: The Regulation of Sexuality since 1800* (London: Longman), p. 220.

11. E. F. Benson (1935; 1970) *Mapp and Lucia* (Harmondsworth: Penguin), p. 132.

12. For a fascinating account of Benson's sexual identity, see John Tosh, 'Domesticity and Manliness in the Victorian Middle Class: The Family of Edward White Benson', in Michael Roper and John Tosh (eds) (1991) *Manful Assertions: Masculinities in Britain since 1800* (London: Routledge), pp. 44–73.

13. Josephine Tey (1950; 1986) *To Love and Be Wise* (Harmondsworth: Penguin), p. 28.

14. Mary Renault (1944; 1994) *The Friendly Young Ladies* (London: Virago), pp. 274–275.

15. The last of her contemporary novels is *The Charioteer* (1953), an account of love between servicemen in the Second World War, which holds classic status in the gay literary pantheon.

16. Nancy Mitford (1949; 1986) *Love in a Cold Climate*, in *The Nancy Mitford Omnibus* (Harmondsworth: Penguin), p. 155.

17. Cedric's precise brand of camp, and its appeal, is summed up by Philip Core: 'In Somerset Maugham, Cecil Beaton, the dilettante actor Ivor Novello, and Noël Coward, we can pinpoint the sort of camp the English upper classes adore: an outrageous but unprosecutable *arbiter elegantiarum* who bullies the world of married society into accepting a homosexual's view of how it should dress, act, entertain and sometimes think.' (Cleto, p. 83).

Afterword

Faye Hammill

This book has emerged from an international research network established by Mary Grover, Erica Brown and myself. When I am speaking of the Middlebrow Network to people who haven't heard of it, I often find myself explaining that it is not in fact a network *of* middlebrows. But this need to explain throws me back on the very set of anxieties and aspirations which the term 'middlebrow' designates. As a professional literary critic, it would be a little dangerous for me to admit to being a middlebrow (if such a thing exists). After all, being a specialist in early twentieth-century literature, I spend a lot of time with people who claim to enjoy reading *Finnegans Wake*. I find it best to avoid quoting from *The Pursuit of Love* or *Cold Comfort Farm* in their presence.

But does a preference for discussing Nancy Mitford rather than 'the *Wake*' (as, of course, it is called by those in the know...) actually make a critic into a middlebrow? Let us return for a moment to the question raised by Virginia Woolf and quoted at the very beginning of this book: 'What, you may ask, is a middlebrow?' My favourite answer to this question is the one proposed by Raymond Williams in *Culture and Society, 1780–1950* (1958): 'There are in fact no middlebrows; there are only ways of seeing people and books as middlebrow.'[1] This is very useful because it reminds us that tastes are constantly being re-evaluated and hierarchies reorganized. I have lately wondered what would happen if we substituted the word 'modernist' for 'middlebrow' in Williams's sentence. It might be provoking to some modernist scholars. Yet 'modernism' is an expanding category, and the new modernist studies embrace many authors who used to be thought of as middlebrow: authors such as Rosamond Lehmann and Anita Loos, Evelyn Waugh and Rebecca West.

The debate as to whether these authors (and, by implication, the scholars who work on them) should be 'seen' as modernists or as middlebrows is not, however, a very productive one. *Middlebrow Literary Cultures* proposes a different approach. It argues that we should instead read these authors in the context of the 'battle of the brows' which marked their era, and acknowledge their active role in those battles. That is, we should understand them as constructing, as well as constructed by, contemporary cultural hierarchies.

Williams's comment also reminds us that, as well as classifying books as highbrow and lowbrow, we also classify other people according to what they read or study, and try to classify ourselves by reading (or at least, walking around with copies of) particular books. Yet, though books and also films, pictures and pieces of music are very frequently designated as 'middlebrow' in the media and in conversation, it is rare to hear somebody call someone else a 'middlebrow', in the way that Virginia Woolf did in the private space of an unsent letter. This may be explained by what William Empson in *The Structure of Complex*

Words (1964) calls 'the return of the meaning of the word to the speaker'. He says:

> most judgements about other people, when you make them public, can be felt to raise a question about how you would be judged in your turn. This is particularly so of inherently shifting moral terms like the miserly-thrifty group; when one man calls another thrifty he is a little conscious of what people would call him. To call someone else clever is rather to imply that you are not clever yourself.[2]

And to call someone a middlebrow implies that you think yourself a highbrow. I have never yet heard it used by someone who was trying to claim to be a lowbrow.

So, in the Middlebrow Network, we do not call ourselves – or other people – middlebrows. But I have still not explained what the Network is. It began as a grouping of about 25 scholars in the UK and the US, who were seeking to explore hierarchies of taste, culture and class in a transnational and inter-disciplinary context. We were awarded funding from the Arts and Humanities Research Council in 2008, and this enabled us to work together on a much more ambitious scale than would otherwise have been possible. The funding allowed us to organize events and conference panels, to produce collaborative publications and web resources and to contribute and connect to a range of initiatives led by Network members, such as the establishment of the Readerships and Literary Cultures 1900–1950 Special Collection at Sheffield Hallam University. The Network's mailing list now includes more than 200 researchers, publishers and library professionals from across Europe, North America and beyond.

The research conducted under the auspices of the Network is by no means limited to literary study, although this book concentrates on the literary part of the project. Middlebrow culture can only be fully understood by bringing together (as we have done) perspectives from social and cultural history with critical analysis of literature, film, music and the media. This is because the tensions surrounding middlebrow are related to discourses of class and taste which range across the whole area of lifestyle choices and cultural consumption, from interiors, gardens, design and fashion to preferences in entertainment and reading material.

This book provides a mapping of the territory for future research into middlebrow cultures. Or rather, it overlays two different maps. On the map of audiences and markets, the middlebrow is literally the middle: the centre ground, a large and influential area of cultural production. On the scholarly map, by contrast, the middlebrow has traditionally been located at the margin: in an area at the edge of the canon, or beyond its reach. (These spatial metaphors are very telling.) The scholarly map is being redrawn now as the analysis of the middlebrow becomes increasingly crucial to the whole enterprise of cultural and literary studies. The middle is connected in myriad ways to the canonical and to the popular, and now, instead of being avoided by scholars, it has become the most exciting location for literary and interdisciplinary study. An impressive amount of scholarship on the middlebrow has been published in recent years, and it is such a rich field of study that we can be sure there are many, many discoveries still to be made.

Notes

1. Raymond Williams (1958) *Culture and Society, 1780–1950* (London: Chatto and Windus), p. 300.
2. William Empson (1951; 1964) *The Structure of Complex Words* (London: Chatto and Windus), p. 18.

Index

academia, 3, 6, 11, 25–36, 70, 116,
    123, 144, 151
Academy, 101, 102–3, 107, 110
Adelphi, The, 79
Adorno, Theodor, 77, 172
advertising, 12, 27, 58, 99, 103,
    120, 121, 123, 131–2,
    141, 154, 159, 161, 188,
    212–13, 215
AE (George Russell), 187, 194
Agate, James, 71
Akins, Zoë, 134, 141
Allingham, Margery, 220
American culture, *see* United States
    culture
American Mercury, The, 11, 141
American Scholar, 151
Anderson, Benedict, 177
Anderson, Sherwood, 117, 122, 134,
    141, 142
Andrews, Julie, 193
Answers, 213
anthropology, 15, 41, 124, 202, 204,
    210, 214
Arnheim, Rudolf, 193
Arnold, Matthew, 13, 85
Asche, Oscar, 61
    Cairo, 61
aspiration, *see* cultural
    aspiration
Atherton, Gertrude, 11
Atlantic, The, 2
Atlantic Monthly, 173
Auden group, 211, 212, 213, 223
Austen, Jane, 106, 190
Australian culture, 14, 176
autodidacts, 59, 99, 104–6, 209
    see also cultural aspiration
avant-garde, 1, 9, 16, 84, 125–6, 127,
    130, 141, 142, 151–2, 156, 162,
    187, 215
awards, *see* prizes (literary)

Baden Powell, Sir Robert, 71
Baillet, François, 4
Baldick, Chris, 56
Balfour, Patrick, 57
Balzac, Honoré de, 16, 95, 106
Barbellion, W. N. P., 107
Barclay, Florence, 109
Barnes, Djuna, 134, 141
Barrie, J. M., 70
Barthes, Roland, 193
battle of the brows, 1, 71, 75, 231
Baumgarten, Sylvia Bernice, 152–3, 154
Baxendale, John, 5, 10, 16, 69–81
BBC, *see* British Broadcasting
    Corporation (BBC)
Beaverbrook, Lord, 55, 65, 82, 88
Beaverbrook press, 5
Beerbohm, Max, 123
Beethoven, Ludwig van, 119
Beisel, Nicola, 138
Belgion, Montgomery, 10
Bell, Clive, 59
Bell, W. G., 107
Benedict, Ruth, 124
Benjamin, Walter, 214–15
Bennett, Arnold, 5, 8, 13–14, 56, 58,
    62, 70, 75–6, 82–97, 100, 133,
    135, 202–3
    Elsie and the Child, 88
    The Glimpse, 87
    Grand Babylon Hotel, 87
    Imperial Palace, 92
    Literary Taste: How to Form It, 85
    A Man From the North, 84
    The Old Wives' Tales, 86, 87
Benson, E. F., 9, 220–1, 225, 228
    Mapp and Lucia novels, 220–1,
    225–6
Benton, Thomas Hart, 124, 125
Betjeman, John, 99, 225
Bingham, Adrian, 4, 16, 55–68
Birrell, Augustine, 107

234

Marx, Karl, 16
masculinity, 10, 94, 157–8, 178–9,
  180, 182, 204, 224, 227
mass culture, 9, 16, 34, 41, 45, 46–8,
  55–6, 59, 62, 72, 77, 87, 131, 154,
  158, 162–3, 172, 202, 222
Masses, The, 121, 122
Mass-Observation, 9, 202–15
Maugham, Somerset, 63, 156, 160
Mayer, Arno J., 3
McKay, Claude, 89–90, 135
  Banjo, 90
McKibbin, Ross, 202–3, 204
Megroz, R. L., 59
melodrama, 172, 176, 180–1, 183
Melville, Herman, 89
  Pierre, 89
Mencken, H. L., 12, 13, 122, 127,
  130–44
Mendelssohn, Felix, 119
middlebrow
  definitions, 1–2, 4, 6–7, 28, 33, 42,
    99, 110, 156, 175–6, 179, 181,
    190, 203, 222, 229, 231
  feminine, 8, 94, 179, 189, 218, 223
  literary form, 8–10, 25–6, 31–2, 58,
    174, 175, 180–1, 188–90
  and nationalism, 14, 176–8, 179
  teaching the, 25–36, 136, 223
  theorizing, 14–17, 138–9
  see also Bourdieu, Pierre; broadbrow;
    cultural aspiration; cultural
    hierarchy; highbrow; lowbrow;
    readerships
Middlebrow Network, 231–2
middle class, *see* class
Millay, Edna St. Vincent, 130, 141
Mill, John Stuart, 131
Mills and Boon, 63
Milton, John, 16, 103, 156, 212
  Paradise Lost, 16
misogyny, 157, 158
Mitchell, W. J. T., 191–2, 193, 194,
  196, 198, 199
Mitford, Nancy, 9, 180, 220, 221,
  227–8, 231
  Love in a Cold Climate, 227–8
  The Pursuit of Love, 180, 221, 227,
    231

modernism, 2, 3, 7, 8, 10, 13, 15–17,
  27, 30–1, 56, 58, 59, 71, 73–4,
  76–8, 84, 87, 90, 108–9, 117, 121,
  123, 126, 130–1, 134, 141, 151,
  156, 157, 160, 171, 172, 176, 181,
  187, 188, 189, 191, 193, 194, 195,
  199, 202–3, 207–16, 231
modernity, 14, 175, 176–7, 178, 181,
  204
Moderwell, Hiram, 118–19, 120, 125,
  126
Montaigne, Michel de, 46–7
Montgomery, L. M., 175, 190
  Anne of Green Gables, 175, 190
Moore, Jocelyn, 180
Morin, Edgar, 15, 41–2
Morris, William, 86–7
Morrow, William, 153
Motion Picture Classic, 120
Motion Picture Magazine, 120
Muller, Jonathan, 154
Murnau, F. W., 88
Murphy, Michael, 123
music (popular), 12, 37, 46, 61, 72,
  118–19, 120, 138–9
  see also jazz
Mylett, Andrew, 83, 94

Nadelman, Elie, 123
Napper, Lawrence, 10, 16
Nathan, George Jean, 13, 122, 131,
  138, 139, 141
Nation, 108
National Book Council, 85
National Film Board of Canada (NFB),
  175
nationalism, 14, 117, 176–8
Nevler, Leona, 153
New Budget, The, 101
New Criticism, 11, 25
New Deal, 125
New Left, 17
New Republic, The, 117, 133–4
News Chronicle (Daily News), 59, 202
newspapers, 4, 55–68, 70, 72–3, 82–95,
  100–3, 121, 136, 142, 154, 172,
  177, 202
  British newspapers, 4, 55–68, 72–3,
    83–95, 100–3, 202

Windsor, Kathleen, 64
Forever Amber, 64
Winfrey, Oprah (Book Club), 33, 173
Winslow, Thyra Samter, 134
Wolcott, James, 163
Woljeska, Helen, 134
Woman, 84
women, 9–10, 26, 27, 62, 154, 158,
   172, 181, 182, 187, 188, 189, 195,
   197, 218, 220–1
Wood, Mrs Henry, 5, 84
Woolf, Leonard, 5
Woolf, Virginia, 1, 2, 3, 5, 7–8, 10, 13,
   42, 43, 47, 58, 62–3, 71, 74–7, 78,
   83, 108–9, 176, 207, 208–9, 210,
   214, 231
   To the Lighthouse, 74
   'Middlebrow' letter to the *New
      Statesman*, 7, 42, 74–5
   'Modern Fiction', 8, 10, 43

'Mr Bennett and Mrs Brown', 8,
      75–6
   Mrs Dalloway, 90
   Night and Day, 108–9
   Three Guineas, 8
Wordsworth, William, 44
working class, *see* class
Wreszin, Michael, 150
Wright, Richard, 131, 135
Wright, Stanton MacDonald, 119, 124
Wright, Willard Huntington, 122–3,
   124, 125, 141
Writer, The, 61

Yeats, W. B., 109, 122, 194
Yellow Book, The, 5, 84
York, Lorraine, 172–3, 174, 177–8
Yorkshire Post, 59
Young's Magazine, 132